Theodosia had turned in her seat when her attention was caught by the officers next to her. Or rather by one officer who sat a little way from the others leaning against the side of his box and regarding her fixedly.

As she met his eyes, Theodosia experienced a physical sensation of explosion in her chest. The effect was one of recognition, of intimate greeting, and yet she knew that she had never seen the man before in her life.

Her mind was in chaos. Who is he? Why do I feel like this? She dared not look again—to the box to her right. She felt his presence there with an intensity that numbed her.

They must meet. She had never had a desire to match this one. More than a desire, it was an ache, a hunger. But how could they meet with her father and fiancé sitting there beside her.

When the curtain fell on a bowing and curtsying cast, she could bear it no longer and turned abruptly under cover of the applause. He was nearer to her now, so that by reaching out her arm she could have touched him. The other officers milled about in the box. He stood aloof in the midst of them, watching her expectantly. She knew that he would communicate with her and felt rather than saw his lips form a question. "Where?"

MY THEODOSIA

Anya Seton

A FAWCETT CREST BOOK

Fawcett Publications, Inc., Greenwich, Connecticut

MY THEODOSIA

THIS BOOK CONTAINS THE COMPLETE TEXT OF
THE ORIGINAL HARDCOVER EDITION.

A Fawcett Crest Book reprinted by arrangement with
Houghton Mifflin Company.

Copyright © 1941, 1968 by Anya Seton Chase

ISBN 0-449-23034-1

Printed in the United States of America

10 9 8 7 6 5 4 3

Aaron Burr to Theodosia Burr Alston.

New York, July 10, 1804.

. . . I am indebted to you, my dearest Theodosia, for a very great portion of the happiness which I have enjoyed in this life. You have completely satisfied all that my heart and affections had hoped or even wished. With a little more perseverance, determination, and industry, you will obtain all that my ambition or vanity had fondly imagined. Let your son have occasion to be proud that he had a mother. Adieu. Adieu.

(Written on the eve of the duel with Alexander Hamilton.)

Theodosia Burr Alston to Aaron Burr.

South Carolina, August 1, 1809.

. . . I witness your extraordinary fortitude with new wonder at every new misfortune . . . you appear to me so superior, so elevated above all other men, I contemplate you with such a strange mixture of humility, admiration, reverence, love, and pride, that very little superstition would be necessary to make me worship you as a superior being. . . . My vanity would be greater if I had not been placed so near you; and yet, my pride is our relationship. I had rather not live than not be the daughter of such a man.

Author's Note

While this story is a fictional interpretation of Theodosia's life, I have tried to be historically accurate in every detail. I have consulted all the Burr biographies, many contemporary newspapers, and have read unpublished Burr letters in the New York and Congressional Libraries, as well as a few which are privately owned.

The *Memoirs of Aaron Burr, with Miscellaneous Selections from His Correspondence*, by Matthew L. Davis, contains the fullest collection of the published letters and has furnished the backbone of my plot, with the exception of the Meriwether Lewis romance for which there are three separate sources.

There is a vast amount of Burr material, so vast and so conflicting that Aaron's character may be interpreted in a dozen different ways. I have chosen the one which seems to me to be truthful and have tried not to distort facts for the purposes of fiction; nor is such distortion necessary—the facts are romantic enough for any purpose.

There are nearly as many theories about Theodosia's fate as there are biographies of Aaron, which is saying a great deal. The most popular theory is the one which has her vessel captured by pirates and Theodosia walking the plank in long trailing robes; there is the theory of the wreck at Nag's Head, of the flight to France or Mexico, and others even more melodramatic.

I have presented the solution to the mystery which I believe to be accurate. It is based on Aaron's own conviction and is considered the most probable by the present Alston family.

I am indebted to many kind and helpful people, especially those in Charleston, Georgetown, and on the Waccamaw Neck, and I particularly wish to thank Mr. Arthur Geiger, of New York City, who has made an exhaustive study of Theodosia and has been very generous to me in suggesting material.

Chapter One

AT SIX o'clock on the morning of Midsummer Day, 1800, Aaron Burr's estate, Richmond Hill, was already well into the day's bustle of preparation for the gala dinner to be given that evening in honor of Theodosia's birthday.

The great kitchens hummed under Peggy's irritable guidance; from the dairy came the rhythmic clop-clop of the butter churns, mingled with more distant sounds of stamps and whinnies from the stables.

The newborn sun shimmered through heat haze upon the mansion's white columns and wrought-iron balustrades. It shone dazzlingly on the Hudson, whose slow-moving waters flowed but a few yards away below the house. Already the river was flecked white with sails, as sloops, schooners, and packets tacked upstream toward Albany with the incoming tide.

Half a mile from the house, in Greenwich Village, a neglected cow lowed for her belated milking. The sound carried to the white bedroom at Richmond Hill, where Theodosia Burr, daughter to Aaron, awoke at last on this morning of her seventeenth birthday to find her room filled with a pungent perfume. She sniffed with sleepy pleasure, and lay quiet on her big bed considering this phenomenon. The gardens were too far away to carry such a decided scent, and anyway there was no breeze stirring.

It smells like roses, she thought, still held in a voluptuous drowsiness. The damask curtains which enclosed her bed were partly looped back, a concession to the warmth of June; so that, without moving, she could watch the brightly blue rectangle of sky through the window beside her.

Sunshine glistened on the linen sheets and touched her braids with red fire. It was of a peculiar color, that hair: now dark brown, now chestnut, yet always enriched by an underlying tinge of auburn.

"Your hair is the color of port wine, Theo," John Vanderlyn had once told her as he worked on one of the countless sketches of her that her father commissioned. She had thought this very funny then, partly because at thirteen all compliments are amusing—if one could call it a compliment—and partly because his heavy Dutch manner and intonation seemed so incongruous. Since then Vanderlyn had spent four years studying in France, and now he was back, having justified her father's faith in him by becoming an accomplished artist.

"Gilbert Stuart is all very well, if you like that swashbuckling style of portraiture," Aaron had once remarked, "but to my mind Vanderlyn will develop the greater gift." And so, with one of his characteristic lavish gestures, he had sent the young wagon-painter abroad.

John Vanderlyn had acquired more arts than that of brushwielding, Theo thought with detached amusement. Last week, she and her father had gone down to the wharves on South Street to welcome him home. As he disembarked from the stout brig which had battled head winds for eight stormy weeks from Le Havre, she had not at first recognized him. Such a beau he had become!—in his plum-colored silk coat, elaborately frilled neckcloth, and jet shoe buckles, and his lanky flaxen hair, that used to be so unkempt, now neatly confined in a beribboned queue.

Vanderlyn had kissed her hand with all the grace of a French courtier, of Talleyrand himself, murmuring: "Ah, glorious Theo! Mais vous êtes vraiment éblouissante! More beautiful than any of the lovely ladies I have seen in France"—with just that blend of boldness and gallantry which signalized a man of the world. But there had been genuine startled admiration, too, in his Dutch-blue eyes.

Her father had laughed complacently. "My little Miss Prissy has turned into a reigning belle, hasn't she? I trust it won't add to her giddy head, or all my theories for bringing up females may go for naught."

Theo had looked up at her father to meet his half-serious, half-teasing gaze. She had made a saucy face at him, and the anxious shadow faded from his darkly brilliant eyes. They understood each other well. Aaron's love and pride sustained her like a great warm river: all-pervading, irresistible. Her being floated on it joyously. And if sometimes the stream turned cold and turbulent, if sometimes his constant concern for her welfare or her intellectual progress seemed harsh or irksome, she simply flogged herself to greater effort. It was unthinkable, monstrous, that she should ever disappoint him.

Her father had been pleased with her lately. She now stretched luxuriously against the frilled pillows, flinging her arms above her head. The hundred lines of Plautus which she had memorized last week had delighted him no less than her spirited interpretation of one of Gabriel-Marie's minuets on the new pianoforte.

"Well done, my dear," he had said, with the gentle smile he reserved for her alone. "Enjoy your morning ride with good conscience."

And she had enjoyed it, she thought with a guilty start, for it was on that day that she had met the strange young man near the Belvidere Tavern on the East River.

Pleasing thoughts of the strange young man and her prospective rendezvous with him this morning were cut short by the white-and-gold enameled clock on her mantelpiece. It pinged seven times, and Theo jumped. So late! Even on a birthday morning would her father forgive the wasted hour and a half? There was her journal to be written up for his critical survey and fifty lines of Virgil to be construed.

She slid from bed onto the waxed oaken floor, gratefully cool to her tiny feet. She flung her nightcap on the bed, and, turning, saw the source of the mysterious fragrance.

A large reed basket stood knee-high on the floor beside her. It brimmed with French roses, golden yellow as cowslip butter around their gilded hearts, and from them rose a perfume warmly sensuous, heavy with the seductive breath of their native Provence.

Theo buried her face in them with a pleased cry. She did not need the accompanying note to tell her who had stolen into her room as she slept and left them there, but the sight of the small familiar writing delighted her.

Happy birthday to my Theo. Lazy slug-a-bed, the most precious hours of the day are wasting. But, this once, I forbear to waken you, nor will I scold you today. If you searched, you might find in the basket a token of my esteem.

Your very affectionate father

A. BURR

The note was characteristic of Aaron, with its blend of love, admonition, and small mystery.

Theo searched eagerly among the forest of thorny green

9

stems. Never had her father failed to provide her with a superb birthday surprise. Her probing fingers found it at last—a silver box cunningly fastened to one of the roses. When she opened it, her breath caught.

An exquisite necklace sparkled up at her from black velvet. It was fashioned of diamonds and topazes, intricately set into gold filigree so as to form a cluster of jeweled rosebuds.

Her hands trembled as she held it to the light. "Dearest Papa!" she whispered. Yellow and white, her favorite colors, and roses, her favorite flower, combined into flashing beauty.

The necklace was magnificent, far finer than anything she had seen of Lady Kitty Duer's or Mrs. Hamilton's. Aaron must have commissioned John Vanderlyn to bring it with him from France. The New York goldsmiths were not nearly skilled enough for this. And how like him to make a pretty ceremony of its presentation! He had the gift of dramatizing life for those around him. He was so generous—so extravagantly generous at times.

Theo sighed, cuddling the necklace against her cheek. Lately creditors had been even more pressing than usual, but this never seemed to worry her father. When he was here at Richmond Hill he handled them all nonchalantly, promising, placating, and occasionally paying strategic sums on account. But during his frequent absences in Albany, Theo had tried to struggle with the complicated household expenditures herself. It took thousands of dollars to run the estate, with its famous wine cellar, stables, gardens, and staff of twenty servants, both white and black. True, Peggy, Alexis, and Tom were slaves, but the others had to be paid their eight dollars a month somehow.

She had tried to curtail the appalling table expenses, but Aaron had checked her. He ate sparingly himself, but his guests—there was never a meal without guests—must be fed lavishly.

Oh, well—they'd manage, as they always did. Besides, there was a great—a glorious probability!

Aaron seldom discussed his political ambitions with Theo —or indeed with anyone—thinking it sufficient that she preside gracefully over his table, amusing and charming without question whatever type of guest he might choose to entertain. "Politics are not becoming to women," he told her once. His full, flexible mouth curved into a teasing smile, one black eyebrow shot up. "Moreover, my dear, you are too young and tender for all the horrid ins and outs of the game."

But now she, and many people throughout the sixteen States, knew that, in view of the New York City elections in May, her father's political prominence had increased a hundredfold, and that, with the presidential elections in the fall, Aaron stood a chance of succeeding President Adams.

"First Lady of the Land!" she thought, and her heart beat faster. Half-laughing at herself, she ran to the cherry-wood mirror above her dressing-table, slipping off her long muslin nightrobe. Clad only in her transparent cambric shift, she fastened the diamond necklace about her neck. Its lowest pendant reached almost to the swell of her small high breasts, and enhanced the luster of her skin, white as new milk, the shade Nature often allies to dark auburn hair.

With one hand she piled her loosened braids high on her head, with the other held out the shift. Her eyes black and shining as onyx, mocked her foolishness as she curtsied regally to the small figure in the glass. "How do you do, my Lady President."

Her room door was suddenly opened, and Theo turned at a horrified cry behind her. "Món Dieu, ma chérie, tu es donc folle ce matin!"

Natalie Delage, Theo's adopted sister, stood round-eyed on the threshold, her pert French face scandalized at this posturing before a mirror in a diamond necklace and very little else. Natalie, product of the ancien régime, and a refugee from the French Revolution, was a great stickler for "les convenances."

Theo laughed, snatching up a brocaded dressing gown. "I'm not mad, Natalie, but it's June, and my birthday, and see what Papa has given me. Isn't he the best and most generous of men?"

The French girl examined the necklace. "Exquisite," she agreed. "A magnificent present. You will look ravishing at your party tonight."

Theo began brushing her finespun web of hair. "I hope so. I shall wear the white India muslin with gold embroidery that Papa likes so much; it will set off his gift. I do hope he will be pleased."

Natalie made a tiny, impatient noise. She leaned against the wall watching the girl with exasperated affection. But she was a child yet—Theodosia!—in everything but her mind and intellectual attainments. These were formidable enough. Miss Burr was celebrated from Albany to Philadelphia for her accomplishments.

But her emotions, thought Natalie—by which she meant

11

flirtation, love-making, the exciting business of eliciting pursuit—were still totally immature. Ever her body, for all its petite femininity, was not fully developed according to the French taste. It lacked a lushness of curve, the hips were too narrow. Still, Theo in the last year had grown extremely pretty, with a vivacious sparkle that immediately attracted. Lately there had been several suitors, but there was something strange about the girl's attitude. She scarcely seemed aware of her conquests.

Natalie sighed, settling down on the horsehair sofa. "Listen, chérie, I must talk with you seriously. You are seventeen now, and a woman. It is not natural to think always, 'Will Papa be pleased?' There should be someone younger than Papa to make your eyes shine like that. Your father is a wonderful, fascinating man, bien entendu, but you are no longer a little girl. You are beautiful and witty, you speak three languages, you play the harp, the pianoforte, you write letters and essays like a Montaigne, and all for what? So your father will be pleased! C'est inouï."

Theo laid down her brush and shook her head ruefully; she had heard all this before. "When I meet another man really worth pleasing, I shall do so." She smiled her quick, lovely smile. "Natalie, please! Don't preach today, and don't look so somber. I have time yet to think of marriage—if, indeed, I must."

"Ciel!" cried Natalie, shocked. "Of course you must marry. Imagine remaining always a virgin, without position, without being rangée, simply the daughter of your father! You are heedless, ma chère, and you have no mother to tell you these things, so I must."

Theo looked at her affectionately. Good Natalie. For all her scant twenty years she was as anxiously maternal as a broody hen. She never forgot the generosity which the Burr family had shown her when Aaron had opened his home to a penniless little émigrée, five years ago.

Theo turned back to the dressing-table. "Will you ring, Natalie? I need Dinah for my hair."

The other girl's hand rose to the embroidered bell-pull, but fell back before touching it. "I'll do your hair for you, petite. Dinah is busy in the kitchen with the others. Là, là! Such a to-do down there getting ready for your banquet this evening."

"I suppose Father has breakfasted already?"

Natalie, pulling and patting the chestnut tendrils, laughed. "Long ago. He could scarcely wait for Selim to be saddled,

12

then he was off to the city like a whirlwind. To Brom Martling's Tavern, I suppose, as usual."

"Oh, yes—those Tammany men," said Theo vaguely. "He has much business with them . . . Tell me, if I piled my hair higher just here, should I look older and taller, do you think?"

They discussed this point animatedly until Theo, opening her great lavender-scented clothes-press, reached for her riding-habit.

Natalie frowned. "You are riding again this morning, in the heat?"

"The heat doesn't matter. A gallop on Minerva will cool me off. Besides——" She paused, one eyebrow shot up in unconscious imitation of her father when he was bent on devilry, her eyes widened with mischief. "You are so anxious to have me feel romantic—well, here is something for you." She lowered her voice to a dramatic whisper: "I am going to meet a young man, very handsome, in the woods across the island!"

"Theo!" Natalie stared; then, with a laugh, "You are impossible. What young man? Who introduced you? Tell me at once."

Theo gave a little trill of mirth, a spontaneous and infectious gurgle peculiar to her. Before she answered, she adjusted the wide skirts of her gray silk habit and pulled her plumed felt hat to its most dashing angle.

"No one introduced us," she said airily. "We just met. And I'm not sure who he is, but I think he's that Doctor Peter Irving's young brother, Washington. You see, we don't know each other well enough yet to exchange names."

With which piece of effrontery she made the thunderstruck Natalie a low curtsy, shutting her ears to the shattering explosion of outraged French which pursued her down the stairs.

She slipped out at a side door, noticing even in her haste the dear beauties of this place that she loved: the splendid oaks and cedars that shaded the house, the soft green lawns with their gentle slopes, even the silly sheep that cropped the grass. There was a pond, too, gracefully marged with ornamental shrubs, and teeming with swans and yellow-billed ducks. Aaron had recently enlarged it to a more respectable size, in keeping with one of the most impressive estates on Manhattan Island. But no amount of enlarging could give it much significance. It was forever dwarfed by the effortless magnificence of the river beyond it.

13

The Hudson. Theo greeted it now with an uprushing of the heart, as she always did. She adored it with a half-mystical fervor that she could have explained to no one—not even Aaron. She had been born within sound of it, in Albany. Her childhood had been spent near it. Many times it had comforted her with its mighty music.

The clouded May night six years ago when her mother died after months of torturing illness, she had stumbled wildly from the house that held that motionless, sheeted figure, alien now and horrible. Her father was away—the end had been unexpected—and she had no one.

She had flung herself headlong on the shaly shore, sobbing with desperate terror, until, at last, the river had brought peace: the peace of inexorable laws. Dimly she felt its message, translating it through her bewildered child's brain. "No matter what happens to me, it goes on and on and on. It doesn't care, because it's too big to care. It just is. Like God."—But God never seemed very real or helpful.

The servants had found her there hours later, asleep beside the river.

But today it was gay and gentle, gracefully balancing its scores of dipping boats. Even the awesome rise of black cliffs on the opposite Jersey shore looked merely picturesque.

Theo stopped at the dairy for a mug of milk, warm and foaming, fresh from the source; and at the stables she found Minerva ready saddled and whinnying her impatience to be off. The gray mare nuzzled her mistress affectionately, and Theo responded with a quick kiss on the satiny nose.

Dick, the Irish stable boy, laced his grimy hands for her to step on in mounting. "Sure, and you look pretty as a peach, this morning, Miss Theo; your seventeenth birthday will be agreeing with you." He spoke with the easy familiarity of all white servants in the first years of the Republic. "Likely you'll be choosing yourself a fine young husband from the elegant throng that's coming to the mansion today." His little eyes leered at her.

"Likely I won't," she replied tartly, flicking Minerva, who darted gladly away down the sandy road that wound through the Lispenard Meadows to the East River.

Marrying and husbands! Everyone acted as though she were at least twenty-one and likely to be an old maid. Besides, there was only one person who had the right to bring up these subjects. And her father would never think of such things. They were too happy together, the two of them.

She loped Minerva easily across the island until she

14

neared the other river, when color flushed suddenly over her cheeks and she raised a hand to tidy her brown hair. The rendezvous was near. Perhaps it was foolish and unladylike, meeting a strange man like this. Her assent to his suggestion had been a mingling partly of bravado, partly of a sense of adventure, and mostly of a genuine attraction to this charmingly sensitive young man whose mind seemed so attuned to her own.

She had met him by chance three days ago. Minerva had caught a hoof in a rabbit hole and stumbled badly just as he appeared. He had been off his mount in a second, offering assistance. Together they anxiously examined the quivering mare, and were relieved to find no serious damage.

As she thanked him, Theo was conscious of his appraising stare. They looked at each other frankly.

He was young, she judged not more than twenty, and though he topped her by several inches, he was not tall: about the height of her father. That gave her obscure reassurance. His dress was careless: his brown pantaloons were wrinkled above mud-spattered Hessian boots; his neckcloth lay askew and seemed none too fresh. He wore no queue or hat, and his sandy hair, cut short to ear length, was well tousled by the wind.

For all that, she knew he was a gentleman, and he attracted her. It might have been the magnetism of his hazel eyes—changeable, vital, and at the moment devouring her with pleased surprise; or the freshness of his skin which blushed as quickly as a girl's; or indeed his mellow young voice which now proclaimed with a flourish, "Don Quixote is always at the service of the fair Dulcinea."

"Oh!" she cried impulsively, "I love that tale!" And they had drifted into talk of many books, both eager and flushed. "Do you know this?" and "Oh, yes, but have you read that?" She confessed to several works that no respectable young lady should have read, Molière, Sheridan, and *Tristram Shandy* but he did not seem shocked. They talked that morning almost as though they had been two young men— almost.

Then yesterday she had ridden that way again, and he had been there waiting at the turn of the road. It seemed natural to rest their horses and chat.

It was strange how well she felt she knew him, and yet they had touched on nothing personal. They had made a little game of the mystery. He called her "Dulcinea," and she called him nothing at all beyond the formal "sir."

15

He was now waiting for her, sitting easily on his big roan, and with his sandy head—much neater today—turned toward Deadman's Rock and the wooded prettiness of Blackwell's Island, which lay like a splinter of green in the East River.

At the sound of Minerva's trot, he jumped off his horse and rushed toward her. "I was in a rare pother, worrying for fear you weren't coming," he greeted her, tethering her mare to a pine stump. He held out his arms to help her down. Her skirt caught on the side pommels and he, perforce, caught her against him to save her from falling. The clasp of his arms, the momentary pressure of his hard young chest, stirred her. Tingling excitement crept over her body, followed by fear. She heard his quick indrawn breath, and was oppressed with a feeling of embarrassment.

There had been nothing like this before in her experience. Natalie's horror at her escapade, which had been so amusing, now seemed to her justified. She was cheapening herself— he must think her vulgar and ill-bred to meet him this way.

She jerked away from him with unnecessary violence, saying stiffly: "Good day to you, sir. I came only because I had promised. I cannot stay a minute."

"But why?" he protested. "We have so much to talk about, and I—I have brought something to read to you. It would amuse you, I think," he added.

Theo hesitated, her round cheeks stained bright with color.

"This is all most unconventional," she said at last. "We don't even know who we are—I mean who the other is."

"Heaven's mercy!" He gave a shout of laughter. "Is that all? And soon remedied. I am Washington Irving, brother to Doctor Peter Irving. I live on William Street, and I am reading law, but I find it excruciatingly dull. I much prefer poetry and romances, and dreams of far countries." He grinned at her. "And I much prefer literary conversations with beautiful young ladies. Now it's your turn, Dulcinea."

Theo dimpled, her poise returned. "I am Theodosia Burr, daughter to Aaron Burr."

He nodded. "I thought as much. I've heard you described: 'A paragon of loveliness and learning.' Now, if the proprieties are satisfied, will you stay a little and let me read to you?"

She smiled assent. After all, why not? Her silly panic had passed. And he was most respectable: Doctor Irving was well thought of in the city. Besides, she liked this young

16

man; he was totally different from anyone she had met.

They seated themselves on a mound of pine needles. He spread his cloak over a lichen-covered boulder and their backs rested against it. It was deliciously cool. Sunlight filtered down through oak and poplar leaves. A small breeze sighed up the river, blowing away the mosquitoes which so often plagued the Manhattan countryside. The air was pungent with the fragrance of wild strawberries and pine. There was no sound except the rhythmic mouthings of the horses, as they edged placidly around their bridle-lengths, cropping the sweet wild grass.

Neither of them spoke for a while. He made no move to start his reading. A gentle peace held them both.

"This is my birthday," she announced after a bit.

He drew his gaze back from the far horizon. "Is it indeed?" He plucked a daisy from a patch beside him, thrust it into her hair. "Here's a nosegay for you, then, and I salute this most auspicious and blessed day. Is it the sixteenth?"

She shook her head, half-annoyed. "The seventeenth."

"Then we are the same age," he said lazily.

"Really?" She was startled. "I had thought you older."

He shrugged his slight shoulders. "This conversation leads nowhere." He pulled a blade of grass and chewed the succulent tip.

"I thought you were going to read to me?" She was puzzled by him; he seemed moody, distrait.

He gestured toward his pocket, but his hand fell back limply. "I was: a silly little tale I wrote about the Dutch country up the Hudson. But it's no good. It wouldn't interest you."

"But it would!" she protested. "Please." Unconsciously she put her hand out to him, pleading. He imprisoned it gently in his, and at her sharp recoil she saw sudden amusement in his hazel eyes.

He released her hand and went on as though there had been no interruption. "I wish I had written a poem for you, Dulcinea, but I am not at home in verse. Dull prose suits me better. Still, I can try."

He propped himself on his elbows, staring at her with a half-humorous, half-tender intensity that discomposed her.

A daisy twinkles from her hair, like star in beechwood forest,
She is the fairest of the fair, and I would fain — fain——

17

He chuckled. "I can't find a rhyme for forest, but no matter."

He sighed and drew himself up, then leaned forward with sudden violence, crying, "Look! Do you see that brig down there?"

She followed his gaze to the river and nodded, astonished by the emotion in his voice.

"That's the *Infanta*." He uttered the name as though it held all wonder. "She's been to Boston, and she's bound for Spain—Spain!" He turned to Theo and spoke passionately: "More than anything in life I wish I were aboard her. You don't know what it is to hunger and thirst for distant places, do you?"

She shook her head.

"No. Why should you? You're sheltered and happy; you're a woman! But every night I dream of the Old World. It's like a fever. England, France, Spain. The very words make enchanted music for me. I shall see them some day—before I die. And I shall write about them, so that others may feel the enchantment as I do.—At least I hope to."

His voice fell flat. But Theo's eyes dilated, her lips parted. "I am sure you will."

For in that one dazzled moment she had seen greatness in the boy beside her, had heard pulsing through his words a longing and a surge that carried her, too, up with him: up to the lonely starlit plateau of genius.

He shut his eyes an instant and turned to her blindly. "You're sweet," he whispered. "I think you do understand."

With one quick motion he laid his head on her lap, and smiled up at her wickedly, as she froze. "Don't look so shocked, my lovely little Theo—is that what they call you? My head is tired and this is such a soft place to rest. I think I could go to sleep."

Her heart beat in thick, painful movements and the white fichu on her breast rose and fell. She tried to think and could not. She wanted to shove his head viciously away, and her muscles would not obey. A shiver shook her.

"What are you afraid of?" he asked softly. "I won't harm you." He gave a short laugh and sat up. Immediately relief flooded her, but with it a shamed disappointment.

He put gentle hands on her shoulders. "You've never been kissed, have you, Theo? It's not such a terrible thing. I think you must have one for your birthday." He drew her quickly toward him and pressed his fresh young mouth to hers. He let her go at once. "See? It's not so dreadful a thing, is it?"

18

She gasped, laughing shakily. Not so dreadful a thing—no. Sweet, piercingly sweet, but unimportant. She had expected the blast of lightning and found a candle-flame, never disturbing the dark secret something that had lain, terror-stricken, deep in her soul. What had it been, what had she expected? She didn't know. Whatever it was, it had passed her by, leaving only a dimming memory of shame, repulsion, and disloyalty.

She smiled at him with calm affection. "I must be getting back now. Father will be home soon. Thank you, good sir, for my birthday kiss."

He surveyed her, frowning, puzzled. She was so pretty with her rose-and-white skin, soft black eyes, and eager smile. He had wanted to kiss her ever since she came this morning, and he had been sure that, barring maidenly modesty and all the rest, she wanted it too. He was not inexperienced in such matters. Now he had kissed her, briefly it was true, as a preliminary, and she had escaped into a bright and all too obviously genuine indifference. There was a strangeness about her, an untouchable quality.

"Theo," he asked, with sudden inspiration, "are you in love with someone?"

"Oh, no." She faced him candidly. "And I mean never to marry."

"Stuff! Of course you'll marry." The sense of humor, that never deserted him for long, returned. "You're not in love with me, that's certain." And he laughed.

She scarcely heard him. She had just noticed that the sun was now directly overhead. She was in a fever to be off. Her father would be astonished, perhaps hurt, if he came back from the city and she were not there to greet him, to thank him for his beautiful present.

When he had helped her to mount, Washington Irving looked up at her. "Good-bye," he said almost humbly. "You do not wish us to meet again?"

"Of course," she answered, with warm courtesy. "Come to Richmond Hill at any time. We shall be so glad to see you." But her small face was preoccupied, her eyes already straining ahead over the mare's ears down the flat sandy road that led toward home.

He stood quite still, watching her go, his hands deep in the pockets of his green riding-coat, his rumpled hair blown back by the freshening breeze. At the bend of the road, she waved once—quickly, and he waved back.

They did not meet again for seven years.

19

Chapter Two

AARON was enjoying a productive morning with a small group of his henchmen at Martling's Tavern. He sat in his usual corner of the smoky, ale-soured room, sipping a thimbleful of port, and looking, in his immaculate blue satin suit, like a sleek greyhound in a kennel of mongrels.

Others of the group were drinking claret or guzzling blistering New England rum and paid their court to the chief, who sat erect with a military precision that was born of army training and long self-discipline. His eyes, glittering black, wandered slowly from one face to another, appraising the potentialities of each. Eyes like Theodosia's, but with an added hypnotic, almost reptilian quality that subdued or fascinated at will.

The miscellaneous band of satellites which surrounded him were known as the "Little Band," or the "Myrmidons," and Theo had also facetiously dubbed them the "Tenth Legion." They covered a wide range of personalities.

There were sachems and braves from Saint Tammany's Society—Matthew Davis, Van Ness, the Swartwout brothers; a sprinkling of artists and dilettantes; and some shady characters—wharf-rats, escaped slaves, and prostitutes. The latter had, naturally, no official standing in the "Little Band," but they were useful—and Aaron was never one to boggle over fine ethical points.

Whatever their individual peculiarities, they were all united by one prime virtue—uncritical obedience to the wishes of Colonel Burr.

Burr's enemies described him as an octopus insinuating slimy tentacles into all the strata of a deluded society, spewing an inky barrage of lies and sophistry to confound the righteous. His friends saw him quite simply as a god, shining, beneficent, and infinitely seductive.

Both views amused Aaron. He knew very well what he

was: a man with a brilliant brain, not unkind, not altogether unscrupulous, but with a genius for manipulating people and events to further his ends.

And the game, to him, was as exciting as the goal.

The goal this time was worthy of his best efforts. Last month he had snatched victory from what had seemed sure defeat, by swinging the all-important New York State to the Republicans. These were now joyfully engaged in thumbing their noses at the furious Federalists, who screamed to the heavens of cheating and foul play.

Now, however, a bigger battle loomed. He and Mr. Jefferson were Republican candidates for the Presidency, and one of them was certain to win. The wily and astute Mr. Hamilton had for once faltered, and the Federalist Party had bogged down into a welter of contending factions. Let them flounder, and a blessing on them! They would never pull themselves together in time to produce a candidate worth a pinch of snuff.

To be sure, the majority of Republicans seemed to take it for granted that Jefferson should be President and Aaron grateful for the small potatoes of the Vice-Presidency. But matters might far better be the other way around—far better.

That lanky, shock-haired dolt of a Jefferson had already been Vice-President for four years. He might well continue in that placid rôle. As it was, he spent most of his time at Monticello, sitting on his backside and philosophizing, or puttering with his idiotic mechanical contrivances, or, worse yet, tending his collection of birds.

Pshaw! thought Aaron, with an inward snort, though not a quiver showed upon his courteously attentive face as he listened to one of Matthew Davis's long-winded stories. John Adams had made muddle enough of his office, too stupid even to recognize that the people loathed his royalist bias. This was no time to elect another visionary. The country needed a man of action, a leader. It should have one!

Precisely as Davis's droning voice ceased, Aaron broke into mellow, appreciative chuckles. "Oh, very droll, my dear Davis. Indeed, I have always said that you have a most ready wit!"

Davis beamed, adjusted his coat collar, flicked an imaginary speck of dust from his pantaloons, glancing triumphantly around the company. They were a set of clods and never appreciated the subtleties of his discourse as Colonel Burr always did.

A newcomer, rough-clothed in homespun, a week-old beard

blackening his foxy jaws, pushed his way to Aaron's table.

Aaron hailed him warmly. "Welcome, Garson. Very welcome. I've been expecting you these three days." He beckoned to the landlord, who bustled up, wiping his hands on his spotted apron.

"A noggin of rum for Mr. Garson, Brom, and one of your finest beefsteak and oyster pasties. He is just back from the Carolinas, and must be in need of Christian food."

Garson laughed. "The Colonel is right, as always. Though they eat well enough in the great houses, I had no taste of it. Nothing but salt pork and corn pone, until my stomach crawled. For I stuck close to the taverns and settlers' cabins as you ordered."

Aaron nodded. Tom Garson was one of his most efficient agents; an Englishman, come over in '95 with a down-at-the-heels theatrical company, and stranded in Philadelphia, where Aaron, ever on the alert for useful men, had picked him up. Garson's training as an actor made him invaluable, as did his cockney shrewdness.

Aaron leaned forward. "You posed as a peddler this time, did you not?"

"That I did—and a pleasant trade it is. I took care to fill my pack with gewgaws for the women, and there was many a fine opportunity for trying the fit of a fichu over a tempting white bosom, or even sometimes a garter around a rosy thigh." He smacked his lips as Aaron laughed.

"I'm willing to believe you made the most of such opportunities, but what of the men? How is the temper of the people? Will they vote for the right party? Will they vote for Aaron Burr?"

Garson drained his rum, wolfed a chunk of steaming pie, wiped the gravy off his mouth with the back of his hand, and sat back, while Aaron waited.

"The Republicans are gaining down there," said Garson at last, "but they know little about you in the South."

"So Timothy Green writes me," said Aaron dryly. "We must remedy that. Go on . . ."

"South Carolina will be the crux; its decision will tell the tale. And it is controlled by a few families, the Middletons, the Rutledges, and the Alstons. Especially the Alstons; they have great plantations up on the Waccamaw River. Gain them and I wager you will gain the state. The small fry will follow their lead."

"The Alstons. Yes." Aaron flashed his brilliant smile. "You've done well, Garson. Your information confirms what

I have already heard. It so happens that young Joseph Alston is in New York, is coming"—he paused for the fraction of a second and went on smoothly—"to my house for dinner this afternoon."

Garson stared. Rum fumes had mounted to his brain, clouding its usual acuteness. Then, as the Colonel's words penetrated, he slapped the table until the mugs rattled, guffawing.

"By God, you're a sly one, you are! I see what you're up to . . . Young Alston to dinner, and the beautiful Theodosia there, too, turning her great eyes his way. She'll use them to good purpose, I warrant, under her father's promptings."

"Sir!" Aaron leapt to his feet. "You forget yourself!" His voice, scarce raised, yet sounded through the tavern like a thunderclap.

Men sat up, murmuring. Garson shrank, his dark skin glistening.

"I—I meant no harm, Colonel," he babbled. "I apologize. It was the spirits."

Aaron's nostrils dilated, but his look became less menacing. "I accept your excuse. Remember"—his piercing gaze swept the whole company—"no man may make light of my daughter's name without having me to reckon with. And I am not unhandy with the pistols."

No one spoke. Aaron relaxed. "Come, gentlemen," he cried, with perfect good-humor, "another bumper all around. Brom Martling, see to it for me. I must go now. I bid you all good day."

As the heavy oak door swung to behind him, Garson grumbled, "How did I know he would be so touchy?"

"'Tis the only subject on which he's touchy," said young Van Ness, with swift loyalty. "Usually he has the temper of an angel."

"He's fair daft about that girl of his," went on Garson, still smarting. "It seems scarcely natural."

"Oh, he's natural enough," snorted Matthew Davis. "He's a great dog with the ladies. Ten to one, he's gone off now to visit that blue-eyed wench he's keeping on South Street. The lucky beggar—she has one of the trimmest ankles I've ever seen. Though I remember once, when I was in Albany, walking down State Street, the door of one of the houses opened, and I said to myself . . ." He meandered on through one of his interminable stories, but this time the Colonel had gone, and nobody listened.

Chapter Three

AARON had not gone to South Street, however, not even thought of it. Little Sally Martin, with her dovelike compliance and devoted eyes of a water spaniel, was useful only as an occasional physical necessity. Brothels offended his fastidiousness, and lately he had not had the time to undertake the complicated and protracted pursuit expected by ladies of fashion. Sally was merely a stopgap. Inexpensive and cozy as a cup of tea—and equally unintoxicating.

Aaron's mind, this morning, was concerned with far more interesting matters. He guided Selim up Broadway at a walk. The stallion's shoes rang on the cobblestones, raising little puffs of malodorous dust, detouring a yapping dog-fight and piles of garbage where pigs rooted, grunting happily. Aaron drew him aside at the sound of a musical horn, to let the Boston Mail go by. He was pleased to see the lumbering coach. It meant letters and newspapers from New England, more news of the political situation.

He turned west on Chambers Street, then north on the Greenwich Road, spurring Selim to a canter now that the cobblestones were left behind. Two miles brought him near Greenwich Village. He passed a handful of wooden houses without seeing them, turning thankfully through the iron gates of Richmond Hill.

The stable-boy rushed up at the sound of hoofs. Aaron mechanically threw him the reins, peering over his head for the small figure that usually came flying down the steps to greet him.

"Has Miss Burr gone out, Dick?"

The man muttered. He wanted his dinner and could not leave until Minerva was back and properly rubbed down. "Been gone since eight, sir, on the gray mare, and yesterday

24

she was gone all morning, and the day before . . ."

"Thank you, that will do." Aaron's quiet voice struck him like a brick.

He opened his mouth, shut it again, and stalked sulkily away with Selim.

Aaron walked thoughtfully up the white steps. So the child was up to something, perhaps, after all. He had heard a rumor. Someone had seen her talking to a youth in the Jones Woods. He had dismissed it as ridiculous. He still thought it unlikely. But in any event he was not much disturbed. She was not one of your giddy little flibbertigibbets. All the same, it was surprising, and Aaron was seldom surprised. As in chess, a game in which he excelled, he found it easy to anticipate his opponent's campagn of play, keeping always two, three, or more moves ahead of him. But Theo was not an opponent. She was flesh of his flesh, an infinitely dear projection of himself.

Frowning, he walked down the white-paneled, picture-hung hallway to his library, and relaxed with the thrill of sensuous pleasure the room always gave him. The stoic and the voluptuary lived amicably side by side in his soul. He could be perfectly indifferent to his surroundings, and indeed, upstairs in his bedchamber he slept on a camp cot, and with no other furnishings except a table, chair, and commode.

But this library was his delight. He had added it himself to the back of the house, when, in 1791, he had acquired the lease to this mansion which had housed the John Adamses and General Washington.

It was a spacious room, with three tall windows that gave eastern and southern light. The walls were lined to shoulder height with books, shipload after shipload of them from the presses of England and France. Soft creamy vellum bindings alternated with the dead leaf-brown of calfskin. Their musty odor of ink and old leather pervaded the room like incense.

The polished oak floor was all but hidden by an ingrain carpet, warmly red, decorated with scattered fleurs-de-lis. Ardent francophile that he was, Aaron had snapped it up at an auction, and had often been sardonically amused at the horror this royalist emblem excited in some of his friends. His convictions, and his interests, were republican enough, but he was no fanatic, and a beautiful carpet was a beautiful carpet.

There were two library tables, a sprinkling of lyre-backed chairs, and a sofa, upholstered in crimson satin, from the fashionable workshop of Duncan Phyfe. An elegant little

25

"traveling-case" on wheels stood near the door, complete with tea caddies and liquor bottles for the refreshment of guests.

The north wall was given over to an enormous fireplace, its wooden mantel painted white and carved with the classic egg-and-dart design. Two Sèvres vases stood upon it, the blues and golds of their porcelain lustrous as jewels. And above them hung a portrait of Theodosia at fourteen. Gilbert Stuart had painted it, and Aaron had been none too pleased with the result. It had caught her dimpled prettiness and the sweet gravity of her face in repose, but failed entirely to give any hint of her vivacity and sparkle. "'Tis a namby-pamby, bread-and-butter miss you have made of her," he told Stuart, whose touchy vanity was thereby so outraged that they had no more dealings with each other.

Still Aaron kept it there until such time as young Vander-lyn could produce a better likeness. He glanced at the picture now, meditatively, seated himself at his writing-table, pulled a sheaf of letters to him, and picked up his quill pen.

In a few minutes there came a timid knock at the door and Natalie's high accented voice. "May I speak with you a moment, Papa Burr?"

He rose with instant courtesy, thrusting his pen into its ruby-colored glass of shot. Natalie slid into the room twisting her fingers nervously. He settled her on a chair and reseated himself. "What is it, Natalie? What is troubling you?"

He smiled kindly at the girl, thinking that it was a pity she was not prettier, though she had a certain style with her retroussé nose and tiny pursed mouth, and she did manage to coax her light nondescript hair into a chic coiffure. She wasn't a Frenchwoman for nothing.

"It's . . . it's about Theo," she faltered.

His eyelids flickered, but his warm smile remained unchanged. "Well, what about Theo? Come, child, you act like a flushed partridge. Out with it."

Natalie gulped and in one excited breath went on: "This morning, she—she said she had rendezvous with a 'andsome young man, but she was not even sure of his name. I could not believe my ears. I tried to stop her, of course, but she would not listen. She ran from me, toute étourdie, laughing comme une folle. I—I thought I must tell you."

Aaron nodded, his eyes sympathetic. "You did quite right, my dear," while he suppressed laughter that would have hurt the earnest and estimable Natalie. So that was all it was.

26

An escapade, a piece of light-hearted foolishment, or she would never have told Natalie.

They both turned at sounds outside, Minerva's unmistakable whinny, then Theo's clear voice, asking eagerly, "Is Colonel Burr at home yet?"

Natalie rose hastily. "You won't scold her too much today, will you? It is her jour de fête."

"I shall not scold her," said Aaron gravely, "too much." Amusement twitched at his mouth as Natalie escaped.

He stood quietly waiting, as light footsteps ran down the hall toward him.

Theo burst in, stumbling a little over her flowing skirt. "Oh, I'm so sorry I was not here to greet you! And, Papa, thank you, thank you, for the exquisite present." She flung her arms about his neck, pressing her warm young cheek to his.

"I'm glad you like it, child. It should suit you." He encircled her chin with his hand, tilting her head back to search her face. Her eyes, brilliant and unshadowed, met his with loving candor.

"Did you enjoy your ride?" he asked quietly, but there was meaning in his tone.

Theo's tiny white teeth caught her underlip. She lowered her lashes, half-guilty, half-laughing. So he knew. It never occurred to her to wonder how. Sooner or later he always knew everything, anyway.

"Well, I did, and I didn't," she answered, choosing her words. "You see, the other day . . ."

"You needn't tell me," he struck in, smiling. "You have my most perfect trust, as you know." He touched her smooth hair in a brief caress.

Suddenly she averted her face. Slow red washed over her neck and up to the curly auburn bang on her forehead.

Aaron stared. His intuition, always sensitive, was triggerquick where Theo was concerned. Damme if I don't believe the minx has been kissed. A surface cynicism masked a disagreeable sense of shock. Imperceptibly his whole body stiffened. "But tell me this, Theo. Will you be riding that way again?" His tone was casual, though he watched her narrowly, intent to catch any secrecy or subtle withdrawal in those transparent features.

And there was none. Her color had ebbed. She perfectly understood the meaning behind his question. She gave her little gurgle of amusement, shook her head. "No, I shall not

27

ride that way again. On the whole, I find the—the landscape not to my liking."

"Ah—" said Aaron, satisfied. He reached over the table, flipped open his silver snuffbox, took a pinch with a well-kept thumb and forefinger, and sniffed it delicately. "Run along now, Miss Prissy." He seldom called her by her childish nickname any more, and she smiled quick response. "I'll let you off your studies today," he went on. "Go and prepare yourself for the party. You must look your loveliest. There will be a rare gathering to do you honor."

When she had gone, he sat quietly at the table, thinking. He appraised Theo's little amourette at its exact worth. Some momentary flirtation, already finished, and leaving her as innocent and unawakened as she had been before. He had been far too wise to force her confidence. To make much of the episode might have lit the spark of perversity that dwelt in every female breast—even hers. Besides, it was not necessary. The chapter was closed, he knew with sure instinct.

But there would be a next time, that was the trouble.

Some obnoxious booby would come along with sheep's eyes and a persuasive tongue to lure Theo into the scalding cauldron of passion. And no one knew better than Aaron that girls, unguided except by their passions, ever entangled themselves with the least desirable men.

He must at all costs protect her from that. He got up, paced back and forth on the carpet. He hadn't realized it, but she was ripe for mating. Already some of her contemporaries were married. Early and brilliant marriage was the crowning accomplishment for a woman.

True, there had been suitors buzzing around her of late, but they were all nonentities. He had not given them a serious thought. Theo must have a husband worthy of her, and worthy of marrying a Burr. And it must be a husband of his choosing, for did he not know, far better than she could know herself, what would be best for her? Had he not from her earliest infancy guided her thoughts, formed her character, and supervised nearly every hour of her blossoming life?

He turned with sudden resolution, went to a mahogany highboy, and, taking a small brass key from his pocket, unlocked a drawer. He took from it a large envelope marked "A," and carried it to his writing-table. There were a number of letters inside and a sheet of paper covered with his own small, precise writing.

The paper was headed "Joseph Alston," and continued

through a complete record of memoranda. "Born: Charleston, November 10th, 1779.—Attended Princeton for one year, 1795. No great scholar.—Three plantations and two estates. Probable net income in excess of forty thousand per annum.—Of an outwardly arrogant and overbearing disposition, but in reality very easily led.—Healthy and well set up. Not unduly addicted to strong drink or venery." And so on, to the bottom of the crowded page.

Aaron read it all over again, very slowly, and his eyes were inscrutable.

Chapter Four

THE GUESTS began arriving at half-past three. The stamping of horses, the creaking of cabriolet wheels, the squeal of brakes on a heavy coach, all floated up through Theodosia's open window. She listened to the delightful bustle and fumed with impatience to be part of it.

She dearly loved the excitement of anticipation, the beginnings of things: parties, trips, or weightier projects. She was never quite to lose that breathless certainty of youth that *this* time something magical would happen, the decisive something for which she dimly longed.

Adonis, the fashionable coiffeur specially fetched from Pearl Street for the occasion, held his tongs near his sweating black cheek to test their heat, and his deliberateness exasperated Theo.

"Do hurry, Adonis," she pleaded. "People are arriving."

The old man threw a contemptuous glance toward the window. "Jus' Republican canaille, mamselle—don' know better zan be early. What do zey know of etiquette?" He snorted, twisting and snipping expertly at Theo's hair. "Parvenus! Like zat Joséphine Beauharnais over in France now, pretending she be somebody. I see her many times in Martinique. Pfoui! Running after any planter who would look at her—no better zan a trollop."

Theo giggled, and he rolled his intelligent, yellowish eyes. "Je vous demande pardon, mamselle, but it is truth. Over zere zey kill ze king, zey kill everybody—and now zey let zis Corsican brigand lord it over zem wiz his—his doxy, cette Joséphine!"

He flung down his comb, his hands shook, their pinkish palms wet.

"Zey even say zis Bonaparte will make himself a king!

It is not possible, zey cannot be as mad as zat—Someday, mamselle—someday zis folie will pass, the Bourbons will come back. You will see, as sure as le bon Dieu watches us up there . . . the Bourbons will be back on zere rightful throne." His eyes watered and he muttered on to himself.

Theo sighed. He was off again, poor old thing. Nothing to do but wait patiently until he took up his comb. Adonis was an artist with the scissors and tongs, by far the best in the town, and the ladies and gentlemen who patronized him all knew his story and put up with his mania. He had been born on Martinique, a free black of some consequence, and with a passionate loyalty to his king. Louis XVI and God were for him merged into one. The Revolution had broken his heart, and he had been hustled off the island by friends just before the newly appointed committee got around to dealing with a trouble-making old black man.

He had landed in New York and taken a mighty vow. Never would he cover his kinky poll until the Bourbons reigned again. Winter snows and summer suns beat alike on his grizzling thatch, while he stalked grimly around the streets, his pockets filled with the implements of his trade, his soul filled with hatred for the Anti-Christs who had murdered his king.

"The Count Jérome de Joliette is coming today," said Theo slyly, beginning to despair of getting her hair finished.

Adonis started, his seamed face crinkled. He picked up the comb. "Ah, c'est bon. Un aristocrat de l'ancien régime. I will make you vairy vairy beautiful for him."

Well, hardly—thought Theo. The Count was a dreadful bore, and quite old, way over thirty. But her bait had served its purpose.

Adonis piled her ringleted hair, dexterously inserted a small white ostrich plume, anchored it with a cluster of rosebuds. He backed off considering. Theo tried to control her fidgets.

"Mamselle has beautiful nose, classique; I have made it more easy to see. And she has magnificent eyes; she should not wear her hair so low on the forehead, only those two little curls, just as I have put them—so. Also zey balance ze chin. Mamselle have ze chin a bit full, a bit too round. Now no one will notice——"

"Yes, Adonis, you've made a masterpiece of me. Thank you, but I must get ready. I see the Hamiltons' curricle coming down the drive, and that means it's late. Peggy will give you your money in the kitchen."

She hustled the old man out and called her maid. They

embarked on the intricacies of her toilette, lacing her tender young body into long stays made of steel and leather. These reached so high as to push her small bosom even higher than its normal position, and they cut cruelly underneath. Theo hated them, and wore them as seldom as possible, fashion or no fashion. Over the stays went a short muslin petticoat, then white stockings with clocks, and tiny yellow satin shoes whose flexible kid soles barely separated her feet from the floor.

The shoes gave her no height, but the Parisian gown did, for it was fashioned very simply in the new mode: a long straight fall of white India muslin, caught high under the bosom with a band of gold embroidery whose gilded vine pattern was repeated at the hem.

And of course there was the necklace, sparkling on her white skin like a shower of raindrops..

When she looked in the mirror, she knew that she was lovely. Her heart swelled with a delicious sense of power. This was her evening, her day. To be admired and fêted against the background of Aaron's fondly approving smile, what greater joy was there in life?

She paused before entering the long drawing-room, looking for her father. It was filled with people. Despite the flooding sunshine outside, the curtains were drawn and all the hundred tapers lighted. They glittered from their crystal pendants, a forest of twinkling yellow flame. The guests made a soft pastel blur of rose and blue and green and violet, accented by an occasional powdered head like that of the beautiful Mrs. John Jay, who clung to a fashion she knew suited her so well.

The buzz of conversation broke off and heads turned to welcome her. Aaron, impeccable in dove-gray satin and white neckcloth, sprang forward from a group.

"Here is Queen Theodosia at last! I suppose we must to-day accord her the royal prerogative of tardiness." He smiled at her with undisguised pride, despite the implied criticism. Aaron had no patience with tardiness, particularly when manners demanded that a hostess should be graciously ready long before guests arrived. Theo was glad to be let off so easily, as he led her forward to stand beside him against the fireplace.

Mrs. Alexander Hamilton came up first, stepping lightly as a girl despite her eight children. She kissed Theo on both cheeks, wishing her many happy returns of the day. Her tall daughter, Angelica, followed more sedately, her melancholy little face already shadowed by the insanity that was later to claim her. Then General Hamilton himself bowed low over Theo's hand.

Theo smiled brightly at his compliments, disguising perfectly the feeling of dislike and fear he always gave her. No reason for it, she knew. He and Aaron were political opponents and had had several bitter public skirmishes, but that was true of many other men whom she heartily liked. Besides, Aaron and Hamilton were friendly enough in private, and called each other by their Christian names. They were rather alike, too, both short men, fastidious and exquisitely dressed, both great gallants with the ladies. General Hamilton this evening was particularly splendid in violet brocade, his sandy hair lightly powdered in the fashion of the Federalists.

"What a very fine bauble you're wearing, Theo," he said, showing his white teeth. "It very nearly rivals the brilliance of your eyes."

"Father gave it to me this morning——"

"Ah—your father is ever one to lavish beauty upon beauty." He spoke smoothly, but she saw a glint in his pale eyes.

One more count against Burr, he thought, as he turned away. Insane extravagance coupled with chicanery. Very like, this ridiculous jewel had been paid for with money swindled from the people in Burr's fictitious water company. If it had been paid for at all. The slippery scoundrel! He must at all costs be checked before he ruined the country with his plunderings and intrigues. God forbid that there should be a chance of his snatching the Presidency. Jefferson was bad enough—but Burr would be monstrous.

He settled himself in a corner and examined the company. Half the town was there. Livingstons, Swartwouts, Morrises and Sedgwicks, Bartows and Prevosts, these latter relatives of the late Mrs. Burr. There was pretty little Katie Brown talking to Burr's protégé, young Vanderlyn, and a handful of young bucks around her too.

He could not honestly object to these guests: they were natural enough selections; but why must Burr ever surround himself with Frenchmen? He glared at the Comte de Joliette: the fellow was rouged and befrilled like a woman; and why the inclusion of the du Pont de Nemours brothers with their wives? They had barely landed and spoke almost no English, and they were of no importance whatsoever.

Hamilton disliked foreigners, and grumpily helped himself

to punch in anticipation of a dull evening.

Victor and Éleuthère Irénée du Pont were unconscious of the great man's disapproval. They were fine-looking young men, tall for Frenchmen, and enthusiastic about everything in the new country. Only this morning, while snipe shooting, Irénée had had a brilliant idea, and he impatiently awaited an opportunity to present it to Colonel Burr for advice. Or, indeed, to General Hamilton, for his shrewd French brain had decided to back the winner. The Federalists were on the way out, Burr and Jefferson were obviously gaining; still, one must be wary of offending expiring monarchs—they have been known to revive.

The great gilded punchbowl circulated rapidly, as black Alexis carried it from one group to another. It contained a Richmond Hill specialty, a mixture of homemade peach brandy and champagne, and it was iced—a newfangled innovation which disconcerted some of the older guests, who were convinced that a freezing liquid could not be wholesome.

Toast after toast was drunk to Theodosia's happiness, and she responded with deep curtsies and laughing eyes. Eyes sparkled, cheeks grew flushed, and still Alexis had not announced that the dinner awaited their pleasure.

Theo signaled her father in surprise, but he shook his head and glanced toward the door. They were waiting for someone, then. Who? She speculated idly, gave it up, and went on talking to the young men who surrounded her.

It was past six before Alexis opened the drawing-room door with a dignified flourish. "Mr. Joseph Alston," he announced.

Everyone turned as a heavy young man lumbered in. Theo stared with the rest. He must be a gentleman of consequence or her father would never have kept this distinguished company waiting for him.

Had she ever heard of Joseph Alston? Something to do with South Carolina, she thought. Political then. He had a pompous air about him; he looked arrogant and humorless. He was of medium height and heavy-set, a circumstance which his bright plum-colored suit did nothing to conceal. It seemed stuffed to bursting across his broad back. His hair was black and cut short à la Brutus; it clustered on his round head in tight curls. Theo thought instantly of a bust of the Emperor Tiberius which she had once seen in a Philadelphia drawing-room: the same thick neck, low forehead, and full, disdainful mouth.

Alston eyed the assemblage in a lofty manner while Aaron greeted him with emphatic cordiality, and drew him over to Theodosia. "Mr. Alston, may I present you to my daughter, Miss Burr?"

Theodosia sketched a curtsy, and the young man bowed. "'S a pleasure, ma'am," he drawled, with a languid blurring of consonants which she knew to be peculiar to natives of the Southern States.

"Welcome to Richmond Hill," she murmured, gave him a bright, conventional smile, and turned back to the group behind her, eager to join in their chatter.

"Theo——" It was Aaron's voice, and, sensitive to its slightest gradations, she heard in the one word that he was displeased with her. "Mr. Alston has but newly arrived in New York. It will divert him to have you tell him something of the season in town, the balls and the theater. He will take you in to dinner."

Her eyes widened. Here was a shattering of precedent. As both hostess and guest of honor tonight, it was fitting that she be escorted by the male guest of highest rank, General Hamilton, Mr. Livingston, or the Count, perhaps. But she was far too well trained to show surprise, and slipped her hand docilely through the arm of the silent young man beside them.

"Indeed, sir, and are you enjoying our city? Is it from the Carolinas that you come? Such a long journey—you must be fatigued." She eyed him with fresh interest. He seemed a prodigiously dull gentleman, but her father was never wrong, and if he wished to do Mr. Alston unusual honor, he must have a very good reason.

Aaron presented his arm to Mrs. Jay, and they all moved toward the dining-room.

The immense table easily accommodated thirty people. Theo, separated from her father by its whole length, felt his admonishing glance as they took their places.

The table was piled high with platters: turtle soup, boiled lobsters that had come by sloop from Massachusetts, three great oyster patties flanked by immense joints, one of beef, the other of mutton. Between them, like the smaller islands of an archipelago, were dotted stuffed pheasants and ducks. There were vegetables, too: boiled onions, tiny new beets, and roasted potatoes.

The guests helped themselves, with the aid of Alexis and his corps of waiters, who facilitated the process when a desired dainty was too far away to be speared with one of

35

the serving forks. This being a formal occasion, individual forks had been provided, but most of the company scorned this French refinement and conveyed food on an expertly piled knife.

Theo made conversation with Mr. Alston, using all her tact to draw him out as her father's look demanded. It was not easy. His responses were slow and ponderous, so that her quick brain had traveled yards ahead of him before he had finished.

Irénée du Pont sat on her left, and from time to time she turned to him thankfully, enjoying both the grace of his sparkling French and the pleasure that her own proficiency in the language gave her.

The party was nearly bilingual, and conversation, led from the center by Natalie and the Comte de Joliette, gradually changed into French. They were all talking glibly until Theo saw her father frown. She started, realizing that Mr. Alston sat heavily silent beside her, sipping his claret with an expression of sulky annoyance.

"You perhaps do not speak French?" she faltered.

Alston wiped his mouth. "I do not, ma'am. Down where we come from we have no liking for foreign taradiddles."

Merciful heavens! thought Theo. What a boor! Fancy a man of education not speaking some French.

Irénée du Pont had watched this little contretemps with amusement. He now struck in across the silenced table, relieving the embarrassment. "I had fonny—how you say—experience zis morning. I was snipe shooting wiz Toussard over by ze river; we shoot all our powder, get no birds. But we are shamed to go à la maison wiz nossing. Sophie will make fon of us." He bowed to his smiling wife. "So we find leetle shop and buy more powder. We see some birds, we aim, we shoot"—he paused dramatically—"and both our guns explode à la fois. Boom! Pan! Boom! comme ça. All in leetle pieces!"

"La! sir," cried Mrs. Jay, leaning forward, "I don't think that funny. Did you not injure your hands?"

Du Pont shook his head. "No, we drop quickly ze guns. But I have idea. I admire much your so marvelous country; only one sing is bad. You make bad powder. So I tell myself someone should make good powder, and why not us? Papa, Victor, and me. We will start a—a usine somewhere to make it."

He looked around for approval, and Aaron said heartily: "An excellent idea, sir. Let us drink a toast to the du Ponts and their powder mill." Glasses were politely raised to lips, and the conversation became general again.

The meal wore on, until the servants removed remnants of the main course and bore in the sweets, fruits, and cheeses, a half-dozen puddings, and a huge salver of rapidly melting ice cream flavored with the vanilla beans that were so costly.

On the other side of Alston sat little Katie Brown, whose provocative dimples usually made havoc of masculine hearts. In desperation, Theo signaled her secretly to help out with the entertainment of the difficult young man between them, but Katie's response was only an expressive rolling of the eyes and a shrug. She had no time to waste on a lout who replied to her best sallies with a bored stare. "Impossible," Katie mouthed to Theo, who was in entire agreement. Still Aaron's eyes were on her, watching and commanding, and she redoubled her efforts, deciding to abandon subtlety.

"Do you not like us, Mr. Alston?" she asked sweetly. "You have not smiled once since we sat at table. Are the victuals ill-cooked, or is the company not to your taste?"

Alston looked up from his plate, and she saw surprise in his heavy face. "Why, the victuals are good, ma'am," he said slowly, "and the company pleasing enough. I do not smile unless I see something to smile at, and that is not often."

Obviously, thought Theo.

"But in South Carolina——" she persisted. "When you are in the company of young ladies, do you not sometimes murmur sweet nothings, and rally them a bit? Or are the young ladies of your country so much more charming than we poor New Yorkers?" She looked archly at him through her lashes, caring little whether he thought her forward.

To her mortification, he pushed back his plate and considered her question as seriously as though she had put to him a proposition in Euclid.

"Why, the young ladies of South Carolina are very well, very well, indeed. A trifle more genteel pallor and delicacy than those up here, perhaps, but these, too, seem amiable and pretty." His prominent eyes examined her blushing face with the first spark of interest she had seen in them.

"Indeed, Miss Burr," he went on solemnly, "I find your appearance not inferior to that of some of our reigning belles. Be assured as to that."

"Oh, thank you very much, Mr. Alston!" Her voice shook, and she dared not look at Katie, who she saw was quivering with ill-suppressed giggles.

Fortunately, the time had come to clear the board. The

servants removed the tablecloth and substituted dishes of fruit and nuts, before placing a clean wineglass beside each gentleman.

Theo rose, and the other ladies with her. They quitted the dining-room in a rustle of perfumed silk and polite murmurs, while the men drew nearer to their host and prepared for the serious business of after-dinner toasts.

Alexis passed a tray of Havana cigars and snuff. Joseph Alston helped himself to a cigar, sniffed it disdainfully, and replaced it with one from his pocket.

Aaron watched him, amused. He now had the young man's exact measure. These wealthy Carolina planters were brought up en prince, having unlimited power over hundreds of black souls, as well as many white ones. They were in fact overlords, and the regal manner came naturally. That they were also narrow and insular, with little interest outside of their own closely guarded society, was natural too. But in this particular specimen he noted that underneath the brusque and irritating manner lay a core of uncertainty. Mr. Alston was ill at ease in an atmosphere unfamiliar to him, and therefore his immature personality was both hurt and hostile. Adroit handling would change that. Moreover, Theo had already made a far stronger impression than she knew. Her vivacity had intrigued Alston, though he had not as yet realized it. Aaron was well content.

He rose glass in hand and smiled his warm smile. No matter how numerous the recipients of that smile, it always contrived to convince each one of Colonel Burr's special regard, and now every face responded—with one exception. "Gentlemen, I wish to propose some toasts. First, the health of our illustrious President, Mr. John Adams."

Glasses tinkled as they drank. Hamilton watched Burr, and his mouth curled.

Aaron went on. "The health of our next President, the great and glorious——" He paused, and a flicker of malicious amusement crossed his face. The men stared. In view of Burr's party, Jefferson's name was surely the only one which could follow.

Aaron began again with leisured relish, "To our next President, the great and glorious unknown." He looked full at Hamilton, who choked, thinking that Burr had contrived this with his usual hypocrisy.

The substitution of "unknown" would be accepted by the other guests as a delicate compliment to the only Federalist present, but Hamilton knew very well that his host had meant, "the great and glorious Aaron Burr." It was a challenge, subtle, of course, as was this insinuating schemer's every act, but none the less a challenge. Hamilton marked it down.

Aaron was amused by his opponent's annoyance. He enjoyed a contest of wits as much as Hamilton hated it, nor did he realize the depth of the other's enmity. Hamilton himself could not have explained the instant dislike he had conceived for Burr from the time of their first association as young officers in General Washington's military family. Though he had resented the similarity between their persons and ambitions, and the contrast between his own tarnished boyhood in the West Indies and Burr's aristocratic background of wealth, education, and respectability, it went deeper than that.

Aaron, still on his feet, proposed another another toast. "And now, gentlemen, I give you one of our company . . . a young man of great estate and ancient lineage, a gentleman of culture and understanding, who is most certainly destined to carve his name upon the tablets of our country's history. I give you Mr. Joseph Alston."

So, thought Hamilton, as he rose with the rest, that's the way the cat jumps now. And for what purpose is Burr shoveling flattery at this oaf of a planter who is obviously destined to carve his name on nothing more enduring than his own rice swamps? He pondered this without result.

In between the toasts that followed, Aaron conversed with Joseph Alston, awakening in him, by the simple method of telling him of them, sentiments that he had not known he possessed.

The young planter relaxed, puffing at his cigar. Colonel Burr, it seemed, thought him wondrous patriotic, found that he had great understanding of the country's needs. Joseph hazarded a few remarks and found that they revealed conspicuous political acumen. Dazzled by this new picture of himself, he suddenly realized that none but Colonel Burr had ever had the penetration to value him at his true worth. A hazy glow of good-will subdued his habitual truculence. He helped himself to repeated glasses of Madeira, until Aaron, who had barely sipped from his own glass, pushed back his chair.

"What do you say, gentlemen, to a game of loo or whist or dicing? Though I believe that the younger ones amongst us may prefer to dance. At any rate, let us join the lovely charmers who await us, I trust, impatiently."

In the drawing-room the ladies upon finishing dinner had divided themselves into two natural groups. At one end by the fireplace, the matrons clustered around Mrs. Hamilton and enjoyed a technical discussion about a difficult lying-in. Even Mrs. Jay inclined her stately head and gave it as her opinion that a drop of laudanum was permissible at such a time. "Though, mind you, I don't hold with coddling. Our Creator intended women to suffer, and has given us the strength to stand it."

Sophie du Pont made a tiny choked sound. "Does eet—is eet so bad?" she whispered.

The ladies looked at her frightened face, and Mrs. Hamilton's softened with quick sympathy. "My dear child, I didn't realize. How stupid of me to talk like that! I can see now, but really with these new styles one can hardly tell, can one? No, of course it's not so bad."

Sophie tried to smile. "But I am so old for a first. Twenty-five."

The ladies clucked dismay; not one of them but had had a full nursery by that time. Still, Mrs. Hamilton launched into detailed advice, for, by virtue of her many pregnancies, she was an authority. Sophie listened respectfully.

At the other end of the long room the girls twittered like starlings. They had intended to try some recently imported songs on Theo's magnificent new pianoforte. Angelica Hamilton and Theo enjoyed duets. But Angelica was more than musically talented, she was touched with genius, and Theo found herself unable to follow the other girl's brilliant performance. So they gave it up. Angelica played soft roulades and chords to herself, while the others abandoned music for more exciting topics.

"La!" cried Katie wickedly, "such goings-on as I have seen here tonight! Natalie making eyes at the Count, and our Theo positively throwing herself at Mr. Whatever-his-name-is from Carolina. I blushed for you, my pet—truly I did."

"I did not throw myself at his head!" cried Theo indignantly. "I was but being polite."

Natalie nodded, her plain little face showing annoyance. "You must not say such silly things, Katie. I only make nice talk with le comte de Joliette to make him feel at ease, and Theo the same for Mr. Alston." She opened her reticule and, extracting a handkerchief to be embroidered, inserted a needleful of silk. Natalie's hands were never idle.

Katie tossed her yellow curls. "Oh, to be sure—I was only teasing. Still, it was rarely diverting to watch Theo." She giggled, drew down the corners of her mouth, and mimicked Alston's ponderous speech. " 'Indeed, Miss Burr, I find your appearance not inferior to that of some of our reigning belles.' What a compliment! Had it been I, I should have slapped him."

Theo laughed. "I nearly did. Still, it's doubtless very good for my vanity to be snubbed."

Katie suddenly sobered, touched Theo's hand. "You have no vanity. You're so pretty and accomplished, and you—you have so much."

"So much?" Theo repeated slowly, squeezing Katie's hand in return. She had never thought of comparing her material circumstances with those of Katie, who lived over a shop in Pearl Street with a crotchety grandmother, and laughingly confessed to scrimping for months to buy the material for one new dress. Theo had always taken her possessions for granted: the horses and servants and abundant table, this new pianoforte, all the splendor of luxury that made Richmond Hill. Then the new gown tonight—it had cost twenty pounds—and the beautiful necklace. These were all part of the safe, pleasant scheme of things, part of her father's cherishing care.

But if she were deprived of everything material, it would not matter, she thought. She and her father could see more of each other if they dispensed with the elaborate panoply of living. There would be fewer people to distract them.

She pictured Aaron and herself relegated to a tumbledown cottage in the woods. She would cook his food over a romantically crackling fire; she could tend him and make him more comfortable than might any number of servants. She saw herself busy, happy, indispensable.

And Aaron—she realized with a shock. What would he be doing? Impossible to imagine him chopping wood or watering stock. Even more impossible to see him clothed in sweaty homespun. Her idyll was ridiculous.

She smiled unconsciously, and Katie trilled with laughter. "I vow you're thinking of John Vanderlyn. On him, at least, your beauty is not wasted. He stares at you ravenously."

"Does he?" She was startled. "I hadn't noticed."

"Lawks!" Kitty's pretty jaw dropped. "I truly believe you hadn't. You are the queerest girl. Hark! Here come the gentlemen now." She straightened against the lyre-backed chair, crossed her feet demurely, and unfurling her ivory fan fluttered it with airy grace.

Natalie patted her already neat hair and shoved her embroidery hastily into the reticule. It was not comme il faut to let gentlemen see one doing anything that savored of domesticity. It would be lamentably bourgeois.

Angelica Hamilton ceased playing, twisted around on the stool, her long face both unhappy and self-conscious, now that she no longer had her music to support her. The other women, including the matrons, all melted into various attitudes. Only Theo had no part in the galvanic thrill which transformed them at the approach of masculine steps and voices.

She watched them with detachment and a twist of envy. They were all, even Natalie, expectant and excited, anticipating pleasure and the delights of flirtation. Yet, for her, the evening had grayed. The magical mood, the breathless joy which had been hers four hours ago when she entered this room, had somehow seeped away. It was a formless disappointment. Something that she ever anticipated was not coming.

She sighed, wishing that it were time for everyone to go home. Then she and Aaron would have their invariable bedtime chat, and he would make her laugh again with his wittily caustic comments on the guests.

The returning gentlemen were preceded by four hired musicians: two fiddlers, a harpist, and a pianist. The string players had brought their pitch-pipe. They were unused to playing with the pianoforte, which they regarded as a most unnecessary instrument. The orchestra broke into hot argument, which Aaron quelled. "Tonight," he announced, "we shall have only cotillions and valses led by Mr. Barks at the pianoforte."

More of this French craze, thought Hamilton sourly. No doubt the minuets and congos were no longer good enough for the magnificent Colonel Burr. He'd be damned if he'd caper around in a cotillion. Let the Republicans make fools of themselves if they wished to. He crossed the room and seated himself beside his wife.

"This gathering nauseates me," he said in her ear. "How much longer must we endure?"

"Sh-sh," whispered Betsy Hamilton. "You are intolerant, Sandy. The young people are enjoying themselves. Soon there will be a party of whist for you. Now behave yourself."

He shrugged his shoulders, crossed his silken legs. She was right, of course. Good breeding demanded that one allow

42

oneself to be bored, insulted, have one's dearest convictions outraged in the name of accepted hospitality. He should not have come. He had let the womenfolk persuade him. They were fond of little Theodosia. Poor child, lashed to the chariot wheels of such a father. He stared at Theo with rising irritation. Spoiled she was. Burr showered gifts on her as though she were a princess—or his mistress. It was preposterous, vulgar.

The musicians after several false starts struck up a recognizable rendition of "The Lass of Richmond Hill." There was laughter and an outburst of clapping. The song had been written in England and referred to a far different Richmond Hill, but its appropriate title pleased Aaron. He took Theodosia's hand and led her forward, started the singing himself, while she stood blushing beside him.

> On Richmond Hill there lives a maid
> More bright than May-Day morn,
> Whose charms all other maids surpass,
> A rose without a thorn.
> This lass so neat, with smile so sweet,
> Has won my right good-will.
> I'd crowns resign to call thee mine,
> Sweet lass of Richmond Hill.

As the song was finished, Aaron put his arm around Theo's waist. "Is my lass of Richmond Hill enjoying her party?"

"Indeed I am, Father." She smiled at him. "They are all so kind, and you are so good to me."

Her lassitude had gone. The sound of the music, the touch of her father's loving arm, had dispelled it. And the prospect of dancing. She dearly loved to dance.

She saw Vanderlyn, Robert Swartwout, and Alston start toward her from different sides of the room with the evident intention of leading her out. She would tactfully choose Vanderlyn, she decided; he would best know the figures, having just returned from France.

The three young men reached her at the same moment. Vanderlyn and Swartwout spoke in undesigned duet. "Miss Burr, I beseech the honor——" and broke off, glaring at each other.

But Alston said nothing, stood awkwardly before her, biting his lips. his face uncommonly flushed. His expression had changed from its former surly indifference. He gazed at her now in a bold way that made her uncomfortable. He must have had plenty to drink, she thought, but would he never find his tongue?

"You wish to speak to me, Mr. Alston?"

He cleared his throat. "To converse with you, yes. I was not going to ask you to dance. I do not like these outlandish dances."

But I do, was at her tongue's tip. She raised her hand toward Vanderlyn who stepped forward eagerly.

Aaron slid himself between them, turning his back on the discomfited young artist, and addressed himself to Alston.

"I quite understand your aversion to dancing, Mr. Alston. I'm sure that Theodosia will be delighted to humor you. My dear"—he turned on her his brilliant gaze—"why do you not show Mr. Alston our picture gallery? It is of some interest, I believe. And he might like to view the gardens, as well. I know that they cannot compare with the beauties of those on his own plantations, but I trust he won't find them too dull."

Disappointment choked her; she raised beseeching eyes to her father's face. Was it really necessary to go on trying to entertain this very boring and unmannerly planter? Must she miss the dancing—and on her birthday too?

Aaron's face softened as he met her look. Unperceived by the others, he shook his head, his lips formed words. "To please me. You may dance later."

She nodded with equal care. Of course, she could do that, or anything to please him. There was a delicious joy in being included in his plans, even though he seldom explained them to her. She gloried in being useful to him—important. But if only she knew his purpose in regard to Alston. She had received no definite hint, though her common sense told her that there was need for flattery, and that he was not averse to impressing the planter with the lavishness of their establishment. It was a rôle she had played before, and she slipped into it expertly now that her momentary rebellion had passed.

"Shall we, Mr. Alston?" Her low voice was now enriched with a tone of intimate persuasion very like her father's. She smiled, glancing at him sideways from beneath her long lashes.

Alston's red face became redder. "Delighted, ma'am," he mumbled, and stalked after her into the hall.

She led the way upstairs to the long narrow picture gallery. It had been fashioned from three attic rooms, and it housed a collection of which Aaron was very proud. There were sketches and three finished portraits by Vanderlyn, rough studies by Stuart, and miscellaneous specimens of French and Italian art. Amongst the latter were two Venuses, and a copy of Titian's "Sacred and Profane Love." This picture, with its clothed and naked females, always tickled Aaron. "How true a realist was this Venetian," he was fond of saying. "See how much more desirable he has made the profane lady, while the chaste one is well-behaved and pallid, very pallid."

Theo had heard this and other comments many times, scarcely listening. The pictures were an old story to her. She enjoyed the rich colors and the surprised admiration of strangers upon first viewing the collection, but familiarity had dulled her interest.

She was, therefore, astounded, after she had lit the candles, to hear Alston gasp as he took a hurried step backward.

They stood before one of the Venuses, a lush blonde adorned only by a necklet of pearls.

Theo had opened her mouth to launch upon her usual little speech of explanation—"Father had great difficulty in procuring this painting; the treatment of the flesh tones is considered very fine——" But her speech was cut off at the source. She stared at her companion.

He turned his head slowly from side to side like a goaded bull, and yet his eyes darted down the line of pictures, passing over the portraits and landscapes to linger surreptitiously on the nudes. He threw her a peculiar sidewise glance and cleared his throat.

She was annoyed. His embarrassment, though she had never encountered the like, affected her by contagion. The brass candlestick trembled in her hands. She became conscious of her own body, her extravagant décolletage. Her irritation increased, though she dimly comprehended that he belonged to a much less sophisticated race than the men she knew.

His reasoning was simple. In South Carolina young ladies did not gaze upon lewd pictures in the company of young men, or at all for that matter. It shocked him, but it excited him as well.

He had never felt sexual interest in a girl of his own class. No gentleman would. There were women, both black and white, provided by a beneficent Providence for such purposes. One married eventually, of course, a girl of suitable wealth and family, and one begat children. But one did not expect to be stirred by one's wife; one sullied her purity as little as possible.

Theodosia's attitude baffled him.

"The pictures are very pretty," he muttered. "Now let us go out to the gardens, as your father suggested."

She nodded quickly, glad to escape.

On the stairs going down he took her arm awkwardly; its bare cool flesh gave him unexpected pleasure. His hand tightened, and she drew away from his hot fingers.

A full moon lit the gardens, painting them with silver and black. Against the darkness of leaves and well-trimmed grass, fireflies made tiny orange lights. The air was sweet with heliotrope and box.

She walked very fast, giving him no time to linger, pointing out the interesting features: the little maze, not yet grown high enough to be mysterious; the sundial from a Versailles garden; the pond, clamorous with bullfrogs. Alston was forced into an ungainly shamble in order to keep up with her swift feet.

"You go too fast," he complained at last, as they entered the grape arbor. "Let us sit down here on this bench."

She hesitated. Through the open windows of the drawing-room music streamed, the mellow harmony of the fiddles, the joyous plink-plunk of the pianoforte. Dancers passed and repassed across the brightly lit rectangles, their heads swaying gracefully to valse rhythm. She saw a blur of smiling faces, heard Katie's unmistakable laugh. They were all having such a good time in there. She yearned to join them. Alston, who had previously only bored her, now made her extremely uncomfortable as well. That moment of mutual embarrassment in the picture gallery had changed their relationship. His attitude had become intimate, and tinctured with a definite flavor of pursuit. And she had no wish to be pursued. Still, her father would be displeased if they returned so soon, or if she refused to a guest any reasonable request. Particularly this guest. Aaron had made that quite clear.

She sighed, seating herself primly on the edge of the bench. Moonlight filtered through the grape leaves above and endowed her with a luminous beauty, softening the slight heaviness of her jaw line and enlarging her dark eyes to supernatural size. Theodosia was pretty by any light, but now she was breath-taking. A siren.

Alston flung himself down beside her and stared. His mouth watered and his heart pounded. New and disturbing impulses besieged him.

He looks, thought Theo impatiently, like a slaughtered

sheep, with his pop-eyes and tight curls, and he has lost his tongue as usual.

"Do tell me more of your life down South, Mr. Alston. Do you have many hunting parties? I have no doubt you are a superb horseman. Have you large stables?"

He neither moved nor answered. He continued to stare as though she were one of the curiosities in Mr. Beller's South Street Museum.

She laughed nervously. "Indeed, Mr. Alston, I asked you a question."

Was he further gone in liquor than she had supposed? She edged farther from him. How unpleasantly audible his breathing had become.

"It's—it's getting chill. I think we had better go in now." She started to rise, but shrank back petrified as he made a lunge at her.

Before she could either run or struggle, he grabbed her roughly by the arms. Her head snapped back as his moist mouth closed on hers. Her hand flew out and landed a resounding slap on his ear. He clutched her the tighter, pressing her against the back of the bench until its rim cut sharply across her shoulders.

Her panic flamed to fury. She beat at his head with all the force of her fists.

Suddenly his arms dropped, limp as though they were broken. He slumped into the far corner of the bench.

"How dare you insult me like that—you yokel!" she whispered, shivering with anger and a sense of defilement. "When I tell my father how you honor his hospitality, he will know what to do. Though I doubt that he will deem you enough of a gentleman to be eligible for the code duello."

A muffled sound came from Alston. He buried his face in his hands and his bulky shoulders shook.

God's mercy! Now the man was crying. Amazement extinguished her rage. This monster who had assaulted her transformed like this into a shamed, blubbering boy.

She distinguished broken words. "Miss Burr—can never make amends. I forgot myself. Apologize—I lost my head. You looked so unearthly beautiful."

She felt a twinge of exasperated pity. No woman can listen quite unmoved to a man who pleads that her beauty overcame him.

"Please forgive me, Miss Burr. Your good opinion means more than I dare tell you." He raised his head, and she saw genuine shame in his face.

Suddenly she felt a hundred years older than he, and impatiently maternal. "Very well, Mr. Alston, I will accept your apology. Doubtless the wine was strong, and the moonlight made you over—over-susceptible."

"You are an angel," he said humbly. "I deserve no forgiveness." He seized her hand and kissed it clumsily. She had much ado not to snatch it away. His lightest touch was distasteful to her, but she was sorry for him, sensing, as her father had done earlier, that beneath his undisciplined emotions and overbearing manner was the heart of an anxious small boy, unsure of himself.

She ran up to her room to repair the damages to her costume.

Two kisses in one day, she thought. Strange that kisses can be so different. The first had been sweet, affectionate almost—and unimportant. She had scarcely thought of it all day. While the second—well, that had been thoroughly disagreeable, hot, sticky, and dirty as the mud springs at Ballston Spa, yet, once over, it had been unimportant too. Why did romances and people make it appear that kisses were soul-shattering experiences—delights of which one never had enough? Though that happened when one was "in love"—whatever that was. Loving was easily comprehended: admiration, respect, perhaps a little fear, the way she felt toward Aaron. An immense desire to please him, a sense of unquestioning happiness in his company. But that state of sighings and blushings and dewy-eyed excitement over kisses, phenomena she had observed in several of her friends, why was that so desirable? Or anything but mawkish?

She forgot all speculation when she returned to the drawing-room. The older people had dispersed to the parlor and tearoom for cards, leaving Sophie du Pont, who did not care for high play, to chaperon the dancers.

Theo stood up at once with John Vanderlyn, and discovered that he did, indeed, know the new steps from France. He complimented her on her quickness in learning them, and she smiled with pleasure.

"I must paint you like that, Theo," he whispered. "You are youth and grace incarnate."

She thanked him absently, engrossed with the pleasure of rhythmical motion.

She turned quickly away as Joseph Alston stalked into the room and seated himself alone in a corner. She had done her duty—and more—by that gentleman; she would take good care to avoid him in future.

48

She could not, however, help noticing that he never took his eyes off her, turning his head so that he might watch her as she passed up and down the floor. When other couples obscured his view, he scowled at them with disconcerting candor.

"You have made another conquest, I see," laughed Vanderlyn. "The haughty young man from South Carolina. I trust you don't reciprocate."

"Fudge!" cried Theo, with an inelegance most unusual to her. "I cannot abide that man. I vow he resembles a sheep. A fat purple sheep." For she included Alston's plum-colored suit in her annoyance. Had he not offended sufficiently without making her conspicuous as well?

Vanderlyn laughed. "Oh, come, you are too hard on him. All men cannot be as slender or as tastefully dressed as your father."

Theo shrugged delicately. "Listen," she cried. "There comes that slow measure. Will you show me once more how to do the reverse?"

Vanderlyn, nothing loath, slipped his arm around her slim waist and they pirouetted gaily down the room.

When the party dispersed at one, the dancers were disappointed, but the card-players had had enough. The du Pont brothers had won nearly a hundred dollars at loo, and were well pleased.

Hamilton, under his wife's minatory eye, had filled in at a whist table, outwardly courteous and inwardly seething. His losses were insignificant, yet, even had he won as much as the du Ponts, he would not have enjoyed the evening. He might have wrested a twisted pleasure from playing against Burr; it would at least have kept him from boredom. But Burr never gambled. One of his maddening affectations, Hamilton considered it. A refusal to risk paltry sums of money when he delighted in risking other people's fortunes —more than their fortunes, their ideals.

Hamilton hurried his wife and daughter's departure, cutting short their polite farewells.

The others followed in a leisurely manner. There were pretty speeches praising the food, the wine, the music, and felicitating Theodosia again upon her birthday.

She stood beside her father in the great hallway, and many of the guests were struck by the resemblance between them. The brilliance of their smiles that uncovered identical rows of perfect white teeth, a brilliance that, though it was not entirely spontaneous, yet had a heart-warming quality which sprang from an interest in people and a desire to please them.

"It has given us the greatest pleasure to have you with us," said Aaron, kissing Mrs. Jay's hand.

"Indeed, ma'am, we have been much honored by your company," said Theo, and her voice, with its caressing breathless quality, sounded as much like her father's as it is possible for the voice of a seventeen-year-old girl to resemble that of a man of forty-four.

Alexis opened and shut the front door a score of times, until Theo, thinking them all gone, at last turned with a tired and happy sigh to Aaron.

It was then that she saw with exasperation that Joseph Alston still remained, half-hidden by the shadow of the stairs.

Aaron also discovered their lingering guest and advanced to him. "I trust you have enjoyed your evening, Mr. Alston. It was kind of you to come. Perhaps you will place me still further in your debt and join me in a nightcap?"

Alston shook his head. "I—I must be going." But he didn't go, he stared at Theodosia instead.

Aaron laughed. "At any rate, sir, we shall see you to-morrow. We shall expect you in the forenoon. My dear"—he placed a warning hand on his daughter's arm—"Mr. Alston is not comfortable at the Phoenix Tavern, and he has most graciously consented to stay here with us during his sojourn in New York."

Theo barely controlled a gasp of dismay, and Aaron's hand increased its pressure. "That will be—be delightful," she managed, after a moment of uncomfortable silence.

When the young man finally took his abrupt, ungraceful leave, she did not raise her eyes or respond to his words except by a vague smile.

Father and daughter walked past the disordered drawing-room to the library, as was their nightly custom. Natalie had long since retired. Aaron settled himself in his favorite high-backed chair, and Theo curled up on the footstool beside him.

"Well, puss—did you enjoy yourself? I found the evening most entertaining."

She hesitated. "Yes—it was fun. Especially the dancing. But——Oh, Papa, why do you show to Mr. Alston so much attention? I don't like him, I find him ill-bred and"—she frowned, idly tracing a whorl on the brocade pattern of her stool as she searched for the word—"and monstrous impulsive."

Aaron raised quizzical eyebrows, reached for his snuffbox and inhaled delicately. "Oh?" He waited for her to continue, but she sat silent, her small face troubled.

He leaned back and crossed his legs. "Alston is one of the richest young men in the country, and would have great political power in the South if he knew how to use it. What did he do that was so monstrous impulsive?"

"I promised, in a way, not to tell you, because I knew you'd be very angry, and he was sorry afterward. But it is impossible to have him staying here. I never wish to see him again."

He was seized by a rare burst of irritation at her. "You are being excessively childish, Theodosia. Spare me these maidenly flutterings. You mean, I suppose, that he kissed you, or something like that."

She flushed, sharply hurt by his tone and bewildered by annoyance directed at her when she had expected it to be all for Alston.

"Well, is a kiss anything to make such a pother about?" he continued, more gently.

Her mouth quivered. "Oh, but it was horrid! He forced himself on me, he was like a—a beast."

"Like a beast. I see. Men often are; it's most reprehensible. And what did you do?"

"I hit him as hard as I could until he let me go, and——" She swallowed, stared unbelieving at her father's face. He was laughing, and it shocked her as much as though he had thrown the candelabra at her. Her hands flew to her throat, she crumpled into a small sobbing heap.

She felt a soft touch on her hair, heard Aaron's voice at its sweetest, infinitely tender. "Poor baby, you're tired. You've lost your sense of proportion, my Theo. You must go to bed now. All shadows seem longer by candlelight. But first listen to me."

He put his arm around her, wiped her tears with his own handkerchief. She rested her averted face against his knee.

He was silent for a moment, considering the best way of dealing with her.

He loved her. She was the only person that he did love, not even excepting himself. But she must do as he thought best. He was, now more than ever, convinced that an alliance with Alston would be of the greatest advantage. Ready

51

money was imperative. Without something tangible with which to quiet his creditors, bankruptcy was inevitable. Public disgrace and the ruin of his ambitions. Disgrace for Theo, too, torn as he would be by the whole pack of envious ravening wolves. They suspected his financial desperation now, but they had no certainty. There was fortunately a very wide gulf between suspicion and certainty.

Alston was a heaven-sent answer. Not heaven-sent in the conventional meaning—Aaron had scant interest in a hypothetical paradise—but one of those remarkable opportunities briefly dangled by Fate which may be snatched by the shrewd and converted into great profit.

Alston had money and political influence, he was manageable, and to cap it all had obviously become enamored of Theo with an even more convenient speed than Aaron had dared anticipate.

That the child had been shocked or revolted by whatever love-making had occurred was a trifle unfortunate. But on the whole it did not displease. He did not quite admit it to himself, but he would have opposed any match with a man whom she passionately desired. He had no intention of transferring her devotion from himself to another. Her worship was the sweetest thing in life. Still, with Alston, there would be no danger of that.

Theodosia's prejudice must be overcome. He did not wish to force her. He considered utter frankness and discarded it. That would be a last resort. Propinquity would do it. The coming weeks with Alston under the same roof. Propinquity, and very subtle pressure.

Theo, understanding nothing of his thoughts, waited submissively for him to speak, thinking that he had not at first realized the enormity of Mr. Alston's offense and was now reconsidering.

She was, therefore, taken aback to hear Aaron say lightly: "I think, my dear, we must forgive Mr. Alston his indiscretion. I am sure that he will not repeat it. You mustn't be a priggish little miss. Men are not angels. I find this young man admirable. You will respect my judgment as you always do."

She raised her head, mutely questioning him. She could not read his smiling face, nor did she understand, but she felt a shadow between them, blotting out their closeness.

Aaron rose abruptly. "Come, Theo. You look like Lady Macbeth. What is there so tragic in the visit of a pleasant young man? Most young ladies would consider it cause for joy. Anyway, remember that, whatever your inner megrims and vapors may be, I wish you to be extremely nice to him."

She, too, rose from her stool, lifting her round chin in a gesture that had unconscious dignity. "I trust that I shall never be found wanting in hospitality to your guests."

She gave him a quivering little smile and moved slowly up the stairs.

Chapter Five

❧ ❧ ❧

THE FOLLOWING morning Joseph Alston swirled up to the front steps with an imposing equipage; his private cabriolet drawn by two perfectly matched bays, followed by a hired coachee crammed with luggage and three slaves: his bodyservant Cato, a cook, and a groom. These were Gullahs; their skins had a bluish hue; they wore strips of scimitar-shaped hair before their ears; and their unusually tall bodies looked picturesque in the Alston livery of red and green. They spoke a dialect unintelligible to the Richmond Hill blacks, who received these foreigners with suspicion and curiosity.

Aaron greeted Alston at the door, ushered him directly to the library, and rolled the traveling decanters over to him invitingly. The young planter relaxed under the influences of cognac and Aaron's concentrated charm. After the requisite interchange of amenities, Aaron brought the conversation deftly around to Theodosia.

"She admires you tremendously—thinks you vastly handsome, you know."

Joseph's jaw dropped; he spilled some of his cognac. "I fear you are mistaken, sir; she finds me intolerable. I—she—I'm afraid she has cause."

Aaron effaced his smile. "Cause, sir? What do you mean by cause?"

Joseph cleared his throat, while a painful red mounted to his close curls. He had not meant to say so much. He was deeply ashamed of his actions in the garden, all the more so as Theodosia now seemed to him a bright and dazzling spirit, infinitely desirable. He remembered the mood, but not the details.

Aaron saw that the young man needed a bit of direction

54

and summoned a portentous frown. "Surely Mr. Joseph Alston of South Carolina has made no overtures to my daughter of which he is ashamed."

Joseph shifted uneasily in his seat. His easygoing father had early promulgated a philosophy for rearing boys. "Let them make their own mistakes, and continually exercise their own judgment; they will learn by experience." This system had worked very well to date as Joseph had never been thwarted or crossed. At Princeton, when he tired of the university's discipline, he had left at once, and studied law for a few months until he wearied of that, too, and amused himself by traveling. His father had not objected. Indeed, Joseph was totally unused to criticism, even implied, as Colonel Burr's remark had been. It worried and yet impressed him.

"Well, sir?" Aaron's eyes were fixed on his embarrassed face with an unswerving glitter.

"I have the greatest respect for Miss Burr, sir. She is the most charming of her sex. I admire her profoundly." He brought it out at last.

Aaron withdrew his hypnotic gaze, allowing his lips to part in a slow smile. "I thought as much, my dear sir. Theodosia has had many suitors. She is very young, as you know, and I would be loath to part with her. Still, I will be frank with you as you have been with me. Your avowal does not displease me."

Joseph was thunderstruck. He choked over his brandy, muttering, "You do me great honor, Colonel." For Burr's meaning was unmistakable, tantamount to approval of a suit for his daughter's hand. A momentary panic seized Joseph. Surely he had not implied anything as decisive as that. Or had he? It must be that Theodosia had, after all, given her father a full account of that miserable episode in the garden. That would explain it.

His slow-moving mind considered this startling development and his panic subsided. He found the idea not unpleasant. She attracted him strongly. She was delightfully pretty and well educated. A trifle free in her manners, perhaps—witness her peculiar complacence before the lewd pictures; still, that could be checked. Her father was famous and likely to achieve even greater political prominence. Moreover, her fortune was obviously ample. His family would be distressed at his marrying a Yankee, but could have no other objections to the match.

Aaron watched the other's heavy face clear and permitted

himself an inward chuckle. Making up people's minds for them proved ever an amusing occupation. With different mentalities one used differing tactics. In this case he had been quite right to feel that finesse was unnecessary, a waste of time. The ground had been well, though unconsciously, prepared by Theodosia.

He refilled Joseph's brandy glass. "A toast to my daughter!"

Both men rose and drank. Joseph frowned, reverting to a previous thought.

"But she doesn't like me, Colonel Burr. She avoids me."

"Pish, my dear fellow! Women are like that. You must go slowly. Recite poetry to her; they love it. Sing duets with her, give her posies, gaze at her with your heart in your eyes—but respectfully. Don't frighten her."

Joseph looked blank, and Aaron went on. "Do exactly as I say, and you will see. Defer to her opinion. Forgive me for saying so, but you are a thought arrogant in your manner. Women like compliments and pretty speeches."

Joseph considered each of these recommendations and finally nodded. "I will endeavor to do as you suggest."

Aaron clapped him on the shoulder. 'Tis a pity he's so deadly serious, he thought. Theo must learn to liven him up a bit. Yet he felt for his intended son-in-law a certain contemptuous affection, for already Joseph was become a part of the Burrs.

After a few days Theo admitted to herself that Mr. Alston improved on acquaintance, and she relaxed her hostility. She began by treating him with frosty dignity which gradually thawed to tolerance. For Joseph in turn treated her as though she were one of Baron Stiegel's blown-glass figurines and might break at a touch. They never referred to the scene in the garden, and its memory dimmed.

Joseph, having had it pointed out to him, realized that he was very much in love with her, but his native indolence combined with nervousness to prevent him from making any specific overtures as yet.

The summer days passed agreeably and Theo grew used to his constant companionship. They rode much together over the sand hills and through the woods of Manhattan Island. Joseph rode well, and felt at his best on a horse where his bulk and awkwardness were less noticeable.

He could not recite poetry, nor yet sing duets with Theo, but he could and did listen. Though music bored him, he hid it with surprising canniness, and kept himself awake while

Theo played by watching the roundness of her white arms, or the enchanting tilt of her chin as she struggled through Bach's inventions or something she called a sonata by a young German named Beethoven.

Natalie kept out of the way. It did not take her long to comprehend the situation, and though she thought the young planter "un peu farouche" and rather dull, on the whole she approved Papa Burr's plan. It was only natural that he should select his son-in-law in the French manner, and, judging by all the evidence, M. Alston was a most eligible parti.

In the kitchen the servants laid bets on the wedding date, and in New York drawing-rooms the match was discussed with interest.

Only Theodosia would not see.

It was on the first of August that Joseph proposed quite suddenly, having screwed up his courage for days. Mindful of Aaron's advice, he had tried to induce Theo to accompany him to some romantic spot. But by tacit consent they both avoided the garden, and his invention was low in the evening, so that his moment came in the full glare of noonday sun, outside the stables where they had dismounted.

Theo, frankly hungry, was making for the springhouse to get a glass of chilled milk, when he checked her by a clutch at her silk-covered arm.

She turned in surprise.

His face was red from heat and the exertion of their ride. His clustering dark curls clung damply to his forehead.

"Miss Burr—Theo, I have something to say to you," he panted.

"Won't it keep until we get to the house?" she asked, amused.

"No!" he shouted, in a burst of desperation. "You must listen to me now."

"Softly—the servants," she laughed, but she had a fore-boding.

He propelled her down the path around the corner of the dairy away from the stable-boy's curiosity.

"Theodosia, I have a most tender regard for you; will you do me the honor to become my wife?" He spoke very fast in one breath.

She stifled an inclination to laugh, thinking that he sounded as though he had memorized the speech for days—as indeed he had.

"You are very kind, Mr. Alston, and I am very grateful for the honor you do me," she answered in the approved formula, "but I have no intention of marrying. Now," she smiled, dropping to her ordinary voice, "let's go to the house."

He was nonplused for a second. "Go to the house?"

"Yes; I wish to change my habit. Then I will direct Alexis to make you some rum punch; it will be cooling," she added, knowing how fond he was of this concoction.

"But you haven't answered me. I wish to marry you."

"I did answer you. I appreciate the honor very deeply, but I have no intention of marrying."

He frowned. "You know very well that that is nonsense. We are virtually an affianced couple. Everyone treats us as such. I had not spoken before because your father said I must give you time."

She jerked around, looking him full in the eyes. "My father!" she exclaimed. "You have spoken to my father?"

"Of course. The day I arrived here. He gave me full permission to ask for your hand. Nay, more, he said that my suit was most agreeable to him."

"I don't believe it!" Her voice was high with anger and sudden fear.

Bewildered, he reached for her hand. She snatched it from him, stumbled down the path and into the house.

Aaron was writing in his library as she burst in, his head bent over the desk. She did not wait for him to turn, but flung strangled words at his back. "Is it true that you wish me to marry Joseph Alston, and that you told him so?"

He sanded the words he had been writing, closed his portfolio, and walked over to her, putting a hand on either side of her face. "Quite true," he said quietly. "And, my dear little girl, I will tell you why."

He told her why. Not the whole truth, yet a near version of it. He marshaled all the arguments, using cold logic, though wooing her the while with his irresistible voice. He talked for nearly two hours until she was beaten and helpless beneath his tenderness and implacable purpose.

"I don't love him," she wailed.

"That's childish, Theo. Love between husband and wife is born of mutual interest, companionship, and children. If you mean that you feel no passion for him, then I say that it is a very good thing. Passion is fleeting, a trick of nature. Nothing more."

"I don't want to leave you. I never thought—thought you would let me go away."

The pain in her cry struck an answering chord in him, too,

though he went on inflexibly: "We shall not be much separated, no more than we have often been in the past. You will come here to me, and I shall visit you. You know, don't you, that you are my chief, my dearest concern, always?"

She tried to smile. "I thought so, yes."

"You know so, surely. Do you remember the letter I wrote you last winter from Albany, in which I told you that the happiness of my life depended on you; for what else or whom else do I live?"

She hid her face on his shoulder.

"And are you not convinced that I know what is best for you?"

Yes. She could never doubt that. As it had always been throughout her life, a momentary rebellion gave way to the seductive joy of submission to his will.

"Oh, Papa, I know that you are the best and wisest of men. I'll do as you think right, of course, but——"

He smiled down at her. "But me no buts, Miss Prissy. Go instead and convert your eager swain into the happiest man in the states. I see him lurking disconsolately behind the hazel bush near the dairy."

After her first reaction to the shock, Theodosia found it not disagreeable to be engaged. No date was set for the marriage, so that could be relegated to a hazy future, and, except that she now called Mr. Alston "Joseph" on occasion and must submit to a respectful kiss on cheek or hand, matters seemed very much as they had been.

Guided by Aaron and his own disposition, Joseph kept his love-making to the minimum, for he knew no middle ground. There was passion, and there was the restrained affection with which one treated one's affianced wife. Moreover, any such regrettable loss of control as that which had overpowered him on her birthday must never be repeated. After marriage, of course, the situation would automatically change. Some combination of the two states of feeling would then appear, and he looked forward to this eagerly. However, he was a languid young man and suffering just now from a mild attack of the fever which periodically afflicted all tidewater Carolinians, and most of his energies were engaged by Aaron.

Joseph and Aaron were closeted in the library every day until dinner-time. The latter spared no pains in grooming his prospective son-in-law for his new political rôle. He initiated

59

him into the intricacies of preferment, persuasion, and promises; he taught him one of his private ciphers and dazzled him with an atmosphere of high drama. He also borrowed money from him, but in such a charming and complimentary way that Joseph felt himself privileged to be allowed to contribute. In other ways Aaron found Joseph more useful than he had dared hope. The young man showed an unexpected talent for letter-writing. He was as verbose and expansive on paper as he was inarticulate of speech.

Aaron, whose own style was always brief and pithy, tactfully pruned many of the classical allusions and involved flights of rhetoric, but he kept Joseph writing letters to the South. Letters to influential families extolling Colonel Burr's aptitudes. These would bear fruit in the elections.

Theodosia, during those hours in the library, was left to her own devices except for the tasks which she must perform. Aaron expected summaries of every book she read, so many lines of Terence daily, a page of Corneille to be translated into "graceful English."

"Better to lose your head than your habits of study," he told her, and found time himself to supervise her work.

After the three-o'clock dinner came the time for gaiety, and there were many pleasures. Turtle feasts on the rocks by Turtle Bay in the East River, with the succulent green meat roasted in seaweed fires. Long excursions on horseback to the Marriner's Tavern north of Harlem, a beautiful old house which had sheltered Washington, but was now in eclipse, not yet bought and rejuvenated by Stephen Jumel and his lovely and disreputable wife, Eliza. There were private parties, soirées, routs, and balls, and there were theatrical performances played by a secondary company until the regular season should start.

The new Park Theater was to reopen that year on September fifth after the summer recess. It was to be a gala night, and all that part of New York society which did not think play-acting immoral would be there. Aaron had reserved a good center box for twelve shillings, and invited the Comte de Joliette to squire Natalie and complete their little party. The box would not be comfortable with more than five occupants.

It was a delicious afternoon, warm and yet with a sparkle in the air which hinted of approaching autumn. They dined early so as not to be hurried in driving to the town. The curtains would rise at seven.

Theodosia had dressed in bird-of-paradise yellow, a color

which accentuated the auburn in her hair, upon which perched a distracting little evening hat of straw and willow-green satin. She wore a set of seed pearls; ring, necklace, brooch, and even buckles on the green kid slippers were all fashioned of seed pearls shaped like tiny cornucopias. She had inherited these jewels from her mother, and their subdued luster became her better than Aaron's flashing diamonds. This she would not admit, however, and would have worn the gaudier ornament except that she did not wish to attract attention from the rowdy element in the gallery and pit.

Natalie, neatly fashionable in a brocaded gown of the new color called cachou-nut brown, followed Theo into the Italian chaise. The three men settled themselves on the seat opposite to the girls.

Aaron, who was as fond of fine materials as a woman, wore his best suit, a gray silk woven at Lyons, and brightened by an embroidered waistcoat. He had directed Joseph to New York's best tailor, so that the planter seemed better groomed and less bulky than usual. Aaron and Joseph were simply dressed as became Republicans, with no frills except the ruffled jabots beneath their chins, but the Count had remained true to powdered hair, frothing lace, and the splendor of paste buttons and shoe buckles.

The coachman slammed the painted doors and they set off at six. Theo hated to be shut in, and would have preferred to gallop to town on Minerva. Yet when they came to the Lispenard Meadows and clouds of mosquitoes rose from the marshy pools, she was glad enough for the protection of the coach.

"These marshes are unhealthy," said Joseph, languidly slapping at his leg. "We have the same trouble at home. Swamplands produce tainted air. You had a plague of fever here last year, did you not?"

Aaron nodded. "We did. People turned yellow as Theo's dress, and died in droves. Still, we are safe at Richmond Hill; the air is pure there. I hope, by the by, that you will not keep Theo shut up on the plantation during the fever months until her constitution becomes accustomed to your Southern miasmas."

Theo, who had not been attending, looked up quickly and her heart jumped. Was it possible that she was really to go so far away to that barbarous land? How could her father speak of it so casually?

"Certainly not," said Joseph impatiently. "We never stay on the plantations in the summer. We go to Debidue across the Waccamaw, to Sullivan's, or sometimes up the Santee."

"O là là!" cried Natalie, laughing. "What fonny names! Theo will have to learn a new language."

Joseph was affronted. "I fail to see anything amusing in those names. Debidue is French, besides. D E B O R D I E U." He spelled it sulkily.

"Tiens," said the Count, flicking his ruffles and permitting himself an amused smile at Natalie. "Eet ees French, most certainly."

"Our place-names up here are equally startling to unaccustomed ears," put in Aaron quickly, seeing that Joseph continued to scowl, resenting both the criticism of anything pertaining to South Carolina and of his French pronunciation.

Theo leaned back against the velvet cushions and thought, How silly this is! What difference does it make what the places are called, these places a thousand miles away from Richmond Hill? O Father, I can't go. You know I can't. Unhappiness clutched her.

Aaron saw her face and understood instantly. He leaned forward and murmured so that the others could not hear above the rattle of the coach: "In the summer you will not be at any of those places, but up here with me."

She gave him a grateful smile.

The chaise entered the city limits on Duane Street, bumping over cobblestones until they crossed Broadway and reached the park in front of the Court House, already called by some ambitious citizens the City Hall.

The theater faced the little expanse of grass and trees on Chatham Street, and there was a tangle of private carriages before its doors; a jostling crowd of servants and loiterers came to gape at the gentlefolk, some beggars, orange vendors hawking their wares, and a long straggling queue waiting to buy the cheaper tickets.

The Burr party went directly upstairs to the curtained-off boxes. These contained hard wooden benches, none too clean, even as did the pit below them.

Theo leaned forward against the wooden rail and examined the scene. The huge crimson plush curtains hung motionless across the dark stage. It was early, but the musicians were beginning to arrive. As each one clambered on his stool, he lit the candle by his music rack, thus adding yet more smoke to an atmosphere that would be dense as a fog in the Lower Bay before the performance ended. Smoke from the candles mingled with smoke from rank cigars which rose from the pit despite the management's interdiction.

A large candelabra hung from the ceiling, illumining its gilded floral design, and making a tempting target for the young ruffians in the topmost gallery, who had come plentifully supplied with rotting vegetables with which to pelt the actors should they prove disappointing.

The gentry sat in one of three rows of boxes, protected from any malodorous missiles. Each box contained a single candle in a glass shade. These were not extinguished during the performance, so that those who were more interested in watching the audience than the actors found it easy to do so.

"There come the Hamiltons," cried Theo, waving across the theater to a stage box; "next to the Schuylers."

The three men in the Burr party rose, bowed ceremoniously. Alexander Hamilton hesitated a perceptible instant, returned the bow in a markedly curt manner, and seated himself at once without a smile.

Joseph's perceptions had sharpened lately. He turned in surprise to his host. "General Hamilton seems less than cordial, do you not think?"

Aaron shrugged, though his lips tightened. "He mislikes my politics, though one would expect a bit more suavity in a social gathering. Still, after all, despite his pretensions and his grand marriage, he's naught but the bastard brat of a Scotch peddler. One must make allowances."

Joseph looked startled at this bald mention of a fact, known to everyone, but never referred to, and Theo cried nervously: "Father, hush! You speak too strongly," astonished that Aaron had been betrayed into a speech so unlike him.

Aaron laughed. "You're right, my dear. I accept the rebuke. One should never be vexed by trifles. The musicians have finally pulled themselves together into a semblance of a tune. I trust this means the play will soon start."

The box beside them had been empty; now the door opened and a party of officers came in with a clattering of sabers and stamping of feet, jesting and swearing good-naturedly as they scuffled for the front bench. There were six or seven of them, Theo observed casually, hoping that they would quiet down in time for her to hear the first lines, for three loud knocks signaled the curtains' rise.

The first offering was *The Grecian Daughter*, with Mrs. Charlotte Melmoth in the title rôle. Her charms were a thought mature for the part, but she was popular with the pit, who interrupted her frequently with bawdy compliments and huzzahs until the climax when the Grecian Daughter strikes to earth the tyrant who is about to kill her father; then the whole house paid the acting the tribute of silence, and a few feminine sobs were heard from the upper boxes.

Theo had seen this affecting tragedy before, and better done: in reality she agreed with Aaron's dry comment, "That is an amazingly silly and old-fashioned piece." Not for worlds would she have had anyone guess that each time she saw it she identified herself with the Grecian Daughter; that her throat closed and she suffered terror while the distracted heroine fought to save her father's life, and that she felt vibrating in her own breast Mrs. Melmoth's cry of revenge as she stabbed the tyrant.

The curtains fell on the reunited father and daughter. I would do that too, thought Theo, and she looked unconsciously to the Hamilton box. Her latent distrust of Alexander was focused suddenly by the aftermath of the play's emotion into hatred. He was her father's dangerous enemy. She knew it, and sensed that Aaron had not as yet fully realized it.

For a second she felt herself exalted, capable of violence, of plunging the flashing dagger as the Grecian Daughter had done. Then her mood was shattered by Aaron's amused, dispassionate voice behind her. He had been discussing the play. "Ah, but you see, my dear Count, life is not in the least like that. Certainly modern life is not. The story is preposterous."

Theo looked again at the Hamilton box and her sense of humor came back. Alexander, engaged in the highly unmenacing occupation of sucking an orange, was beating time to the music with his fingers while his wife and daughter were leaning across him and whispering.

No, life is no longer dramatic, thought Theo, deflated. We are all too civilized. Exciting things don't happen any more.

She leaned back politely in answer to Joseph, who asked if she had ever seen the Spanish dancers who were scheduled for the entr'acte. She answered "No," and turned on her bench in order to talk with him more easily, when her attention was caught by the officers next to them. Or rather by one officer who sat a little way from the others leaning against the side of his box and regarding her fixedly.

As she met his eyes, she experienced a physical sensation of explosion in her chest as though a small musket had been fired. She drew in her breath with a sharp sound. For the effect was one of recognition, of grave, intimate greeting,

64

and yet she knew that she had never seen the man before in her life.

The officer lowered his eyes courteously. She recalled herself with a start and babbled something to Joseph, but she did not hear his answer.

Joy tinged with fear flooded her. What's the matter with me? she thought wildly. 'Tis but the overture to flirtation; he is some philandering officer. But she knew that he was not.

She pulled out her fan to hide her face, made random answers, laughed at everything Joseph said. He was enchanted, thought that he must have become prodigious witty. He had never seen her so responsive.

The officer rose, stood talking with the others, yet she felt that he was as intensely aware of her as she of him.

He wore a blue coat with red facings, the infantry's full-dress uniform, and a gold epaulet on his right shoulder. That proclaimed him a captain. He was lean and very tall; he towered above his companions, and, despite the conventionality of his dress, there was something rough about him, a hint of the frontier. The set of his head and shoulders seemed to resent the imprisonment of his high black silk stock and the affectation of heavily powdered hair which were required of officers.

His profile was stern; his mouth, though full-lipped, held tight and straight as an Indian's. Furrows ran from his nostrils to the point of his sharp jaw. Though he seemed young, there was gravity and an air of command about him that reminded Theo of General Washington, who must have looked much like this in his youth.

She started as the three knocks from the stage announced the Spanish dancers. The curtains were drawn back. The captain sat down and again looked her full in the face. She saw in his intent eyes the same bewildered questioning that she felt in her own. Her cheeks, her neck grew hot, but she could not look away.

She saw his muscles flex as he checked a quick motion to rise, and knew, because she felt the same impulse in her own body, that he had wanted to vault over the people and the railing between them and come to her. Unconsciously she shook her head, and he nodded. His lips parted in a barely perceptible smile as intimate and understanding as though they had known each other for years.

The dreamlike quality strengthened. Her breath came rapidly. Unseeing, she watched the posturings of the blowsy Spanish dancers, who were rewarded with a shower of cabbages and rotten apples before Mr. Hallam the manager pulled them off the stage with his crook.

". . . And high time too, don't you think, Miss Prissy?" asked Aaron jocularly, leaning over her.

She made an inarticulate murmur, unlike her, who usually responded to his lightest word with eager acquiescence. Surprised, he inspected her. Her cheeks were vivid rose. Under the brim of her tiny green hat her eyes shone abnormally bright. He realized, startled, that she looked extraordinarily beautiful, but dazed—moonstruck. His ready apprehensions about her health were aroused.

"Do you feel well, Theo? You're not feverish, are you? It is close in here; shall we leave?"

She stared at him blankly, until, as his words reached her, she managed a gay, natural laugh. "Oh no, Papa. I feel very well. I don't wish to leave. I'm enjoying the performance tremendously."

Aaron was not satisfied. "You could not possibly have enjoyed the performance to date unless your critical faculties are in complete abeyance. Nor did you seem to be attending. Of what were you thinking?"

For the first time in her life she resented his probing of her thoughts, and for the first time since she was ten and told little fibs about the disappearance of comfits and fruit, she deliberately lied to him.

"The Grecian Daughter reminded me of one of Horace's odes. I was trying to remember it."

Aaron chuckled. "See what a little bluestocking you will have to wife, Joseph!"

Joseph grinned fatuously. He was feeling happy, and, for him, excited. He had been comparing Theodosia with the girls in other boxes and decided that not one of them approached her for looks. She would be a wife to be proud of, and her intellectual airs and graces were charming if not carried too far. A beautiful wife who could quote Horace would be an agreeable acquisition to display in Charleston society. Daughter of the President, too, if all went well in the elections.

He felt a sudden urge to establish physical contact with her. She had been much more approachable tonight. Her hand lay beside her on the bench. He grasped it tightly in his, pulling it over so that it was concealed by her skirt.

Her fingers did not move; the little hand rested as passively under his as though it had been a glove.

After a moment he began to feel self-conscious. He looked

at her averted profile. She gazed with strained attention at the crimson curtains before them. Her whole attitude had an unnatural immobility, as though she were holding her breath.

He removed his hand and sank back, disgruntled. Hers remained as before quiet on the bench.

Theodosia had noticed Joseph's caress no more than she noticed the moths which flitted around the candle above her head.

Her mind was in chaos. Who is he? Why do I feel like this? She had a sensation of falling apart, as though her inner essence were rushing out of her toward a point at which she dared not look again—in the box to her right. She felt this stranger's presence there with an intensity that numbed her. The call between them was so strong that she thought it must be visible: a golden flash crackling through the smoky air. Joseph, Natalie, and the Count were negligible. They would not see it. But her father—that was terrifying.

On the stage, Mrs. Melmoth performed again, in a farce called *The Window and the Riding Horse*. The audience in an uproar shouted and slapped their thighs over the broad jokes.

Joseph roared, too, his discomfiture forgotten. Theo heard Natalie give small scandalized gasps, punctuated with "O là, là, que c'est risqué" to the Count. Even Aaron emitted his throaty chuckle. So she laughed, too, at the proper moments, though the speeches were meaningless jumbles and the actors as unreal as figures seen through the wrong end of her father's spyglass.

They must meet. She had never had a desire to match this one. More than a desire, it was an ache, a hunger. But how could they meet? She was immured in the fortress of convention, and, even if she dared break out, there was still Aaron to reckon with.

When the curtains fell on a bowing and curtsying cast, she could bear it no longer and turned abruptly under cover of the applause. He was nearer to her now, so that by reaching out her arm she could have touched him. The other officers milled about in their box finding and replacing their cocked hats, guffawing as they repeated the best lines in the farce. He stood aloof in the midst of them, watching her expectantly. She knew that he would communicate with her and felt rather than saw his lips form a question, "Where?"

"Theo, are you ready?" Aaron's voice came from the back of the box. Desperation seized her, and with it a plan. She whirled, cried gaily at the top of her voice. "Yes, Father—

quite ready. But do not let us go home yet. Let's go to the Vauxhall Gardens. It will be delightful. They have excellent music, and we can eat ices beside the fountain."

She emphasized "Vauxhall Gardens," knowing that *he* listened and would understand.

Aaron bent on her a keen look. "What a gadabout you have become, my dear! I think it time for all respectable people to seek their homes."

"Oh no, Papa, please. It's too early to go home, and Joseph has never been there. He would enjoy the Gardens so much." She cast on that young man a look so compelling and unexpected that his head whirled.

"By all means let us go if Theo wishes it," he stammered.

Aaron's eyebrows shot up. He turned to Natalie. "Are you also interested in this singular little expedition?"

Theo held her breath while Natalie considered the question carefully from all angles before she said: "Why not? It would be amusing, no doubt, and many vairy nice people go there, I think."

Aaron bowed. "I give way to the ladies' wishes as always. But I cannot accompany you. I have business to attend to at home. You four may take the chaise, and I will hire a carriage to drive me back to Richmond Hill."

He waited for Theo's protest, knowing that his absence always diminished her pleasure in any undertaking. There was no protest. She lowered her lashes quickly, but not before he had seen a flash of unconcealed relief. Not by the flicker of a muscle did he show the dismay this caused him. But, as he stood on the paving blocks and helped the girls into the chaise with his customary courtesy, his active brain collected all the scattered incidents of the evening, searching for a clue to Theo's behavior.

At dinner and during the ride to town she had been her normal self, clinging close to him, turning to him for approval or understanding even when she spoke to others, diffusing the atmosphere to which he was accustomed, that he was the only object of importance to her. Something had happened in the theater, then. But what? How was it possible for anything so transforming to have happened in the narrow confines of their box and under his eyes? And yet it had. He had seen hostility in her and a desire to escape from him. Even her looks had changed, burst suddenly into an unearthly glow.

In any other woman he would have understood this. Only one thing produced this effect: the awakening of passion: a lover. Yet that was impossible in this case. Theo had seen no men but those of her own party.

He considered the possibility that she might have suddenly discovered in herself a response to Joseph. Rejected it impatiently. He knew her, and he knew women far too well for that. But then what—who?

When he reached Richmond Hill and shut himself in the library, he found that for once his disciplined mind refused to obey him. He could not work. Dozens of letters demanded careful answer. A communication in cipher from Timothy Green in South Carolina awaited decoding. It was important. It would tell him how nearly the South had been won over by the work he had required from Joseph, how much remained to be done when Joseph went home next week, ostensibly to prepare his family and plantation for the reception of a bride, but also to further the campaign.

Rhode Island and Vermont, too, needed careful handling. They had satisfactorily growing groups of Burrites, but they needed guidance, one of those subtle yet tersely frank letters that he knew so well how to write. Usually he flung himself into these matters, savoring the secret pleasure of manipulating factions, admiring as though it were a separate entity the smooth power of his brain.

And tonight it would not function. He paced up and down the library, his light steps soundless on the ingrain carpet, his fingers twined behind his back. At last he stopped before Theo's portrait, consulting the sweet candid face which looked down on him. His lips tightened. With sudden decision, he went to the bell-pull.

Alexis finally appeared, sleepy and astonished. Colonel Burr, ever considerate of servants, never summoned them at a late hour.

"Yes, sir, master?"

"Wake up Dick and tell him to saddle Selim quickly. I wish to go out."

Chapter Six

THE Vauxhall Pleasure Gardens had recently been moved from town to Bayard's Mount on upper Broadway near Spring Street. Delacroix, the owner, had bought the old Bayard homestead and planted the former farmland with a profusion of ornamental shrubs threaded by brick paths. In the center, dominating the gardens, stood a colossal equestrian statue of General Washington. Around its base were scattered small wooden refreshment tables.

The orchestra and singers were grouped on a high platform romantically erected in a grove of maples, so that their music might give the effect of floating disembodied from amongst the rustling leaves.

Two small fountains splashed into granite basins and sparkled with prismatic lights from fireworks and colored flares that were much admired features of the entertainment.

One of these illuminations was in progress as Theodosia and the others entered the gates. A rocket whizzed up across the black sky, exploded with a deafening bang, and showered the trees with red, white, and blue stars.

"Tiens, c'est joli," remarked Natalie. The Count and Joseph murmured agreement. Theo said nothing. For despite the fitful light of pine torches and candles, she had seen the captain at once. He sat alone at a table near one of the fountains, his long legs crossed, his arms folded, scanning the face of each passer-by. Theo felt as if the rocket had exploded in her own breast.

She saw him start as he recognized her. Her fingers tightened around her fan until one of the sandalwood sticks snapped. They were no nearer meeting each other here than they had been at the theater. Miss Burr of Richmond Hill, hemmed in by a fiancé, a count, and the conventional Natalie, could not make overtures to an unknown captain.

She still retained enough reason to realize that she had somehow been precipitated into an unknown country whose laws to her companions would seem incredible.

Though totally unaccustomed to guile, again her desperation furnished her with a scheme. It would never have worked had Aaron been there, but he—oh, most fortunately —was not.

"Shall we walk around a bit?" she asked Joseph.

"By all means," said Natalie. "It will be agreeable."

Theo pouted. "But Joseph and I want to be by ourselves. You and the Count have an ice here, and wait for us."

Natalie laughed and obediently sat down. It was good to see Theo acting a bit amoureuse, and after all with one's fiancé——

Theo felt a flick of shame at Joseph's pleased smile, at the possessive way in which he pulled her hand through his arm and led her down one of the shadowed paths. But she was caught up beyond shame or pity, or any emotion she had ever known.

They walked some distance, as far as she dared, when she clutched her hands together and cried "Oh!" in tragic tones.

"What is it, Theo?" said Joseph anxiously.

"My seed-pearl ring. I've lost it! It's gone from my finger. Oh, Joseph, go quickly and see if it is in the chaise. Please ——Yes, I'll be all right here. I'll go back to the others. Hurry, do."

Joseph lumbered away.

She stood alone on the path, around a bend which hid her from the main part of the gardens. Music drifted through the windless air and mingled with the call of a whippoorwill from the meadows outside. Above her head from its iron bracket, a torch guttered, shedding orange light on marble urns filled with geraniums and the fragrant white spikes of flowering privet. And these seemed to her like fairy flowers, indescribably lovely.

She waited quietly, without embarrassment, knowing that he would come to her. But when he stood before her, so tall, his black cocked hat in his hand, his powdered hair shining in the torchlight, she could not speak.

"I didn't think I'd ever find you," he said, and his voice was the one she had expected, grave, a little harsh, yet softened now by wonder. She knew what he meant, and that he did not refer to this moment.

"What happened to us?" she said simply. "I don't understand. When I saw you back there in the theater, I felt that

71

I had always known you, that I knew what you were thinking. I had to talk to you. You do not think me common or vulgar that I meet you this way?"

"You know that I don't."

She looked up at him and smiled. "This is passing strange," she said softly.

He nodded. The grim lines about his mouth had vanished so that he seemed young, almost as young as she.

"I've seen you many times before tonight: in the embers of campfires, on the snow-tops of the Alleghenies, reflected in the waters of unnamed rivers. Not your face, perhaps, but you."

His words seemed to her exquisitely fantastic, part of the enchanted borderland in which they wandered together. Louder and more insistent came the wailing of the violins through the trees. A pair of lovers pushed past them and disappeared down the path.

"There is time aplenty to dream in the wilderness," he added, as though she had questioned.

Wilderness. The thought was alien to her and yet beautiful. She repeated it slowly. "Wilderness. And what have you to do with the wilderness?"

He raised his head. She saw his eyes darken. "It has been my mistress, my life. It is where I belong."

He stepped nearer, but he did not touch her.

"I know nothing of women," he said, with roughness. "I do not even think of you as a woman—yet."

"As what, then?" she whispered.

"As a dream made into flesh: the fulfillment of a longing."

Theo thought, the fulfillment of a longing—yes. This moment, this second, is happiness. Nothing must touch it, I must not think or it will dissolve.

"Hark!" he said. "What is that song? It's beautiful, part of this—and us."

She bent her head and listened. It was a recent popular song; she had heard it many times, but it had meant nothing to her. Now, standing beside him, each plaintive tone of the low contralto voice sped to her heart.

Water, parted from the sea, may increase the river's tide,
To the bubbling fount may flee, or through fertile valleys glide;
Tho' in search of lost repose, through the land 'tis free to roam,
Still it murmurs as it flows, panting for its native home.
Heart of mine, away from thee, sever'd from its only rest,
Tosses as a troubled sea, bound within my aching breast.

72

Thou alone canst give release, sprayed my burning eyes with brine.
Swelling e'er with love's increase, let my heart find rest in thine.

The soft notes died away to a distant spatter of hand-clapping.

"Let my heart find rest in thine," he quoted slowly. "Do you understand that—my dear?"

She looked up at him, and her eyes were filled with tears. "Yes, I understand, but——" She broke off with a cry of fear. She heard the light footsteps behind them, even before she heard the voice she knew best in the world, tense with anger.

"Indeed, a most charming little scene," said Aaron. He stood beside them, his face rigid.

"And just who is this individual with whom I find you philandering in corners like a street wench?"

The Captain grew white as the marble urn behind him; his hand flew to his sword hilt, but he said evenly, "I am Meriwether Lewis of the First Regiment of Infantry." He stepped forward, and, presenting his back to Aaron as though he were non-existent, added gently to Theo, "There are two people who call me Merne, persons for whom I care. Will you, also?"

She dared not answer him; indeed, she no longer saw him clearly; her vision was blurred with fear by the fury she saw in her father's face.

"Father—no—please——" she heard her own hysterical cry and bit her lip. That was wrong, that was not the way. There must be a meeting-point somewhere between these two men. Aaron loved her; somehow she must make him understand.

She summoned all her control and forced a nearly natural laugh. "You have no cause to be angry, Papa," she said swiftly. "The Captain and I met here by chance. He doesn't even know my name——"

"So? Then I shall be pleased to inform him. Sir, I am Aaron Burr, and this my daughter, Theodosia. She is betrothed to Mr. Alston. She has, therefore, two men who will be delighted to defend the honor and fair name which she herself seems to hold so light."

Captain Lewis bowed. "At your service," he said coldly. "But your daughter's honor and fair name are not in question. True, I did not know that she was betrothed, yet had I known it would have made no difference; I still would have sought any opportunity to talk with her."

Aaron saw Theo's sharp intake of breath and her terrified eyes. His anger vanished. He was ashamed of the rage which had shaken him; he had long ago learned that one is never master of a situation when possessed by anger. This long cool fellow had so far had the advantage.

He performed one of his bewildering voltes-face, turning on the full force of his magnetism as though from a spigot.

"Come, Captain Lewis, perhaps I've been overhasty. You must in fairness admit that the situation was startling. Still, I'm willing to make allowances for young blood. It is but natural that a soldier should wish to dally with a pretty face."

Lewis did not relax; he threw Aaron a look of contempt. "Ask your daughter if that is all it was."

Aaron went on quickly: "I do not need to ask my daughter. I know very well that she is already regretting whatever moment of folly her youth and the September evening have betrayed her into."

"Colonel Burr, I've heard much of you. I am a friend of Jefferson's. I have heard that you are totally unscrupulous and obsessed by self-interest. I have not liked your reputation, nor the rumors of underhanded conniving which reached me even out beyond the mountains at Fort Wheeling, but I am willing to hope that I was misinformed about you, because you are possessed of such a daughter."

Theo gasped. The incredible words repeated themselves senselessly in her mind: "underhanded, conniving, unscrupulous." That anyone should dare to speak like this to her father! Suddenly she saw Lewis with hostile eyes. Her own behavior became shameful. She moved to Aaron's side, touched his arm timidly, and he, seeing this, laughed with maddening calm.

"My dear, it seems that this backwoods captain sets himself up to be my critic. I think we need scarcely bother with his opinion. Good night to you, Captain Lewis."

Meriwether Lewis did not move. He was sick at heart; he cursed his bluntness and lack of polished manner. He saw the girl's face averted, closed against him, she who had responded so deeply to him for the space of a few hours.

He was a lonely and reserved man, outwardly cold. He had spent most of his twenty-six years in the open, leading the rough life of a frontier officer. His men respected his courage and resourcefulness, but they thought him hard, unsympathetic. And so he was, except in the wilderness, alone. Rivers, trees, and mountains had been his friends. He knew as much of woodcraft and the ways of beasts as an Indian.

No woman had ever before touched his soul. Yet he had told her the simple truth when he said that he had dreamed of her. Deep hidden in him there ran a strain of mysticism, inherited from his Gaelic forefathers.

When he had seen her there in the theater, he had felt his formless yearning satisfied. They had looked at each other and he had seen, beneath her pretty face, the unawakened passion and fire of her spirit. He had not thought of anything so banal as love in the conventional sense. He did not do so now. But he knew that they belonged together; that in each the other would find completion. She had felt it, too, yet now he could no longer reach her. Her betrothal of itself would not have deterred him: he was accustomed to a simpler society, a lawless country where a man takes the woman he wants. It was the change in the girl herself.

He saw her as a prisoner, a willing, eager prisoner who had escaped her chains for a little while, and now rushed back to them bewildered, clinging to the dear familiarity of her confinement.

Yet he could not believe his dismissal. He used the name which he had just learned was hers. "Theodosia——" It was a call so intense and fraught with emotion that Aaron was astounded. How in Heaven's name had all this come about in so short a time? His arm tightened around his daughter. "My dear girl, really—will you be good enough to bid this insistent gentleman good night and Godspeed?"

Theo raised her heavy lashes. Her dark eyes were veiled. They met Lewis's pleading despair, and a hot pain went through her breast. But the sureness and the vision were gone. The pattern of her life could not so quickly be unraveled. Aaron was right, as always. Soldiers did dally with pretty faces, and this backwoods captain had dared to criticize her father.

"Good-bye, Captain Lewis," she said slowly, and turned her head away.

The corners of his mouth bent in a bitter smile. We are not done with each other yet, Theodosia, he thought. Some day we shall meet again. But it will not be the same: our lives will have curved too far apart. He made her a short bow, and walked rapidly off without looking back.

There was nothing to tell her that she had made the most important decision of her life, nothing except a weight of dullness and disappointment. The Gardens which had been so brightly beautiful seemed tawdry. She noticed for the first time that the path was littered with crumpled paper and orange peel. Moreover, it was muddy and had stained the hem of her yellow dress.

"Will you be so good as to tell me the meaning of this extraordinary scene?" Aaron spoke quietly, but his authority, which he knew had for a moment been shaken, sharpened his tone.

She drooped against his shoulder. "I don't know. I'm so tired, Papa, please don't question me."

"No nervous vapors if you please. I am at a loss to understand your conduct. Am I right in conjecturing that you saw this—this fellow for the first time tonight at the theater? And that he was one of the officers in the next box?"

She inclined her head.

"—And that he made sheep's eyes at you, and you were seized with some inexplicable impulse and made them back?"

"Don't please. It wasn't like that."

"Like what, then? Do you expect me to mince words when I find that my daughter has made a vulgar assignation in front of her father and her betrothed? You got rid of Joseph very neatly, did you not? I met him at the gate hunting for your pearl ring, which I now see rests in its usual place on your finger. You have disgusted me!"

His scorn shriveled her. She could no longer recapture the glowing beauty of those moments of communion and realization. She felt blank and terribly tired.

"I'm sorry, Papa," she whispered. "Please don't be angry with me any more. It's finished."

Aaron patted her hand. He had been more upset and hurt by her behavior than he wished to remember. He realized that, despite the apparent impossibility of the thing, this lanky captain had fallen in love with Theo, and that she had not been unresponsive. He would have liked to feel contempt for him; such a display of feeling as the fellow had put into that crying of her name was better suited to effeminate dolts like poets than to a soldier. Still, Aaron seldom underestimated an opponent and he was an accomplished judge of character. He knew that this tuppenny-ha'penny captain, for all his rough speech and rustic air, was nobody's fool. While he doubted the danger of another meeting between the two, for Theo had come to her senses and Lewis had accepted his dismissal, nevertheless he intended to make sure.

In the meanwhile, they must be getting back to their party who would think this prolonged absence exceedingly strange.

"We will forget the whole matter, my dear, and we will not disturb Joseph about your momentary vagary. There is no need for him to know. I told him to wait with the others when I saw him at the gate, for I preferred to find you myself. I am very glad I did. We will let him assume that we have been hunting for your ring and at last recovered it."

"Yes, Papa," she said. She shivered suddenly.

Aaron hastened to pull her little fringed shawl about her shoulders. "You do look tired, child. We will have a glass of wine before we go home." He took her arm and led her briskly back to the tables.

It was late when they got home. Joseph could scarcely stifle prodigious yawns and took Theo's silence as a matter of course. They bade each other sleepy good nights. Candlesticks waited in a row upon a polished table. They each took one and lit themselves wearily up to bed.

All but Aaron. He kissed Theo on her hot forehead, bowed to the others, and vanished into the library. He placed his candle on the writing-desk and sharpened his quill. He then wrote a letter to the commanding officer of the New York garrison, and in it he requested that a certain Captain Meriwether Lewis should have his leave curtailed at once and that he be returned to his frontier post on the morrow.

Aaron reinforced this request with a delicately worded hint: "Matters of army preferment are often brought to my notice, not only because of my official capacity, but because of my friendship with General Wilkinson, your commander-in-chief. I think you will not find me unmindful of favors."

He sanded and sealed this missive. One of the stable boys should speed with it to Fort George at sunrise.

Upstairs in the white bedroom, Theo undressed listlessly. Her head ached. She leaned against the west window, pressing her face on one of the cool panes. The Hudson was gray and shadowy in the half-light. Her heavy eyes rested on it languidly, but presently it brought to her its eternal message of inevitability and peace. He would understand that, she thought suddenly. "Water, parted from the sea, may increase the river's tide."

She thought of him as someone that she had met long ago, a memory of the past. She could not even remember his face.

She put her fingers to her cheeks and found them wet with tears. This surprised her a little. She had not felt them come.

She turned from the window and climbed into her high bed. She sank at once into a heavy sleep, motionless, scarcely breathing for the few remaining hours in that night.

Chapter Seven

♪ ♪ ♪

JOSEPH was to leave soon by fast packet for Charleston. He had hoped that the imminence of his parting from Theodosia would bring them closer together. She would shed a few tears, perhaps, and cling to him. She might even nestle close and look up at him with as much affection as she showed to her father. It would be delightful to comfort her, promising a speedy return, and settling on the date for their wedding.

Joseph was slated for disappointment. On the morning after the theater party, Theodosia awoke with a painful headache which confined her to bed and made it impossible to see Joseph at all. Besides the headache, she had a slight rise in temperature and a total loss of appetite. Doctor Eustis, hastily summoned by Aaron, assured them that the indisposition was not serious—none of the malignant fevers.

As the headache continued, day after day, neither improving nor getting worse, the doctor frankly confessed that its origin baffled him. When calomel failed, he prescribed hemlock and applied leeches to her feet. The purpose of these last was to draw the irritating blood from her head. Theo regarded the slimy black slugs with disgust, but she submitted passively to the treatment.

She hated confinement in bed, and during brief childish illnesses had always chafed against it. Yet now she lay white and quiet, accepting Natalie's anxious nursing with docility.

On the day before Joseph's departure, Aaron decided that perhaps she had had enough coddling and tried bracing tactics.

He entered her room briskly, exuding his usual aura of keen, disciplined fitness. "Good morning, my dear. You look rosier today. Head better?"

She opened her shadowed eyes slowly. "A little better, perhaps," she whispered, trying to smile.

"See what I've brought you."

She turned her head painfully.

He was carrying a cage made of woven reeds, containing a small yellow bird. It cheeped hoarsely, then burst into a cascade of trills.

"Doesn't it sing sweetly?" said Aaron, delighted with his gift. "I bought it off a Portuguese schooner. It comes from the Canary Islands and will cure you by its cheerful music."

"Thank you, Papa. It sounds charming." Not for anything would she have hurt him or let him guess that the bird's shrill singing crashed through her head like cymbals.

Aaron placed the birdcage on a table by the window and came over to the bed. "Now I want you to do something for me."

"Of course, if I can."

"Get up, then, my dear. Just for a few minutes, if necessary. You will feel better—oh yes, you will. I insist. There is nothing really wrong with you, you know. Eustis has made a thorough examination. You will not get well by losing strength. One must make an effort."

Ignoring her protests he placed his arm under her linen-clad shoulders and lifted her up. The room spun around her.

"I get so giddy, Papa—I can't."

But he would not be checked. She slid her bare feet from the bed, feeling blindly for the wooden stool which stood beside it. The bed, nearly four feet from the floor, made the stool a necessity for getting in and out. She touched the edge with her toes, lurched forward, and, despite his support, the stool slid sideways along the polished boards, throwing her to the floor with her left ankle twisted under her. She gave a cry of pain.

"What is it?" he said sharply, trying to lift her.

"My ankle—oh, it hurts!"

The ankle was badly sprained, Doctor Eustis announced when he arrived post-haste. Complete rest was imperative. There could be no thought of leaving her bed for some time.

When the physician had gone and the bustle of preparing hot compresses and herb tea had died away, Theo was surprised to discover that the headache had vanished, quite suddenly and unnoticed. She felt weak, but hungry and peaceful, except for the ache in her ankle.

79

Aaron was full of compunction, and, though he never reproached himself—or others—once an unfortunate circumstance had passed, he redoubled his tenderness toward Theodosia. That afternoon he made a special trip into town, where he stripped the shops along the waterfront of their latest imported delicacies. He bought French comfits made of marzipan, a basket of dried dates and figs from Smyrna, and a large fuzzy coconut from the Spanish Main. The sea captain who sold it assured him that the liquid inside was considered most wholesome and would surely strengthen Miss Burr.

Aaron also procured a small packet of China tea perfumed with jasmine, and he had been unable to resist a pair of gilded kid slippers embroidered with white silk butterflies and reputed to have been made for a French marquise.

As he re-entered the house, followed by a servant with his bundles, he encountered Joseph gloomily descending the stairs. Joseph had been excluded from the sickroom and allowed only an occasional peek at Theo through the partly opened door. Always her eyes had been closed, and she had been unconscious of the glimpse which was all that Natalie's ideas of propriety would allow him. Even a fiancé may not enter a young girl's bedroom! "Ce n'est pas convenable," she told him, and though he never quite understood her French, her meaning was made plain enough.

He had, therefore, spent the last days of his stay wandering disconsolate around the house and grounds, neglected even by Aaron, who had been busy with upstate political leaders when not engaged in worrying about Theo.

Aaron was recalled to his duty as he saw the young man's air of sulky dejection.

"You look a bit mopish, Alston," he said kindly. "But you mustn't worry about the girl. She'll be right as a trivet once this ankle heals."

"Can't I even see her to say good-bye before I go?" said Joseph, with resentment.

"Of course you can. I will go and prepare her, then take you to her at once."

Joseph's face cleared. "I hate to leave her for so long." During his stay at Richmond Hill he had grown side whiskers, glossy black tufts on his cheeks. He was proud of the dignity they gave him and very conscious of them. In moments of embarrassment he fingered them absently, tugging and smoothing. He did so now. "She may forget all about me."

"Nonsense," said Aaron heartily. "Of course she won't.

Write her love-letters, the moony stuff women like. Quote poetry. Tell her about your heart, how fast it beats when you think of her. Tell her you are in a fever of impatience for the wedding day. By the by, have you two decided on that blissful date?"

"No, sir. I've tried, but she only says she doesn't believe in early marriages, and quotes Aristotle to prove it."

Aaron laughed, divided between amusement and exasperation. What a lover—cowed by Aristotle! No wonder the child put him off. But it was vitally necessary that they should be married as soon as Alston could finish his business and family arrangements and get back North. Creditors were still imperfectly appeased, and he could borrow no more from Alston at present, though the young man would come into a substantial sum upon his marriage.

And from the political angle a close connection with South Carolina was imperative. Though it had occurred to no one else, Aaron foresaw the possibility of a tied electoral vote between himself and Jefferson. In this event South Carolina's influence might easily swing the election.

These considerations were not, however, the most important. There was Theo herself. If her little episode with the unknown boy by the East River had caused him to think that it was high time she married the right man, the shocking incident with this Captain Lewis the other night had confirmed his opinion with regrettable emphasis. She must be anchored at once in a safe port where the chance winds of passion could not reach her. He had not the smallest doubt that his decision was right, all the more so since it gave him pain to part with her.

"Write to her by every packet," he went on, knowing that Theodosia would be far more receptive to a courtship by letter. "Very often one expresses oneself better on paper, and Theo is an excellent correspondent."

"I'm not," said Joseph gloomily.

"But indeed you are, my dear boy," contradicted Aaron quite sincerely. He considered Joseph's facility with the written word to be his one native asset.

Theo accepted her farewell interview with Joseph placidly. During these days of illness she had managed to forget about him, as she had forgotten everything except the headache. Still, when her duty had been pointed out to her, she admitted the reasonableness of Joseph's request.

Aaron overruled Natalie's objections. "I admire your sense of propriety, yet these circumstances are exceptional," he said, and Natalie finally allowed that they were. So she brushed Theo's hair and braided it into tight auburn plaits, straightened the bedclothes, pulling them up to her chin so that no inch of the high-necked linen nightdress might show. Then she stationed herself in a far corner of the room with Aaron.

Joseph, when summoned, shuffled to the bedside and stood there uncomfortably, trying to think of something to say.

Theo was unexpectedly touched by the anxiety in his face. "I'm much better, you know, except for this stupid ankle."

The gentleness of her voice flustered him anew. She seemed so young, lying there between her long braids, her pale little face upturned and defenseless.

"I'm sorry you're going tomorrow. I shall miss you very much," she added, from an impulse of pure kindness, and realized as she said it that she did feel more kindly toward him than she ever had.

His heavy face flushed. "I'll come back soon, soon as ever I can. Will you be glad to see me?"

She smiled up at him. "Of course, very glad." That was true, too. She would surely be glad to see him when the time came. It was a long way off: three months or more—an eternity.

"We'll write each other often?" he insisted.

"Yes, indeed we will."

He moved uneasily. Her soft pink mouth tempted him, as did the innocent relaxation of her body, outlined, despite Natalie's care, by the bedclothes. He glanced nervously toward Aaron and Natalie. They were chatting in low tones, politely unconcerned, but his courage failed him.

He bent and kissed Theo on her cool cheek. "Good-bye, Theo."

She touched his shoulder lightly. "Good-bye, Joseph." And as that seemed inadequate and he still looked unhappy and dissatisfied, she added, "I shall count the days until your first letter."

With this he had to be content. No one could express vehement emotion in the face of sickness. Neither of them suspected that the pattern for their whole marital life had been set. Theodosia had discovered the power of weakness and illness, the release they gave from intolerable circumstance, and though she fought this consciously, never recognizing the evasion, she was to be many times defeated.

Joseph, his Gullah servants, and his fine carriage sailed next day on the *Veronica* for Charleston. While the vessel awaited the tide's turn, he and Aaron shared a flagon of Trent wine at the Tontine Coffee House, and the latter rehearsed his prospective son-in-law's instructions.

"Communicate with me in the cipher I gave you if you wish to write indiscreetly. I need not tell you to guard your tongue: you are not overtalkative. But do not be niggardly with your letters, either to me or to Theo."

Joseph again gave his assurances. The prospect of soon seeing his homeland and pangs at parting from Theodosia had induced in him an unusual state of emotion.

His eyes were moist as the *Veronica* set sail, and he strained them to get the last glimpse of the New York skyline—a jumble of low, clustered red and brown rooftops, dominated by the high-flung spire of Trinity Church.

He mused sentimentally for a while, leaning on the after rail and watching the swirling wake, until the *Veronica*, tacking, rolled halfway over in a ground swell, and his meditations were disagreeably replaced by a queasy feeling in his stomach.

He loathed the sea, and his vexation increased at finding his cabin smaller and dirtier than he had expected. Cato, his bodyservant, crouched on the planks, was already retching with the seasickness which assailed all the blacks.

"Don't you dare puke here, you worthless nigger!" shouted Joseph, pointing his command by a hard kick on the Gullah's backside.

When Cato had staggered out, Joseph locked the door and hunted for his escritoire. Difficult though it was to recapture the nostalgic yearning of an hour back, he dipped his pen and set bravely to writing the first pages of his first letter to Theodosia.

She received the letter a month later. As Aaron had expected, it surprised her by its eloquence. Beneath the ponderous phrases ran a current of real feeling. He told her that he missed her; he described his voyage and his reception on the Waccamaw; he hinted at their wedding date.

Theo's ankle healed slowly, and this cut her off from most of her normal distractions. No dances, no rides on Minerva, no gay expeditions to Turtle Bay. She had much time for reading and pursuing her studies as directed by Aaron. And she had plenty of time for letter-writing.

Joseph's image softened and acquired a romantic blur. Relieved of his bodily presence, she discovered in him virtues that she had not previously noted. It would have been strange had she not, for Aaron daily pointed out these virtues. He commented on Joseph's proficient horseback riding, on his aristocratic appearance, on his growing political aptitude. "Mark my words," said Aaron, "he will be Governor of his State some day, unless I can find for him a loftier situation. Which is entirely possible."

This was as close as Aaron ever came to mentioning his ambition, even to Theo. He was engaged in a perilous political balancing act, and his native discretion had deepened to complete secrecy.

There was nothing actually unconstitutional in trying to take advantage of the existing method of voting. Separate ballots were cast in the Electoral College for the candidates for President and Vice-President, but the candidate receiving the highest vote was chosen as President. If by some fortunate circumstance the vice-presidential candidate should receive more votes than the presidential one, the positions of Jefferson and Aaron would automatically be reversed. Nothing either heinous or unconstitutional, and yet the country at large, both Federalist and Republican, persisted in acting as though there were. Heated orators held forth on "the will of the people," and the tragic consequences of a "possible miscarriage of justice," until the public gradually convinced itself that Jefferson must be the only, the divinely appointed, choice.

The returns trickled in through November and December, delayed by weather conditions and different voting days throughout the States. It became increasingly apparent that the result was to be as inconclusive as it was anticlimactic. The votes for Jefferson and Burr showed a tie.

Aaron sat tight awaiting developments, guarding his speech and his writing, while most of the press, led by Hamilton's *New York Evening Post*, exploded into outraged editorials.

Aaron kept very quiet, but Jefferson did not. He wrote to his rival an extraordinary letter barbed with distrust and fury, and in a calmer tone he wrote to James Madison.

". . . The election in South Carolina has, in some measure, decided the great contest, though as yet we do not know the actual votes of Tennessee, Kentucky, and Vermont, yet we believe the votes to be, on the whole, Jefferson 73, Burr 73. . . . There will be an absolute parity between the two Republican candidates. This has produced great dismay and gloom . . ."

Jefferson was right. There was indeed dismay, and with

it gloom. It disconcerted Aaron to discover the rising strength of public opinion against him.

It was declared that he had been intriguing with the Federalists and was a traitor to his party. Well, what if he had? thought Aaron. A judicious tempering of sentiments was always allowable. Even the great and noble Mr. Hamilton, who now cried "Shame!" had not been above circulating a secret pamphlet vilifying his own party leader, John Adams, when it suited his purpose.

Never given to self-pity or sickly introspection, Aaron was not crushed by the hullabaloo against him. He accepted it stoically and retired into dignified silence. Never at any time in his career did he trouble to explain his actions. What was done was done, be it right or wrong, and recapitulations bored him.

But there were moments when he felt puzzled and hurt by the hostility of the nation's leaders. Many years ago Washington had taken one of his dark, unreasonable dislikes to him, blocked his military advancement, and refused him an appointment as Minister to France. Adams disliked him. Jefferson, who had once been friendly, now hated him, and as for Hamilton——But he was so accustomed to hostility from that quarter that he underestimated it. Nor did he as yet suspect how much Hamilton's influence had contributed to stifle his career.

By January the tie-vote excitement had mounted into hysteria, yet Theodosia, tranquil at Richmond Hill, was scarcely aware of it. Snowdrifts piled high across nearly impassable roads; raw damp air blew up the Hudson and stopped all thoughts of venturing out. The quiet winter days followed each other without outward change. And yet imperceptibly there had been change, for Theo had come to accept the inevitability of her marriage. Time, Aaron's pressure, and a constant interchange of letters with Joseph had overcome her resistance.

After a talk with Aaron, who must shortly leave for Albany and the legislative session, she capitulated in the following note:

NEW YORK, *January* 13th, 1801

I have already written to you by the post to tell you that I shall be happy to see you whenever you choose; that I suppose is equivalent to very soon; and that you may no longer feel doubts or suspicions on my account, I repeat the invitation by a packet as less dilatory than the mail; but for all these doubts and suspicions I will take ample revenge when we meet.

I yesterday received your letter of the 26th of December, and am expecting your defense of early marriages today. My father laughs at my impatience to hear from you and says I am in love; but I do not believe that to be a fair deduction, for the post is really very irregular and slow—enough so to provoke anybody.

We leave this for Albany on the 26th inst. and shall remain there till the 10th of February. My movements will after that depend on my father and you. I had intended not to marry this twelvemonth, and in that case thought it wrong to divert you from your present engagements in Carolina; but to your solicitations I yield my judgment. Adieu. I wish you many returns of the century.

THEODOSIA

The following day Alexis brought to her bedroom the letter from Joseph that she was expecting. It was immensely bulky and spotted with red seals. It covered thirty manuscript pages, and Joseph had sat up all night composing it. He flattered himself that he had turned many a neat phrase, displayed an "elegant" knowledge of the classics, and answered all her objections.

He began ceremoniously:

CHARLESTON, S.C., *December 28th*, 1800

"Hear me, Miss Burr." [And he quoted from one of her letters:] "Aristotle says that a man should not marry before he is six and thirty; pray, Mr. Alston, what arguments have you to oppose to such authority?"

It has always been my practice, whether from a natural independence of mind, from pride, or what other cause I will not pretend to say, never to adopt the opinion of anyone, however respectable his authority, unless thoroughly convinced by his arguments; the 'ipse dixit,' as logicians term it, even of Cicero, who stands higher in my estimation than any other author, would not have the least weight with me; you must, therefore, till you offer better reasons than the Grecian sage himself has done, excuse my differing with him.

He went on like this for several pages, and Theo sighed as she waded through paragraph after paragraph of his sprawling handwriting.

He talked a great deal about himself; he quoted a poem by Benjamin Franklin; in one unrestrained moment he addressed her as "My Theodosia," and told her that he anticipated marriage with rapture; that it would form "so perfect a heaven from our uniting in every study, improving our minds together and informing each other by our mutual assistance and observations."

But now, having polished off the subject of early marriage, Joseph abandoned the personal note and embarked on an essay, nearly three thousand words long, refuting her objections to South Carolina.

"Alas! Beautiful and romantic hills of South Carolina—fair and fertile plains interspersed with groves of the orange, the lemon, and the myrtle, which fling such healthful fragrance to the air, where are ye fled?" wrote Joseph, soaring into dizzy heights of rhetoric. And there was a great deal more of this, until Theodosia, a quarter of an hour later, reached the postscript.

> The arrangement you speak of, proposing in your letter for an interview, has determined me. I shall, therefore, sail certainly in a few days. Winds be propitious!

Theo folded together the scattered pages and carried the letter to her father, as a matter of course. Aaron sat in the library composing a speech on taxation for the session at Albany, but he turned to her with the instant whole-hearted attention that was one of his greatest charms.

"From Joseph," she said ruefully, half-laughing. "There's a vast lot of it."

"There is indeed." Aaron surveyed the crumpled pile of paper. But he read it at once, while Theo pulled a book from the shelves and lost herself in the sprightly pages of a new romance.

Thank Heaven, thought Aaron, as he plodded on and on, that Alston does not speak as he writes, or my poor Theo would soon be buried under an avalanche of verbiage. I could have said all this in a tenth the space, and far more seductively. Still he hid his amusement, finished reading the letter, and replaced it on the table.

"A masterly dissertation. I see that we are to expect your betrothed very soon. He will, no doubt, follow us to Albany. In fact I have written him to that effect."

Theo nodded, still deep in the pages of her romance. The fortunes of Rinaldo, who had scaled the castle wall on a silken ladder to elope with his lady fair, were far more important than Joseph's possible advent.

"Moreover," went on Aaron, with calculated lack of emphasis, "you and Alston will be married in Albany in about a fortnight, I should think."

She jerked upright. The novel slid from her lap to the carpet. "In Albany!" she repeated blankly. "Why, that's impossible! It's too soon."

"Not at all. What is there to be gained by waiting? He is coming North for the purpose, is he not?"

"Yes, I—I suppose so. But I always thought I should be married from Richmond Hill, and not in the middle of winter——"

"Neither location nor climate has anything to do with marriage, my dear. And though I do not wish to sound vulgar, I must tell you the truth. I cannot afford to give you a wedding appropriate to our position at Richmond Hill. The whole town would have to be asked."

Which was true enough, though Aaron had another motive for desiring an Albany wedding. At this critical period, with his name on every thinking man's tongue and the hostile press yapping, it would confound them all when it became known that he was quietly pursuing his legislative duties in Albany, and that, far from being engaged in the tie negotiations or intriguing for the Presidency, he was engrossed by a charming domestic affair—the marriage of his beloved only child.

He went to the highboy, and unlocking a small drawer drew from it a bag of coins. He put them gently in her lap. "Consult with Natalie as to your wardrobe, then buy yourself some pretty gowns. That new French modiste on Chatham Street will make them up in a few days. Stint nothing. And if you need more money, I will find it for you gladly. I want my Theodosia to be the most beautiful of brides."

Chapter Eight

THEODOSIA and Joseph were married in Albany, on Monday, February 2, 1801, in the low-ceilinged parlor of the little house Aaron had leased for the session.

Afterward Theo never could remember much about the ceremony except a sharp sensation of surprise that marriage, which seemed such a soul-shaking step to contemplate, could in the happening seem so casual and undramatic. She had expected heartache, palpitations, perhaps even the mystical joy one read about. She felt nothing at all.

It was dusk and snowing fast against the tiny-paned windows. The parlor glowed with a crackling fire. At one end of the small room the half-dozen guests murmured politely as though awaiting the arrival of the tea service and decanters. There was no atmosphere of special festivity.

Aaron, exactly as usual, made graceful desultory talk and quietly supervised everything. Joseph in a new coat of buff brocade seemed precisely the same young man who had left Richmond Hill four and a half months ago, silent and embarrassed. He had arrived yesterday evening, and Theo had not seen him alone. She herself wore a fine muslin frock embroidered in brilliants, one of those bought in New York before they left. But this was not unusual either. She had had many new white dresses, and this one could not compare in elegance to the one she had worn for her birthday party.

Only Natalie, who had of course accompanied them, experienced any of the emotions proper to a wedding. She huddled in a corner behind the fire screen, her handkerchief to her eyes, her kindly little mouth working. "Pourvu qu'elle soit heureuse, cette pauvre Theo," she horrified herself by murmuring. For Theo's total lack of animation, with none of the shy radiance one expected in a bride, smote Natalie's

89

practical heart with dismay. She touched the crucifix around her neck and prayed for Theo to the Holy Mother who understands all things.

The Reverend Mr. Johnson swayed back and forth in front of the fireplace as he intoned the service. His long black coattails all but raked across the burning logs, and Theo watched them fascinated until he prompted her to each response.

Suddenly he stopped swaying. His ponderous Bible shut with a thud. It was all over.

Theo felt her father's arm draw her close to him, and in the same moment that she realized his arm trembled a little she looked up to see his eyes bright with moisture. He put his long delicate fingers on either side of her face and kissed her forehead. "God bless you, my dear," he whispered.

"Father——" She clung to him frantically, an hysterical sob crowding into her throat.

He shook his head slightly and put her from him. Beneath the tenderness of his gaze, she saw the familiar air of admonishment. "Go to your husband, Theo. He is waiting to embrace you."

Husband! The word struck through her brain. This thick-set stranger with the curly black hair and petulant mouth— Husband! Terrifying and yet ludicrous too. Almost she could have laughed, as he stepped forward clumsily and kissed her on the mouth.

A smile rippled through the company, the half-sentimental, half-bawdy amusement reserved for weddings.

I'm quite alone, she thought, profoundly startled. No one understands—not even Father!

"Let us away to the wedding feast," said Aaron lightly, herding them into the dining-room and lifting his glass in the first toast to the young couple.

At nine o'clock Natalie led Theo upstairs and helped her change into her traveling clothes. She draped a violet velvet cloak over Theo's shoulders, tied bonnet ribbons under her round chin. The bonnet was of violet velvet too, and beneath its brim the girl's face shone ghostly white.

Natalie kissed her. "Don't be afraid, chérie," she whispered unhappily. "It can't be so—so bad. All ze married women in zis world have—subi." She blushed scarlet.

Theo smiled faintly. "I'm not afraid, Natalie, dear."

For now again she felt nothing but a weary blankness: a complete detachment as though she stood far outside herself watching the antics of tiny, not very interesting puppets.

This sense of isolation carried her through the leave-taking. Aaron had prepared himself to deal with this difficult moment, soothing her, and reminding her that they would meet again in a fortnight. His precautions were unnecessary. She seemed scarcely more aware of him than she did of the others, and her brief, almost casual farewell dismayed him. He wished her to adapt herself to her new circumstances, of course, yet where had she acquired this sudden remoteness? It invested her with a surprising maturity. For one instant he felt misgivings—he checked them instantly. Of course she would be happy—ambition and determination produced happiness under any conditions. She must learn this.

He flung open the door and ushered the bride and groom to the small cutter which was waiting outside. The horses stamped and blew with the cold. But it had stopped snowing. High above a frosting of stars twinkled tiny as spangles, diminished by the chill air.

Theo seated herself in the cutter and Joseph clambered in beside her. The horses started off briskly with a cheerful jingling of sleighbells.

"Good-bye, Godspeed!" Most of the company had returned indoors, unwilling to brave the cold or the night air, but Aaron stood bareheaded on the Dutch stoop until the cutter disappeared around a corner.

It glided smoothly on its runners over the fresh snowfall toward the docks. Aaron had booked a stateroom for them on the New York packet, and had informed Joseph of it upon his arrival the evening before.

"Theodosia loves Richmond Hill," he had explained, "and I have made arrangements for you to go there at once. It will be easier for her to go by boat, even though ice on the river may delay you. The overland journey is too rigorous at this time of year, and the taverns are impossible."

So Joseph had found his honeymoon arranged for him in every detail. He had accepted it without protest, recognizing that it was sensible and saved him trouble. But he was astounded, on entering the large and commodious cabin which Aaron had booked, to find it transformed out of all resemblance to a ship's cabin. A Turkish carpet covered the floor, and the dingy curved timbers that formed the walls had been whitewashed to shining purity. There were two small armchairs with needlepoint seats, and on the hinged table by the berths stood an enormous bowl of Christmas roses.

Theodosia broke her silence with a little cry. "How pretty it is! I didn't know a ship's cabin could look this way. Did

91

you have it fixed this way?"

He shook his head sulkily. "No." After a moment's silence he added, "I presume that your father did."

She walked over to the stove, pulled off her mittens, and held her chilled hands to the blaze.

Of course it was her father. Who else would have taken such pains to insure her comfort? Who else would have thought to send her roses, the only kind that could be procured in midwinter, a trifle shriveled and puny, but roses none the less? Messages of cheer and comfort.

Joseph flung his cape on one of the chairs and stared unhappily at Theo's small unconscious back. His mind was not analytical, but he found himself irritated by Aaron's thoughtfulness. There was something faintly ridiculous about starting married life in a bower of a father-in-law's devising. And deeper than that lay a disquiet that he could not quite drag to light.

Now and then at Richmond Hill, he had mulled over the single-hearted devotion that Theo showed her father. And often, when they were together, he had felt himself excluded while the two of them escaped into an apparently delightful atmosphere which he did not understand and slightly resented.

Still, you couldn't resent so admirable a thing as love between father and daughter; it was most proper and becoming. Always, he had told himself, it would be different once he and Theo were married. Theo would then automatically transfer that eager admiration, that breathless responsiveness, to her new master. Girls always did.

He had vaguely pictured his wedding night, seeing Theo starry-eyed and shy, shedding a few natural tears, perhaps, as she parted from her father. But, after all, they were to see Aaron again so soon. He had pictured himself as drying those tears tenderly, carrying her off in a high manner. Then they would be alone at last, freed from all other influences.

But Theo had neither blushed nor cried. Since the ceremony she had not spoken to him at all—until now, to express pleasure over the transformed cabin, with which he had had nothing to do. Neither did he like the transformation. A ship's cabin should be a ship's cabin. This looked like a stage-setting, specious and theatrical. It made him uncomfortable.

Theo continued to warm her hands at the stove; her back, under the cape which she had not removed, was both remote and rigid. She seemed totally unapproachable: a polite little stranger.

From the deck above their heads he could hear the trampling of sailors' feet. Six bells rang from somewhere, there came a musical shout, "Heave away," followed by the flapping of the mainsail. The vessel creaked.

He cleared his throat. "We—we're getting under way."

"Why, yes, I believe we are," she answered, not moving.

He walked over beside her. "Won't you take off your bonnet and cape? It's warm in here."

She obediently untied the ribbons beneath her chin. He took the cape from her, hung it on a bracket near the door, taking as much time as possible to do so. He was increasingly uncomfortable. Damn it all, they were married, she was extremely pretty, she was his wife. He had dreamed of this moment. There had been nights in Carolina when he had tossed sweating on his bed, consumed with desire for her. For love of her he had refused to go to the brothels with his friends in Charleston.

But now he felt no desire. Her pale fixed little face, with its great staring eyes like—like a sleepwalker's almost frightened him. He could no more imagine embracing her than he could one of the cold marble statues in his plantation garden.

Yet this was a bridal night. On bridal nights a man must be masterful, vigorous, no matter the unresponsiveness of the bride.

Joseph paced a few uneasy steps across the cabin and made a pretense of peering through the porthole into the blackness outside. A light or two pricked out from the shore; the leaping flames of a huge bonfire moved slowly past, and out of sight. The packet glided downstream with velvet quietness. There was almost no motion. The inner uncertainty and fear of being inadequate, which had bedeviled him from childhood, now gnawed at Joseph's heart. He took refuge in the brusque, arrogant manner that was half-temperamental and half-concealment.

"I'm going to have a dram of negus," he said abruptly, scowling at Theo as though she had forbidden it, "if I can find a servant to make it for me on this damned boat."

Theodosia turned her small head, her eyebrows raised in cool surprise.

"Alexis is waiting out by the saloon, you know. You have but to call him. He makes excellent negus."

Alexis, of course. He had forgotten. Aaron had provided his own servants for them too. Joseph, suddenly swept with unreasonable anger, threw open the cabin door, and shouted in a voice that was an insult, "Alexis!"

The black man came running. "Yes, sir. Yes, sir."

"I want negus. And be quick about it, damn you."

Alexis bowed with dignity, resentment in every line of his stiff body. Aaron treated his servants with invariable kindness and courtesy. The black did not like Mr. Alston, but he saw that the bridegroom was unhappy. He felt a trifle sorry for him, but a whole lot sorrier for Miss Theo. She'd got herself a dull-headed, ill-tempered bull of a husband for fair: him and his passel of Gullahs with their singsong jabber and their heathen charms.

He came back in a few minutes bearing a steaming bowl of negus, fragrant with lemon peel, port wine, and nutmeg. Miss Theo was sitting in one of the chairs, her chin on her hand, mooning over the Christmas roses Colonel Burr had combed Albany to find. Mr. Alston was leaning against the far wall, frowning at the carpet. Neither looked up when Alexis came in, so he placed the bowl of negus beside two china cups on the wooden bench, and bowing disappeared.

Joseph ladled out the smoking-hot liquid. "You will join me," he ordered sharply. "We must drink a toast to our marriage."

"Certainly." She accepted the cup, touched her lips to it. Joseph gulped his, poured himself another, and another.

This isn't real, Theo thought. Soon I shall awaken and I will find myself in my white bedroom at Richmond Hill. Father will be up and dressed already, down in the library writing. He will be a little cross with me for being late to breakfast, and he will tease me by forbidding me another cup of tea. But after breakfast we will walk out onto the porch together; the air will be crisp and sparkling; Minerva will be waiting for me, whinnying at the hitching-post. Our pond will be thinly iced, with new pussy-willows around its margin, and behind I shall see the Hudson.

My beautiful river! But I'm on the Hudson now! The realization came with shock, yet it brought comfort. Her river that she loved cradled her now on its mighty waters: waters that flowed relentlessly on like Time that could not be checked or diverted.

Merne. The short blunt name which she had never used slid into her thoughts. It gave her sharp pain. All these months she had kept his memory away from her. She pushed it back now with violence. It didn't happen the way I thought it did. There was no magic, no enchantment. It was trivial and cheap: Father said so. I must never think of it. For Time and the river have brought me on here to this clipped moment, and even now it slips into the past as I try to hold it. "What must be must be, and there is no going back." That is the river's eternal murmur.

"Theo!"

She looked up slowly to meet her young husband's eyes. The wine had given him courage. He flung across the room and seized her roughly by the shoulders. "Kiss me!" he shouted, and his trembling fingers fumbled at her bodice.

She shrank convulsively, pushing against the chair-back. Her flesh seemed to gather itself up and recoil from his hands. She gave a moan of terror. "No, please——"

His face flamed. "What's the matter with you? You're my wife! You look——" His voice thickened, was nearly unintelligible. "You look as though you hated me." He dropped his hands and sank to his knees beside her chair. Theo huddled as far from him as possible. The sound of his heavy breathing filled the cabin.

"Theo——" His voice cracked. He swallowed.

Her heart pounded in sickening strokes. Slowly, inch by inch, she turned her head toward him. He was grotesque, crouching there, this great panting animal, an enemy, a wild beast. Suddenly his face pierced through the thick mist of fear. His mouth was twisted like that of a small child that has been unbearably humiliated and does not understand. His eyes, bewildered and desperate, slid quickly away from hers. But before his mouth hardened back into its customary defiance, she had seen, and it cut through her own terror. He was not an enemy, not a wild beast, but a groping, unhappy human being, unsure of himself or his real worth. Her throat closed with pity, for she knew in that second that, under his clumsy show of masculinity, he was as frightened as she.

"Poor Joseph," she whispered. The two words trembled between them. He stared, unbelieving, on guard. Tears filled her eyes and she smiled at him, the compassionate smile of maternal women through all the ages.

They did not belong together, their bodies had for each other no chemical attraction, their souls no communion. But they were both caught. Equally helpless bits of jetsam on the forward-surging river of life. And for well or ill they must remain together, nor hurt each other too much. She closed her eyes and, stretching out her arms, drew his head gently against her breast.

Chapter Nine

♫ ♫ ♫

ON MARCH fourth Theodosia and Joseph arrived in the new Federal City to witness President Jefferson's inauguration. They wedged themselves amongst the wildly excited crowd inside the Capitol, craning and jostling with the others for a clear view.

Aaron, splendid in black silk, as presiding officer of the Senate made a brief, graceful speech presenting the new President, for his inauguration, to the assemblage and to the new Chief Justice, John Marshall, who administered the prescribed oath. Jefferson's lanky, unkempt figure towered over him, yet Theo was not the only one in the Senate Chamber who felt that Aaron would have better suited the high position, and that Jefferson would make but an uncouth and grotesque representative for the growing nation.

It's all wrong, thought Theo bitterly. It should have been Father. Why are people so blind—so stupid?

Though Aaron privately shared this opinion, neither to friend nor enemy did he ever show the slightest disappointment at the eventual outcome of the tie vote. On the contrary, during the last weeks, when the election had finally been thrown into the House of Representatives, and that harassed body had doggedly cast indecisive vote after vote for thirty-five ballots, and on the thirty-sixth the Federalists voted in sufficient numbers to elect Jefferson, Burr had taken pains to disclaim all personal interest in the matter, assuring everyone of his dismay at the situation. "How monstrous," he said smoothly, "that the plainly expressed will of the people for Jefferson should be blocked by a technicality."

Aaron was a good loser, and if one avenue closed, his natural optimism at once suggested another. He had lost the Presidency by one electoral vote. Maddening—yes. Still, it

96

was lost; he accepted the inevitable with his usual composure and made plans for the future. There would be other elections, other opportunities for dazzling achievement in this vast and unexploited country.

His cheerfulness infected Theodosia, and, for the three days that she and Joseph spent in Washington, the celebrations, receptions, banquets, and parades gave her no time to think of the approaching separation from her father. During the past month she had been able to make at least a partial adjustment to her marriage relation. She never quite lost the maternal compassion she had discovered on her wedding night: an emotion new to her, who had spent all of her seventeen years in the rôle of dependent and worshiper. It gave her strength to endure Joseph's ill temper and inept love-making.

The Alstons left Washington on the seventh. Joseph, fretting to be off, managed by his impatience to soften the pain of Theodosia's parting with Aaron. She clung to her father, repeating all the trivial instructions which occur to one at such moments—"I forgot to give Katie the book I promised; please tell her I will send it at once from the South. And tell Natalie that my white cashmere shawl was forgotten on the top shelf of my cupboard at Richmond Hill. I want her to use it herself as long as she wishes, and——"

"The horses are waiting, Theo," interrupted Joseph. "We shall be late for the ferry."

Aaron smiled wryly. "Your husband is anxious to carry you away from me to his rice swamps, but I'll be down to see you soon, and in the meantime write me, madam, often and legibly. None of your careless scrawls, please."

"Oh, I will," she promised. "And you, Papa, I shall count the days until I hear."

Joseph scowled, angrily flicking tiny icicles from a bush. "You said all that last night. Will you please to get into the coach, Theo?"

"I expect that Joseph is right, my dear," said Aaron. "It is never wise to prolong farewells." He kissed her quickly and hurried away, his footsteps almost noiseless on the wooden planks that formed the sidewalk.

Joseph handed Theo brusquely into the coach; the horses strained forward into yellow mud that sucked around their hocks; the cumbersome vehicle moved sluggishly toward the Potomac ferry. They had started on their sixteen-day journey to Theodosia's new home.

This journey blurred into a tiresome haze of bumping

coaches, dirty taverns whose unsatisfactory meals upset even their young stomachs; the general discomfort heightened from time to time by moments of danger when they forded rivers swollen by spring thaws.

Joseph was a difficult traveling companion, intolerant and demanding, treating all underlings in the imperious way that he treated his slaves. By a natural consequence he received grudging service. Post-horses were delayed; he never seemed able to engage adequate accommodations in the crowded inns; he and Theodosia were given the dregs in the wine flask, the last cut on the roast.

Traveling with Aaron had been very different. Theo had had no conception of the effect of her father's lavish use of his personal magnetism upon all human contacts. And on the rare occasions when he encountered discomfort which he could not remedy, he accepted it good-humoredly. But Joseph sulked. Or, if he did not sulk, he fumed, railing against the weather, the roads, the folly of trying to travel in this barbarous fashion.

"If we had waited for a packet to sail from Alexandria, would it not have been easier?" Theo suggested once.

"Certainly not," retorted Joseph. "You know very well that I dislike traveling by water. This journey is hard because we are traveling like peasants. I am not accustomed to waiting on myself. It's undignified. I'm extremely uncomfortable."

And so am I, she thought. But already she had become wise enough not to point out that their lack of private servants was due entirely to his own decision. On this trip to the North he had brought none of his slaves, having found them a nuisance on the previous visit, nor had he allowed her to take any of the Burr servants, saying with truth that more than a plenty awaited them on the plantations. In consequence they shifted for themselves and were a travel-stained, disheveled couple on the morning of March twenty-third, when they finally reached Yawhannah, and left the Lumberton–Georgetown Mail.

The Alston chaise awaited them, on its box a glistening black coachman resplendent in the family livery—red and green stripes with brass buttons and a tall, shiny black hat.

"This is your new mistress, Pompey," said Joseph, giving a groan of relief as he stretched his legs in the chaise.

Pompey grinned and murmured something unintelligible to Theo, who smiled helplessly, and, turning to Joseph, laughed, "I can't understand a word he says. It might be Chinese for all of me."

Joseph was not amused. "He bade you welcome and wished you good luck. You must learn the Gullah dialect at once. You will be mistress of more than two hundred niggers and will have many duties amongst them."

"Shall I?" She was startled. She had had little to do with the servants at home. Peggy and Alexis managed the household and neither expected nor welcomed supervision. Peggy, a highly intelligent mulatto, wrote nearly as good a hand as Theo did herself and competently dealt with all emergencies.

How little I know of this life I am going to lead! she thought, and barely suppressed the thought which followed: How little I wish to know of it! She gave herself an inward shake. "No fears, no nerves, no self-indulgence." That was one of Aaron's favorite maxims.

"What duties shall I have?" she asked, trying to sound enthusiastic. "I thought an overseer looked after all the Negroes."

"The overseer is responsible for the field hands and the artisans, not the house servants. Besides, there are many other things——" He sighed. He was tired, and as every mile brought them nearer home, he began to feel misgivings which had never occurred to him up North.

Just how would Theo behave as a plantation mistress? What impression would she make on his family—the family which was even now gathered twenty strong at his father's plantation? They would be cordial and courteous, of course, but would they approve of his choice? In so far as his nature permitted, Joseph was very much in love with Theo, yet these doubts provoked his ready distrust. He was seeing her through his family's eyes—an alien. That she was very pretty and charming and daughter to the Vice-President would, after all, count for little down here. The Waccamaw Neck was a principality in itself. He had married a foreigner, and one without money at that.

He had not known this latter awkward fact on his trip home in the fall. It was not until after the marriage that Aaron had exposed his deplorable financial condition. Nor, to do Joseph justice, had the discovery much upset him. He had money enough of his own. Yet the family might think differently.

Theo, watching, saw him frown.

"You must bear with my inexperience, Joseph," she said quietly. "I shall try to learn. But please remember that every-

99

thing is so different down here. Even the landscape," she added, shuddering a little.

They had descended into the swamplands that bordered the tangle of rice rivers, the Peedee and the Waccamaw. She looked in amazement at the dense vegetation unlike anything she had ever imagined—vines as big as her arm writhing about twisted black branches, and everywhere hanging fronds of ghostly gray moss. Here sunlight scarcely penetrated; the effect was mysteriously sinister and threatening.

Joseph stirred, crossing his legs. "Theo," he said abruptly, "I've been meaning to speak to you on this subject." He paused, fingering his cherished whiskers. "Your upbringing has been quite unlike that of the ladies here. You must guard your speech or they will think you immodest. You discuss many subjects that are not here considered in good taste."

"Do I? I don't understand what you mean."

"I suppose not. Your father has seen fit to allow you great freedom of thought. For one thing, do not let them know you do not attend church. Down here you will go to All Saints' every Sunday."

"Of course, if it is the custom. Father and I are not particularly orthodox. He always says he was steeped in too much dogma in his youth. His grandfather, Jonathan Edwards, was a renowned preacher, you know. Still, I have gone to several churches out of curiosity—the Roman Catholic, the Dutch, the Friends Meeting House——"

"Preposterous!" cut in Joseph. "That's just what I mean. There is only one church for a gentleman—the Anglican. And another thing. You must not refer to—to an expected birth in the loose improper way which seems to be permissible at Richmond Hill."

Theo colored, but her mouth was mutinous. "I think what you say is silly. You hinted yourself that your stepmother was expecting another baby; it must be about due now. I don't see how one can ignore the fact."

"You will ignore the fact," he snapped. "You will not mention it at all. They would think you lewd."

She subsided. "Very well, Joseph." For after all, what did it matter? She realized that the approaching ordeal worried him. She, who had met so many different people and gained their liking without effort, found his anxiety to have her appear to advantage both amusing and pitiable.

"Don't look so solemn," she said lightly. "I will act pious as a preacher and avoid all inconvenient subjects, I promise you." She touched his square, blunt-fingered hand with her little glove.

His face cleared. Always he melted at one of her rare caresses. He put his arm around her slender corseted waist and squeezed her tight. She submitted, smiling.

"Are we nearly there?" she asked.

He shook his head. "Not for some time, but we are nearing the Waccamaw Ford."

She gazed curiously at the river of which she had heard so much. She knew vaguely that the fortunes of her new family were rooted in the thick mud that bordered its tidal banks, and that all their plantations depended on it. But she was unimpressed by the small rust-colored stream which they forded without difficulty. Joseph assured her that it grew much larger farther down, but she was disappointed, thinking of the magnificent river at home. She shut her eyes and tried to picture the dearly loved rooms at Richmond Hill, each one pervaded by her father's presence. What was he doing now? He must be back there soon. He was to leave Washington soon after they did.

"You might at least look at the country that is to be your home." Joseph's annoyed voice startled her.

She jumped guiltily. "Indeed I have been. But there is not much to see—just trees and swamp and that horrible hanging moss. It gives me the shivers. It looks like a scene from Dante's *Inferno*; I can almost hear the wailing of the lost souls."

"I do not know to what you refer," he said stiffly, "but we consider the moss beautiful. There is much of it around the Oaks."

"Where is the Oaks?" she asked quickly.

"A mile down the road, but we shall not stop there today."

She wondered why. The Oaks was Joseph's own plantation, left him by his grandfather, and was to be their home eventually. But today they were bound for Clifton, the home of Colonel William Alston, her new father-in-law.

"But isn't the Oaks on the way to Clifton?" she insisted. "Couldn't we just look at it?"

"No," said Joseph shortly. "The family are waiting for us."

The family. Only in the last week had she begun to realize the importance of that phrase. As Joseph neared home, it appeared with chilling frequency. Still, one would have thought that the family, having waited all day, might have

101

spared an additional half-hour while a bride inspected her own new home. She was far from guessing that Joseph was ashamed of his plantation and its small tumble-down house. It had been untenanted since the death of his grandfather in 1784, and seventeen years of Carolina weather had not improved its appearance. Moreover, the slaves, laxly supervised for so long, had run wild over the whole estate.

Clifton, on the other hand, was a well-regulated plantation with a mansion hardly inferior to Richmond Hill. Had not General Washington stayed there in '91 and written that it was "large, new, and elegantly furnished"?

Accordingly they passed the entrance to the Oaks without comment and continued south on the river road. The tiring horses plodded ever more slowly on its sandy surface. The sun beat down upon their carriage top, converting the interior into an oven. On either side the trees, now scrub pine, now live-oak, pressed in on them, shutting off any possible breeze.

The Waccamaw Neck, a narrow finger of land, pointed south to Winyaw Bay and Georgetown. On the west ran its river and the rice plantations, while on the east, five miles across the peninsula, was the sea.

I shall go there often, thought Theo. I love the ocean. For a moment she imagined that she caught the tang of salt.

"I smell the ocean," she said eagerly. "How soon can we go and see it? Tomorrow?"

"What for?" answered Joseph. "We never go to the seashore until May."

"But I want to go. It's only a few miles."

Joseph mopped his dripping forehead and scowled. "Theodosia, I trust that you will conform to the wishes and plans of the family. I beg that you won't upset them with sudden impulsive whims."

Theo suppressed the retort which rose to her lips. After all, they were both hot and tired. She would manage "the family"; and anyway, surely she and Joseph would be in their own home in a day or so. She would be her own mistress.

She felt faint and her head throbbed when at last they dragged around a bend in the road and came to high wooden gates. A cluster of blacks slouched against the posts or sprawled limp on the scrubby grass. At the sound of carriage wheels they sprang to attention—a motley handful, big and little, some in the Alston livery, some in cotton shifts. They

102

waved and cheered. "Welcome, Maussa Joseph! Welcome, Mistiss!"

Joseph smiled and, leaning out of the carriage window, greeted some of the grinning blacks by name. Such ridiculous names, thought Theo—Romeo, Cupid, Orpheus, Amoretta. She tried to copy Joseph's air of affable condescension, wondering how in the world he ever told one black face from another. Each seemed to have the identical assortment of protruding lips around enormous white teeth, slate-black skin, and rolling eyes.

As the carriage turned into the plantation drive and headed for the river, the blacks shuffled along behind them, laughing and chanting snatches of a rhythmical song. Soon the cavalcade entered an avenue of enormous live-oaks so lavishly festooned with gray moss that the trees were almost obscured. Pompey flicked the horses into a trot and they drew up with a flourish at the steps of a large white-pillared house.

"Clifton," said Joseph majestically, but Theo noted that his voice trembled. With sudden sympathy she squeezed his moist hand as he helped her down.

At once they were surrounded by an exclaiming, gesticulating throng, adults and excited children. So many, that Theodosia, dismayed, stood uncertainly beside Joseph waiting for guidance.

In the babel of welcome she heard her own name many times repeated and prefixed by different tags of relationship —"Cousin Theodosia," "Sister Theodosia," even "Aunt Theodosia" and "Daughter."

"I'm so very glad to meet you all," she laughed, turning from one to another, "but won't you please tell me which is which?"

"Of course, my dear." A spare middle-aged man with grizzled hair detached himself from the group. He took her hand. "I am William Alston of Clifton, Joseph's father. Mrs. Alston is awaiting you upstairs in her chamber. She is unfortunately ailing today. Now for the others—Maria, my child——"

A tall, decided-looking young woman in her twenties stepped forward.

"This is my daughter, Lady Nisbett," said Colonel Alston, stressing the title with evident satisfaction. Maria kissed Theo coolly on the cheek, made a civil murmur.

"These are your brothers-in-law, William Algernon and John Ashe." He presented two beardless young men who resembled Joseph, though their complexions were far lighter.

They bowed one after the other, eyeing her admiringly.

"And this is Charlotte, youngest of my children by my poor lamented first wife," continued the Colonel.

A plump and giggling miss of fifteen bounced up to Theo, delivered a shy smack, and retired to a corner, where she stared openmouthed at her new sister-in-law.

These, then, thought Theo, are Joseph's full brothers and sisters. But there were still a dozen adults unidentified. Nor did she manage to remember their exact status after she had met them. They were, it seemed, Middletons, McPhersons, Flaggs, and Hugers, all related in some way to the Alston family.

Her face ached from smiling, and her back could scarcely support her by the time her father-in-law indicated the assorted children with a careless wave of the hand. "Little John Nisbett, Maria's son, and my children by my present wife—Rebecca, Thomas, Pinckney, Charles, and Jacob Motte."

Six small faces looked up dutifully. "How do you do, Sister Theodosia," they chorused, before rushing thankfully back to a far corner of the piazza where sat an enormous turbaned black woman swaying and crooning to herself. One of the small boys flung himself onto the vast aproned lap. "She's real pretty, Mauma, ain't she?" he shrilled, "but she got mighty queer clothes. She got naked bosom."

The old woman gave him a reproving shake. "Hush yo' mouf, yo' naughty chile! Plat-eye goin' ter git you, effen yo' talk like dat."

Theodosia laughed. Her clothes probably did look queer to the child, in that, though rumpled and travel-stained, they were of the latest Parisian cut and very different from those of the Alston ladies. They still wore modest fichus, sashes around the waists of their muslin frocks, and their hair fell in loose curls, product of both art and as much of nature as possible—a fashion of three years ago.

Theo, with her hair piled high, and elaborately embroidered violet velvet traveling gown, cut low in the neck to outline her breasts, drew surreptitious and scandalized glances from the assembled ladies. And her scanty skirt exposed two inches more of ankle than did theirs.

"Ah!" cried Colonel Alston. "Here comes the lime punch, at last."

Theo turned with the others to see a procession of servants filing onto the piazza, a solemn parade headed by a butler bearing an enormous cut-glass bowl, while three black boys followed behind with trays of glasses.

Theo, appalled at the prospect of a lengthy drinking ceremony, rose to her feet, murmuring tentatively, "Perhaps I'd better go upstairs and repair my costume——" She looked around for Joseph, but he was of no help. He lounged against the railing, discussing the rice crop with his uncle by marriage, Benjamin Huger, who came from the adjoining plantation of Prospect Hill. He would not look at her and her imploring glance was wasted. Her father-in-law ladled out the punch.

She gulped down the sour-sweet liquid and put her glass definitely back on the tray. But the family were not to be hurried. They drank toasts to the bride and groom, to the absent Mrs. Alston, to a great many other people of whom Theo had never heard, as well as to President Jefferson, Governor Drayton, and belatedly, with bows to her, to "Our illustrious Vice-President, Colonel Burr."

Oh, Father, she thought, I never would have believed that I should be laggard in drinking a toast to you, but in truth I shall disgrace myself before my new family if I touch any more of that concoction. The punch mingled with her exhaustion to produce giddiness and nausea. She longed for the cool and quiet of a secluded bed somewhere, anywhere.

But when Lady Nisbett arose at last, Theo found that her ordeal was not yet ended. Mrs. Alston awaited her; she must of course pay her respects to her new mother-in-law at once.

"Are you fatigued?" asked Maria Nisbett, noting Theo's lagging walk. Her cool voice was clipped and affected in imitation of the English accents in her husband's family. And where the rest of the Alstons showed a typical Southern languor, laziness bred half by climate and half by the superabundance of service which they commanded, Maria stood out sharp, decisive, and self-important. She always knew what she wanted and managed to get it.

"A little fatigued," replied Theo, clinging to the stair rail. "It has been rather a long journey, you know."

"To be sure," replied Maria. "I think you very brave to have withstood it so well." She smiled a quick, tight-lipped grimace which was meant to be ingratiating and patted Theo's shoulder, which she topped by a good five inches. "And how did you leave the dear Vice-President? Sir John—my husband, you know—has every intention of waiting on him in Washington. Though Sir John has not been home to England in some time, he is conversant with British affairs. Perhaps he may be of use to your father."

Or *vice versa*, you mean, thought Theo cynically. She was not drawn to her sister-in-law, who struck her as both spinsterish and pretentious.

"I hope Mrs. Alston is not seriously ill," she offered.

Maria flushed. "Oh, no—just a slight indisposition. Here is her chamber." She knocked and they entered in response to a murmur.

The cause of the "slight indisposition" was immediately apparent even to Theo's inexperienced eyes. She gave a little shocked cry, as she saw the clumsy figure on the bed. Her husband's stepmother was a faded blonde, with weak, watery blue eyes and an obvious desire to be both welcoming and kindly, but her forehead was beaded with sweat, the hand she held out to Theodosia shook, and even as Theo clasped it, the woman's face contorted and she gave an involuntary moan of pain.

Theo turned sharply to her sister-in-law. "But Mrs. Alston is——" she stammered. "Isn't she—I mean, isn't anyone helping her? She's suffering."

Maria drew herself up. "Maum Chloe is taking care of her." She indicated an old black woman who sat back in the shadows muttering to herself.

The crone raised her head and shuffled forward, thrusting her wizened face up into Theo's. "Maum Chloe brung heap o' babies, buckra, nigger, all come dis same way. Mistiss she doin' fine. Knife under she bed cut pains."

Bewildered, Theo followed the gnarled pointing finger. The high four-poster bed on which lay Mrs. Alston cleared the floor by two feet, and in the exact center beneath it lay a long sharp butcher's knife.

Theo turned indignantly on Maria, who stood silent and apparently bored beside the window. "But that's barbarous," she cried. "Surely you will get a doctor—someone to help Mrs. Alston besides this superstitious old hag."

Maria frowned. "Maum Chloe is very skilled," she said coldly. "And I cannot think what you mean by a doctor. No modest woman would endure the presence of a man at such a time. You must have very strange notions of propriety up North."

Theo swallowed an indignant answer remembering Joseph's warning, but she thought, When—and if—I have a baby, I shall have all the doctors that can be got and the Alstons may whistle for their propriety.

"Don't look so worried, child," said a weak voice from

the bed. "I'm sorry that my—my situation is as it is right now. It is quite unexpectedly early. I would not have chosen to greet you like this." She smiled apologetically.

Theo started to reply, but the old black woman interrupted. "You're early, Mistiss, 'case you'm got two of dem in dere and dey's rarin' to git out. De loggerhead he call twice from de swamp las' night. Dat mean twins. Bimeby buckra see Maum Chloe say true. She know better den highfalutin po' white trash doctor."

She darted a resentful look at Theo from her rheumy old eyes and hobbled over to her mistress. Mrs. Alston was tossing monotonously from side to side, no longer conscious of her visitors.

Theo, embarrassed and torn by pity, tried to signal to Maria. If they could do nothing, surely they should leave. But her sister-in-law had moved to the far corner of the shadowy room and was engaged in snuffing a guttering candle, meticulously collecting any small wax drippings which might make an untidy appearance.

How can she be so heartless! thought Theo angrily, and turned to go, when she was held motionless by a strange scene at the bedside.

Mrs. Alston cried out once, sharply, and the black woman bent over her muttering. Neither patient nor midwife seemed aware of Theo's startled exclamation, while Maum Chloe drew a small object from within her dirty blouse, murmured to it, then placed it ceremoniously upon the sheet which covered Mrs. Alston's abdomen. She held it there with one skinny hand, and her head weaved back and forth in a snake-like motion. Her shriveled lips parted as she muttered a whispering chant—guttural syllables repeated over and over like the thumping of a hidden drum.

Theo's spine prickled. She peered at the object on the sheet, unwilling to believe that she could be seeing truly. It was a small crude doll made of dried mud. The chant stopped. The old woman cocked her head as though she were listening.

Mrs. Alston struggled up from the pillows. "How much longer will it be, Maum Chloe?" she panted.

Maum Chloe thrust the doll back into her bosom. "Conjuh say not till fust cock-crow, Mistiss."

The woman sank back on the bed with a sobbing sigh. "Such a long time—I don't know if I can——"

"Sho yo' kin, Mistiss. Yo' jus' chaw on dis bit o' conjuh root. He gib yo' sleep." She thrust a hand into a bag that dangled from her apron strings and fished out a twisted black root. Its pungent smell filled Theo's nostrils.

Mrs. Alston let the black woman put it into her mouth and sucked on it feebly.

"Good, Mistiss, enty? En Maum Chloe e'en cut de pain mo'." She fumbled beneath the bed, brought up the knife, thrust it rhythmically backward and forward a foot above the tossing, restless figure. Mrs. Alston grew quieter, her eyelids fell slowly.

Maria returned from the mantelpiece, a pile of wax pellets and fuzz in her cupped hand. "Those worthless niggers— they never think to clean, unless you stand over them every minute. I found dust near half an inch thick over there behind the clock. If this were my house, I'd order ten lashes apiece for the whole parcel of them. They'd soon mend their ways."

"Oh, hush," begged Theo. "Mrs. Alston is sleeping, and I —I'm very tired. Won't you please show me my room?"

When Maria at last complied, Theo dropped down on the bed too exhausted to remove her dress. The fatigues of the long journey, her difficulties with Joseph, the ordeal of meeting the Alstons, were all overshadowed by the weird scene she had just witnessed in the great front chamber. How could intelligent people accept all the huggermuggery and black magic of the African mind for their own! Twins because a bird had called twice, a brandished knife and a dirty piece of root to deaden pain! Most monstrous of all, the hideous doll that was supposed to prophesy the exact moment of deliverance!

She pictured her father's incredulous amusement when she should tell him of this. She knew so well his hearty scorn for superstition, his calm, realistic approach to fact. Yet with it he had immense sympathy for suffering. He would have been as appalled as she by Maria's callous indifference, and the rest of the family's elaborate ignoring of Mrs. Alston's danger. Mrs. Alston. But I am Mrs. Alston too. This is now my family, my home, my country.

She buried her face in the pillow. "I hate it here; I want to go home," she whispered, and at the sound of her own voice she burst into tears.

She did not hear the door open, and started as Joseph touched her, saying, "Why, Theo, my dearest girl, what is the matter?"

He raised her, holding her quivering body close to him. "What in the world has happened?" he insisted.

She could not tell him that she was lonely and frightened, that she longed bitterly for her father, but she was grateful for the comfort of his arms about her. Her head fell against his breast, her sobs quieted.

Finding that she would not speak beyond a murmur of "headache," he kissed her and dismissed the matter as female vagary.

"The family are pleased with you," he said presently, and went to the mirror to rearrange his stock. "They find you pretty. My father and brothers agree that they have never seen so fine a pair of dark eyes, and Mrs. Huger— Aunt Allston that was, of the double 'l' branch—says you are a sweet creature."

Theo wiped her eyes on her cambric handkerchief. "I'm glad of that." She watched him with a certain mournful amusement as he rolled up his sleeves and washed his hands in the Wedgwood basin. He whistled tunelessly and dried his hands with a flourish. She realized that he was pleased with himself and her. He was, in fact, in a very good humor, had enjoyed playing the traveled man of the world before his brothers, had been delighted to hear that his overseer, Mr. Smith, at the Oaks saw prospects of a bumper rice crop, and that seven black wenches at the plantation had produced healthy brats—fertile slaves were mighty good assets.

Yet deeper and more important than these, more important even than Theo's initial success with his family, lay a simple primitive emotion. He was glad to be home. The Waccamaw Neck was dear to him. He had been born there, had romped and hunted over every foot of it. He knew each one of the thirty plantations strung in a row down the river like green beads on a brown silk cord—Brookgreen, Turkey Hill, True Blue, Hagley, Forlorn Hope, Rose Hill—their very names pleased him, and every one was connected with Alstons or Allstons. And, he thought complacently, his own place, the Oaks, was the original one; from the Oaks both branches had spread like creepers along the banks of the Waccamaw.

Tomorrow, or maybe the day after, he would ride up to the Oaks and inspect the young rice, at the same time deciding what must be done to make his house habitable. No hurry for that, however. They could stay at Clifton indefinitely.

It suddenly occurred to him that Theo was exceedingly quiet. He looked around to see her sitting dejectedly on the edge of the bed, staring out the window into the murmurous Carolina spring night.

"Theo, rouse yourself. 'Tis nearly time for supper. Surely you wish to change your dress—though wait, I had almost forgot. You need a maid, of course. We no longer have to live like savages."

He clapped his hands. Cato, his bodyservant, appeared and waited deferentially for orders.

"I ordered a maid sent from the Oaks for your mistress. Bring her here. Who is it, by the by?"

"Venus, Maussa. Li'l Venus, Big Venus' gal. Li'l Venus she'm sma'test wench in de quarters."

Joseph nodded dismissal.

Theo looked up, smiling a little. "Oh, Joseph, must I really have a maid named Venus? I fear I shall laugh every time I see her black face."

Her husband paid no attention to this attempt at frivolity. He was carefully brushing pomade into his cherished side whiskers preparatory to having Cato curl them, and he saw no point to her remark.

When Venus presented herself in a red-and-green cotton dress and bandanna, Theo felt no inclination to laugh, for the girl had the lithe grace of a tiger cat. Her skin, not black but copper-tinted, covered a face far different from the splay-nosed, thick-lipped Gullahs. She was a Foulah, the Arabic strain plainly written in her aquiline nose and delicate bones. Her parents had been abducted, not from Angola like the Gullahs, but from the wild North African interior, twenty years ago, before Venus was born. After the first wild misery and rebellion they had accepted slavery in the strange new land, but Venus, who knew nothing else, had not.

She burned for freedom, her heart festered with resentment against the buckra. She hated them, and she hated her stupid companions in the "street" of slave cabins at the Oaks, because they accepted their degradation so placidly. Almost she hated her parents, who had been chieftains in Africa, despising them for their quiescence.

She had come now under orders from the overseer to be maid to the new white mistress from the North. Her first rebellion had quieted when she realized that there would be advantages. She would learn buckra ways, she would insinuate herself craftily into their smug lives, until the time came when she could strike for freedom, perhaps even—far sweeter thought—for revenge.

Theo, knowing nothing of this, yet saw that her welcoming

110

smile was tardily answered. She saw the look in the long sensual eyes slide from hers, while something inimical flickered in their depths. She felt rather than heard the hypocrisy in the slurring submissiveness of Venus's speech, and she knew from that first moment that her maid hated her. It scarcely mattered, she could dismiss the girl tomorrow: it was foolish to mind. But she did mind.

Like the black trees outside writhing amongst their spectral moss, like the fever-breeding swamps whose tainted air even now seeped through the windows, like Maum Chloe's conjuh, this slave girl's causeless hostility added to her desolation. She reasoned with herself, quoted Aaron's brisk sensible maxims, yet she could not shake off a sense of foreboding, formless fears which rendered sleepless and miserable her first night on the Waccamaw.

Chapter Ten

THEODOSIA continued to have new experiences in the next few weeks at Clifton—most of them unpleasant. The family were kind, but there were so many of them, even after the uncles, aunts, and cousins, who had come only to view the bride, had packed up and left for their respective plantations.

There was no privacy anywhere, even in her bedroom. Maria Nisbett assumed that Theo would be grateful for her company at any time, and Charlotte followed her around wide-eyed and admiring in the throes of an adolescent infatuation for the beautiful new sister-in-law.

The children swarmed all over the house like monkeys, chattering, screaming, and quarreling, eternally eluding their fat mauma, who waddled after first one and then the other, scolding and blandishing by turns, but powerless to control them.

Joseph, his father, and two brothers escaped from the turmoil during the day. They rode far and wide upon Waccamaw Neck inspecting the plantations, but Theo was not invited to accompany them. She was expected to amuse herself with proper feminine occupations—whatever they might be: apparently nothing except needlework and gossip. She was bored, and her nerves were frazzled by the constant pressure of people and noise.

A new noise had been added to the clamor on the morning after her arrival. Mrs. Alston had been duly delivered of twins a few minutes after the first cock-crow, and the incessant wailing of sickly babies now pervaded the house.

No one but Theo seemed astonished at this exact fulfillment of Maum Chloe's prophecies. Nor was anyone surprised three days later when the tiniest of the baby girls gave a brief feeble cry and was suddenly stilled forever. Maum

Chloe had foreseen that too. Her conjuh had told her.

The little body was tucked into its oak coffin and buried that day. For an hour or two the men went around with solemn faces, and from the "street" of slave cabins rose an outlandish keening for the dead, but even the mother did not mourn long. There had been so many babies, and she was too tired and spent to feel much. Besides, her arms were not empty, there was still a baby left to fill them: little Mary Motte, her own namesake.

But to Theodosia this casual acceptance of birth and death was painful and frightening. She wrote to her father about it, and in time had one of his breezy letters full of advice and common sense. "You must not indulge yourself in morbid fancies," wrote Aaron. "Adapt yourself to the customs and temper of mind that you may find in your new environment. It would be wiser to be less critical, more tolerant, though indeed I know my little Theo well enough to be sure that she would never show outward discourtesy of any kind."

Theo sighed as she read this. It wasn't exactly a question of criticism or intolerance. She was trying to adapt herself, but the ways and outlook of the Alstons were so alien. Nor did they make any effort to understand her.

She went out for a walk by herself one morning after breakfast and tried seriously to think out her problem. To get off alone had brought on a minor crisis. Maria had asked where she was going and why. First Charlotte and then two of the younger children had tried to accompany her and had had to be discouraged.

"At least," said Maria, "do not take any of the paths leading to the rice fields, because the field hands would think it most unseemly to see Mrs. Alston wandering around at such an hour. Do not go off the plantation road. Take one of the servants with you, or Venus—the proprieties will thus be better observed."

Theo gently refused. She wished to go by herself, and she certainly did not want Venus. She saw more than enough of her maid as it was. Joseph had flown into a passion when Theo had suggested getting rid of her. And, in truth, she had been unable to give any good reason. Venus was remarkably deft and efficient and prompt to answer a call: too prompt. Theo was convinced that the girl listened at doors and hid herself in corners, she moved so swiftly and quietly.

Theo longed for Minerva and the happy days of wild free rides across Manhattan Island. She might have ridden here; there was a large stable of horses—but not alone! Oh, never!

A decorous trot, accompanied by one of the grooms, was all that was permissible, and that was considered eccentric for a married woman.

"Order a carriage if you wish to go somewhere," said Joseph carelessly.

Theo had as yet seen nothing of the country except Clifton, and she longed more than ever for a sight of the sea. But it turned out that that was not so simple. The horses needed rest, or the coachman was drunk, or a spoke had broken in one of the wheels; the latter a simple matter to fix, thought Theo, in her first innocence, until she discovered that an excess of service often resulted in nothing being done. If the wheelwright was ailing, as he usually was, then the wheel must wait until he felt better. No one else would dream of touching it.

How different it will be when we are in our own home, thought Theo. Yet here, too, lay cause for disquiet. Though she had not yet seen the Oaks, she had now heard enough about the place to realize that it was uninhabitable in its present state.

"Then let us start at once to make it habitable," she urged Joseph. "If the roof leaks, it can be mended. If, as you say, the house is too small, we can build a wing."

"To be sure," he answered readily. "But little can be done during the summer. The fever months will soon begin. In a week or two we shall move southward to Sullivan's Island."

"With the family?" she asked in a small voice.

"Of course with the family." Joseph stared; and she said no more.

Today, having momentarily escaped them, Theo walked swiftly down the plantation road toward the river, hurrying lest she should be caught by any more delays or admonitions. Once out of sight of the house, she gathered her muslin skirts high and ran in an access of freedom and released spirits. Her yellow chip straw hat flopped crazily about her face. Panting, she laughed at herself and ran the faster, plunging off the road and down a shady bypath into the forest. She reached an open clearing beneath a grove of long-leaf pines, sank down on the moss, and fanned her face with her hat.

It was enchanting to be quiet and free: ecstasy to be alone. The thought startled her. She began to count back. She had literally not been entirely alone for more than half an hour since her marriage. Even her one delight, the letters she wrote to and received from her father, were read or written surrounded by white faces or black.

And at night, of course, there was Joseph. Dear Joseph, she thought guiltily. She was fond of him, to be sure. She wanted to please him and to make him happy. She knew well how insecure was his hold on happiness, how easily upset he was, how liable to be hurt and to react to hurt with anger. That he needed and loved her increasingly in his own way, she could not doubt. And she needed him too, down here where he was the only link with a happy past, the only person who knew her father, and with whom she might sometimes talk of him. Only here there never seemed any opportunity to talk with him. He was away all day with the other men, and at night he was either sleepy or amorous.

She picked up a little stick and began absently to make small designs with it on the turf beside her. Sullivan's Island would be the same or worse: noisy children, wailing babies, hordes of slaves, Maria's inescapable and acid tongue, Mrs. Alston's vague complaints. And only two topics of conversation for each sex: domestic detail and family gossip for the women, race-horses and rice for the men.

She tossed the stick aside with sudden resolution. The Alstons might go to Sullivan's Island if they liked, but she had other plans. Richmond Hill was waiting: Richmond Hill and Aaron. They had exchanged many letters about it. "Of course you must spend the summer with me," he had written. "You will contrive some way to bring your husband to our way of thinking, I have no doubt."

Yes, indeed she would contrive! In the burst of joy at the prospect of liberation she thought, And I will be patient with them, and make them love me, even if they do weary me. I must learn to like this place too. After all, in its way, I suppose it is as beautiful as the North.

For the first time Theo looked about her with unprejudiced eyes. Spring had sprinkled the forest with flowers—fragrant yellow jasmine, wild violets, and the flaunting scarlet redbud. A mockingbird, high in a hickory tree, was trilling its varied music, and she listened entranced. Even the everlasting moss did not seem sinister today, for spring sunlight had flecked its grayness with vivid green.

She got up and sauntered aimlessly, enjoying the soft air and the peace, parting the hanging fronds in front of her until she saw through the interlacing branches a brown expanse of light. That was the Waccamaw down there, a great sluggish river like molasses. It was banded by the rice fields, emerald now with their waving masses of unripened rice.

115

She gathered a handful of violets and buried her face in them. Fragrance as always gave her keen sensuous joy. Then, spying a charming red-berried vine, she tucked the violets into her bodice, and darted through tangled bushes to reach the vine. She stretched out her hand to pluck when a peculiar noise stopped her. A dry, sharp sound from the ground beside her foot, half rustle and half rattle. Puzzled, she searched for its source. Again came the noise, and turning her head she gave a moan of fear. Her heart stopped beating, sweat broke out on her forehead. Not two feet from her lay coiled an enormous mottled snake. She froze into a block of terror, motionless as the trees around her except for the tiny chattering of her teeth. And her paralysis saved her. The rattlesnake slowly uncoiled and glided away into the underbrush.

Sobbing, stumbling, she fled back to the path, to the safety of the dusty plantation road. As her terror subsided, her gratitude for deliverance left one violent emotion behind: a loathing for this treacherous country. Her one effort to appreciate its beauties had been too brutally thwarted.

She was to endure some more years of it, to accept it, and even to some extent to look upon it as home. But peculiarly sensitive to her environment, she had felt from her first glimpse that the Waccamaw Neck was hostile to her, and now she was sure of it. She told no one of her experience, knowing only too well that there would be scant sympathy, and that, in Joseph's case, fears for her safety would react as anger. But she never walked alone in the woods again.

Theo escaped that summer as she had planned and spent a few happy weeks with Aaron at Richmond Hill. Soon after her arrival, Natalie sailed for France to see her mother from whom she had been separated for six years. Theo missed her adopted sister, yet it was delightful to be entirely alone with Aaron. Almost she could forget that she was a wife. The Waccamaw Neck blurred into unimportance.

In August, however, Joseph arrived in his own carriage, and this time with a full retinue of servants: a pleasanter, more tolerant Joseph. He had missed her more than he had thought possible, and during her absence it had even occurred to him that she had not been entirely happy on the Waccamaw. He had puzzled over this, finally admitting to himself that for a girl unused to a large family, his had perhaps been a bit overpowering. Accordingly he had ridden to the Oaks, decided upon the necessary improvements, and given orders for work to begin.

"When we return South, we shall move into the Oaks," he told her. "I am having the establishment enlarged so that it will be fitting for people in our position."

"Oh, I'm so glad," she cried, kissing him gratefully. She pictured an airy, spacious mansion, exquisitely furnished, for Joseph assured her that the original furnishings needed but a little polishing and repair to hold their own with those of Richmond Hill. She saw herself, composed and gracious, inspiring the slaves to efficient service, assisting Joseph in his budding political ambitions by adroit hospitality. There would be a well-stocked library and music, intelligent, sparkling conversation. A salon, perhaps—a small center of sophistication and culture, thought Theo, enthusiastically ignoring the isolation and the unpromising material she had so far discovered on the Waccamaw. "With energy and ambition all things are possible." Had not Aaron said so a hundred times?

After these romantic dreams the reality proved bitter. She and Joseph arrived at the Oaks in November, and she could not hide her dismay. She had shut her eyes to the tangle of unmowed grass, to the unfilled holes which rendered the plantation drive a bumping torture, but at her first sight of the house she turned on Joseph incredulously. "But it's so small, scarcely bigger than our gardener's cottage at home, and—what's the matter with the roof?"

The roof, half-covered with the original weathered shingles, and half-renewed with the raw yellow of unpainted pine, presented a singularly spotty and raffish appearance.

"They haven't finished it," said Joseph unhappily.

Indeed, they had finished nothing. The porch still sagged, two of the six small rooms were littered with lumber and paint pots, and Theodosia suspected that evening a fact which she later repeatedly verified: fifty slaves could not accomplish as much as one skilled Yankee workman.

They moved in, anyway. Discouraged as she was, Theo yet definitely vetoed Joseph's suggestion that they go to Clifton "until the place was ready."

"No. Obviously we must be here to supervise." And Joseph, ashamed of the failure of his plan, agreed.

The house gradually became habitable. She sent to her father in New York for ornaments and furniture, Joseph's heirlooms having turned out to be few and rickety.

"With energy all things are possible." Yes. But what to

do if the energy is lacking? thought Theo. The glowing health and enthusiasm with which she had arrived on the Waccamaw ebbed day by day.

By the end of November she knew that she was to have a baby, and she wrote to Aaron at once. He was delighted, wrote letter after letter of advice. He exhorted her to watch her diet, to attend to her teeth, and to take exercise.

"You must walk a great deal. I do entreat you to get a very stout pair of overshoes or short boots, with one button to keep them on; thick enough, however, to turn water. . . . Without exercise you will suffer in the month of May. . . . Walk, if you must be in form, with ten Negroes at your heels."

Theo tried to follow his advice in this, as in everything, but it was difficult. Not only was her body apathetic and heavy; but her mind also. Every movement, every thought required an expenditure of effort that appalled her. For longer and longer periods she lay on a sofa in her chamber, staring out of the window at the eternal drip, drip, drip of the gray moss. Books no longer interested her; she gradually gave up her attempt to fulfill the duties of plantation mistress. Even in the first month at the Oaks, before her health declined, she had not seemed able to cope with these duties satisfactorily.

The slaves, outwardly docile, yet treated her orders with a bland indifference. Phoebe, the fat cook, listened to Theo's planned menus, said "Yas'm, Mistiss," then produced exactly what she pleased. Nor was she a good cook, but slovenly and inept.

"The mistress of a plantation should order and direct the servants, should dispense supplies, should visit sick Negroes and prescribe for them, should arbitrate disputes amongst the wenches, and occasionally deal out punishment." This she knew from Joseph, and also from observation at Clifton. She had tried to follow this program. But when she visited the "street" of slave cabins their laughter or singing was at once stilled, doors closed quickly at her approach, to open reluctantly at a knock, when a black child would thrust his woolly head through the crack, murmuring that Mammy or Granny or Sis was out. They made her feel like an interloper, and completely superfluous.

In the management of household detail she was no more successful. She tried to institute certain reforms. Every morning at about eleven, thumpings and bangings shattered the quiet air for half an hour, while three kitchen wenches pounded the unhusked rice in wooden mortars made from tree-trunks. They pounded one day's supply at a time, enough for the buckra table and the household servants.

"On Monday morning," Theo directed, "call more girls from the quarters and pound enough rice for the whole week. We shall be spared this daily racket, nor will there be the constant nuisance of flying chaff and dust through the house."

They stared at her blankly, but the most intelligent one at last nodded. Next morning the pounding continued as usual. Theo remonstrated sharply. Next day there was no pounding, but there was also no rice on the table. This mattered not at all to Theo, but Joseph was furious.

When she explained her plan, he retorted irritably: "Let them alone. They always pound the rice every day."

"Well, can't they do it somewhere else except under my windows?"

"Of course not; the flagstones outside the kitchen house are the proper place."

So they pounded the rice each day; just as they made bayberry candles on a string instead of using the molds which Theo had had sent from New York; just as they refused to scald the plantation piggins—shallow wooden buckets in which all staples were carried. It was bad luck: it might sour the wheat, or mold the coffee beans, or rot the precious everlasting rice. A great many things seemed to be bad luck. If Phoebe heard a screech owl in the woods, she could not possibly set bread that night, it would never rise. If the laundress on her way to the house from the quarters encountered a rabbit, or a black cat—or almost anything at all, it seemed—there could be no washing that morning. Lizette returned to her cabin.

"A plantation mistress should give her people simple religious instruction."

In the first burst of enthusiasm Theo had tried to follow this precept too. On her second Sunday at the Oaks, she dutifully accompanied Joseph to the little parish church three miles away, endured an interminable sermon, then in the afternoon summoned the black children from the "street" to the big house for Bible stories.

The children wriggled and squirmed, rolling longing eyes back toward the cabins, while Theo felt foolish and apologetic. She knew nothing of their previous Christian training —if any—and was suddenly conscious of her own deficiencies as a spiritual teacher.

119

Aaron had only an amused tolerance for orthodox religion, and such matters had not been included in her education. Still, it was surely an easy matter to read a Bible story, and she embarked bravely on Jonah and the whale.

When her voice stopped, all the kinky little black heads jerked, forty pairs of round eyes gazed at her unwinking.

"So you see," she added, feeling that some pointing of the moral was indicated, "God punished Jonah for his wickedness."

The faces continued to regard her blankly.

"You understand the story, don't you?"

No answer for a moment, then a weedy ten-year-old broke into a pleased smile. "Yas'm, Mistiss."

She turned to him gratefully. He was the only child she recognized, Phoebe's son. "You know what a whale is, don't you, Chance?"

He nodded, beaming. "Ole wil'cat he wail in de woods."

"No, that's different. I told you this was a big fish. It ate Jonah."

Chance nodded intelligently. "Sho wil'cat eat'um big fish, many time."

She looked around at the others. "Didn't any of you understand what I read you?"

They lowered their eyes, digging dusty toes into the porch planks. Someone giggled.

She sighed. "Well, you may go now."

For a moment they did not move until Chance nudged them, and then she realized that not only had they failed to comprehend what she had read them, but that they did not understand her speech. The field hands talked pure Gullah. It was only with the house slaves that she could communicate at all.

Gradually, she gave up her efforts to manage the blacks. As her pregnancy advanced and increasing malaise and lethargy overpowered her, she could not feel the tolerance for their shortcomings that was requisite to dealing with them. "Just treat them as children," Maria Nisbett admonished her impatiently, when she once ventured to discuss her troubles. Still one wearied of being surrounded by, and dependent on, children. Also children eventually improved under tutelage, outgrew pilfering and lying and laziness. But the blacks didn't, they were always the same, and she found them tiresome or worse, as in the case of Venus.

Theo had no idea that part of her difficulties in handling the slaves came from Venus's influence. The girl did her best to spread mutiny throughout the two hundred blacks who served the Alstons at the Oaks. She made little headway; the blacks only laughed at her, and their loyalty to Joseph, their hereditary ruler, was unshakable. Nor could she incite them against the overseer, who was a just man and understood their psychology. But the "Yankee mistiss" was another matter. Was their allotment of groceries a trifle scant, or the temper of a new hoe not so keen as those dealt out last year? It was the foreign mistiss who had ordered it thus, said Venus. Old Fortune's rheumatism and Hagar's bloody flux, for which Theo had tried some Northern remedies, hadn't they got worse at once?

And she had laughed at conjuh, telling them it was foolish, hadn't she? said Venus, who secretly had no use for conjuh herself, but understood this most powerful of all arguments. That was because young miss didn't believe in anything. She was no better than a heathen. Night after night, said Venus, she had waited and peeked to see if young miss said her prayers. But she never did. She never even opened the Good Book and read. She went to church only when maussa made her. She was bad, was young miss.

All this made less trouble than she had hoped, for Venus was not popular in the "street," the women were jealous of her looks, and resented her air of superiority. The men were afraid of her, particularly those who had tried to bed her, and on whom she had turned scratching and snarling like a catamount.

Yet Venus's campaign had its effect and increased Theo's troubles. She gave Theodosia no overt cause for complaint, kept her clothes in perfect repair, obeyed orders with promptness, but with a sort of silky defiance and sullenness that was intangible. Until one day in March.

Joseph's next youngest brother, John Ashe, had just been married to a girl from the Santee country, Sally McPherson, and had brought her back to the Waccamaw. Colonel William, according to custom, had presented his son with a plantation, Hagley, and the young couple were now in residence.

Theo's health had not permitted her to attend the wedding, and she and Joseph set out on this March afternoon to pay their respects. Theo liked her new sister-in-law at once. Her giggles, curls, and vivacity reminded her of little Katie Brown at home. For an hour or so she forgot her discomfort and laughed with Sally. They whispered and made silly jokes like the eighteen-year-olds they both were.

But by five o'clock Theo was exhausted. Her brief access of spirits vanished. She was within two months of her term, and her physical sufferings were insistent. She loathed her body as it had become—swollen, heavy, even the once trim ankles and tiny delicate hands. She could have endured this and the backaches, giddiness, and laboring heart, which everyone said was quite natural, if it had not been for the frequent clouds of depression. They floated down on her like masses of thick black gauze, stifling her, and flattening life into an endless gray wasteland.

The blackness descended on her now, and she pulled herself clumsily to her feet, murmuring excuses to Sally. She wanted only to crawl home to her own room, to her soft sofa. There she could lie in peace without effort, if possible without thought.

Sally was much concerned and wanted to call Joseph. The two brothers had gone walking over John's plantation to inspect the rice stand in the far fields.

"Oh, no," protested Theo, trying to smile. "Please don't call him. Pompey is waiting and can drive me home, then come back for Joseph later."

Sally reluctantly agreed. She was worried. Theodosia looked badly, so pale, and her features blurred and puffy. It was hard to believe John Ashe's statement that the poor girl had been extremely pretty some months ago. Still, of course in that condition—Sally felt very mature and matronly—one must expect to lose one's looks, and one must be forgiven sudden crotchets like rushing back to the Oaks before the men had finished their visit together.

No one at the Oaks expected Theo back so soon, and the house seemed deserted and very quiet. Even Cuffey, the little errand boy, whose duty it was to open the front door, was nowhere to be seen. Far off, from the quarters, she heard the sound of laughter and singing, the strumming of banjos—African instruments the blacks made themselves. They were all down there, no doubt, as usual rejoicing at any opportunity to escape from work. She sighed wearily.

When she had dragged herself upstairs, panting and resting on each step, she noticed without surprise that her room door was ajar. She had given strict orders that it should be kept closed, for the day was uncommonly chilly, and she wished the room to retain all the heat from the little fire. But the servants never remembered anything for ten minutes at a time.

Her kid shoes made no sound on the carpeted floor as she

trod painfully down the hall, and, putting her hand on the doorknob, pushed open the door.

There was a flash of sound, a streak of movement from within. Theo gave a startled cry and hung onto the doorknob. Venus confronted her, backed up against the long gilt mirror before which she had been posturing. The girl's eyes were dilated with fear and hatred. She flung her head back defiantly, glaring at her mistress, but she had thrown her arms high across her chest and around her throat in a quick gesture of concealment.

It took a moment for Theo to grasp the meaning of this tableau. Then she gasped. Her eyes slowly focused on Venus, and then she suddenly understood. "You've got my dress on! My dress——" she whispered. Not that dress, the white gown embroidered in gold which she had worn on her birthday night at Richmond Hill! The beautiful gown that she loved so much that she had never worn it since, but had kept it wrapped in linen in her cedar box! She shut her eyes dizzily. Horrible—dark brown arms, a brown column of throat against the whiteness of that dress.

Nausea welled in her, her face contorted. "Take it off, you slut!" she panted, her hands twisting and untwisting on the doorknob.

Venus did not move, her thin mouth curled, her cheeks glowed dusky scarlet.

Theo darted forward. "What have you got on your chest—what are you hiding?"

For a second the girl shrank, hugging her arms tighter about her throat. Then her chin went up, her lips parted in a malevolent smile, supremely insolent. She dropped her arms. Glittering and fiery on her dark bosom lay Aaron's diamond necklace.

Rage brought a rush of blood to Theo's head. If she could have killed, she would have. She beat Venus across the face with her small swollen fists, dragging the necklace off with such violence that the clasp tore through the brown flesh.

"You're vile—vile! I hate you—I hate you——"

Her voice cracked, the room swirled around her, and she fell forward on the floor, cradling the necklace against her cheek. The other servants found her lying there, crumpled and still, when they returned from the "street" later. They were frightened and placed her gently on the bed, applying rude restoratives.

When Joseph came home she was conscious and in pain: a grinding pain that tore through her at intervals and made speech impossible. Joseph sat on the bed beside her and patted her hand nervously. He was worried and upset, but he could not understand what had happened, nor did he realize what was likely to happen until Phoebe the cook, who hovered near the bed, remarked with gloomy satisfaction: "Look lak dat babby comin' right now, Maussa. Yuh better fotch Maum Chloe fum Clifton, enty? Mistiss she gwine hab bad time."

Joseph started. "You think it's that? Send for Pompey at once, tell him to gallop to Clifton. Tell him——"

Theo opened her eyes. "Joseph, no." Her whisper held a desperation that checked him. He turned to her uncertainly.

"I'm not going to have the baby now. I—won't."

Not till May when Father will be with me—I need him —I won't live through it if he's not near me.

Phoebe chuckled, shrugging her fat shoulders. "Yo' kain' stop 'em, Mistiss, wen dey wants ter come."

Theo lay very quiet. Inside her racked body she gathered her will, consciously drawing strength until it flooded her with a compelling power. The pain receded.

"Joseph——"

He bent down quickly. "What is it, my poor little Theo?"

"Laudanum," she whispered. "A big dose, now. And don't fetch Maum Chloe. I won't let her near me. I'm not going to have the baby yet. I won't."

Nor did she. For three days and nights she lay almost motionless on her bed. The pains gradually died away.

Chapter Eleven

ON THE fifth day after the averted crisis, Theodosia sat up, and Joseph was relieved to find that she felt much better. He drew a chair to her bedside and at last broached the subject of Venus.

"She told me the whole thing, my dear, and I was extremely angry with her, of course. I told her that she was not fit to be a house servant again for some time. She shall be punished by staying in the quarters until she has learned her lesson."

Theo stared at him, astounded. "But Joseph—don't you realize what she did? She can't possibly remain on the plantation. I want you to sell her. Oh, don't you understand—the girl hates me."

"That's unreasonable, Theo," he said patiently. "The wench was not going to steal your things, she has too much sense for that. She was simply trying them on; very impertinent, of course, but scarcely a crime. She is very pretty for a nigger, and I dare say has female vanity like others of her sex."

Theo slumped back against the pillows; she was very weak and tears pricked her eyelids. It wasn't so much that the girl had got around Joseph by a clever flank attack, or even that he should be so willfully blind to Venus's hostility, but that he couldn't realize that the dress and the necklace were not any chance part of her large wardrobe. They were her most cherished possessions. Venus had known it, that was why she had chosen them. And now they were desecrated. It was a part of herself that had been rubbed against that oily brown skin, had covered a heart that seethed with hatred and the passion to hurt.

There was no use explaining. Joseph would never understand. She had not the strength to argue with him. Yet there was one point she must make clear.

"I suppose you will do as you like about the disposition of Venus, except that she will never be a house servant again in any house that I occupy—never." She paused a moment. "Joseph—I've been thinking. Father might get me a French maid. I would like someone to speak French with—a French chef too, perhaps. You know Governor Drayton has one, and several of your father's friends in Charleston," she added quickly.

"What's the matter with the victuals Proebe provides?" he snapped, ruffling.

What indeed? thought Theo, except that she can apparently cook nothing but rice, fried pork, and kitchen greens swimming in grease.

"Phoebe cooks well enough, Joseph, but sometimes something a little more elaborate—when we entertain, I mean. I believe that Father could procure us a chef," said Theo, who had already discussed it with Aaron.

Joseph was silent. He deplored her manifest inability to manage the blacks, and thought it foolish to import expensive white servants from the North, but on the other hand one must not cross women in her condition, they were always unreasonable, and his vanity was tickled at the thought of French servants. They would undoubtedly lend a certain luster to his plantation.

He lit a fat black cigar, leaned back on his chair, and changed the subject. "When is your father coming South? Have you heard?"

She smiled suddenly, her strained eyes softened. "Of course I've heard." Unconsciously she touched her bosom, and Joseph saw a corner of a letter through the opening of her nightshift.

His mouth tightened. Anger seized him. He tapped his foot impatiently. "When, then?"

"The first of May. That should be plenty of time. The baby isn't—shouldn't come until the middle of the month anyway." She turned away, adding very low, half to herself, "I know I wouldn't come through it if—he weren't here."

Joseph expelled a great mouthful of smoke with the effect of an explosion. "That's nonsense, Theo! Ridiculous! What has he got to do with it? It's unseemly to have men around at such a time anyway——"

He flung his cigar into the fireplace, and glared at her. Why must she always be different from other females? Why could she not accept this normal business of women in the natural way, as Mrs. Alston did, and his sister, and every other woman he had ever heard of? They kept their embarrassing condition as unobtrusive as possible, never mentioning it, never fussing, until at the proper moment they quietly disappeared from masculine eyes, and eventually reappeared with a new addition to the family.

Sometimes, though, they did not reappear. It occurred to him suddenly that his cousin Mary had died in childbirth. A trickle of fear extinguished his irritation. He examined Theo anxiously, consciously seeing her for the first time in weeks. She did not look right. Her small face was both puffy and pinched. Her glorious eyes had lost all their brightness. And her cheeks between limp auburn braids were as white as the newly plastered wall behind her.

His heart contracted. "My darling——"

She raised her eyes, startled at his tenderness. "Yes, Joseph?"

He looked down, embarrassed, touched her hand clumsily. "Theo, we'll go to Charleston, as soon as you can travel. You shall have a——" He hesitated: the family would be shocked and contemptuous. He swallowed and went on. "You shall have Doctor Debow, if you wish. I don't want you to worry. You must take care of yourself, I——" His face crumpled. "Damme!" he shouted at her, "why haven't you taken better care of yourself? You've had none of that medicine Maum Chloe made up for you. Look at it, there's the bottle—full!"

He pointed angrily at a viscous mixture of swamproot and chopped snakeskin which the Alston midwife had sent over to the Oaks.

Theo shook her head gently; her eyes glistened as she smiled at him.

"Poor Joseph, I do cause you a lot of trouble, don't I? You are good to me." She raised her arms and, pulling his head down close to her, she pressed her pale lips softly against his whiskered cheek.

Six days later, Theodosia and Joseph made the trip to Charleston. It was not so difficult as she had feared. Pompey and Cato carried her on a litter from the house through the tangled woods to the Oaks Landing on the creek. A huge flatboat awaited them, and she was made comfortable upon it, while skilled boatmen rowed and poled it along the winding creek to the Waccamaw.

The tide was running out and swept the heavy craft downstream to Winyaw Bay, fifteen miles away, where they labored against the currents and whirlpools around the point, then up the Sampit River, to tie up at last beside the Alston Wharf in Georgetown.

Here a schooner awaited them, already loaded heavily with the precious rice, two hundred barrels of it, rough-polished and ready for sale in Charleston. Theo was carried on board, and the *Live-Oak* set sail, skimming along with a following wind the whole sixty miles.

They entered the Cooper River just as the Charleston city lights began to prick yellow against the darkening spring sky. Theo admired the graceful cluster of houses with its lofty church spires—slender, pointed silhouettes—but she never saw it without a sick yearning for that other skyline so many miles to the north. The two cities were so maddeningly similar in many ways—both built on points with two encircling rivers, both with batteries at their tips.

But the other was home, and this one, though more beautiful and certainly cleaner, was not. And never would be—for her.

They went, as a matter of course, to the great Alston House on King Street. The lovely Georgian mansion which Charlestonians still persisted in calling the Brewton House after its original owner, though Colonel William had bought it ten years ago when he married his present wife, Mary Motte, whose family had inherited it from the Brewtons.

Since it was customary for all the planters to spend at least two months of the year in Charleston, and since Joseph could well afford it, Theo had prodded him into getting a house of his own on Church Street. But it was not ready for them, of course. Nothing was ever ready on time, and only Yankee blood would expect the impossible.

So they drove, perforce, to the family mansion, and found to Theo's immense relief that Colonel William was there alone.

He greeted them with absent-minded cordiality and complete oblivion to the cause of their visit. "Delighted to see you, my boy. Delighted. And Theodosia—how well you look!" He did not look at her at all, but at a point above her head. "How unfortunate that you have just missed the others! They left yesterday for Sullivan's, where you will no doubt join them in a day or so."

Oh, no, we won't, Theodosia thought. I'm not going to have my baby in that cramped beach cottage and in the company of Mrs. Alston, her six children, and Maria and Charlotte.

"The servants will show you to a room," continued the Colonel vaguely. "There must be one vacant for once. How did you leave things on the Waccamaw? I must run up there in a day or two. Hubbard writes me that the trunks need repairing on the west fields at Clifton. Can't have the young rice flooded at the wrong time, eh?"

Theo escaped from the rice talk and went upstairs to bed. Her father-in-law was kind and courteous, but he was so dull. He had but three topics of conversation—rice, his fighting days under General Marion, and his race-horses. They all bored her, though she hid it quite successfully. During race week in February she had made pretense of sharing the delirious excitement which apparently gripped the whole of South Carolina, but it had not really seemed very important that Colonel William's Maria was unaccountably beaten by Trumpeter for the Jockey Club Purse. Yet to the Alstons, including Joseph, it seemed to be stark tragedy. They had talked of nothing else for weeks.

Imagine Aaron, who lost the Presidency with airy grace and humor, being cast into deepest gloom at the loss of a trifling purse. There were so many more interesting things in life than rice and racing or prosy details of inconclusive battles fought long before she was born.

She sighed, turning her unwieldy body slowly in the bed, searching for a cooler spot. A melodious clangor of church bells jangled across the city. Saint Michael's, Saint Philip's, and the Huguenot Church one after another struck the hour. Only nine o'clock and a long night ahead. Of late, though she felt dull and heavy all the time, and occasionally drifted without warning into a dreamy stupor, yet real sleep eluded her.

I wish Father would come, she thought miserably. I want him so.

She struggled up from the bed, and fetched the small leather box in which she kept his letters, to re-read the last one. He had been upset by the carefully unalarming bulletins from Theo about her health. "Why have you not gone to the mountains as I wished you to?" he wrote. "All places on the Carolina seacoast are subject to excessive heat and fever at this time of year."

To Joseph he had written more strongly: "I learn with a good deal of regret that the mountain plan is abandoned. . . . With Theodosia's Northern constitution she will bring you some puny brat that will never last the summer out; but, in your mountains, one might expect to see it climb a precipice at three weeks old. Truly I mean to be serious, and beg to know whether you have, in fact, resolved, and whether the resolution has, in good faith, been the result of reflection or of inertness."

Joseph had resented this particular attempt to regulate his conduct. Had he not already shown excessive caution by bringing Theo to the city long before it was necessary, and in granting her leave to consult a doctor? Moreover, he intended to transfer her to Sullivan's Island, as his father suggested. He was amazed to find that Theo had no such intention, and that to all his arguments she presented a quiet inflexibility. She would risk the fever, risk the waxing heat, but she would not leave Charleston until Aaron arrived.

The renowned and popular Doctor Debow waited upon young Mrs. Alston two days after her arrival. During these two days Theo had been feeling increasingly ill, and she had not realized how eagerly she had counted on the physician's visit, how much she had depended on his advice and help, until Joseph ushered him into her chamber.

"I'm so glad you've come, Doctor," she cried. "I don't feel well, I mean even in the circumstances, and I'm sure you can help me."

The doctor bowed. He had flowing white hair, and in his fur-collared black robe he looked both impressive and priestly. "Your confidence does me great honor, madam. It is natural for ladies in your—ah—delicate situation to be concerned over trifling manifestations. You must not disquiet yourself. Secundam naturam, my dear Mrs. Alston. Secundam naturam, you know." He balanced himself on his heels, crossed his fingertips upon his corpulent belly, and regarded her benevolently.

"Exactly," said Joseph. "Just what I tell her."

"Oh, I know," said Theo unhappily. "I don't mean to make an unnecessary pother, but my head aches almost constantly, and I can't seem to see very well. It is as though little black flecks floated across my eyes."

"Ah—visual disturbances, madam, are by no means uncommon. You must keep your strength up. Plenty of good red meat, copious libations of hearty wine, between repasts as well as while partaking of them. It is wise to force one's inclination a trifle. You are providing nourishment for —ahem—for two, you know." He swayed ponderously, beaming at her.

130

"But I can't eat more," she protested. "Food makes me ill, and I am getting so fat anyway."

He nodded affably. "Quite natural—quite. Hic et ubique. Corpulence is an encouraging sign."

"I suppose so," she agreed hesitatingly. "Yet my feet and hands are so swollen that I can wear neither my shoes nor my gloves, and it is a peculiar kind of plumpness, when I press it.—Look." She thrust a small puffed foot from beneath the bedclothes, touched the taut white flesh: the dent from her finger remained for some seconds.

Joseph made an impatient sound and turned to the window, but the doctor's eyes flickered, his tolerant smile slipping for an instant. "Possibly a slight dropsical condition. Perhaps it would be as well to——" He paused, glanced hastily at Joseph's disapproving back, pursed his lips delicately, and went on in a lower voice, "Pray do not think me offensive, but we should perhaps examine the—ah—water——"

She cut him short. "Of course, Doctor Debow. I quite understand."

Yet after she had silenced Joseph's shocked objections and induced him to wait in the hallway, the examination proved to have been quite unnecessary. The doctor put on his silver rimmed spectacles, held the vessel to the light, peered at it and through it, wagging his head, then placed it on a table. "Entirely satisfactory, my dear madam. Entirely. Nullius addictus jurare in verba magistri," he added, rolling the rich syllables over his tongue.

Theo had a fleeting impulse to giggle, immediately quenched by uneasy disappointment. If only she might consult Doctor Rush in Philadelphia, or Doctor Eustis at home. Would they, too, think her a silly, fanciful woman, unwarrantably, almost indecently concerned about her condition?

"Nature, salubrious and omnipotent Mother Nature, will dispose of all these little inconveniences of which you complain. They are," said the doctor, describing a sweeping gesture, "the inherent concomitants of parturition. Nil disputandum. I will compound for you some Balm of Gilead, a sovereign remedy for nervous disability. Partake of it frequently, and remember"—he waggled his plump forefinger —"Mens sana in corpore sano."

He bowed himself out, after assuring her that he would await summons, "whenever—that is—when circumstances force you to suspect that new developments may be imminent."

Joseph accompanied the doctor to the front door and returning said to Theo: "A most gentlemanly physician, and learned too. Now that he has set your fears at rest, I hope that you will show a little more spirit. So much lying in bed can scarcely be good for you."

She smiled wanly. "I know, Joseph; I'll try."

Theodosia dragged herself through the next week, forcing herself to eat and drink, fighting against the constant throb in her temples, the ever more frequent dizzy spells, when the world blurred and her eyes seemed filled with darting black flashes.

On the sixth of May, she felt better and her spirits burst through the chains that weighted them when she received a letter from Aaron. He had arrived at Clifton, where her father-in-law had entertained him. He would be with her in three days.

At once she plunged into feverish activity. She called the servants and impressed them with the unparalleled importance of the occasion, directed the sweeping and garnishing of Aaron's bedchamber herself. She harried the cook, ordering menus far beyond that placid black woman's comprehension, and finally in desperation engaged the best caterer in town for Thursday.

"You are wearing yourself out," said Joseph crossly. "Your father will hardly expect such an elaborate welcome."

They were together in the drawing-room on the second floor, for Theo preferred this room to all others. Its graceful beauty gave her pleasure and some measure of peace. It always seemed cool there, for its cypress-paneled walls were tinted pale blue, and gold brocade draperies softened the pitiless heat from five tall windows, while in the center of the ceiling hung a gigantic chandelier like a reversed fountain of crystal ice. It held twelve candles, and lighted, as they were now, they threw tiny jets of color through the sparkling prisms to the polished floor beneath.

Theo was bending over a small walnut desk, checking lists, her eyebrows puckered. She had not heard Joseph's remark. "Father does not care for this type of Madeira," she said. "If this is all there is in the cellar here, we must order more." She made a note.

Joseph was sprawling on a sofa, chewing the end of a cheroot, since he could not, of course, smoke in the drawing-room. He removed his cigar and frowned. "That Madeira is good enough for my father, so I cannot see why Colonel Burr should object to it."

Theo looked up and smiled. "Oh, Joseph, don't be out of

temper. It's just that I wish everything to be perfect for Father. After all, he has never been South. I want him to see how well we live, what luxuries and elegance you provide for me."

Joseph grunted, replacing the cheroot.

"We must give a party for him," she went on. "Governor Drayton, the Richardsons, the Pinckneys, the Rutledges, they'll all be delighted to honor the Vice-President. How beautifully this room will lend itself to entertaining!" She saw it filled with brilliantly dressed guests, laughter, music, flowers, and Aaron in the midst of them standing against the black marble mantel charming them, investing the most trivial conversation with interest.

"You surely do not propose to appear in public at this time," cried Joseph.

She flushed. For one blessed moment, she had indeed forgotten.

"I suppose the party must come afterward," she said slowly. She put down her pen, pushed back the paper. Afterward. After this strange thing which has transformed my poor body shall be painfully wrested from me. After I shall be released and alone again. But how if there is no "afterward"? If the shadows which are closing on me should at last forget to lift? What then? This room will be here just the same. There will be laughter and music and flowers in it just the same—for others, even perhaps after a while for Father.

"What is it, Theo?" Joseph hoisted himself from the sofa and strode over to her. "Why do you look like that?"

"I'm frightened," she said. "Frightened."

"Of your confinement?"

She nodded.

His face cleared, and he patted her shoulder encouragingly. "Nonsense. You are in splendid health; Doctor Debow said so. After all, this happens every day. Every mortal being in the world has come the same way and——"

"Such fears are only the natural hypochondria of my condition, I know," she finished, with a wry little smile. "I'll try to be good."

Theo spoke little during the next few days and spared Joseph all morbid fancies. On Thursday afternoon Aaron was expected. She dragged about her room and struggled to make herself presentable. She hid her distorted figure as best she could with an embroidered India muslin scarf, made repeated attempts to pile her hair into the coquettish mass

133

of ringlets which Aaron was used to seeing. But she could not lift her arms so high, and the little black maid who had temporarily replaced Venus was stupid and clumsy.

When she was ready, she went into the drawing-room to wait, and paused before the huge carved mirror which covered the southern wall.

How ugly I look, she thought, and how old! The flesh around her eyes had puffed and darkened until they appeared small, and her skin was the color of putty.

It was warm today, even in this room, and flies buzzed monotonously around the great chandelier's tempting glitter. From time to time the high whine of a mosquito made obbligato to the buzzing of the flies.

Theo sank down on the sofa, trying to listen for the first clumping of horses' hoofs down King Street, but gradually a rushing and roaring in her ears, which had bothered her for long, obscured all other noises. Her heavy head tipped sideways against the arm of the sofa. She shivered. How strange that she should be cold! In some way she must surmount this aching, agonizing languor. I must not sleep, she thought, and, thinking that, fell into a stupor so heavy that no sound could touch her, even that for which she longed above everything on earth, the bustle of Aaron's arrival. And he, dashing from the carriage and up the massive oak stairs ahead of Joseph, found her like that.

"God's blood, sir, what have you done to her!" he shouted, turning on Joseph furiously.

Joseph's face darkened. "I don't know what you mean. She's asleep. She sleeps a great deal."

"Look at her, you fool! She's ill, fearfully ill."

"It is but her condition; you have not seen her before. There is nothing alarming."

Aaron gave him one terrible look, and leaned over the sofa. "Theodosia," he called, with a tenderness that Joseph thought angrily was almost womanish.

A long convulsive shudder shook her body. Her lips moved, but she did not rouse.

Aaron gathered her up; he and the now alarmed Joseph carried her down the hall to her bedchamber. As her head touched the pillow, her muscles twitched, she jerked from side to side, her breathing stopped, while her face became suffused with a horrible dusky blue.

"What ails her?" Joseph gasped. "She was never like this before."

Aaron flung around violently. "Don't stand there gibbering! Summon the doctor! Get hot water, brandy, blankets!" He bent over Theo, shaking her gently, chafing her cold arms, calling to her.

When the excited servants ran in, he dashed brandy in her face, and forced some drops between her rigid lips. He piled blankets on her. "Bring all the warming-pans in the house, fill them quickly with hot coals. We must get her warm."

Little by little Theo relaxed, the bluish hue fading to pink.

When Joseph returned running, with Doctor Debow, she was breathing quietly, while Aaron paced up and down the floor beside her bed and his forehead glistened with sweat.

The doctor was puffing, his flowing hair disordered, his fur collar awry, yet, despite the alarm and uncertainty in his eyes, he produced his bland smile, made Aaron a sweeping bow. "Mr. Vice-President, it is indeed an honor——"

"My daughter is very ill, sir. She has had a convulsion. She has come out of it this time, but I fear very much for the consequences if she should have another. What is the cause and what is the remedy?"

The doctor drew a deep breath, arranged his spectacles, and bent upon Theo a portentously grave look. He touched her pulse with his fat fingers, tapped her chest.

"Mirabilium est natura," he remarked at length. "One must expect that under certain unforeseen circumstances, when dealing with situations of a pertinent nature, there may perchance occur an unexpected discharge of either gaseous or bilious humors into the circulatory system, a certain effluvia——"

"You are a fool, sir." Aaron's words spat out. "A fool and a charlatan. You do not know what to do for Mrs. Alston. You are dismissed."

He spun on his heel and, to Joseph: "Is this fat prating ass the best physician your city has to offer?"

Joseph, pallid and miserably frightened, started to speak. Aaron interrupted him. "Bring them all to me here, at once. I will interview them—all."

Joseph's jaw dropped; he hesitated.

Aaron took two strides, clapped his hands on his son-in-law's shoulders. "My boy, do you not realize that your wife is in grave danger? I have heard of these convulsions which sometimes accompany childbirth. They almost invariably prove——" His voice thickened. He compressed his lips, strode rapidly to the window. With his back to the room he finished the sentence with a coldness and lack of emotion that were more terrifying to Joseph than tears would have been. "You will lose both your wife and your unborn child unless there is a miracle."

The miracle was wrought, and wrought by Aaron.

From the four other physicians in the city he selected the only one who seemed to his keen insight to have sufficient knowledge or intelligence to be of help to Theodosia: Doctor Ramsay.

The doctor was installed in the house and spurred to extraordinary effort by Aaron's unceasing vigilance. Aaron supervised everything that was done for Theo, held the basin for the blood-letting, washed and tended her, slept on a chair in her room, alert for her feeblest cry. All through a blur of gray days and nights when she was sometimes wandering and sometimes in stupor.

Doctor Ramsay thought it to be some failure of the renal function.

"Then she must have water," cried Aaron, "to dilute the poisons. But city water is often impure. I long ago noted that tea-drinkers have fewer maladies. It is a more wholesome fluid."

So he forced Theo to drink frequent draughts of weak tea, and gradually the swelling in her limbs subsided, her head grew clearer, her strength came back a little, and then one afternoon toward dusk labor commenced.

Through a suffocating red mist of new pain she heard noises of muted confusion through the house, servants running, shouted orders, the constant jangle of bells. There were faces, many faces. Dimly she recognized her mother-in-law and Maria peering nervously, murmuring.

They must expect me to die if they have come back from Sullivan's Island, she thought impersonally. Death no longer seemed important.

In a pause between pains she heard a dialogue at the door between Maria and Aaron.

"Colonel Burr, I understand that Theodosia is in danger, but I must request you to leave her room. Your presence here is most unseemly at such a time. My father and Mrs. Alston are extremely distressed; they asked me to tell you."

Theo drew herself up—"No, Father! Don't leave me—please." Her voice was high and thin.

"I have no intention of leaving you, my dear child. Lady Nisbett, I deplore any wound that I may give to your sensibilities, but I shall do what I think best for my daughter."

"It is her husband who should be with her if any man must be," returned Maria angrily.

"When Theodosia asks for her husband, I will call him at once. She has not so far done so." There was a faint edge of satisfaction in his cool speech.

No, she had not called for Joseph; he seemed unreal and far away. He could not give her strength as her father did. Nor could he hold her hand and by the sheer force of his magnetism and desire keep her from slipping over into the bottomless gulf.

So Joseph sat alone in the dining-room downstairs, as far as possible from the clack of disapproving women in the drawing-room, his stock thrown into the corner, his face buried in his hands, except that now and again, when a sharp scream penetrated through the ceiling from the floor above, he reached for the half-empty brandy bottle at his elbow.

When Saint Michael's church bells clanged six times across the fragrant May morning air, Doctor Ramsay decided that Mrs. Alston could stand no more. He fished in his dusty black bag and brought out a pair of iron forceps.

Aaron winced, the corners of his nostrils indented sharply. "Is it necessary?" he whispered.

The doctor nodded. "It is necessary. I assure you that I would not interefere if it were not. I notice that the incidence of childbed fever is greater when instruments are used. I don't know why. But we must risk it." He rolled up his sleeves.

Theo moistened her parched lips. "Father, I can't. Not any more—I can't stand——"

Aaron moved quickly to the head of the bed. He took her wet hand in his. "Courage, Theodosia. What is to be must be. You *shall* stand it." He spoke in a voice of cold parental authority, the voice which had always ordered her life, and to it there was only one response—obedience.

She gave a choked, mewing cry, gripping his hand until the bones cracked, then was quiet. Aaron sat beside her pillow, his head averted, rigid as though molded in lead, until an incredible sound echoed through the room—the fretful wail of the newborn.

Theo's hand fell open, releasing his; she sighed, and, turning a little, fell at once into profound sleep.

The doctor looked up, his sweating face triumphant. "All's well, Colonel Burr. 'Tis a fine, bouncing boy. Be so good as to call one of the women to tend him."

Aaron arose and walked lithely to the nested sheets where the doctor had laid the baby.

Minute and dusky red, it stilled its restless cry as he looked down. Its slate-gray eyes stared back at him unwinking. Aaron bent closer. Deep in his heart there moved a strange joy. The baby, with the peculiarity of the newborn, showed a greater facial resemblance than it would again for many years. It was like Theodosia. It was like himself. It was pure Burr, with no hint or taint of Alston.

Aaron drew a deep inaudible breath; his eyes softened as they had never done for anyone but Theodosia.

At last I have a son! He softly touched the damp auburn fuzz on the baby's head. I will raise them high above ordinary mortals. I will make them great—through me: Theodosia and her baby.

He turned, and walking to the window gazed unseeing over the waking city's roof tops. The ways and means were not apparent yet, but one cannot hurry, though one may control destiny. Nothing was impossible to a disciplined, indomitable will. Nothing.

Chapter Twelve

THEODOSIA'S strength came back more quickly than anyone had thought possible. The eighteen-year-old body, freed of its burden and attendant poisons, surged again with vitality. Her convalescence was happy. She lay quiet in the big bed, lapped in the peaceful aftermath of childbirth, the actual agony faded to a dim, scarcely remembered haze.

She delighted in her baby. The tugging of his lips at her breast gave her a physical delight keener than any she had ever known. She had indignantly refused the black wet-nurse that Mrs. Alston and Maria engaged. "I wish to suckle him myself," she averred, with a gentle firmness against which they could make no impression, either by frowns or pleadings. So they gave it up. It was but one more of Theodosia's outlandish, immodest ways. They took themselves back to the beach, and left her to delicious quiet and the company of the three beings she loved: Aaron, the baby, and Joseph.

Yes, Joseph. For when he had come to her on the day after the baby's birth and held his little son in his arms, she had seen how sharply hurt and unhappy he was. His face was haggard, his clothes disarranged, his eyes bloodshot.

"Thank God, you're safe," he muttered, and sank to his knees beside her. She pulled the baby close into the crook of her arm, where he nuzzled, settling down with a tiny sigh. The other arm she threw around Joseph's neck. And in that moment she felt close to him, of one mind, caught up together by the miracle of their parenthood.

"Isn't the baby beautiful?" she whispered. "Father says he is the most perfectly formed infant he has ever seen."

Joseph stiffened. "Colonel Burr behaves as though the child were his."

Theo started to smile, but checked it. She realized something of Joseph's resentment: that the whole process of her illness and confinement had frightened and disgusted him, and that nevertheless he had been hurt by his exclusion. He loved her, had during the last hours been wild with fear for her safety, and yet she had not wanted him, had apparently not remembered his existence.

"Father saved my life, Joseph——" she began, watching his scowl.

He made an impatient gesture, but he knew she was right. He could say nothing.

Theo felt new tenderness for him as the days went by; tenderness not unmixed with guilt. For Doctor Ramsay had made it very clear that she could fulfill no more wifely duties for some time.

"I cannot answer for your life, madam, if you should be brought to bed with another baby before the system has regained its full health. It shall be my painful duty to tell Mr. Alston so."

She was shamed at the uprush of relief and joy this gave her. Oh, to be free—free—free! Protected from those painful, revolting moments in the dark when only her pity and sense of duty could sustain her. Free to show her husband the affection she truly felt for him, without the fear of kindling by her touch a passion which she loathed, and could not even remotely share.

So Theo was happy, doubly happy because this time there loomed no immediate separation from her father. He had booked passage for the middle of June, and she and the baby were to go with him. The annual epidemic of fever was getting under way in Charleston, and it was manifestly dangerous to stay there a day longer than was necessary. As for Sullivan's Island, which Joseph presented as alternative, there was fever there too. Charlotte even now was suffering from ague and chills.

"The whole of your Carolina low country is unhealthy in summer," said Aaron, and Joseph could not deny it.

"I suppose you and the baby must go, then," he agreed grudgingly, "since your father has made the arrangements, but I shall not be able to join you this year. It will be a long separation."

"I shall miss you," she said softly, squeezing his hand. "But I am so proud of your political interests, Joseph. It is fitting that one of the wealthiest and most consequential men in the State should have a voice in that State's government."

"Quite so," agreed Joseph. He had recently decided to run for the state legislature, and had embarked on his campaign with the seriousness which characterized all his actions. The final impetus had come during the weeks of Theodosia's lying-in. With the passing of the anxiety and tension, Aaron had had time for social matters in Charleston. There had been many dinners and banquets, much speechmaking. The town had exerted itself to honor the Vice-President. Joseph basked in reflected glory.

He did not think in so many words, "I too can be a statesman. She shall see that to be wife to Joseph Alston is as important as to be daughter to Aaron Burr." Yet some such thought was in his mind and at last conquered his native indolence. He was temperamentally unsuited to politics—domineering, tactless, and unperceptive. Moreover, now and for some years to come public speaking was torture for him. Self-consciousness swamped him, his tongue thickened into a ludicrous stutter, he tugged at his side whiskers and shuffled his feet until the audiences squirmed in unconscious imitation. Nevertheless, in this summer of 1802, when he was not yet twenty-three, he decided that neither furthering his father-in-law's career nor leading the life of a typical rice planter gave sufficient scope to a man of his abilities, and the seeds of ambition which Aaron had planted at Richmond Hill at last germinated.

On June sixteenth, the brig *Enterprise*, being full-laden and finding gentle southerly breezes, set sail from Adger's Wharf.

At the moment of parting from Joseph, Theo was filled with unexpected emotion. It would be many months before she saw him again. Still weak and shaky, she sat on the forward hatch with the baby in her arms and her eyes misted as she looked up at her husband.

"I'll miss you very much," she whispered. "Write me often, won't you?"

"Certainly."

"You speak so coldly. You're not vexed with me, are you?"

Joseph did not reply. Around them rose the many sounds of the waterfront—the shouts of sailors, the creaking of windlasses. Next to the *Enterprise* a ship from the West Indies was discharging its cargo of bananas and coconuts, and the latter, escaping from their wicker baskets, rolled and bounced merrily along the wharf, while the sweating black porters pursued them, cursing and laughing. Farther along the wharf stacked bales of sea-island cotton crowded a hundred

141

rice tierces which awaited shipment to England. Beside the rice stood a factor in tall hat and blue frock coat arguing violently with a sea captain. The factor—invaluable middleman—attended to all business details for the planters, receiving, dispatching, and financing the plantation crops.

Joseph's eyes lingered on the familiar scene without seeing it. Even when the factor shook his knobbed cane in the captain's face, and the latter dancing with rage brandished a cutlass, Joseph's attention was not caught. The disputed cargo was not Waccamaw rice, and that was not his factor. Joseph, in fact, was engaged in an uncomfortable attempt at self-analysis. For he *was* vexed with Theo, vexed with her for leaving him, vexed with her determination to name the baby Aaron Burr Alston, when he had confidently expected that it would be Joseph, or perhaps William. Vexed at her indifference to the shocking fact that his son had not yet been baptized. There was no time, she argued, and the ceremony could very well be deferred to the fall, when it could be performed in the parish church on the Waccamaw; nor did this concession soften the fact that she held the rites of the Church very lightly. "Agnostic, free-thinker," whispered the horrified Alstons, and Joseph had not been able to refute them convincingly.

"Joseph, please, don't be angry now," pleaded Theo, seeing that his face remained black and that he showed no disposition to speak. "You know that it is only for our health's sake, mine and the baby's, that I leave you."

Her soft voice touched him as it always did. He turned slowly and looked down at her. Under the brim of her gray satin bonnet her small face smiled beseechingly. She had regained all her beauty, and her magnificent eyes under the curly auburn bangs on her white forehead shone bright and dark as dewberries. Except for the fullness of her bosom and an indefinable maternal bloom, she might have been thirteen and the baby on her lap an oversized china doll.

Joseph's stocky body relaxed; and he sat down beside her on the hatch. She moved the baby so that his head rested partly on his father's lap, and she leaned against Joseph's shoulder.

For a moment they were quiet, oblivious to the barefooted sailors who padded past them on the narrow deck. Aaron had gone aft and stood near the helm talking with Captain Tombs.

"You look pale, Joseph," she said at last anxiously. "You will be careful of your health, won't you? If you must go

142

into town, do not do so before or after the middle of the day. I have somewhere heard that persons are less apt to catch infectious disorders at that time than any other, because sunshine acts to dissipate the noxious vapors. And pray smoke all the time you remain in the city; it creates an atmosphere and prevents impure air from reaching you."

"I will be prudent," said Joseph, smiling.

"I can scarcely yet realize that we are to be so long separated. The month of October appears to me a century off," she added sadly.

This sadness continued to oppress her during the hurried farewells while the captain bellowed orders, sailors swarmed up the masts unfurling the courses, hawsers creaked straining to be loose; and Theodosia, leaning against the taffrail, waved to Joseph's diminishing figure as the brig slipped away from the wharf, until he merged into the blur of pink and yellow houses behind.

On the seven-day journey up the coast Theo thought about Joseph a great deal oftener than she had ever done before. It was easier to see him in a romantic light when at a distance from him, yet it was more than that. At this period her love for the baby extended itself to the father. It was, after all, the same sort of love, deepened by a year and a half of companionship, and sharpened when she reached Richmond Hill by Aaron's absence. For after he had established her in New York, his affairs took him to Washington and Philadelphia. She was much alone, her activities restricted by the demands of her son's hungry little mouth.

So she wrote to Joseph, tender, affectionate letters, partly the product of her own feelings and partly from a desire to reassure him and make him content. "You do not know how constantly my whole mind is employed in thinking of you. Do you, my husband, think as frequently of your Theo and wish for her? Do you really feel a vacuum in your pleasures?" And later she wrote: "How does your election advance? I am anxious to know something of it. But not from patriotism, however. It little concerns me which party succeeds. Where you are there is my country and in you are centered all my wishes."

Joseph, when he received this, was gladdened, and yet in another letter she had not been able to refrain from enthusiastic praise of her own home place. "Never did I behold this island so beautiful. With the beauty of the country it is impossible not to be delighted whether that delight is expressed or not, and every woman cannot fail to prefer the style of society."

Will she never learn to appreciate the Carolinas too? thought Joseph, and his heart was sore.

On Monday, July fifth, the whole country burst forth into riotous celebration of Independence Day, because the Sunday had naturally precluded festivity. Richmond Hill and all the other estates were thrown wide open, guests streaming through the house drinking joyfully of brandy punch in the dining-room or Madeira in the library. Outside on the lawns there was a din of gunpowder explosions, and later fireworks. Parades marched by on the Greenwich Road, and the air continually jigged with the strains of "Yankee Doodle."

In the midst of the hubbub, Theo heard her baby's plaintive wail and, excusing herself, she disappeared upstairs to perform her pleasurable duty.

She looked up astonished as Aaron, after a hasty knock, walked in.

"News from Paris, Madame," he said, holding out a letter. "News about one of whom we talked only this morning."

"Natalie?" she asked anxiously. "There's nothing wrong, is there?"

"On the contrary. Natalie, it seems, is married, and to whom, think you?"

Theo digested the first part of his sentence in silence for a moment. Amazing somehow to think of Natalie married, amazing and dismaying. She would then perhaps never again see the kind little elder sister. She had missed her, appreciated her far more after she had sailed, and often longed for her return. There were so few people to whom she was deeply attached.

"I suppose she has married some French nobleman," she answered at last. "It is what her mother always wished."

"Quite so, her mother always wished it, and is apparently angry that Natalie has not obeyed. Natalie has married young Thomas Sumter of South Carolina."

"A Carolinian!" cried Theo, astounded. "But she's in France."

Aaron laughed. "So is Mr. Sumter. He is secretary to the American Legation. They met on the trip over. Judging from this ecstatic letter, they are very much in love.—Look." He handed the paper to her.

A paragraph caught her eye. "Dear Papa Burr: I never dreamed that there could be such happiness; all day long I sing and laugh. He is so handsome, so kind, and yet so much the master—my Tom. You will not think me foolish to tell you that I love him more than anything in life, or life itself."

Theo folded the page quickly. How could the quiet, self-contained little Natalie write with such abandon! She angrily denied to herself a stab of envy, and moved by an unreasoned impulse she hugged her baby so close that he stopped feeding and emitted a reproachful squeak.

She kissed him apologetically and said, "How strange that we should both marry Carolinians! She will live there some day, I suppose."

"Yes, at Statesburgh. She will return home next year, she writes, and how delightful for you all will be the reunion."

Theo sighed. "Yes, but Statesburgh is two days' journey from the Waccamaw. I wish she had married an Alston; it would be heavenly to have her on the next plantation. There would be someone to talk to."

Aaron gave his daughter a keen look. "I know that you do not find your Southern life congenial, but you should rule circumstances, not allow them to master you. A little more spirit, my dear, a little more initiative, and you will be able to create about you whatever atmosphere you desire."

She shifted the baby to her other arm, and nodded slowly. "I know, Papa. And when I go back again in October I mean to try very hard."

She did not, however, return in October because in the late summer her strength declined alarmingly, and Aaron sent her to Ballston Springs to take the waters.

On September the eighth Aaron wrote to Joseph

> Doctors Bard, Hosack, and Brown join me in opinion that she ought immediately to wean her child. This she peremptorily refused, and the bare proposition occasioned so many tears and so much distress that I abandoned it. Within the last three days, however, she has such a loss of appetite and prostration of strength, that she is satisfied of the necessity of the measure for the sake of the child, if not for herself; and I have this day sent off a man to the country to find a suitable nurse.

Aaron found a nurse, a stalwart French peasant girl of twenty-three. He did not find her in the country, but huddled, miserably homesick, in a frowzy little boarding-house by the waterfront. Sophie du Pont de Nemours, who interested herself in all her immigrating countrymen, had told Aaron about her, and he engaged her the minute he saw her. Her apple-cheeked healthiness, her shrewdness and air of quiet capability were her references, and Theodosia, who had been prepared to dislike any woman who usurped her own place with the baby, lost all resentment at the first sight of Eleanore in her starched white headdress. Its streamers whisked through the air as the red work-scarred hands reached out to the baby with brisk, reassuring tenderness. "O, c'est un petit amour, Madame," she crooned, dandling the baby. "We will make heem gros et fort, nous deux." Nous deux! We two! From that moment it was always that for Eleanore, she and her mistress. Her loyalty and affection never wavered during the ten years of life which remained to them both.

On November the twelfth, Theodosia sailed back to the Carolinas, and again on the *Enterprise*. Besides Eleanore and the flourishing baby, she had with her a French chef whose reputed culinary prowess would surely inaugurate a new era on the Waccamaw.

This time, thought Theo, with renewed optimism, everything will be different. The Oaks had been refurbished, and would be infinitely more comfortable with the addition of the two French servants. She would be insulated from the slaves and from Venus. Surely Joseph would no longer refuse to send the girl away. He would understand how Theo felt, because their letters had brought them close. They would begin together a new and sweeter relationship.

She sat on deck, well bundled up against the November wind, and thought happily how well she would now manage her life. No more morbid fancies or childish fear of the moss-hung landscape. No more lying on couches, or neglecting plantation duties. She would be the paragon of wives—and mothers. The darling baby—the thought of him melted her heart with love. He should be the most brilliant and famous man in the world. As a first step, Joseph must build a library at the Oaks. Even now in the hold were stacked a dozen books which Aaron had bought as a nucleus. Already at six months the baby was precocious, and though she did not quite share her father's opinion that the child should recite his letters at a year, yet it would not be long before she could begin teaching him. She smiled to herself, trying to picture him at two—at five.

The brig plowed steadily southward, rocking easily over the smooth Atlantic combers. A single yellow star sparkled in the eastern sky, hung trembling against the dark. How pretty it is, she thought idly, and then suddenly, as though

146

it had been a bolt of lightning from out that gentle sky, her mind twisted with sharp pain.

Why? She asked it half aloud, and, bewildered, stared around the empty decks. How could one feel poignant sorrow and not know its source! The recognition lagged behind the fact, but it came gradually. In the fo'castle some sailor was playing on his flute. She had been hearing the music for some time without noticing it. The sailor had just now changed his tune, and it was this new soft strain that hurt her. Yet why? She still did not recognize it. It was something she had heard long ago, but where——

And then the words slipped quietly within the melody, and she heard again the rustling leaves in an enchanted garden, felt intolerable sweetness and yearning.

Water, parted from the sea, may increase the river's tide——

That song—but she had not heard it since, nor thought of the captain in many months. Why, then, should there be pain?

Heart of mine, away from thee, sever'd from its only rest,
Tosses as a troubled sea, bound within my aching breast.
Thou alone canst give release, sprayed my burning eyes with brine.
Swelling e'er with love's increase, let my heart find rest in thine.

She flung off the rug which wrapped her.

"Eleanore!" she called sharply.

The French nursemaid came running, her broad peasant face anxious. "Oui, Madame?"

"I'm cold. I wish to go to my cabin. And tell that sailor who is playing the flute to stop it. He makes a hideous noise, it vexes me."

147

Chapter Thirteen

JOSEPH stood on the wharf at Georgetown, awaiting the brig, and he was surrounded by Alstons. Theo counted them ruefully while the vessel slid up to the dock: Colonel William, John Ashe and Sally, William Algernon, Lady Nisbett, Charlotte, a collection of milling children, and black servants.

Her heart sank. She had pictured their reunion otherwise, this reunion that was to start for them a new and closer married life.

And Joseph had altered; for a moment she had scarcely recognized him. He had always been swarthy, but now in his new indigo-blue suit his skin had a greenish tinge. He had grown fatter. And why, she thought impatiently, had he had his hair cut so short as to stand up like a fan from its own wiry coarseness?

They greeted each other with constraint, exchanged a brief kiss, before all the relatives crowded around to exclaim over the baby. Theo was once more swamped in Alstons. Fifteen minutes after she had landed, Colonel Alston was talking rice again. "We have had a most unusual fall freshet, my dear. We thought for a few hours that the fields at Rose Hill would be quite ruined, but fortunately it subsided in time. How, by the way, is the price holding in New York?"

It was the only question they asked her about her voyage. Their lives, she thought, were bounded by the Waccamaw Neck, even though their bodies could and did move around elsewhere, occasionally.

Theo and Joseph went home to the Oaks by barge, poling and rowing up the river even as she had descended it over six months before. Only then, she had not yet had the baby. She looked at him, rosy and sleeping in Eleanore's arms, his deep auburn curls stirred enchantingly under his little cap by

148

the breeze off the water. He shouldn't be caught by the deadly monotony of this country; he should grow up, in spite of them, alert and broad-visioned, worthy of his Burr name. If only—if only——A confused terror stole over her. A baby's life was tenuous, so easily assailed by the creeping evils that lived in these swamps. On the ship she had felt brave, confident that nothing could touch them. A little effort of the will, a few precautions, and this place would be as healthy as anywhere. After all, there were diseases and fevers in the North too.

But as the cumbersome barge veered slowly from the Waccamaw River into the Oaks Plantation creek, she felt the old foreboding and melancholy which she had thought conquered. Here every manifestation of nature was dark, weird, and fantastically shaped. The inky water, stained by the gnarled black cypresses, gave forth no reflections. The moss hung down above them like gray tresses of witches' hair. When one of these clumps brushed her cheek, she bit her lips so as not to cry out. The barge progressed ever more sluggishly, butting its prow into the soft mud, first on one bank and then the other. The six blacks who propelled it burst into a minor chant—"Yowdah . . . Rowdah . . . De weary, weary load." Their mournful wail mingled with the sucking of the water on their oars. The fetid odor of the swamp and drained rice fields stole around them.

Eleanore, who had been watching the blacks with startled eyes as they sang, shuddered suddenly. "Je n'aime pas ce pays, Madame. C'est triste."

Joseph turned from contemplation of his rice fields. "What does she say?" he snapped. "Tell the woman to talk English."

Theo smiled faintly. "She says it's sad here. I'm afraid she doesn't like it, and no more does Louis." She indicated the gloomy chef, who crouched morosely at the far end of the barge, his chin on his hands, his nose wrinkled in a disgusted sniff which never left him during his stay on the Waccamaw.

Joseph shrugged. The management of the servants was Theo's business, and their emotions interested him not at all. He had been, moreover, exceedingly upset by an occurrence of the morning. His anger had overshadowed the reunion with Theo.

Once they gained the house and the baby had been settled into his cradle, Joseph ordered himself a glass of rum punch and requested Theo's presence in the drawing-room

"Whatever is the matter, Joseph?" she asked, sitting down.

149

"You have seemed preoccupied and out of sorts ever since my arrival. Is there anything wrong?"

He nodded curtly, leaned his elbow on the mantelpiece and drummed with his fingers, scowling fiercely at the top of the gilt clock.

She sighed. "It isn't the elections, surely. You got your seat all right, did you not?"

Again he nodded.

"Well, then, what is it?" She began to be alarmed. She knew him too well to think that he was angry with her; at those times his behavior was quite different. Could it be some financial disaster, had a rice cargo been lost, or the factor proved dishonest?

Suddenly Joseph jerked a cigar from his pocket, bit off the end, and spat savagely into the fireplace. "Venus has run away."

Theo stared at him blankly, then, before she could check herself, laughed. Thank Heavens! she thought. Is that what he is making all this fuss about? She hastily composed her face, as she saw his expression.

"I'm so sorry, Joseph. I did not mean to laugh, but you see I expected some terrible occurrence, and this is not so serious, is it?"

"Not serious!" shouted Joseph, beside himself. "Have you no comprehension at all? No Alston slave has ever run away. My father will be scandalized. It's a shameful occurrence. Shameful!" he repeated, glaring at her.

"I'm sorry, Joseph," she said again lamely, wondering if it were her own relief at Venus's absence, for any reason, which made it impossible to understand his violence. Or was it but another of those inexplicable differences in their viewpoints? There had been many of these, and yet they never ceased to astonish her.

Accustomed as she was to her husband's sudden rages, she was appalled at his vindictiveness. A vein throbbed in his forehead and his voice shook. "The ungrateful bitch! I was too lenient with her last spring. She should have had the lash. Now when she's brought back, she shall have more than the lash. She shall have a chain around her yellow ankle, and at the other end a fine mate. I shall breed her to the Ape."

"Oh, Joseph, no! Don't speak like that, you frighten me." Theo stared at him horrified. The "Ape" was a slobbering and dangerous idiot who dwelt in a remote cabin under the care of Maum Reba, his unfortunate mother. Even for

Venus, Theo could not imagine such a fate.

Joseph slumped suddenly onto a chair, scowling at the floor.

"Couldn't you just let her go?" Theo ventured after a minute. "What difference does one slave make? You can afford it."

"Just let her go!" mimicked Joseph furiously; then he added more quietly, "You don't know what you're talking about. She's worth near a thousand dollars, though that's not all. How long, think you, would our plantation system endure if runaway slaves were let go? How long before they would begin to feel themselves equal to the whites? Do you want an insurrection? Would you like the Oaks to be run by niggers?"

She shook her head. "But do you think you can find her?"

"She cannot have gone far. I've sent an advertisement to the *Gazette* and the *Courier*. She'll be hard to hide; she's an uncommonly handsome wench."

Theo looked up quickly at something in his voice, but she saw that he had been unconscious of any unusual intonation, unconscious, too, of her recoil as he repeated slowly: "When she's brought back, she shall have a taste of the cat on her deceitful yellow back, then she shall live with the idiot until such a time as I choose to sell her to the Spaniards in Florida. She shall see the rewards of disobedience and ingratitude."

But the weeks went by and Venus was not found, though Joseph continued to advertise, and his overseer made many fruitless trips through the surrounding country.

The winter dragged. Theo's early energy vanished. In March she had a stiff bout with la Grippe, emerging white and weak, to lie once more on the sofa and long for her release in June. For that she would again go North to her father had come to be an accepted fact. She was much alone that winter while Joseph spent a great deal of time in Columbia pursuing his legislative duties; and the various Alstons spent two months in Charleston. But for this Theo was glad. Try as hard as she could—and she did try hard —she could not seem to establish any enduring basis of common interest or deep sympathy with them. She knew that they disapproved of her. Even her initial kinship with Sally, John Ashe's bride, had lapsed. For Sally was interested in nothing but her husband, and Theo found it difficult to sustain enthusiasm over John Ashe's peculiar preference for eggs roasted rather than boiled, or his distaste for French pomade and Virginia tobacco. Besides, Sally, along with the rest of the family, had decided that Theo was eccentric and gave herself airs. Witness the inordinate amount of time which she spent in reading and writing. Witness, especially, her slack methods of housekeeping and her French servants.

In truth, these latter presented problems which Theo had not anticipated. Eleanore was invaluable, but she would in no way co-operate with the blacks, and Louis, after a few weeks, did no work at all. He discovered that the blacks stood in awe of him and were prepared to obey him implicitly. So he gradually came to spend all his time in an armchair in the kitchen, languidly directing the operations of his underlings, while sampling Joseph's best wine and chewing on Joseph's best cigars. He lightened his boredom by a few affairs with the more personable of the wenches and a short-lived pursuit of Eleanore. But that shrewd peasant would have none of him, so that there was a state of war between the two. Eleanore loathed the Waccamaw; only her affection for Theo and her immense devotion to the baby kept her moderately contented. She, too, longed for June and the trip North.

Their release came sooner than they had expected. In the third week in May the *Enterprise* unexpectedly put in at Georgetown, and even Joseph agreed that this opportunity for sailing North on the familiar vessel should be seized. Especially since the fever season had begun early this year. Already a damp, suffocating heat had settled on the plantation. Green mold appeared upon the walls and upon their clothing. Meat spoiled in one day, and milk soured—the precious milk upon which the baby depended. Theo hung over his cradle and felt his little forehead a dozen times a day. It remained cool. The fever had so far spared them all except Louis. The unhappy chef no longer went to the kitchen house at all, but shivered and sweated in his attic room. He was, of course, to sail with Theo, Eleanore, and the baby.

"And kindly do not engage any more gibbering French monkeys," said Joseph to Theo on the day before sailing. "You must confess that the experiment has been a total failure. I wish you to get rid of Eleanore too. My son should have a mauma, as do all the Alston children."

Oh, no, she thought. No dirty African wench is going to tend my baby, teaching him Gullah or frightening him with conjuh. This place is dismal enough without the added terror of spooks and plat-eye. But she had long ago learned the

152

folly of combating Joseph openly, and she feared blighting their parting with one of his rages.

"You are entirely right," she said gently. "Louis has indeed been a failure. I was foolish to bring him. When, think you, will you arrive in the North? I shall be monstrous glad to see you."

Joseph, this summer, was to join her as soon as the legislature adjourned.

"I'm not sure," he answered, forgetting as she had hoped the subject of servants. "When I leave Columbia, I shall go to Charleston. I'm not satisfied with the factor's accounting. He got exceedingly poor prices on the last rice shipment. We shall be beggared at this rate."

She listened patiently to this familiar theme, fixing on him a look of bright interest, while she mentally tallied the trunks, bundles, and boxes which waited ready packed in the hall for conveyance down the river to the *Enterprise*.

The sturdy brig made her usual quick voyage to New York. So quick that, when Theo disembarked, she found that Aaron had not been able to meet her. He was in Philadelphia and must stop in Washington before returning home. She was greatly disappointed at this delay until she thought of going to Washington and awaiting him there.

Accordingly she, Eleanore, and the baby took a packet to Alexandria and arrived two days later. At the wharf she hired a coachee, and they ferried across the Potomac, then bounced over dusty roads to Aaron's lodgings on Independence Avenue. He was expected from Philadelphia "maybe tomorrow or the day after," the landlady informed them, and in the meantime she had a small apartment to place at Theo's disposal.

So Theo happily established herself in three pleasant rooms on the second floor and prepared to surprise her father. She well knew what delight the unexpected reunion would give him, and arranged the details in a happy bustle of anticipation. She bought an armful of early roses from a flower vendor at the market and scattered them through their rooms. She laid in a stock of Aaron's favorite Cuban cigars and ordered a cask of the Trent wine he preferred to all others.

She regretted that she could not buy herself a new gown for the occasion. All her dresses were sadly out of date, and Aaron dearly loved to see her dressed modishly. He took an eager interest in feminine apparel. During her short stay in New York she had noted that tunics had come in, necks were not so low, and bow trimmings had replaced embroidery. Yet she had not had time to have a gown made, and there were no dressmakers in Washington, nor any shops in which to buy fine goods.

In fact, the Federal City had improved little since her visit there for the inauguration. Her lodging windows overlooked the Capitol, and she thought it quite impressive. The President's unfinished "Palace," too, gave promise of eventual grandeur, but between these two lay a welter of unpaved, barely discernible streets. They gloried in fine names, Pennsylvania, Maryland, Constitution, but led nowhere except into mud flats or stubbly fields. There were a few partially finished residences, a handful of lodgings and Stelle's Hotel, these latter scandalously expensive. And that was all. All except a city plan so ambitious and ridiculously far-flung as to provoke bitter mirth from the foreign ministers who dwelt irritably and uncomfortably in the inadequate quarters provided by this uncouth village.

Theodosia, however, was indifferent to the town's appearance. Inasmuch as it would soon contain her father, it justified its existence.

She felt well and young for the first time in months.

Chapter Fourteen

ON THE morning after her arrival in Washington, Theo awoke at five o'clock. There was freshness in the June air, and sparkle. She jumped from bed, ran to the cradle in the next room, and kissed the sleeping baby.

Eleanore poked up a frowzy head from the near-by bed. "Madame rises herself so early?" she cried, astonished.

"Yes, Eleanore. It's such a glorious day. Come get me dressed. I'm going out for a walk."

The maid, grumbling a little, obeyed. This was a new thing for Madame, getting up with the sun. Down in Carolina she often remained in bed all morning. Still, down there it would be hot already—but hot! Thick odorous heat that choked one like fog. Heat like that of l'enfer itself, no doubt —only damper, and rendered quite unbearable by the high, maddening hum of mosquitoes. Ce maudit pays!

Eleanore had a sharp nostalgic pang for her native Touraine, but it passed. She could no longer conceive of an existence apart from Madame and the baby. For them she would drag around the country on vessels and coaches and flatboats; for them she would endure, when she had to, the discomforts and fevers of the Waccamaw.

"Ça y est, Madame," she said, as she finished tying the ribbons on Theo's kid slippers. Theo thanked her and waved good-bye. Arrayed in a "Conversation" bonnet of yellow chip straw, a willow-green walking-dress, and a small India shawl, she let herself out of the sleeping house and walked rapidly down Maryland Avenue to the river.

As she walked, she hummed, joying in the sense of physical well-being, in the glowing June dawn, in the clear note of a meadowlark which mingled with her own voice. "Cherry Ripe! Cherry Ripe!" she sang, laughing as the bird seemed

155

to imitate the notes. Cherries were ripe now too, and Aaron liked them. She must send Eleanore to see if there were not some for sale in the market.

She crossed a bridge, and the road narrowed as she approached the river. Soon she glimpsed blue water between the trunks of hickory and oak trees. Not the sprawling, moss-dripping live-oaks of the South, but great sturdy trees that flung their leaves proudly to the sky. As trees should.

She came upon a field of daisies and Queen Anne's lace. Half-amused at her childishness she plucked a handful of these flowers and wove their stems together into a wreath. The white petals were studded with dew. She rubbed some of it upon her cheeks. Early morning dew is supposed to make one beautiful, she thought. I trust it improves my color or Father will scold.

She raised her head quickly as she heard galloping hoofs thump toward her down the road, and saw an enormous bay with a tall rider in a white shirt. Some other early riser, she thought indifferently, averting her head until he should pass and leave her again to the quiet beauty of the morning.

But he did not pass. The horse gave a quivering, resentful snort as he was pulled up short beside her.

Astonished, she turned. As she recognized the rider, she gasped, her fingers fell open, and the wreath dropped to pieces on the grass.

The man flung himself off the horse and stood staring down at her. His mouth smiled a little, but his gravely questioning eyes transcended convention with their same message of intimate understanding as when they had met in Vauxhall Gardens. The three years that had passed collapsed like the twig houses that children build. Theo felt again the trembling joy and the fear of that September night in New York.

Have I always known that this would happen? she thought. Was it for this that I awoke so gay, so happy today? And at once an inner voice chimed in: I will not make a fool of myself again. I was a silly child then.

She recovered herself, struggling frantically for composure. "So we meet once more, Captain Lewis. I had no idea that you were stationed in Washington." She spoke in precisely the cool voice she would have used to greet one of her father's less important political satellites.

Lewis bowed slightly, the light behind his eyes vanishing. He replied in a tone equally impersonal, though it was sharpened with the faintest edge of amusement. "Indeed,

Mrs. Alston, this is an unexpected pleasure. I am not stationed here. I am Mr. Jefferson's private secretary. I lead a life of pampered ease and uselessness. Not, however, for long, I believe."

"Oh, indeed," she murmured inanely, annoyed to find that his coolness had destroyed hers. No longer an insignificant frontier officer then, but secretary to the President. She could think of nothing to say. She stood there tongue-tied as a country girl, and her knees felt weak. How stupid I am! she thought angrily.

There was nothing about him so to discompose her. He was not handsome in the least: his features were too rough and gaunt for that. And he was immoderately tall. She liked neither tall nor fair-haired men, and he was both. His hair was sun-bleached to a hueless, ashy tint that nearly matched his chill gray eyes. And his dress was most careless. No gentleman should be so careless. No coat, no vest: nothing but buckskin trousers like a backwoodsman, and a cambric shirt thrown open to disclose a heavily muscled brown neck that shocked her with its naked maleness.

The stallion nickered impatiently. She grasped with relief this subject of talk. "A fine animal, Captain Lewis. Do you ride much here?"

"Every morning. This is Mr. Jefferson's Wildair. In addition to my more sedentary duties I have to exercise the stallion. And you—do you often walk abroad so early?"

"No, in the South I never do. But this morning was different. I longed to be out to see the sun rise. I wanted to see the river. I love rivers——" She broke off. What nonsense!

Lewis smiled suddenly. "So do I. Let us walk and see the river, then."

In the midst of trying to say that it was getting late, that she must return, that no doubt she would have the pleasure of meeting him again sometime at the President's mansion, Theo found herself strolling down the road at his side, while Wildair stamped resentfully at their heels.

When they reached the riverbank, Lewis tethered the stallion, and turning quickly peered into the brush. She heard a tiny rustle.

"What is it?" she asked.

"Fox. A little red vixen. Look!" She followed his pointing finger, but her untrained eyes could see nothing except a tangle of underbrush.

" 'Tis a pity you have no gun," she remarked politely.

157

Lewis frowned. "Why so? I do not shoot animals, unless I need them for food. I don't think killing a sport."

Her surprise at this unfamiliar viewpoint held her quiet a moment, then she said, "But you must have killed many men. You're a soldier."

"That's different. Men can take care of themselves. And a good part of mankind," he added calmly, "should be shot."

"La, mercy on us! How fierce you sound!" cried Theo. "I trust you do not include me in that number." She fluttered her eyelashes. Perhaps, after all, a tone of airy flirtatiousness was the easiest to maintain.

He gave her a long, cool look. "Don't coquet with me, Mrs. Alston. It does not become you."

She reddened, her eyes flashed. "You're insolent, Captain Lewis."

He laughed grimly. "Then I apologize. But there is that between us that forbids coquetting or gallantry."

Her heart gave a frightened thump. She stiffened, twisting her fingers together. "You talk folly. There is nothing between us. I have never seen you but once in my life, nor—nor thought of you since——" She faltered, remembering the strange stab of blind pain dealt her by the sailor's flute on the *Enterprise*.

He shrugged. "I believe you. For you would never admit a thought which was not approved by your father, would you?"

He spoke with a quiet matter-of-factness which robbed his words of offense. But they hurt her sharply.

"You seem to forget that I have a husband and son as well as a father," she answered coldly. "Or perhaps you did not know that I had a son?"

He nodded. "I had heard it."

He was silent, staring out over the bright Potomac in front of them. He was disagreeably surprised at the emotion which the sight of her had again aroused. Women as romantic creatures had no place in his life. He had nothing but contemptuous amusement for the philandering of his brother officers, and complete boredom with the nebulous state called "love."

And yet this girl—for she was still a girl—affected him profoundly. She plucked at some chord in him that was deeper and richer than desire, though it contained desire. When he had suddenly come upon her again, he felt, as he had in those brief September hours, that they belonged to each other.

He had not thought about her often in the years since their single meeting. He had had no time, nor was he a man to sentimentalize over a girl who had dismissed him. Still, he had heard her mentioned now and then over the teacups and wine bowls to which his present situation as Jefferson's secretary often condemned him, and of late the mention of her name no longer brought a pang. He had been indifferent to it.

And yet the sight of her small graceful figure in the daisy field had aroused in him a troubling emotion. It was not her beauty or fragile femininity. The few women who had attracted him during his rigorous career had been tall, resplendent goddesses, forthright and frankly primitive— women of the unsettled country accustomed to hard work, quickly responsive and unshocked by man's need for mating.

Theodosia had none of these qualities, and yet he wanted her. The realization angered him. This was no time to allow himself to be upset by a woman, when at last his confined and uncongenial life in the President's mansion was nearing its end, and when he was about to embark on the dangerous enterprise for the accomplishment of which he would need the full exercise of his mental and physical qualities.

Even now, there was a pressure of work awaiting him. The President would have had breakfast and be getting impatient, yet he lounged her beside her like a gawking schoolboy, unable to leave her.

"Tell me of your life," he said abruptly. "Are you happily married?"

She flushed. "Of course."

He watched the slow color flood her neck. She averted her candid eyes from his gaze, but not before he had seen the flicker of uncertainty in their dark depths.

"I don't think you are," he remarked calmly. "I don't believe you know anything about true mating."

"Your speech is offensive, Captain Lewis, and ridiculous. You forget that I have a child."

He gave a short, hard laugh. "Any fifty-cent doxy can have a child. Do you give yourself to your husband with rapture? Do you belong to him body and heart and mind?— Have you ever felt about him as we felt about each other that evening in New York?"

He snapped his lips closed, turned impatiently from her. What insensate impulse was driving him to these foolhardy probings? She was right, there had been and there could be nothing between them. Why, then, this desire to cut and thrust into the shimmering smooth bubble that imprisoned her. He must leave her alone. But he could not.

"You have not answered me, Theodosia?"

She swallowed, her wide, startled eyes sliding over his face. She got up. "I don't understand you, sir. I must be going back now. The sun is high."

He sprang to her, put a rough hand on her white arm. "Wait!"

She stood still, trembling, staring down at his hand.

Wait for what? They neither of them knew. The myriad sounds of the awakening forest swelled around them, sounds that for Lewis each held meaning, had he heard them, but he was deaf to everything except the thick beat of blood through his temples and the voice of bitter desire for this woman who was neither of his kind nor his ken.

" 'Thou alone canst give release,' " he quoted harshly, scarcely knowing that he spoke. "Do you remember?"

She shut her eyes. "I remember, but let me go—please—please——"

He shook his head. His grip on her arm tightened; he pulled her toward him. She felt that her whole being was dissolving into the rushing of resistless waters. They looked into each other's eyes and saw deep shadows and the call of their longing. Tears scalded her lids as she lifted her mouth to his.

In that moment of physical communion, they escaped from themselves to become another, which was both of them and yet neither in a unity beyond time or place or thought, compact with bliss.

Then he put her from him. God's blood! he thought savagely. That's done it, you fool! Why did you not let her go?

Her head fell against his shoulder. She clung to him in blind submission. "Merne," she whispered, "I'm so happy." She looked up at him with the sweet languorous eyes of new passion. Her face now seemed to him achingly beautiful, lit by the radiance of the woman beloved. He touched the bright smoothness of her loosened hair, but his voice was harsh.

"Happy!" He spat out the word as though it burned his mouth. "Neither of us is marked for happiness, my dear one. We must do without that."

She stirred against him, scarcely understanding. "But we can be happy for a little while; we can see each other; we can be together often. There must be ways——"

He sighed. The furrows deepened in his cheeks. "Theodosia, we are not some John and Sally of the tavern who may make love in corners and none the wiser. Would to God we were!" He paused, and went on with a stony desperation. "Why didn't you listen to me in New York when we met? That was our moment, but it slipped away. We are destined now to march forever on different trails. I am leaving in a fortnight to head an expedition to the West. I shall be gone for years. Very like I shall never come back."

"Oh, no!" She twisted from him, frightened. "What do you mean? What expedition to the West?"

"Louisiana Territory, and farther, to the Pacific Ocean. A country so vast that it staggers the imagination. It is ours now, since the little French Consul has sold it to us. Didn't you know?"

She shook her head. "I arrived but yesterday, and news is slow to get to Carolina."

"It is not yet generally known, and there are many to criticize, saying that Jefferson has beggared the Treasury to buy millions of worthless desert acres that will make us the laughing-stock of nations. But I don't think so. I believe that this gigantic new land holds the key to our future."

What has this to do with us? her heart cried. What do I care for the future of the nation? Let it take care of itself, as it must, anyway. It is our future that matters. Our present.

But she could not say it, for he had withdrawn from her, his eyes, grown coldly gray, gazed up the river toward the West of which he spoke.

"Why must you go, Merne?" she whispered. "I don't want you to."

He turned on her passionately. "And if I stayed? What is there for us now? Shall I make you my mistress? Shall we find some hidey-hole in Alexandria or Bladensburg where we may snatch an hour together, trembling at every sound? Or shall I follow you back to your home and call out your husband——I am a fair shot with the pistols, or——"

"Don't—!" She flung her hand over his bitter mouth. "You know I mean nothing wrong. But surely we may just see each other, here by the river. Can't we pretend for a little while that we have just met—as it was three years ago —to be together and talk? I know so little about you. I long to know so much. Merne—please."

He caught her by the shoulders, and, as she shivered under his touch, his hands dropped clenched to his sides. "What a child you are, Theo!" he exclaimed with fierce tenderness. "And what a fool I am! But it shall be as you wish. Meet me here tomorrow." He gave a curt laugh. "Perhaps by tomorrow the stars will have turned back in their courses, the sun have forgotten to rise, and our love will be simple and easily satisfied with talk."

He strode from her, loosed the stallion's bridle, and jumped into the saddle with one swift motion. He did not look back.

Theo, with her hands pressed tight against her breast, stood where he had left her until the mounting sun blazed through the leaves above her head.

Chapter Fifteen

ELEANORE was astounded at Madame's behavior that afternoon. She laughed for no reason, she sang, she grabbed the baby and smothered him with kisses, only to put him down and pace through their rooms with a light, dancing step. She seemed unable to keep still. All the languor and lethargy which Eleanore had thought characteristic vanished like smoke.

Strangest of all, when the evening stage from Philadelphia arrived without Monsieur Burr, instead of the sharp disappointment which the maid expected, Madame said nothing at all. She scarcely seemed to understand.

What had caused this extraordinary change? The climate? thought the puzzled Eleanore. But the climate did not make one spend hours before a mirror brushing one's hair and trying new coiffures, did not make one ask with a sudden anguish: "Am I really pretty, Eleanore? Do I look sallow or old, do you think?"

Old at twenty! The maid laughed as she gave sincere reassurance. Still, it was true that in the Carolinas Madame had looked older than her years. But today her eyes danced, her cheeks were pink, she glowed with a sort of bloom one could almost touch.

Could this transformation come entirely from the expected joy of meeting Monsieur the Vice-President? To be sure, Madame was far more than commonly attached to her father, her devotion was beautiful. But still——

The explanation came at bedtime, as she helped Madame into a loose embroidered nightshift.

Theo twisted suddenly, saying with an embarrassed little laugh, "Eleanore, were you ever in love?"

Aha! So it's that, thought the maid. Her plain face splintered into a grin. "Once, Madame. With the butcher's boy in Chinon."

"Tell me," commanded Theo. "Was it——How did you feel?"

"Feel?" The maid chuckled. "I felt as though my sabots had wings and skimmed of themselves through the streets; that the black bread and soup that I shared with Pierre were changed into delicate food fit for the angels; that all the countryside smiled at me and wished me well—the birds, the river Vienne, even the pigs—all things smiled."

"Then what happened?"

"Nothing, Madame. Pierre married the daughter of a rich farmer. The pigs and the birds ceased smiling. The wings dropped off my sabots. I came to America."

"Oh." Theo was deflated. She was in that state of new love which yearns for a confidant. She felt that she must speak of him. "Eleanore, this morning I met a man—I have not seen him in three years—but when we saw each other it was like—as you say. Only more—so much more. Not like anything I ever imagined." Her voice trembled suddenly. "I think I love him."

The maid looked troubled. "Ah, Madame, it happens like that sometimes. Will you—see him again?"

"See him again!" repeated Theodosia slowly. "How can you ask me that? I tell you I love him. I could not live if I didn't see him again."

Eleanore frowned, smoothing her apron. She thought it entirely justifiable that Madame should have une petite liaison, un cavalier, if she wanted one. It was for sure hard on her to be married to that fat, whiskered planter, and no one could blame a beautiful young woman for looking elsewhere a bit. But there was that in Madame's voice and manner that was disquieting: too much intensity, too much passion.

"Madame must be very discreet, then."

"Oh, discreet—yes. I suppose so," murmured Theo, with a lack of conviction that Eleanor found both irritating and touching. "I can't think beyond tomorrow morning when I'll see him again. Nothing else matters."

A great deal else mattered, thought the maid. La pauvre petite would soon have to come down to earth, very soon. Monsieur son pere would see to that, not to speak of all the clacking tongues and curious eyes of this little town. But she held her peace and tended her mistress in silent sympathy.

For three days longer Aaron delayed his arrival. He was held in Philadelphia by business and the semi-serious pursuit of a lady called Céleste. Theodosia was relieved at his absence. Yet the relief was not sharp. Engulfed in a blur of unreasoning bliss, she had lost touch with reality. She even thought vaguely that, when her father came, she might tell him of this thing which had happened to her. But the past and the future were cut away. She stood on a narrow pinnacle alone—except for Merne.

Each morning at sunrise they met by the river. For those few hours he allowed his clear-headed common sense to be submerged and closed his mind, as she did, to the world outside their oak-shaded riverbank. Her curiously virginal quality awakened all his idealism. It transmuted his desire for her, and they were together as young innocent lovers. For both of them it was new.

He made for her a seat of pine boughs and moss, and once, when the early morning was chill, he built a campfire, and they sat beside it joying in the sweet, resinous smoke. Sometimes they walked a little way through the forest together, and always she was startled at her own blindness and ignorance, for every broken twig, every well-nigh invisible footprint on the loamy soil had a message for him. He knew the habits of the wild creatures, the identity of each plant, even the tiny herbs which she could not discover until he picked them for her. Then sometimes he told her their Indian names and uses. When he had been stationed at Fort Pickering, he had lived much amongst the Chickasaws and come to know their ways. When a bluejay chattered at them he made her smile with a Chickasaw legend about the impudent bird, or he told her the story of the battle between red squirrel and weasel.

She listened eagerly, her eyes on him with worshiping admiration. But it would have been the same had he wished to expound theology or teach her Chinese. For nature itself, beyond a romantic response to scenery, meant little to her.

Bit by bit she drew him on to tell her of his life. And this was hard for him. He had never talked about himself. Yet his taciturnity melted under her fascinated interest.

He had been born in Albemarle County, Virginia, twenty-eight years ago in a log house that clung sturdily to the lower slopes of the Blue Ridges. The wilderness pressed around them, and his earliest memories were of the heart-cracking struggle to maintain their little plantation against its encroachments. His people were gentry, had owned slaves and been fairly prosperous, until his father died when Merne was four. Then the widow Lewis had had a hard time. They grew very poor.

"One winter, I remember, we had naught to eat except the rabbits and 'possums that I snared. We got so lean, Mother and I, that our bones were like to rattle together."

He gave one of his rare laughs at Theo's expression of horror.

"There are worse things than an empty belly, my dear one. You would know nothing of that, though."

He paused, struck by his own words. How wide was the gap between them! She knew nothing of struggle or hardship. She had never felt hunger, thirst, or the clean, wit-sharpening fear of tangible danger. Impossible to imagine her raising a musket against looters, or braving a mountain blizzard as his mother had done many times.

"Yes—and what happened then? Did your circumstances not improve?" she urged.

"For a while they did. When I was ten, Mother married John Marks, a fine man. I liked him well enough, and our situation was much better, and yet there were matters——" He stopped again, frowning, then added: "I escaped often into the forest. Always I found peace there."

Later he told her of his struggles with learning. His indomitable Scottish mother had sent him daily on a ten-mile walk to the cabin of an old preacher, turned hermit. "I had no liking for books, no mind for spelling or fine speech. But I was quick at figuring, and the study of maps came easy. In a few months I learned all the geography and arithmetic the old man could teach me, and I would not go back to him. Mother soon found she could not force me for all her scoldings and switchings. So she let me be."

"I think no one could force you to do anything, Merne," said Theo softly.

He shrugged. "Maybe not. I've always gone my own way."

He told her of his one close friend, Billy Clark, a lad four years older and yet the gentler and more biddable of the two. So that it was Merne who commanded and Billy who followed. They were separated awhile, when Billy went to soldiering, then, as soon as his age permitted, Merne followed his friend into the army. They fought together in the Whiskey Rebellion in '94. After that for a few years Merne acted as regimental paymaster. The life had suited him. It gave him travel, danger, constant opportunity to exercise his alert, resourceful brain.

The safe transporting of the gold was no easy task. With his saddle-bags bulging with gold eagles, he rode regularly from Philadelphia to the forts at Pittsburgh, Wheeling, Cin-

cinnati, and even on to the rough new blockhouse at Detroit. Often he was without escort and had many a brush with marauders both white and Indian. Yet his record was unstained. Not only did he safely deliver the government gold, but, far more remarkable in a soldier, he never made a mistake in accounting or apportioning. His books balanced to the last ha'penny.

Jefferson had known him as a boy, for Monticello was not far from the Lewis homestead. After Merne received his captaincy, Jefferson kept in close touch with him, until two years ago, when he had offered him the post of presidential secretary.

"'Tis not much in my line," said Merne, with a wry smile, "crouching over a desk, smoothing down touchy ministers, handing teacups to the ladies. I cannot say I do it well or find it congenial. But it has pleasured me mightily to be near Jefferson in any capacity. He's a great man, and a good one."

"Father doesn't think so. He thinks him a dolt and overfond of shilly-shallying." She spoke without thinking, repeating words she had heard many times from Aaron.

Merne's face darkened. "Colonel Burr——" he began roughly, but checked himself. "We do not see alike on a great many matters."

Lewis fully shared Jefferson's distrust of the insinuating little man who had all but intrigued himself into the Presidency, and was even now beckoning to the discomfited Federalists with one hand, while he flourished the Republican standard with the other. That Burr was a trouble-maker, Jefferson was convinced. Small puffs of intrigue and disloyalty arose from his vicinity, wherever he might be, like smoke from a smothered campfire. A situation all the more annoying because there was nothing tangible. He discharged his official duties with dignified efficiency, and presided well over the Senate, as even his enemies were forced to admit.

"Why do you speak of my father in that tone?" said Theo sadly. "You have been listening to scandal, the lying tongues of his enemies. You do not, surely, believe the ridiculous allegations of Alexander Hamilton and his cat's-paw, Cheetham. He is well named, 'Cheat 'em.' There is no truth in any of his scurrilous articles."

Lewis was silent. Doubtless no man could be the monster of iniquity which Cheetham in the *American Citizen* represented Aaron as being, but though Lewis and Jefferson agreed with Hamilton on little else, they did agree with him in his estimate of Burr's character. There was no purpose in discussing the subject with Theo. It would but give them both pain.

"Merne," she insisted, "if you understood Father, you could not help but admire him. He is so brilliant, so learned and brave. He is the soul of honor and unselfishness. He is a great man. I know he is. In the years to come everyone will acknowledge it." Her voice faltered. "You do agree with me, don't you?"

He could not lie to her, so he kissed the soft mouth that pleaded with him, murmuring lightly, "He has earned my eternal gratitude by begetting you, my Theo."

She was not satisfied, but his caress effaced everything for the instant. And she was quiet.

They did not speak of Aaron again, nor did they ever speak of the future. Once he tried to tell her about his expedition to the West, but to this one thing she would not listen. "Why must you go, Merne? Who cares what lands lie beyond the Mississippi? The risk seems to me so useless and so foolish. If Jefferson wants this thing done, let him find someone else to go."

"The expedition has been my dream since I was fourteen, Theo. And I think there are perhaps no two men so well suited to this particular undertaking as William Clark and myself."

"What good will it do?" she repeated desperately. "You say yourself no other white man has ever been through those regions; why, then, should any white man ever go there?"

He sighed, yet, because he loved her, he answered patiently. "We shall take title to those lands for our country. They will become part of the United States. We shall stretch from one ocean to the other, a mighty nation, unified, of one tongue. Does this mean nothing to you?"

"All I know is that you wish to go far away and into certain danger. Don't talk of it now—please." She reached her arms out to him, and he drew her gently to him, allowing her to lead him into the tender murmured nonsense which delights lovers.

Still, he knew with grim clarity that this idyll of theirs was a piece of beautiful folly that could not last. Each day when he left her, he turned tirelessly to his plans—the ordering of supplies, the meticulous directions to people in St. Louis, from which town the complete expedition would eventually start up the Missouri. And he spent his evenings in the study of astronomy, latitude and longitude.

Yet each day it was harder to leave her; they put off the parting hour until the forest lay hot and muted under the noon heat. Jefferson did not question his tardiness, Merne enjoyed his complete trust, but his tired old eyes wondered, and Merne threw himself savagely into the accumulated work, cursing his own weakness.

It could not last, and it did not.

On the fourth afternoon Aaron returned, and, with the first glimpse of his spare, energetic figure and his delighted smile, Theodosia was jolted from her dream.

"It's most kind of you to shorten our separation, Miss Prissy," he said, embracing her warmly. "I scarcely dared suggest that you meet me here, knowing your fondness for New York, and knowing, too, your love of comfort. I fear Washington has little of that to offer as yet."

"Indeed, I have wanted for nothing," she said briefly. "We have not been uncomfortable."

He put his arm around her waist. "And how is the really important member of the family?"

She smiled and led him upstairs to view the drowsy baby, who opened his dark eyes at once and, seeing his grandfather, crowed with pleasure.

"I believe he actually remembers you!" cried Theo, laughing.

"I have always said that he was a singularly intelligent infant. Look——" He pulled a small silver rattle from his pocket, jingling the bells. "See what Gramps bought for you in Philadelphia."

The baby lunged forward, his fat fingers closing around the toy. "Gampy," he said joyfully, bestowing on Aaron a seraphic smile.

"He means you, I think," said Theo. "He calls himself Gampy, but he calls your picture Gampy too, the one I always carry with me."

"So," said Aaron, pleased. "Then we share even our nicknames. We are both Gampy." He stroked the child's curls. "Just so fiery red was your hair, Theo, at his age. Little Gampy is much like you, only a great deal handsomer, of course."

His eyebrows shot up in their characteristic quizzical manner when he teased. She smiled at him, thinking how young he looked for all his forty-seven years. Over the fine bones the flesh was firm and ruddy, scarcely marred by a wrinkle. Though his hair had receded a trifle from his forehead, it was still brown and abundant. He never lost or gained a pound, nor had he since his eighteenth year, having long ago found the secret of his interior chemistry. He looked young and buoyant, in some ways younger than Merne, she thought with dismay.

But she couldn't think of Merne now.

Seated with her father at the other end of the supper table, she slipped insensibly into the old familiar pattern, stirring the sauces as he liked them, watching anxiously for his approval of her choice of wine, responding to his affectionate banter with eager amusement. Deep underneath, her love for Merne throbbed poignantly, but she dared not even think of it now.

That she could have been with him this morning, close in his arms, his lips on hers, seemed incredible while Aaron sat there chatting of Joseph, or telling her witty stories of his pursuit of the lady Céleste.

"The lady leads me on," said Aaron, chuckling; "then, as I gallantly approach, she runs for cover, cheeks mantling, eyelids fluttering as though she were fifteen instead of—well, I shall not be so cruel as to hazard a guess. She bids me begone, then summons me back with vague little notes which I cannot fathom. What, ma chère, is your opinion of all this?"

Theo sipped her wine and pretended to consider. "Well, here is my opinion. She meant from the beginning to say that awful word YES, but, not choosing to say it immediately, she told you that you had furnished her with arguments against matrimony, which means, "Please, sir, to persuade me out of them again." But you took it as a plump refusal and walked off. She called you back. What more could she do? I would have seen you in Japan, before I should have done as much."

Aaron laughed. "No doubt you are right, my Minerva. Perhaps also she sensed that her five thousand pounds dowry attracted me more than her full-blown charms. I must find me some more congenial way of raising a little money."

Theo frowned. "Is it so bad? Were you really considering marriage seriously? I thought it all in jest."

" 'Tis no jest, alas, I'm hard-pressed again. Barring a rich wife, which I really cannot stomach, I fear I must sell Richmond Hill."

"Sell Richmond Hill!" she cried, thunderstruck. "Oh, no! Surely things cannot be so bad as that. It's like a part of ourselves. I can't conceive of your not owning it, of our not being able to go there. It's home. No other place on earth could ever be that to me."

"I know, my dear. The thought pains me too. But we must face the crude, unpalatable fact. I am financially embarrassed."

She had never questioned this familiar predicament. All her life periods of prosperity had alternated with periods of retrenchment and anxiety, but they had never before threatened her personally or threatened Richmond Hill.

"But surely you can think of some other way," she said, miserably, then brightened. "There's Joseph. He'll help, I'm sure."

Aaron's mouth quirked. She had no idea of how much Joseph had previously helped, and of late the young planter had become increasingly difficult, had shown a regrettable tendency to hang on to his money. In short, he had tried Joseph already.

Aaron pushed back from the table, wiped his mouth delicately on his cambric handkerchief. "Let us speak of pleasanter subjects. I shall manage some way. I always do. What have you been doing with yourself during these days here while you waited for me?"

Had she really in her purblind folly thought that she might tell him of Merne? Father, I have met Meriwether Lewis again. I love him. What shall I do?

She turned a little, shading her cheek with her lace fan. "I have seen no one, gone nowhere. It has been very quiet."

Aaron shrugged. "Quiet, yes. I suppose so. I'm not in very good odor with our society here. Our worthy President disapproves of me, the cabinet and senatorial ladies follow suit. Only Mrs. Madison remains kind."

"Mrs. Madison is always kind," said Theo. "Papa, why are you unpopular here? I cannot understand it."

"Nor I, my dear, except that, egged on by the excellent Hamilton, who apparently has naught else to keep him busy at present, they do me the honor to consider me a dangerous man. A very Lucifer of villainy and corruption."

"Why should people believe this? No statesman but has had his politics impugned, had derogatory articles printed about him. It is the usual thing, is it not?"

Aaron smiled at her calmly. "There are always some who believe what they see in print, and besides it is more than my public life that has been attacked. I am thought monstrous lewd. It is said that I consort with niggers, because, indeed, I allowed my good Peggy and Alexis to give a party at Richmond Hill for their own people. It is said that I keep a secret collection of indecent pictures with which to debauch

171

the young men who visit me. This, my dear, is our poor picture gallery. It is said that the brothels of New York are filled with the victims I have seduced, not to speak of my unbridled assaults upon virtuous ladies of fashion." He gave a contemptuous snort. "I fear that they vastly flatter my virility."

"But it's so monstrous!" she cried. "Deny all this! Write counter-articles!"

He shook his head. "No. I hate apologies and explanations. They do no good. They but fix the matter more firmly in the public mind. The time may come when I shall have to take action, and then I shall act, you may be sure of that, but in the meantime I shall not dive into the sea of ink." He added, with bitter humor, "At least no one can take exception to the manner in which I fulfill my office. I am a confounded good Vice-President."

She smiled with him, but her heart ached. He was so gallant, so devoid of self-pity. He was fashioned to be a ruler of men, a king, instead of an insignificant understudy to a man who disliked him, and who constantly blocked even the scant authority which his office gave him.

She went to him and kissed him. "It will not always be like this, Father. I think—I know—your star is but beginning to rise. Some day you will be the greatest—the very greatest in the world."

Aaron smiled. "You are a loyal little partisan, my dear. Mayhap you're right." He was silent a moment, went on with sudden force: "You're the one being on whom I can depend, from whom I have no secrets. What should I do without you?" He took her hand in his, kissed the small white fingers briefly. For a moment they were held in silence, she leaning over his high-backed chair, the two faces, that so much resembled each other, close and filled with the same expression of brooding tenderness.

Then Aaron stirred, releasing her hand. "I have not yet told you of the treat in store for you tomorrow afternoon," he said lightly. "I am bidden to dine with Jefferson. You will, of course, accompany me."

Theo sank into the opposite chair, her heart pounding. She would see him there—Merne. The unthinking spurt of joy died down. But how should they meet as strangers? How comport herself through a state dinner without showing her feelings? How conceal those feelings from the all-seeing eyes of Aaron?

"It's—isn't it late in the season for official dinners?" she

172

stammered. "There cannot be many people left in town."

"The Gallatins and the Madisons are still here, at any rate, and the foreign ministers. We are all in a rare pother over Jefferson's remarkable negotiation with Bonaparte. You haven't heard, I suppose?"

He went on before she need answer. "He has swapped some fifteen million of our hard-won dollars for a tract of country so far away and so vast that no one has ever seen it. I have no doubt Bonaparte was delighted to get rid of the burden, and is now sniggering up his sleeve at us, poor gullible fools. The Spaniards, moveover, are enraged. It is the beginning of a mort of trouble. How like Jefferson, who never can make up his mind, to choose for an exception a piece of unbridled bad judgment. And he did it, too, against all advice."

"But does it not add to the prestige of our nation? We shall be larger than the whole of Europe."

"Pish," said Aaron impatiently. "We had too much land already. Far more than can be governed from this ramshackle village here. Even a thousand miles away, on the shores of the Ohio, I hear that they are resentful of our pretensions. Think you that the bears and the wolves and the savages in the territory beyond will be an asset to us? If indeed that unexplored country supports any life at all. For no white man has ever penetrated most of it. No—the purchase was a piece of egregious folly."

Yet one white man was preparing to explore this new territory, thought Theo. For the first time she felt a thrill of pride in Merne's ambition, followed quickly by sick dread. Her father, too, thought the purchase was folly, and this confirmed her own instinctive judgment. The expedition was foredoomed to failure. Merne's lot would be not only foolhardy danger but ridicule. How can I stop him? she thought desperately. Somehow I must make him listen to me. I'll plead and reason, use all the influence of our love. Yet, even as she made incoherent plans, she knew how helpless she was.

Aaron, staring abstractedly at the floor, went on, half to himself, "Before long this unwieldy mass of land will divide into its logical parts. There is no government now or in the future which can cope with such geographical differences. The lands beyond the Alleghenies will break away. Those mountains form a barrier far more formidable than the arbitrary divisions in Europe."

"Do you think so?" said Theo politely. She had only one

173

interest in the land beyond the Alleghenies, and that was not political.

"I think so," said Aaron thoughtfully.

With his daughter he shared the feminine trait of boredom with impersonal concepts. His own idle prophecy had swung ajar a window which opened on an attractive new vista. He instinctively considered it in relation to himself. The disaffection of the West, the resentment of the Spaniards— could they not be used to advantage by an ambitious and farsighted leader? But how? To this there was for the moment no answer. The idea had after all been only a foolish fantasy. And he had no patience with impracticality.

His course for the immediate future lay clear ahead. He would continue to be an excellent Vice-President, and he would run for the governorship of New York State. In the event of his winning—and he felt confident of doing so— he would find this key position a far better political springboard than any he had as yet tried.

He now dusted a few flecks of tobacco from his black silk breeches, and rose with quick litheness. "I'm going to bed, my dear; the highway from Philadelphia is enough to weary Apollo himself. Do you go and retire, too. I wish you fresh and shining for the President's dinner tomorrow." He saluted her gallantly, but turned back as a thought struck him. "By the by, do you remember the overgrown captain with whom you coquetted at Vauxhall Gardens?"

She drew a sharp breath, looked up at him, and then down at her lap.

Aaron regarded her confusion with amusement. "I know it is cruel to taunt the sedate Mrs. Alston with the indiscretions of her salad days. But you will meet him again tomorrow. He is secretary to the President."

She moistened her lips, managing a brittle little laugh. "Oh, is he indeed? I—I will try to behave myself with perfect decorum this time."

Aaron chuckled. "I should hope so." A yawn caught him. "Pleasant dreams, my dear." He went to his room and thought no more of it.

If he had ever permitted himself retrospection, he would have been mildly ashamed of the anger and violence into which he had been betrayed on that September night in New York. The incident had been too trivial to warrant them. But he never looked back, or carried around with him the trailing ends of spent emotion. It was perhaps the secret of his youthfulness.

Chapter Sixteen

🍃 🍃 🍃

IT WAS raining when Theo awoke the next morning. She stared out the window at the drenching summer rain and thought with bitterness that it solved one problem anyway. Merne would not expect to meet her beside the river in this downpour. Yet, even had the morning been as brightly beautiful as the others, how could she have slipped away?

Aaron was already stirring. She heard his light footsteps in the room above. She shut her eyes again and tried to sleep, but she could not. A feeling of desolation enveloped her. For the first time she realized the utter hopelessness of their love, seeing the situation objectively, as Lewis had done from the beginning.

"We are now fated forever to travel on different trails," he had said. It was the simple truth. She knew it, and yet——He was only a mile away from her; they might still see each other, as they would this evening. Somehow they would arrange to have a few more of those ecstatic hours alone together. And that was all she asked, she thought passionately, just to hear his voice for a little longer, to have him kiss her gently, and smile for her his rare slow smile.

Deep within her heart, she knew she lied. That was *not* all she wanted. Her awakened body ached for him. Her lips whispered his name with a longing that frightened her. Turning on the bed, she buried her face in her arms.

All day the rain stabbed down like silver knives, cutting at the roads until it had reduced them to a pulp of yellow mud. It was damp and cold. The baby was cross, and wailed dismally, resisting all Eleanore's and Theo's efforts to amuse him. The monotonous cries resounded everywhere through the jerry-built house; one of the many which had been run up anyhow for temporary occupancy and never properly finished.

Aaron supported the racket with his usual good-humor, finally going out into the pelting rain to scour the town for toys.

By noon Theo was exhausted. "Darling, won't you please stop yelling?" she implored the red-faced infant. "Could there be anything really wrong?" she asked Eleanore anxiously, as they hung over the cradle. She felt a ghastly clutch of fear. This was the critical "second summer," and so many things could be wrong: fevers and fluxes and convulsions.

The maid put a square knowing hand on the child's forehead. "He's all right, Madame. It's the weather, and the little tooth that is coming. C'est tout." Her brisk positiveness was balm.

Theo turned wearily. Her head ached. The day was interminable. Matters were not improved by the receipt of a letter from Joseph. She had no wish just now to think of Joseph, and this letter was unusually affectionate, even passionate, beneath its pompous and weighty verbiage. He missed her, it seemed, immoderately. And he had arranged his affairs so as to join her up North "very soon." He thought that he might catch the next packet.

She sat perfectly still, staring at the thick ink-scrawled paper. If he had caught the next packet, he would arrive in a week or so. She saw him suddenly as though he stood in the low room beside her: his glossy whiskers framing the dark heavy face, his thick-barreled body stuffed into his favorite indigo-blue coat, his truculent eyes, suspicious as those of a maltreated dog. She saw details which she had never consciously noted: the black hairs in his nostrils, the pudginess of his hands with their blunt, insensitive fingers. But he was her husband, and he loved her. She knew that she and the baby were the only things he loved. As always she felt a remote pity for him. Poor Joseph. They said pity was akin to love. Sometimes she had very nearly come to believe it. She would never believe it again. Passionate love between man and woman was not compounded of pity. It was storm and lightning and beauty and desire, not pity, with its implicit condescension and superiority.

"Aha," said Aaron, coming into the room, his greatcoat streaming, his arms full of sodden packages. "A letter from the South, I see."

She noded. "Joseph is coming North to join us."

176

His quick black eyes glanced at her curiously. She did not look the picture of an eager wife about to be joyously reunited with her husband. Nor for that matter did Joseph's advent fill him with any elation. The grumpy young man bored him, and was at present not particularly useful. Still, one must make the best of things.

"Capital!" he exclaimed heartily. "Look, Theo, I found a Swiss music-box for Gampy. Though I see that the young gentleman has at last mercifully ceased to roar. I think, by the by, that you're not feeding him right. All that pap, and porridge, and sugar teats. He needs goat's milk. I bought a goat, just now; the stable boy is tethering it in back. Give the baby goat's milk twice a day."

"Oh, Father!" she exclaimed, half-laughing. "You'll be telling me how to diaper and physic him next."

"No doubt I shall if I think you are not doing it properly. I think you will admit that my ideas are usually sound."

"Indeed they are," she agreed sincerely.

Aaron unwrapped the Swiss music-box. It was an intricate affair of trilling birds and dancing peasants and from underneath issued the pleasing tinkle of folksongs.

"It's delightful!" she cried; "but wasn't it very dear?"

"It was," agreed Aaron cheerfully. "It cost twenty-five dollars, and I haven't a sou left. I bought also a volume of Burke's *Vindication of Natural Society* for you. It's high time you did some more serious reading, lazy baggage. I was scandalized to see a silly romance like *Castle Rackrent* on your table. I'll wager you haven't construed a line of Latin since I saw you last."

She shook her head. "It's so hot down there, and I—I never feel very well, somehow. It seems an effort to open a book. The days slide by—one into the other——"

"Why don't you make your husband take a place up in the mountains?" he interrupted, frowning. "That unhealthy swampland is suicide for you; only the niggers can stand it."

Theo sighed. "We've talked about it, you know. But it never happens. We have three estates already, and, besides, Joseph must be on the Waccamaw, unless he's in Columbia or Charleston."

Aaron snorted. "You are the two most spiritless young persons I ever knew. I believe you never muster up enough energy to do anything but lie on a sofa with a nigger wench waving a peacock's tail over you. I'm ashamed of you."

She smiled at him sadly. "Don't be angry with me, Papa."

He bent over and pinched her cheek. "You're a worthless

hussy, but I forgive you. Mind you sparkle tonight with your old liveliness. I wish you to do me credit before the brilliant assemblage of disgruntled diplomats and unkempt statesmen."

"Not unkempt," she protested, "surely."

Aaron gave a short laugh. "Wait until you see our magnificent President."

At four o'clock that afternoon Theo and Aaron in a hired coach bounced and splashed through puddles down Pennsylvania Avenue to the President's mansion. This house built of reddish-gray freestone was large and of pleasing proportions, but it was still unfinished. It stuck up crude and naked from a sea of mud dotted with piles of lumber and brick. The grounds were unembellished by either tree or shrub, and their desolate rainswept expanse was enclosed by a weathered post-and-rail fence that awaited an appropriation from the reluctant Congress before it could be replaced by a more dignified stone wall. For the same reason the entrance steps were still of rough planking, the east rooms were unplastered, and the slate roof leaked dismally. On a wet day such as this one visitors were assailed in the vestibule by an odor of damp mixed with more unpleasant effluvia of which the hearty smell of boiling cabbage and the stench of a garbage pile beneath the kitchen windows were the least disagreeable.

Theo and Aaron, after waiting some time in the rain, were ushered in by a black butler whose greeting seemed to Theo astonishingly unceremonious. "Good day, Mistah Vice-President. Howdy, ma'am. Nice weather for frogs," he said chattily. "You'm a mite early. Massa Jefferson he still figgerin' in his study. You all wanta go there or you wanta wait?"

"We'll wait, Henry," said Aaron. "Kindly announce us to the President—Mrs. Alston and myself."

"Sho' I will, sir. Sho'." He shuffled away, leaving them to stand by the door.

Aaron laughed at Theo's astounded face. "Just a taste of Jefferson's perfect democracy, my dear. You will see more of it before the evening is out."

She drew her shawl around her and shivered. Her nose wrinkled. "What a malodorous barn! I should think it hardly worth while being President if one must live here."

"Ah," said Aaron softly, placing his hat on a frayed red damask chair for want of any other place. "If I were President, this would not be a malodorous barn. Nor, I assure you,

178

would I make a cult of rudeness and boorishness in an endeavor to impress people with my democracy."

"It is indeed very rude to leave us standing here like this," cried Theo with sudden indignation, as it occurred to her that this cavalier treatment might be an intended slight directed at her father.

Aaron shrugged, taking a delicate pinch of snuff from his snuffbox. "You look charming, my dear," he observed with satisfaction. "Eleanore did wonders to that gown. The green touches become you mightily."

Eleanore's clever fingers had refurbished a last year's ball dress with scraps of green silk from an old negligée. The white tunic was edged with it, and emerald bows chased each other like butterflies down the front. She had wound a strip of the green silk in amongst Theo's hair, which was closely twisted about her head à l'orientale. On her bosom sparkled the diamond necklace. She had not worn it since Venus's desecration, and before donning it tonight she had scrubbed it viciously with soapy water. From this it emerged all the brighter.

And still they waited, and Theodosia's nervousness grew. Where was Merne? She longed and yet dreaded to see him.

Shouts and rumbles and stampings outside announced the arrival of other guests. The door opened and Dolly Madison swept in, laughing. Her spare little husband followed in her wake like a sparrow pursuing a bird of paradise. On her dark hair she wore a yellow satin turban, with ostrich feathers, and a topaz brooch. Her pleasantly buxom figure was encased in white satin trimmed with swansdown and she exuded a strong odor of musk. Her kind blue eyes widened as she discovered the Burrs.

"Why, Colonel!" she cried, rushing forward. "And Theodosia, how do you do, my child! How pretty you look! Whatever are you two doing out here, and with your wraps on?"

Aaron kissed the bejeweled hand that was held out to him. "We haven't been invited to go anywhere else, as yet, ma'am," he said dryly.

"La!" She favored them all with her charming smile, not excepting her husband. "Isn't Jefferson wicked! He has no manners at all, I vow. But 'tis my fault. As official hostess, I should have been here sooner. Jemmy—you know Mrs. Alston?"

Madison bowed stiffly and gave her a tight smile as Theo dropped a curtsy. His wizened face seldom changed expression except when he looked at his wife, when it assumed an expression of tender admiration which illumined it.

"Come, let us all go up to the drawing-room," cried the lady. "The President may find us there."

She shepherded them upstairs, deftly avoiding a puddle on the landing, summoning a maidservant from somewhere to take their wraps, and drew Theo beside her to the sulky little fire that smoked at one end of the huge and meanly furnished room.

"'Tis four years or more since I've seen you, child. Tell me all about yourself. You have a husband, I know, and a baby. I do not need to ask whether he is an intelligent and beautiful child. He could not help it, with such a mother." She rattled on, dimpling and laughing with so much spontaneity and kindliness that the sprightliness, which might have seemed unbecoming to a buxom middle-aged matron, became completely endearing.

"How well your father looks! I protest, he gets younger and handsomer every time I see him. He is a remarkable man."

"I'm glad you, at least, are his friend," said Theo, with a touch of bitterness; "he seems to have many undeserved enemies."

"Oh lawkes—enemies! What statesman has not! Of course I am Colonel Burr's friend. Do I not owe him a great debt of gratitude? He introduced me to my Jemmy, you know." She threw a fond glance toward the Secretary of State, who was deep in what appeared to be gloomy converse with Aaron.

"Here come the Gallatins," she cried as the Secretary of the Treasury and his wife entered the room, unannounced. Dolly greeted them warmly, both hands outstretched, and introduced Theo, who examined the brilliant Swiss curiously, thinking that he was extremely ugly, with his bald head and long beaked nose. Nor was his manner engaging. He murmured, "Enchanted, Madame," in a heavy French voice and, turning his back, sauntered off to join Aaron and Madison in their corner.

Mrs. Gallatin impressed Theo not at all. She had been a typical American girl, and was now a typical American matron, a trifle colorless, a trifle bigoted, an excellent wife and mother.

Peder Pedersen, the Danish Chargé d'Affaires, arrived alone in a magnificent general's uniform, and made up for Gallatin's coldness by kissing Theo's hand with lingering gusto, attaching himself firmly to her side and breathing amorous platitudes down her neck. He fancied himself a great dog with the ladies.

Henry, the errant butler, reappeared with a rush in time to announce the last two invited couples. He might have spared himself the pains, for the names of the French and Spanish Ministers emerged as a kind of gibberish that inspired Theo with an hysterical desire to giggle.

Turreau de Garambonville, Bonaparte's newly accredited representative, was a slim lizard of a man with cruel, glancing eyes, and dripping with lace and gold embroidery. His lady scuttled timidly behind him, her pale mouse's face crumpled into an expression of perpetual terror.

"They say he beats her," whispered Pedersen delightedly in Theo's ear, "and makes his aide play the flute to drown her screams. She was the jailer's daughter, you know, and helped him escape from some prison. He married her. She should be grateful for that and overlook the beatings."

"Of course," said Theo, laughing mechanically, and wishing her admirer would leave her in peace; "a mere trifle like that."

If the French and Danish representatives were resplendent, the Spanish Marquis Casa de Yrujo was dazzling. He never appeared without the panoply suitable to a grandee and to a representative of Charles IV—curled and perfumed wig, gold-headed cane, medals and decorations which were crowded into a glinting jeweled mass upon his changeable rose brocade coat. His Castilian blondness and the aristocratic delicacy of his features gave him a deceptive air of effeminacy, as did the Castilian lisp which he had transferred from his native tongue into his carefully correct English. Except for a curt nod he ignored Turreau. There was no love lost between France and Spain just now.

The Marchioness, his wife, was lovely, and though born Sally McKean of Philadelphia, oddly enough looked more Spanish than her husband, for she had dreamy dark eyes, olive skin, and black hair.

"We are all here, I see," said Dolly, consulting a list which she pulled from her reticule.

"Exthept the President," drawled Casa Yrujo. "He is perhaps to busy with matters of thtate to attend to his guests. I hear that of late he has been *extheptionally* busy." His silky voice made no effort to hide the barb in this speech, and Dolly laughed.

"La, my lord! Let us have no politics or foreign affairs

tonight. This is but a social gathering."

"Ah, indeed?" said the Marquis, his glance roaming over the guests. "We are a remarkably thmall gathering."

"Mr. Jefferson likes it so. He detests large dinners, you know."

"I am thurprised to note that there is no British representative present."

"Ah, but there will be soon," said Dolly quickly, "when the Merrys arrive in September. We are all looking forward to the advent of the new British Minister and his lady; they will liven up our society, give us fresh interest and diversion."

The Marquis permitted himself a disdainful smile. "I hear that Mr. and Mrs. Merry are much given to theremony and etiquette. It is they who will be interested and diverted, if the President treats them to one of his pêle-mêle dinners. Tho refreshing for them to be initiated into the—delights of true republicanism."

Dolly threw Theo a quick, naughty glance of humorous dismay and whispered: "The Marquis is inclined to be critical tonight. You must help me charm him into a kinder mood or we shall have a cat-and-dog fight on our hands. It's really vexing of Jefferson to be so late."

Theo started to reply, but the words wavered and died away. Two tall men walked quickly into the drawing-room together. But her eyes slid over the first one blindly.

Lewis stood motionless, a foot or two behind his chief. He was in his dress uniform as she had first seen him— blue coat with red facings, dead white vest and breeches, white bindings and buttons, the white Captain's epaulette on his right shoulder. His hands were gloved in white, too, contributing to the impression of severe immaculateness. His high black boots, the dangling scabbard, and very tall stiff collar added to his already considerable height.

Her heart dissolved within her, as he gave her one long penetrating glance, a half-smile, and then looked away. Confused, she gazed quickly at the others, half-expecting that they would be staring at Merne with the same transfixed admiration that she felt. He was so commanding, so impressive. He dwarfed all the other men.

But the company was not looking at Lewis, it was greeting Jefferson, who leisurely progressed from one to another bidding them "Good evening." As he approached her, she understood the angry gasp which she heard issue from the Marquis, who stood behind her.

The President, pursuant to his stubborn policy of "no fuss

or feathers, simplicity and democracy before all else," had come to them straight from his study.

His big loose-jointed frame appeared shrunken inside a wrinkled brown coat, that looked as though he had visited the stables in it—as indeed he had. His thin sandy hair was indifferently combed, there were inkstains on his fingers. Far worse than all this was his footgear, and Theo reflected Dolly Madison's look of dismay when she discovered, as did all the guests with varying degrees of horror, that the President, whose corns hurt him, was shuffling about in heelless and stained carpet slippers that made small flapping noises on the bare floor.

Even Dolly, who was accustomed to the President's deliberate indifference to dress, was stricken dumb by this innovation. The reactions of the cabinet members present did not, of course, matter. But the diplomats would be outraged: were outraged already. The French and Spanish Ministers, for once in accord, stared pointedly at the ceiling with glassy eyes. Their gold frills and perfumed laces quivered indignantly.

"I am sorry to have kept you waiting, ladies and gentlemen. It was unavoidable. You must all be hungry. We will go down to dinner at once, informally," said Jefferson.

Dolly sighed. "Another one of these higgledy-piggledy dinners," she murmured to Theo. "If he would only let me or Captain Lewis seat the guests properly. But he likes them mixed up together. I vow he makes a fetish of informality."

"You mean I may sit where—with whom I like?" asked Theo, her color deepening.

Dolly had time to nod before the President returned smiling. "Come, Mrs. Madison," he said, capturing her arm, "we will lead the way."

"If I sit beside you, I shall scold you, be warned of that, sir," answered the lady archly, tapping him with her fan. They progressed down the room.

There was an instant's embarrassed silence, before the Marquis, with a frozen face, bowed to his wife and proffered his arm.

Theo saw Pedersen approaching her, smirking. She turned her back on him, her heart thumping. Oh, why didn't Merne come for her? He must. She willed him to her with a convulsive inner spasm. But Lewis was cornered by Gallatin. She saw his fair head bent courteously toward the Secretary of the Treasury, who was emphasizing a point with gestures. She couldn't keep on ignoring Pedersen. She must do something. She threw discretion overboard, glided across the floor as unobtrusively as possible.

"Perhaps Captain Lewis will be so kind as to escort me down to dinner," she said lightly, turning on Gallatin her most brilliant smile, as excuse for interruption. "Captain Lewis and I used to know each other long ago in New York, Mr. Gallatin. We must renew our acquaintance."

The Swiss bowed. "Of course, Madame." His accented voice was chill. He did not like being interrupted. Those Burrs—he thought—like father like daughter—models of effrontery.

Lewis quietly took her hand and tucked it beneath his arm. "Neatly done, my dearest," he murmured.

She leaned against him, faint and dizzy from the joy of his nearness. "Oh, Merne," she whispered, "it's been such a long dismal day without you. Did you miss me?"

"I did."

The crisp dryness of the two monosyllables delighted her, more convincing than any amount of flowery protestations. She laughed, a low trill of happiness.

They were descending the stairs, Aaron a few steps behind them with Mrs. Gallatin on his arm. He could not hear what they said, but he heard Theo's laugh, and he had missed nothing of her boldness in demanding the Captain's escort. His eyes narrowed. He failed to comment on Mrs. Gallatin's anecdote about the cleverness of her little son, and the good matron was astonished. Whatever else Colonel Burr might be, she had always before thought him the acme of attentive courtesy.

When the confusion of seating had died down, Theo found herself between Lewis and Pedersen near the center of the table. The Marquis and Marchioness de Casa Yrujo sat together in haughty disapproval at the foot. Aaron had seated himself next to the Marquis, whom he thought it worth while to cultivate. From this position he could also watch Theo.

"What a remarkable room," observed Pedersen, endeavoring to get her attention. "Have you ever been here before, Mrs. Alston?"

She turned reluctantly from Merne.

"No, I haven't. But what is there so remarkable about it?" She had in fact not observed the room at all. Her surroundings were of cloudy unimportance. Even Aaron was out of focus. She was quite unaware of his veiled inspection.

"Look around you, fair lady," said the Dane, pushing his flirtatious pug face closer to hers. "Potted flowers, birds, one would think oneself in a conservatory were it not for the ingenious mechanical contraptions. Look—see, the wall is opening!"

Indeed, the wall was opening or rather revolving. Jefferson had introduced an enormous "lazy Susan" between the kitchen and dining-room. At the touch of a spring it revolved, to the accompaniment of creakings and rattlings, and disclosed shelves full of laden platters and dishes, steaming from the stove.

"I believe he has many such inventions," continued Pedersen. "They say there is a species of lift or elevator which runs on pulleys, and is strong enough to carry a man up two or three flights. Though this I haven't seen."

"How very interesting," observed Theo tepidly. Why didn't the man eat his dinner? What did she care for the President's contrivances, or his birds, or his horticulture, when the precious moments were passing; Merne sat so close to her, and yet they could not get a word with each other!

The dinner was good and the wines excellent. Mr. Jefferson's passion for plainness stopped short at the culinary department. Rice soup was followed by platters of beef, ham, veal, mutton cutlets, turkey, fried eggs, and a new Italian dish called "macaroni" pleasantly flavored with onions and cheese. This delicacy at last silenced Pedersen, who subsided with his mouth full. Theo pushed back her untouched plate and turned again to Merne. He had been waiting for her, watching the pure oval of her averted cheek, the distracting little tendrils of auburn that escaped from her green bandeau and nestled against the whiteness of her neck. He, too, made no pretense of eating.

"Theo," he whispered, "this is a hideous farce. I must see you alone—once more."

Her face went white. She raised frightened eyes. "Once more," she whispered. "What do you mean? I'll slip out somehow. It's hard now Father is here, but I'll manage. We can meet by the river again——"

"No, my darling." His lips barely moved. "We cannot. We were seen. By one of Jefferson's servants. I managed to shut his mouth, I think. But there might be others. I cannot let you run the risk. Besides, I——"

He and everyone else at the table except Theo suddenly stiffened and craned forward. Jefferson was speaking in a raised voice, designed to include them all. From the depths of a devastating misery Theo heard phrases, without understanding or caring about them.

"In this intimate gathering it does no harm to state openly what most of you know already. It will be public knowledge on Independence Day . . ."—"Fortunate acquisition of territory without firing a shot . . ."—"Our excellent sister nation, France . . ."—"Spain, our illustrious neighbor to the south . . ."

Aaron, sure of his listener, murmured to Casa Yrujo, "He is like a cat with a dish of cream, is he not, my lord?"

The Spaniard's lips curled. "But this tho-called purchase is not permitted by your Constitution. He ignores that. It is illegal from beginning to end. Thpain will not allow this. There will be war."

"You think so?" said Aaron softly, hoping to draw more interesting indiscretions. But the Marquis veiled his eyes and tapped the head of his cane in angry silence.

Jefferson's voice continued: "It has long been my ambition to send an expedition through the westward lands to the other sea. It has been tried three times, only to end in failure. Now that the title to these lands has most fortunately devolved on us, I feel such an expedition to be of unparalleled importance. The new expedition had been organized, and this time I think it will not fail, for it will be led by two intrepid young men who perfectly understand the nature of their undertaking: my aide and secretary, Captain Lewis, and his friend and comrade at arms, Captain William Clark, who will join him later."

There was a polite buzz of interest. Everyone looked at Lewis, except Theodosia. She sat rigid, staring at the tablecloth.

"Ladies and gentlemen," said Jefferson, rising, "I give you a toast to the success of the expedition, and to its leader."

He sent the reddening Merne a smile of sincere affection, and went on: "He is of courage undaunted, possessing a firmness and perseverance of purpose which nothing but impossibilities can divert from its direction; careful as a father to those committed to his charge, and yet steady in the maintenance of order and discipline; intimate with the Indian character, customs, and principles; habituated to the hunting life; honest, disinterested, liberal; of sound understanding, and of a fidelity to truth so scrupulous that whatever he shall report will be as certain as if seen by ourselves.

"Ladies and gentlemen, I give you Captain Meriwether Lewis!"

The company murmured congratulations and drank, while Aaron thought, All this for a country bumpkin of a backwoodsman who is about to be swallowed up forever in the wilderness. Good riddance to him! He was annoyed by the flash of what looked like pure hero-worship that he had seen on Theodosia's face. And he found to his surprise that he had not overestimated his previous dislike of Lewis. It had surged back with full force.

The talk now became general at the President's end of the table. Madison was asking Lewis questions about the expedition, and Dolly kept up a running obbligato of comment and admiration. "What a wonderful adventure it will be, Captain Lewis! How brave you are to attempt it! It quite makes me shudder to think of the hardships you will have to endure. Still, men thrive on hardships, do they not?" Her blue eyes sparkled, and she laughed her infectious laugh.

Jefferson leaned back in his chair, beaming at his protégé, and relaxed as he always was by Dolly's cheerful chatter.

The Secretary of the Treasury addressed himself to the dessert. Jefferson's cherished project did not interest him, and inasmuch as the appropriation for it was but twenty-five hundred dollars, he felt no wish or need to oppose it.

Theodosia smiled blindly, and tried to force an appearance of attention, but the chatter, the private currents of thought swirled by her. She felt herself alone and desolate. Merne did not belong to her. The sweet isolation of their little time together had had nothing to do with his real life; while for her, it had come perilously near to being life itself.

A feeling of anguish possessed her. She felt herself detached from this roomful of people. For a moment she saw them all objectively, each with his dominant thought written large on his face. They were like characters in a morality play: Jefferson—Complacency. Dolly Madison—The Social Graces. The Casa Yrujos—Affronted Indignation. Mrs. Turreau, who had not uttered a word since she sat down, was Anxiety, as her husband was Cruelty. Slowly her gaze traveled over them: Pedersen—Gluttony. Gallatin—Shrewdness. Even Merne was outside, and far away from her. His face expressed nothing except the "firmness and perseverance" of which Jefferson had spoken.

Only Aaron's face she could not read. She knew him so well, and yet she could not tell what thoughts dwelt beneath that blandly smiling mask.

Her throat closed, and she looked at Merne. "Come back to me. Come back," she cried at him silently. But he would not hear.

It was only when Mrs. Madison gave the ladies the signal

to rise that he turned to her under cover of the scraping chairs. "Fix some safe meeting-place," he whispered urgently. "I will meet you wherever and whenever you say. Send your maid here with a note. I will get it."

"When are you leaving?" she asked hopelessly.

"Tuesday at dawn."

Tuesday, and this was Friday night. She made a smalll choked sound.

"Come, my child." Dolly Madison swept her up with an affectionate arm around her waist. "We must leave the gentlemen to their port. I fear they are eager to be rid of us poor females."

The girl allowed herself to be led upstairs, walking, thought Dolly, with a too docile precision. Her dark beautiful eyes were blank and fixed. She seemed not to hear when Mrs. Gallatin addressed some civil remark to her. Dolly's kind heart was dismayed. She kept Theodosia close to her, covering the girl's behavior with a graceful screen of tactful chatter.

When the other ladies had withdrawn a little, and there was opportunity, she gently patted Theo's hand. "You're not happy, dear. What is it? Can I help?"

Theo started, her small face convulsed. "Happy!" she cried, with explosive bitterness. "Is anyone happy?"

Dolly smiled. "I am. You won't believe me, dear, you're too young, but happiness comes from acceptance, from ceasing to struggle with things you cannot change. And it lies in small, unconsidered joys, the beauty of flowers, a cup of tea beside the fire with a friend, the pleasure of good conversation, music——" She spoke with unaccustomed seriousness. But she saw that it was of no use. The girl was deep in an emotional crisis, where she could not be reached by tame philosophizing. Dolly had formed a shrewd idea as to the cause of the trouble. Lewis and Theodosia had been transparent enough to her worldly-wise eyes. But there was nothing to be done about that. It would pass, as all violent emotions passed. One worked through them somehow to peace.

"At any rate, smile, Theodosia," she urged affectionately. "You must never let the world read your pain, whatever it is. Nakedness of the spirit in public is far more lewd than nakedness of the body."

Theodosia reddened. The gentle reprimand was deserved. She had been false to her father's training, false to her own ingrained social discipline. "I'm sorry, ma'am. You're quite right."

Dolly nodded approval, pulled a tiny gold snuffbox from her reticule. "I am now about to indulge in one of the small joys I spoke of," she laughed. "I believe many people are shocked by it, but it gives me pleasure and I am stubborn."

She applied a hearty pinch to each nostril and sniffed with a sort of humorous voluptuousness. This produced the effect she had intended. Theodosia smiled a little.

"That's right, my child. You have a lovely smile. Now let us join the other ladies, whom I hear chattering in French for the sake of poor Mrs. Turreau. I know that in languages you are most proficient, and, alas, I am not. So you must assist my stumbling efforts."

She drew Theo with her and joined the other ladies.

Chapter Seventeen

IT DEVELOPED next day that Aaron had an engagement at the Union Tavern in Georgetown, and, though this was to be a masculine political dinner, he urged Theodosia to accompany him, suggesting that she might visit either the Stodderts or the Carrolls until he was free to rejoin her. But she pleaded headache and fatigue so successfully that he reluctantly gave in.

His absence would be providential. There would be some free hours in which to see Merne. But how? And where? The rain continued. Their meeting-place by the river would have been impossible even had Merne not vetoed it. She considered summoning him to the boarding-house, but rejected it at once. The landlady was a renowned gossip and possessed of a fierce curiosity about the comings and goings of her boarders.

Theo locked her chamber door and paced up and down nervously. It can't just stop like this, she thought. We've had so much beauty, it can't be all over. If we can be alone and quiet once more, I can bear it afterward. There's so much we haven't said to each other. Just once more—please. Then I'll be good. I promise I will.

She didn't know what entity she was trying to propitiate in this old childish formula; she was beyond coherent thought.

It was Eleanore who provided the solution. She tapped on the door to ask some question about the baby's clothing, and when Theo finally unlocked it, the maid ran to her mistress with a cry of sympathy.

"Mon Dieu, Madame. Qu'avez-vous?"

She soon found out the trouble and, while her sympathy deepened, it became tingled by the amusement which passion always inspires in those not involved. La pauvre petite! So now her fine lover was going away. Papa had returned, le mari would soon be here, and the lover must leave. Madame wished to say farewell in private: most natural.

"Mais c'est tout simple, Madame. There is a house in the woods by Rock Creek where they take couples embarrassed as you are. The owner is bien discret. No one will be the wiser," said Eleanore, who had her own channels for finding out things.

Theodosia flushed. "You mean it is a house of assignation?"

The maid shrugged her stalwart shoulders. "Ah bien, one may call it what one likes. But when one is starving, one does not examine a crust of bread too closely, n'est-ce-pas?"

"I suppose not," said Theo slowly. For, after all, what difference did it make, as long as they would be together?

She wrote a brief note and handed it to Eleanore with instructions.

"Soyez tranquille, Madame. I will arrange everything. How fortunate that monsieur votre père is going elsewhere tonight. When the cat's away, the mice will play."

Theodosia sprang to her feet. "Hold your tongue!" she blazed.

Eleanore's jaw dropped; she was too astonished to feel indignant at the first anger she had ever seen in her mistress.

Theo slumped back on the chair and covered her face with her hands. "I'm sorry, Eleanore—go now."

She couldn't explain, that, put in the maid's crude words, the thought of deliberately deceiving Aaron had twisted her with sudden hot pain. Self-loathing sickened her; but much stronger was her longing for Merne.

Merne arrived first at the house near Rock Creek, and went through the necessary business of hiring a room with cold distaste. He knew the place by reputation and had been astonished by Theodosia's note, designating it for their meeting place. For a moment he had been seized by a normal male reaction of triumph. Surely this could mean only one thing: tacit surrender. Invitation to spend their last hours together, not in the idyllic romantic haze of their days by the river, but in the frank consummation of their passion. On reflection he knew that he was wrong. She was incapable of such cold-blooded planning. She must have picked the place because she could think of none else. Nor for that matter could he. But the frowzy, leering atmosphere of the house revolted him.

He stood by the dirty cracked window of the bare room assigned him, and saw Theodosia, her face concealed by a dark hood, slip from a carriage and walk uncertainly to the door below. It opened silently at her approach.

'Tis like a stinking French play, he thought angrily: intrigue and shoddy gallantry: "The Officer and the Married Lady." Phaugh!

The room smelled of countless unwashed bodies, and from the rumpled bed there rose an odor of patchouli. The furnishings, frankly practical, consisted only of bed, table, and slop bowl. Through the flimsy partition which separated this room from the adjoining one came excited squeals of laughter punctuated by male grunts and guffaws.

Merne opened the door at a sharp knock. The fat proprietor entered, smirking. Theodosia, shrinking into her hooded cape, followed him.

"Here's your little lady, sir. Anything more I can do for you?"

Merne drew Theo against him, encircling her with a protecting arm. "Yes. Make me a fire," he ordered sharply. "This dismal hole is damper than a cellar."

The man shook his head. "Can't be done, sir. I ain't got no wood. Don't pay to cut none in summer. Anyways, the folks that comes here don't need no fire. They got something better to keep 'em warm."

Merne's fist clenched, as he felt Theo tremble against him. "Get out!" he shouted violently. The man scuttled from the room. The door slammed to.

Theo stirred, looking up at him piteously. "Oh, Merne, this is terrible. I didn't dream it would be like this."

"I know you didn't," he said quietly. "It can't be helped." He untied the ribbons of her wet cloak, laying it across the worm-eaten footboard of the bed.

She stood silent, more beautiful than he had ever seen her. She wore a plain gown of dark blue silk from which Eleanore had removed all trimming so that in case of mishap it would not be recognized. Her skin against the unrelieved blue took on the thick white luster of a dogwood petal, except on her cheekbones where excitement had tinted it pink. Her bronze hair disordered by the hood lay loose about her neck and at the temples small tendrils, curled tight by the dampness, gave her face a luminous delicacy.

The force of her beauty unnerved him. A honeyed lassitude swept over him and into his brain. His hands shook suddenly. He scowled, and, turning sharply, lit the candle on the table, consciously prolonging the small business with the flint and steel and tinder.

He came back to her and drew her gently to the bed. She shrank, with a slight embarrassed sound.

"There's nowhere else to sit, my darling," said Merne, with grim humor.

She looked about the dingy room. The wavering candle-flame flickered to the rafters from which hung cobwebs and dust in long furry shreds. Cockroaches skittered across the floor. The couple next door who had been murmuring burst into raucous song. This was followed by the clink of bottles.

Theo sank on the lumpy bed beside him. Her eyes filled with tears. "I wanted it to be so beautiful, Merne: our last hours together. A memory to live by, to hold in my heart forever. It should have been as it was before: the sun, the trees, the river that we love. I never felt shame there. But here——"

Her head drooped against him. He pressed his lips silently to her hair.

"Don't go West," she whispered. "I can't let you go. Stay near me, my beloved, even if we cannot see each other. You'll be safe. And sometimes we could meet."

He raised her face so that she must see his eyes. "Sometimes we could meet," he repeated bitterly. "How, Theodosia? In places like this?"

She flung away, burying her face in the corn-husk mattress. Her arms curled around her head in a gesture at once so childish and so full of despair that it turned him to water.

"I thought you loved me," she cried, with the complete unreason of women.

He leaned over her. "I do. There will never be anyone else. Don't you know that?"

She turned her body slowly so that she could look up at him. Her warm breath scarcely passed her parted lips. Her face was stilled by a sorrowful tenderness. "Yes, I do know that," she whispered. She raised her arms. He kissed her then as he had never kissed her, even on that first day by the river, with the brutality of desire long held in check. Suddenly she stiffened; he saw beneath the answering passion in her eyes an agonizing fear.

He jerked away from her, strode across the room. He yanked at the small crooked window. It stuck fast. He drove his fist savagely through one of the panes. There was a crash and the diminishing tinkle of broken glass. The fresh damp evening air swept by him. The jagged cut on his hand

193

gave him a fierce pleasure. It hurt, and the hurt relieved him.

Theo lay with closed eyes where he had left her, motionless except for the sharp rise and fall of her breasts beneath the blue bodice.

"Theodosia," he said roughly, "there is one way: one thing we can do."

Her eyes opened; her pale mouth formed a question.

"Come away with me: out beyond the mountains. No one asks questions there."

"Out beyond the mountains?" she repeated slowly. "How could we?"

He made an impatient gesture. "We shouldn't be the first couple to run away from entanglements, take new names, and start afresh in the wilderness."

"You mean to leave my husband, my baby, and my father——" She frowned a little as though trying to understand. "And you, Merne? Would you, after all, give up your expedition, forfeit the President's trust, and your honor——"

He laughed through tight lips. "Obviously. One does not run off with another man's wife and enjoy the blessings of the community. Yet it would be far harder for you——"

He stopped, overcome by the impossibility of this wild proposal into which his passion had betrayed him. Theodosia in a log cabin struggling to cook the game he brought her, toting water, tending the corn patch: she who expected service from underlings as unquestioningly as she expected air to breathe. Even more impossible to imagine her alone for days as she would have to be, without hope of help in case of illness or danger, dependent only upon herself.

Many gently bred women had found within them the strength to lead this hard frontier life, but much as he loved her, Lewis knew that Theodosia could never be one of these. Adversity would break her. And in this case, physical hardship was the least of it. How long could her love endure against the inevitable remorse? She might abandon her husband with no sufferings except those that sprang from outraged convention, but never her child—or her father.

I've been a fool, he thought, a mawkish fool. And he looked at her with suddenly hostile eyes.

She understood his look and smiled sadly. "Yes, it's impossible, Merne. Soon we should hate each other. You would never forgive me if I went with you. I think you would never forgive anything that turned you from your purpose. We can't wrench the pattern of our lives as violently as that. Perhaps some day it will be different. We're both young.

You'll come back from your expedition—I know you will——" Her voice wavered and broke.

He took her into his arms, holding her now with a pure tenderness, grateful for her wisdom, passionately grateful that she had understood. "Of course I'll come back. You vastly overestimate the dangers."

"You'll think of me, Merne: nights when you sit beside your campfire, when you hear the sound of water, the mighty new rivers that you will find out there in the far country."

She straightened suddenly, staring past him out of the shattered window into the black night. "What is the message of rivers? Why does it mean something so deep, so disquieting and yet fulfilling—I can't express it. Yet it's in that song, 'Water, parted from the sea . . . Still it murmurs as it flows, panting for its native home.' The rushing waters panting for the sea. They mean love to me, but they mean life too— and fear. What is the sea, Merne? Is it peace—or death?"

"I don't know, my darling," he answered, smiling. "Perhaps both at once, for death is peace, I think. You're a little pagan. The Indians have much the same feeling about rivers that you have."

He spoke with determined lightness, but he understood her. Again she had touched the mysticism in his own soul. Sometimes, not often, when alone in the forests, he had felt all the manifestations of nature to be endowed with an inner meaning. He was half-ashamed of this, believing it to be puerile sentimentality. Yet he loved her best as she was now, withdrawn from him, unapproachable, her fragile face lit by a brooding beauty.

He was profoundly glad that he had not possessed her. Whether the aftermath would have been disillusionment or a compelling ecstasy which would have bound them fast— he could not tell. In either case their love would have crystallized into a new, more rigid form from which they could not have escaped. Now they were still free.

The candle sputtered suddenly and Theo turned her head. She gave a cry and jumped to her feet. "Merne, look! The candle! It's nearly gone. It must be very late. Oh, what shall I do if Father comes home before I do! What will happen?"

"Eleanore will think of some excuse for you. Don't be frightened, my dear one." He kissed a strand of her long shining hair. But in truth he thought that she had better go. Their hour was rounded and finished. Since it must be, it was time for them to take up again their separate lives.

195

She bundled her hair under the hood, fastened the ribbons on her cloak. Her fingers shook with haste. When she stood ready, they looked silently at each other.

These things, she thought, I must remember. The silver-gold of his hair, as it springs back in just that little whorl from his forehead. The way his gray eyes soften when they look at me and yet are cold as slate to others. The brown leanness of his hands with their strength to bruise and their gentleness to caress.

"Good-bye, my love," she whispered. "O Merne—I——" Her voice cracked and she ran from him, slipping through the door like a dark wraith. He heard the soft patter of her feet descending the stairs. From the window he saw her run to the waiting carriage. Its heavy door slammed.

As he came slowly back from the window, the candle guttered and died. A devastating sense of loss and loneliness seemed to fill the sour, darkened room. He flung himself out of it and from the house in headlong strides. It was a tavern he wanted, a tankard of cold, tingling ale, the companionship of males, forthright masculine talk. There, perhaps he would find surcease and forgetfulness.

He reached the Washington Tavern just as Aaron returned to his lodgings on Independence Street to find Theodosia wan-faced in her white dressing-gown and about to retire. The headache was still bad, she said, as she quickly kissed him good night. He sent her to bed without suspicion.

For the only time in her life Theo had successfully deceived her father. She felt neither triumph nor compunction nor shame any more: nothing except a physical weariness so overwhelming that her legs ached and her brain was stupefied.

Meriwether Lewis left Washington before the sun had risen on July the fifth. He left alone, and as quietly as though he were setting out on one of his early morning rides. He was to meet William Clark at Harper's Ferry, and for the two of them there were to be long months of preparation while they trained men, built boats, and waited for the winter to pass in St. Louis, before they could actually start up the Missouri.

Merne checked his horse as they came to the ford over Rock Creek. He turned in his saddle to look back at the sleeping town. The unpainted dome of the Capitol glimmered through the early morning mist, and behind it, invisible to him, was the house where Theodosia slept. He gazed long in that direction. Farewell, my dear, he thought, and sighed, yet his mood was a mingling of sadness and relief. For it was not only to her that he said good-bye, but to a whole way of living. Luxuries and refinements, subtleties and intrigue, he left them behind now.

He tautened the reins, and the horse darted forward, eager for speed. "Not so fast, my friend," said Merne, pulling him down. "We have a long way to go." Then, struck by the aptness of his words, he laughed grimly. A long way to go: thousands upon thousands of miles ending very like in death. He thought with sudden amusement of Dolly Madison's romantic flutters about the expedition. She had persisted in regarding him as a hero: mighty little romance about it. For the hundredth time he ran over figures in his head. So many pounds of provisions, so many of ammunition, the capacity of the flatboats, the canoes.

He pulled out a leather-bound notebook and began to figure in it with a piece of sharpened charcoal. The horse, accustomed now to a slower gait, jogged on unguided. The trail beside the Potomac ran up the river and westward—steadily westward. And westward Merne would continue to face for three harsh years.

Chapter Eighteen

𝒯 𝒯 𝒯

JOSEPH arrived in due course, and with him, to Theo's dismay, he brought his father and brother William Algernon. They all left Washington at once, Aaron to go on necessary journeys which ranged from Philadelphia to Providence, while the Alston family repaired to Ballston Spa to drink the waters.

In this atmosphere of anxious health-seeking, Theodosia found her own health deteriorating again. Aaron wrote worried letters of advice, Joseph consulted the resident physicians and personally supervised her visits to the springs, where she drank gallons of the salty, sulphurous liquid.

Eleanore watched these proceedings sympathetically. When one is unhappy and bored, one is apt to be sick, and who could help being unhappy and bored in the company of those three stupid men? Particularly now that the fine lover was gone; and le père too, with his gaiety and good-humor. No wonder Madame was like a small snuffed candle: there was no fire around to kindle her. The Alstons were invariably solemn and repressive. En masse they were enough to make anyone sick.

Theodosia gradually improved. Time dimmed her first desperate longing for Merne. She once more accepted the pattern of her life and tried to make the best of it. But she was a trifle less compliant and had more trouble hiding her impatience.

The Alstons went back to South Carolina by land, and the long uncomfortable trip produced constant friction. Day after day the five of them were shut into the heavy family coach, while it rocked and rumbled southward. Colonel Alston and William Algernon sat with their backs to the horses. Joseph, Theo, and the fretful baby rode on the opposite seat. Little Gampy at a year and a half was as active and restless as are other children of that age, and Theo exhausted herself trying to quiet him. Moreover, he was teething and his resentful wailing was difficult to bear. Frequent drizzles made it impossible to give him to Eleanore, who rode behind in the open spring wagon, so the four adults in the coach endured the child according to their various natures. The Colonel and William Algernon talked horseracing when they could hear each other above the din; when they could not, they said nothing, but their long faces were set in heavy disapproval. Joseph occasionally dandled his son irritably until his scanty patience was exhausted. Then he dumped him back onto Theo, who soothed and rocked him, racking her brain for new stories and songs with which to quiet him.

From Lumberton, South Carolina, she wrote to Aaron on October twenty-ninth: "Thank Heaven, my dear father, I am at Lumberton, and within a few days of rest. I am sick, fatigued, out of patience, and on the very brink of being out of temper. . . . We travel in company with the two Alstons. Pray teach me how to write two A's without producing something like an ASS."

This state of irritation was hardly lessened by Joseph's belated admission that they were not bound for the Oaks, which was being plastered and would not be ready for them. "We will spend a few days at Clifton with the family, then visit John Ashe and Sally at Hagley, before we go to Charleston," said Joseph.

"I think you might have told me sooner," snapped Theo. "Why is our own plantation never ready? You know very well that the baby and I need rest. A round of family visits is scarcely conducive to that."

"I don't see why not," retorted Joseph. "You've been away all summer and can now do as *I* wish for a change."

Her sense of justice silenced her. According to his lights Joseph was an exceptionally indulgent husband. After a bit she smiled at him apologetically. "I'm sorry I was cross. This trip has been hard on all our tempers." She sighed, and to change the subject brought out the first topic which occurred to her. "I suppose you have never heard anything of Venus?"

A long silence followed this chance remark. Theo looked up at her husband, surprised. They had been sitting together in their room at the little tavern in Lumberton. Gampy slept in a trundle bed beneath theirs, her father and brother-in-law had already retired.

"Have you found Venus?" she repeated, increasingly amazed at his expression.

Joseph looked both triumphant and sheepish. "Venus came back of her own accord, poor girl," he said at last. "She was painfully thin and ill. She had spent a year hiding in the savannas. I don't know how she managed to exist. She implored me to take her back."

Theo, remembering his violence when Venus ran away, his threats, his vow to sell her to the Spaniards, said wonderingly: "And you've taken her back? Didn't you even punish her?"

"She's learned her lesson," said Joseph quickly. "She's suffered much. You should have seen her kissing my hands in gratitude, heard her heartbroken cries. She says she wishes for nothing in life but to serve me—and my family, of course."

Theo opened her lips to protest, but thought better of it. She would not disturb Joseph's picture of himself as kind, compassionate master. Perhaps the girl had suffered, perhaps she was contrite and would behave. Yet the thought of that sleek golden-brown trouble-maker once more ensconced in the quarters made her angry and unhappy.

"I know you have a prejudice against Venus, but I thought you would be pleased at my forgiving her. You are always preaching tolerance in the treatment of the other slaves." Though Joseph scowled, there was a note of genuine hurt in his voice. He tugged at his whiskers, and, turning a little so that she could not see his face, he added slowly, "Sometimes I feel that nothing I do pleases you."

She looked up quickly, touched by his rare humbleness. "Do you really care to please me still? We have been married three years."

He stirred, turning still farther from her. "You've seemed so cold, so indifferent of late. Even your letters——"

She drew a sharp breath. Oh, why, she thought passionately, wrapped up in our separate worlds, do we all hurt each other? Insensitive as he is, he has felt the change in me. Now that I know what love is, I can no longer pretend to myself that I feel it for him. Yet he's my husband, the father of my baby. Even if I am unhappy, we need not both be so.

She rose and went over to Joseph and, taking his resisting hand in hers, pressed it gently against her cheek. Gradually his rigidity relaxed, his expression changed into one which was too familiar. He pulled her violently against him.

This is all there is to marriage for anyone, she thought, tolerant affection and this—this degrading submission of the body. Even with Merne it would surely have come to this in time. She clung desperately to this theory, using it as anodyne. It carried her through the visits to Clifton and Hagley. It enabled her to write cheerful letters to her father, but it lost its potency when she reached Charleston on December third. For there she met Natalie again, and no amount of feverish self-deception could blind her to the fact that her adopted sister had found in marriage, not tolerance or submission, but passionate love.

Natalie and Thomas Sumter had at last arrived from France, bringing with them a baby daughter. Joseph's own house on Church Street was for once in readiness, and Theodosia was delighted to be able to welcome the travelers in her own home.

After the bustle of greeting and the first excited exchange of news, the two young women settled down in the drawing-room to take stock of each other.

"How delicious it is to see you again, Theo!" cried Natalie, kissing her enthusiastically. "Do you see how well I speak English now, since Thomas wants me to? What do you think of my Tom? Is he not handsome?"

Theo agreed politely. She thought Thomas Sumter a pleasant-looking young man with agreeable manners, though hardly the paragon that Natalie considered him. The French girl had grown thinner, but her pointed face was radiant, her staidness and small spinsterish ways had vanished. She bubbled with an irresistible joy.

"I'm so happy to be back here in my Tommy's home, though I am happy anywhere with him. Marriage is heaven, Theo, is it not, chérie?" She paused a moment. "You are happy, are you not, with good Joseph? He seems so fond of you."

"Yes, of course," said Theo briefly.

"And he is so rich, too, your Joseph," added Natalie, laughing. "This splendid town house and all your plantations ——We are not so rich, but it matters not a bit to me. We have enough." She leaned forward suddenly. "Le bon Dieu has blessed me in every way. My beloved husband, my baby, and now——" she laughed, touching her stomach in a frank gesture.

"Another one so soon!" cried Theo, half-shocked. She

could not recognize the prim Natalie, particularly when she answered gaily:

"Why not? What greater happiness is there in life than sleeping with the man you love and in bearing him children?"

Theo did not respond. For a moment she hated Natalie. What right had anyone to be so blatantly sensual or so maddeningly pleased with her lot? She was ashamed of her annoyance, however, and patiently bore with Natalie's rhapsodies during the week in which they remained together at Charleston. It was disconcerting, though, to find that the Charlestonians took Natalie to their hearts in an impulsive, affectionate manner which they had never shown toward Theodosia. The young Sumters were exceedingly popular, which the young Alstons, though possessed of far greater wealth and position, were not.

I suppose it's my fault in some way, thought Theo wearily; everything always is, but I can't help it.

She was sorry to say good-bye to Natalie when the Sumters left for their home in Statesburgh, yet for once it was a relief to get back to the Waccamaw. She settled down for that winter of 1803-04. She was no longer actively unhappy. Her days passed quietly. There were small pleasures —new books from England, Gampy's Christmas party, and, as always, Aaron's letters.

In February Aaron became a candidate for Governor of New York State. He wrote of it to Theo in his most airy manner, adding in one place, "Hamilton is intriguing for any candidate who can have a chance of success against me." He would be, thought Theo angrily, when she read this, but as Aaron made no more mention of the campaign in his next letters, she thought little about it.

On May first, casually inserted into the middle of a chatty letter, he wrote one sentence, "The election is lost by a great majority: tant mieux." So that the affair seemed unimportant to her. There were always elections and political contests. If he failed this time—well, next time would be better.

She was far more interested in the plans they were again discussing for the annual trip to the North. Aaron, by borrowing another strategic amount, had managed to stave off his most urgent creditors. As always at the temporary release from money pinch his spirits soared. And he still retained possession of Richmond Hill. What, then, more delightful than that they should pass the summer there again, Theo and Gampy and himself!

But a little later he suddenly ceased to mention this

project, and while his letters continued brightly affectionate, there lay over them a thin film of evasiveness. His plans, it seemed, were unsettled after all. Perhaps rather than go to Richmond Hill in June she had better spend the forepart of the summer with Natalie at Statesburgh. This puzzled her, but she decided that it must have to do with financial embarrassment as usual and did not press him.

Aaron gave her no inkling of his purpose, nor of the grim interchange of notes between two estates on Manhattan Island—Richmond Hill and the Grange. Hamilton's hatred had finally subdued his caution, his attacks could no longer be ignored. For years Aaron *had* ignored them, disdaining to notice rumors or oblique references. Cheetham's scurrilous articles could not be certainly traced to Hamilton, and they had become so violent as to defeat their purpose anyway.

But one of Cheetham's published taunts had rankled: "Has the Vice-President sunk so low as to permit himself to be insulted by General Hamilton?" That appeared in the heat of the gubernatorial campaign. Aaron, completely contemptuous of the source, had tried to dismiss it from his mind along with the other slanders. It was not so easily dismissed, however.

He could treat with disdain attacks on his morals, his politics, even on his reputation, but his physical courage had never before been impugned. His one real vanity lay in his military record for conspicuous bravery during the War of Independence.

On June fifteenth he sat in his library at Richmond Hill with a newspaper open on his desk before him: a newspaper that had been brought by young John Swartwout. The young man's face was red with indignation; his voice quivered as he flung the sheet before Aaron. "Look at this, sir. By God, it's too much!"

Aaron's eyebrows shot up, and he smiled. "What now, my hot young friend? More insinuations against the Vice-President?"

"This is more than insinuation, sir. This is too direct to be overlooked."

Aaron ran his eyes over the letter which had been printed without comment: a letter from an unknown Doctor Cooper to a friend.

General Hamilton and Judge Kent have declared, in substance, that they looked upon Mr. Burr to be a dangerous man, and one who ought not to be trusted with the reins of government. . . . I could detail to you a still more despicable opinion which General Hamilton has expressed of Mr. Burr.

Aaron's face was impassive. He leaned back in his chair and offered his snuffbox to the excited young man, who was watching him anxiously.

Swartwout waved the snuff aside, crying: "But what are you going to do, sir? You can't let it pass. You will be derided, people will think you are afraid——"

Aaron shook his head. "Softly, John. There is nothing new in this. Hamilton, it seems, is forever interested in labeling me with 'despicable, and more despicable.' I am flattered that he finds me of such enduring interest."

"But this is different, sir. It's in print, a direct quotation!"

Aaron laughed. "Even so. It's in print, and that makes all the difference. Don't look so woebegone. I do not intend to let it pass. My patience is indeed exhausted."

Swartwout brightened. "What will you do, sir?"

"Point out to General Hamilton the necessity of a prompt and unqualified acknowledgment or denial of the use of any expression which would warrant the assertions of Doctor Cooper."

The young man frowned; he worshiped Aaron, thought him without flaw, and yet any temporizing in this instance seemed to him almost shameful. "Why do you not call him out at once, sir? He has given you unendurable provocation."

Aaron shook his head, smiling wryly. "Don't be alarmed, John. I have a feeling that you will not be cheated of the bloodshed you desire. But one must observe the proper decorum. You needn't be in such a hurry. You may safely," he added, with a trace of annoyance, "leave the vindication of my own honor to me. Come, pour yourself a glass of Madeira from the decanter over there, and then go, for I have much to attend to."

On June seventeenth, Aaron summoned his friend, William Van Ness, and gave him a letter for Hamilton, who answered evasively and unsatisfactorily, averring that he could not be held responsible for the inferences drawn by others from whatever he had said of a political opponent in the course of fifteen years' competition, and that he could not enter into any explanation on a basis so vague. In short, he denied or affirmed nothing, and the letter, though partially conciliatory in tone, also managed to be subtly insulting. Letter followed letter, and each one carried the two antagonists nearer to the inevitable climax.

On the evening of July tenth Aaron locked himself into his library and, though it was warm, he kindled the fire which lay ready on the hearth. He sat down beside it and watched the orange-and-gold flames. Tomorrow at this time, I may be quite dead, he thought, and the crudity of the thought gave him sardonic amusement. His hand was steady, and, except for a slight persistent chilliness, he felt fit and normal.

He thought of Hamilton up at the Grange, surrounded, no doubt, by his wife and children, and the picture gave him an unaccustomed pang of loneliness. Above the fireplace a new portrait of Theodosia had replaced the one by Gilbert Stuart. Vanderlyn had painted it two years ago, and Aaron liked it. But the face was turned from him in profile, and the expression was grave, almost judicial. It gave him no sensation of communion tonight. Still, he poured himself a glass of wine and drank to the picture. "It is to you, my dearest Theodosia, that I am indebted for a very great portion of the happiness which I have enjoyed in this life," he said aloud. And he thought of the first Theodosia, her mother. Ten years since she died, and he no longer missed her, or thought of her often. Yet he had been fond of her and had made her a good husband.

I was faithful to her, he thought, and it surprised him to remember this. Since her death there had been so many women, casual, unimportant: affairs of a few weeks or months. Still, in each case when the thing ended, there had been no recriminations. No ex-mistress bore him any ill-will.

There were, however, embarrassing letters about. He must dispose of them. It was one of the tasks which confronted him this evening. He rose and went to his secretary, and took from it sheafs of envelopes and six blue boxes which contained his private correspondence. When he had finished with these, he wrote to Theodosia and Joseph, long letters of direction and farewell, calmly affectionate and unemotional.

They would never be seen unless he fell. Again the thought of death impressed him as melodramatic and ludicrous. It happened to others, but it held no immediate significance for oneself. That is no doubt a childish feeling——He shrugged his shoulders, and, removing his coat, slipped on a light silk dressing-gown and stretched out on the sofa before the fire. Tomorrow what was to be would be. In the meantime, it was late and he was tired. He closed his eyes and fell into a sound sleep.

Chapter Nineteen

J J J

IT WAS only a few miles across the Waccamaw Neck from the plantations on the river to the string of sandy islands in the ocean, and yet those few miles made the difference between health and fever in summer.

Many of the planters had built themselves summer homes upon the ocean side, and Colonel William Alston had followed suit with a pretentious cottage. Because of its squat gables and unusual size for a beach house, it had come to be called the "Castle." This the Colonel had built on Debordieu Island, which lay nearly opposite to his own plantation. He seldom used it, however, for his family preferred Sullivan's Island near Charleston.

In the summer of 1804, the "Castle" being vacant, Theodosia moved the baby and a portion of her household over to Debordieu, while she awaited word from Aaron as to their northern plans. She had considered joining Natalie at Statesburgh, but Gampy had not been well. He had had a fit of the ague, and though it passed quickly, it left the child pale and listless. She dared not travel far with him. Even the carriage ride from the Oaks and the short row across the creek which separated Debordieu from the mainland tired the little boy.

But when they reached the house and saw below them the surf creaming on the sand two hundred yards away, he revived. His dark eyes glowed with excitement. "Gampy like this place," he informed his mother solemnly in his clear little voice.

Theo smiled, kissing him quickly. "And so do I, darling."

From the first hours on Debordieu Island she knew a peace she had never before found in the South. The "Castle" had grace and informality. It was built on a mound of oyster shells and raised high on brick piles, so that the servants' and kitchen quarters beneath the house were always light and cool. The house proper had but one floor—two great rooms with octagonal bay windows at either end, connected by a central hall and four small bedrooms. The two twenty-foot rooms were, respectively, Theo's bedroom, which she shared with Gampy, and a living-dining-room facing upon the ocean.

The island was covered with crab grass, relieved by a few stunted cedars, scrub oak, and the pretty red-berried cassena bush, but all this shrubbery was low and in no way checked the constant salt breeze. A wide porch spread across the house front, and on the afternoon of their arrival Theo curled up in a chair on this porch, took deep breaths of fresh salty air, and listened contentedly to the ceaseless booming of the sea.

Presently a delicious odor of frying oysters stole up from the kitchen below. She realized that for the first time in weeks she was really hungry and eager for supper. There were three servants down there in the kitchen—Dido the cook, her husband Hector, and their little son Cupid. Theo's selection of these particular slaves had annoyed Joseph. Neither they nor any of their forebears had been house servants; they were field hands, and that was that.

"But can't they be promoted?" urged Theo. "I wouldn't dream of taking Phoebe away from the Oaks or disturbing the arrangements there. And I know Dido can cook. I visited her cabin the other day when she was stewing a rabbit that tasted most delectable. Anyway, Eleanore can teach her."

"The regular house servants will resent your interfering with their caste system," objected Joseph.

Theo sighed. "I'm afraid they resent anything I do, any-way——Oh, it's not anything tangible," she added quickly, seeing Joseph's frown deepen and wishing to forestall the usual criticisms of her plantation management. "It's just that I should like to start fresh at the beach with new servants who will be tractable and grateful for their eleva-tion."

She did not add that she had overheard Dido referring to Venus as a yellow wildcat who would be the better for a good lashing. She was slightly ashamed of herself for the warmth which this remark kindled in her toward Dido. Since Venus's return and restoration to favor, the girl had kept out of Theo's way. But she spent hours with Phoebe in the kitchen house, and she wielded an even greater influence over the

208

slaves than she had before her escape. That this influence was hostile, Theo now knew definitely. The murmurs, the dark, quickly averted glares, the tardy and resentful obedience to her wishes—all these had begun again amongst the slaves. And yet there was nothing specific, nothing with which to confront Joseph. He remained oblivious. The blacks always obeyed *him* promptly enough. As for Venus—the girl's topaz eyes dewed with gratitude when they turned on maussa; in his presence her thin, voluptuous face wore a look of eager worship, highly flattering.

Theo knew that, to Joseph, Venus represented continual proof of his generosity, his humane treatment of his people; that he experienced a pleasant glow when he thought of her.

But I'm not going to think of Venus now—or anything disagreeable, said Theo to herself. There is peace here by the ocean and no worry.

No Joseph either. He had left for Columbia three days before. That his absence also contributed to the delightful relaxation of these days at the beach she did not admit to herself. In fact, during the next few weeks she scarcely thought of him at all.

Gampy grew plump and happy as he collected shells and dug holes in the sand with the wooden spade that Hector made for him. Dido justified Theo's confidence and produced delicious food. Hector and Cupid went fishing or crabbing daily, returning with succulent prizes. The household feasted on turtle eggs, oysters, clams, shrimps, and the delicate stone crabs. These Dido boiled in wine, flavored by a little herb which she had gathered herself upon the mainland. They all ate and slept prodigiously; even Eleanore was contented and ceased to grumble about le sale pays.

The ocean was for Theo a living presence, a companion. Its rhythm entered into her blood. Despite the horrified Eleanore's remonstrance, "You will turn red as a boiled crab, Madame—so much sun is bad," she lay long hours on the dazzling white beach, soaking up warmth and listening drowsily to the sea's thunderous music.

Lulled in this way by a rare sense of physical well-being, time lost its significance. Therefore, though she sent Hector to Georgetown twice a week for mail and was regularly disappointed at receiving no word from her father, it was not until August that she became seriously disquieted.

She woke one morning shocked by a sudden realization. Not only had she heard nothing from Aaron in nearly two months, but it had been a fortnight since she had received a letter from Joseph.

A faint unease oppressed her that day. She was restless and could not settle down. She tried to reason with herself. Letters from Aaron had been longer delayed than this. A packet might have encountered storms, or, if he had used the post, the mail might have been lost or stolen. As for Joseph's silence, there could be a dozen explanations. And yet it was surprising: he usually wrote her by every post. Perhaps he has gone to see the Sumters at Statesburgh, she thought, or unexpectedly to Charleston. That must be it.

For the moment she was relieved, but the relief did not last. She had been calmly happy, and now quite suddenly she was apprehensive. The sun that evening went down in a red haze. Fog rolled in. The "Castle" was shrouded in dripping dampness. Theo ordered Hector to light a fire in her bedroom. She pulled a chair close to the driftwood blaze and settled herself with the baby on her lap for the nightly ceremony of lullaby-singing. His soft weight snuggled against her and quelled the sense of foreboding. She bent her head, resting her cheek on his bright curls.

"Sing 'Robin Adair,'" he commanded, as he always did, looking up at her expectantly. She laughed, amused by the child's passion for this mournful ballad.

> *What's this dull town to me?*
> *Robin's not here.*

She followed the familiar song without conscious thought. But as she finished, Gampy asked, "Why did she want Robin to be there?"

"Because she loved him, pet."

He digested this in silence a moment; then he asked, "Who do you love? Is his name Robin?"

She squeezed him, laughing. "I love you and you're right here and your name isn't Robin."

He accepted this and lost interest, but she sat silent, staring into the fire. Its blue-and-green flames blurred, running together like shaken jewels. Bitter longing stabbed her, as it had not done in months. Merne, my beloved, where are you? Oh, why does it have to be this way!

She shut her eyes. From without came the muffled boom of surf through the deadening fog. And otherwise—silence: heavy, creeping silence.

"Your face looks queer, Mama——Sing some more."

She sighed, opening her eyes. "I will if you'll go to sleep."

One by one she sang his favorites, "The Silver Moon," "Au Clair de la Lune," and "Bye-Low, Baby Bunting," until his lids drooped and his breathing quieted. Then she carried him to the trundle bed which was pulled out in readiness from underneath her own.

As she turned from the sleeping child, there was a commotion outside her door, a sharp rap. She threw it open. Dido stood there panting from the exertion of climbing the kitchen stairs. Her fat face glistened with excited fear. "Somebody comin' in boat acrost the creek, Mistiss. Hector gone see 'um. Muss be bad news, anybody come dis time night in fog. Enty?"

Theo's mouth went dry. Bad news—yes. It could be nothing else. She went to the window. Dimly through the gray mist she could see the flare of torches down by the landing. "Go and see that we have refreshment to offer—whoever it is," she said hiding her disquiet. Even Dido would blow up into hysterical panic if given the slightest chance.

Dido waddled off. Theo flung an embroidered blue shawl over her informal gown, and as she ran out on the porch, she heard a familiar voice calling, "Theo."

"Here I am, Joseph," she answered into the fog. Relief and anticlimax smote her at once. That was why she had not heard from him; he had been on his way. After all, her uneasiness had been ridiculous.

He stamped up the steps, embracing her briefly.

"I'm delighted to see you," she said, smiling. "I had worried at not hearing from you; it never occurred to me that you might be on your way. I thought the legislature was to keep you in Columbia."

"It should have," he answered glumly.

She was puzzled by his manner, which seemed even more than normally brusque and ill at ease. His clothes were stained and wrinkled as though they had not been off him for days.

"What is it?" she asked, with renewed fear. "Has something happened?"

Joseph tugged at his whiskers in the habitual gesture which indicated that he was uncertain of his course. "There is news, yes—but it will keep until I've eaten. I'm famished. Can that damned Dido produce anything palatable?"

"Certainly."

She clapped her hands, and when Cupid appeared, gave him hurried orders. "Some corn pone, a few slices of ham, perhaps some boiled shrimp with the rice, and make some negus

211

for your master. He's chilled through."

She came back to Joseph, clasping his arm urgently. "Now tell me, please. What is the trouble?"

Joseph moved uneasily, averting his face from her anxious scrutiny. He had made careful plans for telling her tactfully, but could remember none of them.

"It's your father," he blurted out, and then cursed himself as he saw the blood drain from her face, leaving it gray. Her hand dropped limp from his arm.

"He's—he's ill," she whispered. "Or—or worse. For Heaven's sake, Joseph, can't you speak?"

"I'm trying to. He's not ill. *He* is in perfect health."

Even through the tide of relief that left her knees shaking, she noted his contemptuous emphasis on the pronoun. She collapsed onto the sofa, lacing her hands together.

"Then it can't be so bad, if he is well."

"Bad enough." Joseph gloomily lit himself a cigar. "He's killed Hamilton."

She stared at him blankly. "I don't understand."

"He challenged Hamilton and they met at Weehawken July eleventh. Burr fired first and shot him in the side. He died two days later."

"But what about Father?" she cried, comprehending but one aspect of this astounding news. "Are you sure he wasn't wounded? How can you be sure? Oh, Joseph, for God's sake —speak!"

"I'm trying to tell you. He was not wounded. Hamilton's pistol was discharged into the air. I know because I have had two letters from Colonel Burr, and, besides, the papers are full of it."

"That's why he didn't write me," she murmured. The numb uncomprehension passed. She began to understand what had happened. She looked at Joseph. "Thank God, I didn't know beforehand. I should have been mad with terror. But it is well over. Hamilton was always his enemy. He gave him, I know, unbearable provocation. I always hated the man," she added on a lower key, remembering the Creole's cold, disdainful eyes, the covert sneer in his voice.

Joseph impatiently flecked a cake of dry mud off his boot. "It's not as simple as all that." He was exasperated by her attitude, which seemed to him both callous and casual. "There is a tremendous hullabaloo. The country has been incited by the press to consider the Colonel as a ruthless demon. And——" He hesitated. He had meant to break it gently, had spent three uncomfortable days and nights of travel worrying as to the best way of telling her. But her airy reception of the news changed that. She might as well know it all at once. "Your father is being prosecuted for murder, Theodosia. He has fled from New York to escape hanging."

She caught her breath sharply, springing to her feet. "How can that be? It was a fair and honorable duel."

Joseph shrugged his massive shoulders. "I have no doubt it was, but they say not. At any rate, there has been a jury, and they have brought in a verdict of willful murder."

"But it's incredible!" she cried. "Duelists are never prosecuted. Why, General Hamilton's own son, Philip, was killed by George Eaker three years ago, and no one dreamed of prosecuting Eaker."

"I know. The Colonel himself is amazed at the outcry against him. I confess I do not understand it, but there is no doubt of the seriousness of the matter."

"Where is he now?" She paused, swiftly considering. "He must come to me, here," she said decisively. "He will be safe. I will write him at once, but it mustn't be trusted to the mails. We can send one of the servants to take the letter direct."

"That won't be necessary," said Joseph coldly. "He is already on his way to you. A roundabout way, for he is off the coast of Georgia. He dared not travel overland until the hue and cry dies down. Major Butler has offered him asylum on Saint Simon's Island. I have a letter to you from him which was dispatched from Philadelphia and sent in my care."

He rummaged in his pockets while she watched him in a fever of impatience. Aaron, persecuted and in danger, Aaron in flight——These things were incredible. She scarcely felt fear for him, so monstrous did it seem that he could find himself in any situation of which he was not the cool master. His note both reassured her and yet confirmed the facts as Joseph's bald statements had not seemed to.

PHILADELPHIA, *August 3rd*, 1804

You will have learned through Mr. Alston, of certain measures pursuing against me in New York. I absent myself from home, merely to give a little time for passions to subside, not from any apprehension of the final effects of proceedings in courts of law. They can, by no possibility, eventually affect my person. You will find the papers filled with all manner of nonsense and lies. Among other things, accounts of attempts to assassinate me. These, I assure you, are mere fables. Those who wish me dead prefer to keep at a very respectful distance. No such attempt has been made nor will be made. I walk and ride about here as usual.

A. BURR

She put the note in her bodice. "As always, he makes little of his troubles," she said softly. "Oh, Joseph, you do think he's safe, don't you? He does not write thus only to reassure me?"

"Oh, he's safe enough where he is in Georgia. They had no love for Hamilton down there."

"And he must come to us, at once. You must write, too, so that he will be assured of welcome."

"I suppose so," said Joseph unenthusiastically. The visit of a debonair Vice-President had been one thing, but the harboring of a disgraced fugitive with a murder charge, however unwarranted, hanging over him was quite another: particularly in view of Joseph's own growing importance in the legislature. Moreover, he was tired and hungry and sick of the subject, which had been disturbing him for many days.

"How can you speak so coldly?" she demanded with resentment. "Were it one of your own family who was in trouble, you would stop at nothing to help him."

"My own family wouldn't get into a mess like this," he snapped.

Her eyes flashed. "That's because they're a spineless, lily-livered lot without a thought in their heads except horse-racing and rice-growing."

His face blackened, his underlip shot out. "Thank you, madame, for the compliments. Spineless and lily-livered they may be, as you so sweetly put it, but at least not one of them is eternally trying to squeeze money from me as does your worthy father. He's a first-class leech."

She gasped. Blind with anger they stared at each other.

Joseph was sorry to have said so much. After all, the financial arrangements between himself and Aaron were no woman's concern. They had always had a tacit agreement to keep her in ignorance. He had tried to make allowances for her natural upset at his news; it was in order to minimize the shock that he had come himself to tell her. But she was infuriating in her eternal concentration on her father and indifference to his own reactions. How pretty she looked, though, with her eyes sparkling instead of brooding and remote as he so often saw them.

Hector walked in then, staggering under a loaded tray.

214

The sight of approaching food mollified Joseph. He seated himself at the table and ladled a huge helping of shrimp and rice.

"Let's not quarrel, Theo. Sit down and join me. I judge from the looks of the victuals that Dido is indeed a good cook," he said, offering an olive branch.

Theo was too angry and hurt to accept it. That he should dare to criticize her father! That he should dare to begrudge any financial help which Aaron might need, and needed, she knew, only because he was so foolishly generous at times! Joseph was rich: he could well afford to be generous too: but he wasn't. He was compounded, she thought passionately, of small niggling traits, like the rest of his family. Caution, convention, prudence, with no trace of imagination or vision or genuine sympathy.

"I have already eaten," she said angrily, "and if you will forgive me, I think I shall retire. I am tired and the news has been a shock."

He gulped a great tumbler of wine, wiped his mouth on his handkerchief. "I'll come with you, Theo. I, too, am tired. We will go to bed immediately."

She turned to face him, and the inward shudder of repulsion seemed to diminish her body, so that she looked smaller, suddenly eclipsed.

"Eleanore will make the bed for you in there"—she indicated one of the small bedchambers. "The boy is sometimes restless in his sleep. You will rest better, and I—I have a headache."

"By God!" He banged his hand on the table so that the dishes rattled. "I have not seen you for weeks, and this is the way you receive me! It is always the same story, is it not? Always a headache, or you are tired, or the boy may be disturbed. I will not stand for it, I tell you!"

Even as he shouted at her, he knew that his anger and bluster were futile. In a way he admired her frigidity toward him. It was a desirable feminine trait—all pure women should feel that way—and he never approached her without a feeling of guilt. She had nearly died in childbirth. But it was damnably hard.

"I'm sorry, Joseph," she whispered, with one of the quick voltes-face of manner which she inherited from her father. Now her voice was gentle, and she wistfully smiled at him. "I know I'm not a very satisfactory wife. You should have married Anna Pinckney or one of the Middleton girls. They are bred to the plantations and would have managed far

better than I. They could have given you a dozen—children."
She added, with a touch of malice, "Their fathers, I'm sure,
would never have proved troublesome to you."

It was true, he thought, with a sensation of shock; perhaps
he should have married one of the Middleton girls. But he
hadn't wanted to, and, in spite of everything, he did not wish
he had.

He put his arms around her almost timidly. "I don't want
anybody but you, Theodosia, you and little Burr"—for he
could never bring himself to use Aaron's nickname of Gampy.
"I—I love you," he said, stumbling over the word which he
could use on paper, but which, when spoken, made him feel
like a fool.

Her heart contracted. She touched his coarse crisp hair.
He kissed her eagerly.

"Theodosia, I will write your father. He is always more
than welcome to any home of mine."

"Thank you, dear," she said. Sometimes he was so like the
sheep dog which Vanderlyn had long ago said he resembled:
a dog that has snapped and snarled and is now trying once
more to ingratiate himself.

"Good night," she whispered.

Her rose perfume crept to him and stayed with him after
she had gone into her room, shutting the door quietly behind
her.

Chapter Twenty

𝒯 𝒯 𝒯

IT WAS October before Aaron finally arrived. An early sharp frost had made possible a return to the Oaks before his coming. Frost cut the fever, though no one was entirely agreed as to the reason. Either it "froze the poisonous miasma which exuded from the swamplands," or it "produced a change of electrical fluid in the air and neutralized the excess acidity which was conducive to disease."

At any rate, this October frost had rendered the plantations safe once more. The river road up the Neck swarmed with homecoming planters in coaches, while the house servants who had accompanied them on the summer exile were packed, along with the movable household goods, into mule-drawn spring wagons.

Colonel William and his family returned to Clifton. John Ashe and Sally, the family augmented now by the baby, William, reopened Hagley. William Algernon took possession of Rose Hill, the plantation next but one to Clifton. His father had just given it to him in anticipation of his marriage to a charming widow who was also a cousin. Polly Young, née Allston, from the double "l" branch, was a buxom matron of twenty-eight, five years older than her prospective husband and encumbered, moreover, with a little girl, Eliza. But the staid William Algernon saw no disadvantage in that, particularly as Mrs. Young was possessed of a considerable fortune. He was all eagerness to establish himself and waited impatiently for Polly's second year of widowhood to end, that they might marry without offending convention.

Theodosia, drawn perforce into the whirl of family reunions, watched the delighted fuss being made over Mrs. Young's imminent entrance into the family and illogically was hurt. It was "Polly dear" this and "Darling Polly, what

217

do you think of that?" No gathering was complete unless Polly were there. And they petted and made much of little Eliza, who was not even direct kin, paying her far more attention than they did Gampy.

Theo was fair enough, however, to realize that she had never been able to muster much appreciation for the Alstons. Still, human nature being what it is, it is one thing to withdraw from a group because you find it unattractive and quite another to have it withdraw from you. Particularly now, when Aaron needed all the friends and backing that could be had. Since Joseph's visit to the island, she had been startled out of her indifference to newspaper reading and had sent Hector on constant trips to Georgetown after the latest news. Though most of it was local, there was occasional mention of Aaron, and she had been appalled at the venom displayed. Decidedly he needed friends.

For some time the maddening difficulties in communication had made his exact arrival uncertain; their letters crossed, or hers arrived after he had left. But she at last heard definitely that he was in Savannah and would board the first packet for Georgetown. He would be at the Oaks in five days, allowing for the ship's inevitable stop-over in Charleston.

She had acquiesced in Joseph's wish that her father's projected visit should not be mentioned to the family. The Oaks, an hour's ride from the other Alston plantations, would provide quiet asylum until Joseph could see how the land lay. His family never mentioned Aaron to Theo, but they did not disguise from Joseph their horror at the murder charge. If the papers said that the duel had been wickedly unfair, that Colonel Burr had most shamefully conspired to murder his enemy in cold blood, why, it was doubtless true. There was, at any rate, something fishy about the matter, and they preferred to ignore for the present the unfortunate relationship with which Joseph had saddled them.

Perhaps, thought Joseph hopefully, Colonel Burr may not arrive at all; he was apparently having much difficulty in finding transportation, or the money for it. So he tried to forget the matter.

He did not know about Theo's recent letter, and had no inkling of her decision that willy-nilly the family should assist at Aaron's welcome. The Vice-President in hiding at his daughter's home—never! Aaron was no skulking criminal, but a much-wronged man; he should be received with honor. But unfortunately one must first proceed with guile.

"I think we should give a party for William Algernon and Mrs. Young," she announced one evening at dinner.

Joseph was surprised and pleased. Her share in the family hospitality had never been as whole-hearted as he wished.

"Splendid! I must go to Columbia next week, but when I return——"

"That is too long to wait," she interrupted. "I was thinking of Saturday. No," she went on quickly, as she saw protest forming. He never liked sudden plans, particularly when they did not originate with him. "I shall take care of everything. I have already written all the invitations. Pompey shall deliver them this evening. Besides, if we wait too long, Mrs. Young may be gone. She is contemplating a trip to Charleston to buy her wedding finery, you know."

He nodded unwillingly. "Well, but it seems hurried. We must do the thing right. It would never do to be niggardly. We entertain so seldom here."

"Of course. We'll give a magnificent party. Waccamaw Neck will never forget it, I promise you."

Especially after they discover who is to be the real guest of honor, she thought, secretly mirthful, and set about her plans.

It was to be a truly magnificent party. Everything from the food to the entertainment was to be as perfect as she could provide from the limited resources of the Waccamaw. This was to be none of their stodgy dinners of fried meats and rice washed down with rum punch, and followed by a desultory card game, or the plunkety-plunking of the children on the harpsichord. She would startle them out of their smugness, show them that, when she chose, she could entertain with lavishness and brilliance.

The invitations were all accepted, as she had known they would be. Social gatherings were scarce on their remote neck of land, and the family approved of her wish to entertain for the affianced couple, though they attributed this idea to Joseph.

Theo impressed Eleonore into service, and between them they bullied and inspired the servants to activity. Ever distrustful of Phoebe's cooking, Theo imported a free black caterer from Georgetown. Dido, of course, was not permitted by Phoebe in her kitchen, but even Dido could not rise to the culinary heights to which Theo was soaring. She was delighted to find that the caterer was capable of a dish on which she had set her heart. It was called "Preserve of Fowl," though this title in no way did justice to its intricate mysteries. It was fashioned like the nest of Chinese boxes which Aaron had once given her for a toy. A dove must be inserted into a partridge, the partridge into a guinea hen, this into a wild duck, then into a capon, the capon into a goose, and last all the amalgamated birds were enclosed in a mammoth turkey. Each fowl was first boned and seasoned with herbs and rich gravy. There were to be four of these creations, and Theo delegated a small army of helpers to the perspiring caterer—for the preparation took days.

She supervised the garnishing of the rooms herself. The floors were polished until they gleamed like brown mirrors. She impounded all the supplies of myrtleberry candles for the candelabra, and on Saturday afternoon filled every cranny of the rooms with massed armfuls of whatever blossoms she could find untouched by the frost.

She surveyed her handiwork critically: the rooms still looked a trifle bare. An idea struck her. She ran out to the clustering live-oaks and dragged from them great bunches of the hanging moss. She draped this over the branched sconces to try the effect; then, calling two of the servants, she had them bring in basketfuls and fasten the greenish-gray streamers to the ceilings, until the rooms were filled with a cloudy, swaying mistiness. The Alstons so admired their everlasting moss and considered it, for no reason at all, yet another proof of their superiority to the North. Well, they should have it, she thought, plenty of it!

Joseph came in from the rice fields just as she was finishing. He had been watching the women burn the stubble of cut stalks—necessary fall procedure to prepare the land for its fresh crop. He stopped dead in the doorway.

"What is the world have you been doing? What's all this truck in here for?" he demanded, with marked displeasure.

She pushed back her disheveled hair with one hand and turned on him a flushed and laughing face. "I wanted some decorations, and we have no bunting nor enough paper to make streamers, so I thought of this. I think it's pretty. And our ceilings aren't properly finished yet: this hides them."

"I think it's confounded silly," he snapped. "Lot of vegetable matter in the house, sure to bring bugs." But the effect was attractive, and there was no doubt that the ceilings were in a bad state. He had been rather ashamed of them, for the recent plastering had already scaled into brown patches. He abandoned the subject for one more urgent. "I wanted to give Ishmael some orders and was told he had gone. It seems you sent him to Georgetown with six of our men in the big barge. Pray, why did you do that?"

She bit her lips and busied herself straightening a china shepherdess on the mantel. Ishmael was their best boatman, and she had hurriedly dispatched him that morning to wait beside the Georgetown Wharf until Aaron's ship docked, then bring him posthaste up the river to the Oaks. Though Joseph would find all this out eventually, she did not wish him to do so yet. There was still time to stop the guests from coming, as he would certainly do if he knew.

"I discovered that we were out of some essential supplies," she said lamely. "I sent Ishmael, because he's so much quicker than the rest."

Joseph grunted. "I wish you would not do such things without consulting me, it's most inconvenient. What things did you need so badly?"

She was saved from answering by the wheezing chime from the corner clock.

"Oh, it's late!" she cried, escaping. "I must get dressed."

She had hoped to startle her guests, and she succeeded. The hordes of arriving Alstons and near Alstons were literally struck dumb by her arrangements. She greeted them all with a charming, unconscious smile, as each group stopped in the doorway and stared at the transformed rooms, which looked as though they had suddenly grown long gray hair. It gave the place a weird eldritch air, a fantastic unreality that shocked their conventional minds.

"What a peculiar thing to do," whispered Maria Nisbett to Mrs. Huger, as they divested themselves of their wraps upstairs. "Really outrageous, I think it. Just what one would expect of——" She gave an eloquent shrug. "And, my dear, what in the world is that noise downstairs?"

They both paused to listen. Rhythmic strumming assailed their incredulous ears, an obtrusive barbaric rhythm that was strangely disquieting. The strumming was accompanied by the chant of soft male voices.

The ladies looked at each other. "It sounds like niggers," cried Lady Nisbett. "It sounds like a Saturday night on the 'street.' But surely she couldn't——"

She not only could, but had, they discovered when they went downstairs. Six black men crouched together in a corner of the drawing-room, partially but by no means sufficiently shrouded in long fronds of the moss. They were playing on their uncouth, homemade instruments, heathen monstrosities called banias or banjos, identical with those their fathers had twanged in Africa.

"Lawkes!" murmured Maria, drawing herself up after one outraged stare. "Niggers in the drawing-room and the hideous racket! I cannot imagine how Joseph can allow—surely she cannot expect us to listen to that. It's insulting."

Her lips drawn tight, she swept pointedly past the musicians, gathered up the other bewildered Alston ladies and retired with them to the farthest corner of the library, where they fell to indignant whispering.

Theo saw this maneuver and was discomfited. She had expected them to be amused, and, when they got used to the unfamiliar sound, pleased with her innovation. She thought the African music stimulating. She recognized in its mournful harmonies some genuine beauty. Their music was the only thing about the blacks for which she had much sympathy, and she had been delighted with her idea of having them provide a musical accompaniment to the party. Particularly as it was impossible to get conventional musicians on the Waccamaw, and surely in their hearts the isolated planters must be as sick of their own blundering renditions of murdered classics as she was.

It seemed that she was wrong. The Alston backs were without exception rigid and disapproving, not a single foot tapped unconscious time to the infectious rhythms. Theo sighed and directed the banjo players to stop for a bit.

Perhaps punch would thaw the Alstons. She ordered the servants to bring it in. Not their inevitable rum and lime punch, but the Richmond Hill specialty of iced peach brandy and champagne. This innovation, too, had in prospect seemed brilliant. She watched them eagerly as glasses were raised to the first toast: "To the happiness of Mrs. Young and William Algernon."

They scarcely touched the bubbling liquid. Maria, indeed, gave an exaggerated start of surprise and put down her glass with a decided thump.

You'd think I was trying to poison them, thought Theo, trying to hang on to the vanishing shreds of her sense of the ridiculous. It was of no use, she was angry and hurt. The party was a failure, and far from the merry convivial setting she had imagined. Here was no laughter, no relaxation. She had been a fool to think of delighting them with novelty. They weren't dazzled, they were affronted. Even the sight of her splendid dining-table evoked only a few polite murmurs, then astonished silence.

She had been so proud of that table. The caterer had outdone himself. Besides the four "Preserves of Fowl" there were great bowls of cooter stew with the terrapin's luscious green fat swimming in sherry sauce. There were piles of roasted eggs and fried oysters fresh that day from the creek behind Debordieu. And there was rice: huge sculptured mounds of the flaky white grains. Even Theo had not dared serve a meal here without rice.

These delicacies were but pale triumphs compared to the two centerpieces. The center, imbued by artistic fervor, had fashioned on one platter two lifelike doves of blancmange, hovering upon a mammoth nest of shredded and candied orange peel; while on the other platter towered a huge cake in the shape of a castle, and the Alston coat of arms was picked out in colored comfits upon the iced walls. Theo had meant this as a delicate compliment, or, if they chose, a touch of humor. It produced no emotion at all except astonishment tempered with suspicion.

True, Polly Young said, "How beautiful! It almost seems a shame to eat such pretty confections"—and smiled her wide, good-natured smile. But Maria with an audible sniff remarked to Mr. Huger on her left: "How strange to serve food tortured into such unnatural shapes. I doubt that it is wholesome. I'm sure I shall not eat a bite of it." Though she did manage to consume a goodly amount under cover of an air of chill disapproval. If Theodosia was trying to impress them, she might save her pains. She might far better, thought Maria, comport herself quietly and inconspicuously in all ways in view of her father's disgrace—nestling with humble gratitude beneath the outer tip of the family's wing, not putting herself forward. Thank Heaven, Sir John had not got himself mixed up with that man, after all. That Sir John had at one time made every effort to secure patronage from Aaron she conveniently forgot.

The general drift of Maria's thoughts was obvious to Theodosia. What an atmosphere in which to introduce Aaron! The plan had been mad. Instead of furthering his cause, it would hinder it. For Aaron there would be humiliation, averted eyes, perhaps even insult. It would be better, after all, to smuggle him upstairs to her bedroom if she could. But how? The stairs were in plain sight of the company. How stupid I am, and how badly I've managed this! she thought. Why didn't I offer them the same dull fare and dull entertainment to which they are accustomed? Or, better yet, why did I invite them at all?

She cast a nervous glance at the door. She had told little Cupid to wait down by the landing and warn her by a secret signal the moment he heard the splash of oars approaching on the creek. It must be nearly time. Her guests at least had eaten plenty. The men, indeed, had paid her food the compliment of silent and concentrated consumption. They now pushed back their plates and wiped their mouths. Colonel William extracted his gold toothpick from his pocket and plied it vigorously. The white doves had vanished, their nest was demolished, and the proud cake castle had crumbled to pathetic ruins.

As Theo rose, and the other ladies with her, she saw Cupid flash by the door, his small black face twisted into a grimace of conspiracy. She nodded, and, leading the way to the drawing-room, instructed the banjo players to strike up a tune. The ladies would not like it, but no matter. She no longer cared what they thought, and the noise would help to cover her retreat and Aaron's arrival.

"Will you excuse me a moment?" she murmured, and without waiting for their stiff bows slipped out of the room. She caught up a long black cloak from a corner of the porch where she had hidden it and ran down the path beside the house. Cupid joined her with a lantern, and they scurried together on the hard trampled quarter-mile to the landing.

The barge had already been tied up to the dock. She saw the black, half-naked figures of the boatmen by the light of their torch, and then, detached from them, advancing toward her, came Aaron, erect and lithe as ever in a dark gray suit and beaver hat that showed not the slightest trace of his grueling travel.

"Father, darling!" she cried, flinging her arms around his neck. "Oh, I'm so glad to see you! So glad!" Her voice broke. She had not known how much she had longed for him, or the full extent of her worry about him, until she saw him. It was all right now. What did the Alstons matter, or the failure of her silly party? He was here with her, and between them they could manage or defy the world. Joy washed over her like a golden wave.

He kissed her tenderly and laughed. "How now, Miss Prissy, do you greet me with tears? I should hardly have traveled a thousand miles to you for such a reception." But her joy was reflected in him too.

"Where is your estimable husband?" he asked.

"Up at the house; we have guests. I—I didn't tell him you were coming today."

224

"So? And why not, pray?"

She hesitated, then tucked her hand through his arm. "Father, we have so much to talk about, I don't know where to begin. Let's not go back to the house yet. I want you for myself a little while."

"Willingly, but just where do you propose that we talk? It's dark and passing gloomy out here, and I see no place to sit."

She frowned. It was true, there was no place where they might sit alone and talk. She bade Cupid hold high the lantern, while she searched for a fallen log or stone. Then her gaze fell on the silent little graveyard. "Over there, Father, we can sit."

Aaron laughed. "I find your choice a trifle macabre, but so be it."

He followed her through the wrought-iron gate; they took the lantern, and dismissed Cupid, who scuttled away terrified by the possibility of 'hants.' Aaron spread his traveling cloak over one of the raised horizontal slabs, and they seated themselves on it.

"This is a mournful and eerie place," observed Aaron, contemplating the hemming trunks of live-oaks and their burden of weeping moss.

She shuddered. "I know. I hate it. I never come here. I confess I'm afraid of the place—not of the quiet people who already lie here, but I think I'm afraid of the future ones: of those to come. I don't want to lie here——" She broke off. No, she didn't want to lie here under the weeping trees with people and in a country that were alien. For a second terror seized her. All those people up there at the house, the Alstons, how many of them were destined to end here in this mouldering plot—? And I, too; they'll pull me in and bury me here, because I bear their name; my body will fester and crumble next to theirs, we shall mingle together to form yet more of this hateful black earth.

She caught her breath in a little sobbing gasp. "Promise me, Father, that you won't let me be put here——"

"My dear child," said Aaron briskly, "you are being not only exceedingly morbid but very foolish. You are twenty-one, and I am forty-eight. It is, therefore, unlikely that I shall have the opportunity of directing the disposition of your remains. If you can't think of more pleasing topics of conversation, I move we go elsewhere." He belied the severity of his words, however, by putting an arm around her and giving her a small affectionate shake.

Her terror vanished at his touch. "Forgive me," she said, and managed to laugh. "Tell me of your journeys; the letters were so few. The heat down in Georgia and the Floridas must have been frightful. And you were miraculously lucky to have escaped the fever."

Aaron shrugged. "I did, at any rate. I confess that my four hundred miles of travel in an open canoe became a trifle tedious, but I'm none the worse for it and brown as a mulatto, as you'll see when we get into the light."

"Father——" She hesitated, fearing to open a topic too painful, but she had to hear from his own lips. "Will you tell me of the duel? There have been so many rumors and—slanders. I have no clear account of it. You never mentioned it directly."

Aaron nodded wearily. "I am sick to death of the subject. I wish to forget it, but I recognize your right to question me, though I recognize no one else's. I need not go into the provocation to you, I think. It has been continuous for years."

"Yes, I know. Even as a child I realized that Hamilton was your bitter enemy. Before you did yourself, I think."

"Yes, perhaps. I was stupidly blind for too long a time. At any rate, before I challenged him, I gave him ample opportunity to apologize or explain. He declined to do either and stated that he was willing to abide by the consequences. I know he did not wish to fight, but it's not true, as many say, that he had no intention of firing at me. He discharged his pistol as my ball took effect. The shot went wild, but that it went deliberately so, I do not believe."

"Then how can they say that the duel was unfair?" she cried passionately.

Aaron sighed. "I don't know, my dear, except that, as I have told you before, 'they' can say anything. Every detail of our meeting was according to the code. Van Ness was my second and Pendleton his. Doctor Hosack was the surgeon—all respectable men, but their words are ignored. It has seemed desirable to the Federalists and to some Republicans, too, to make of me a criminal and a murderer. The States of New York and New Jersey are engaged in a charming dispute as to which shall have the honor of hanging the Vice President."

"Oh, don't! How can you speak of it so flippantly? It—it terrifies me."

"It need not," he said, smiling at her. "You needn't have the slightest fears for my safety. There is not a shred of legal evidence if it should come to trial. But it won't."

They were silent a moment, while the lantern flickered beside them, and a chill breeze stirred the moss above them.

Theodosia moved. "I do feel great pity for Mrs. Hamilton and the children, especially Angelica; she adored her father almost as—as I love you."

"Yes, I know. But Hamilton's health was none too good; he might have dragged out in gradual decay instead of dying what the public is pleased to call a martyr's death. His career was in eclipse, his influence waning, but now through the act of being shot he has become a hero; the nation resounds with his plaudits. He may thank me"—Aaron's voice sharpened—"he may thank me," he repeated, "for I made him a great man."

Theo's throat contracted, a passion of loyalty surged through her. Her father's momentary bitterness hurt her doubly, because it showed the pain which he would never admit. He would not allow of sympathy, would permit no recriminations or self-pity from himself or her. It was his pride to accept adversity with the same cheerful, bantering equanimity with which he had taken good fortune, and she admired him for it with a vehemence that had in it at that moment something of worship.

She took his hand and laid it softly against her cheek. "It is you who are the great man"—she tried to speak with lightness, knowing his dislike of sentimentality, but her voice shook.

He said nothing, though he was profoundly moved. Her faith in him was sweet and more necessary to him than he would allow himself to know. Still, he had ample faith in himself, too—in his ability to surmount this present unfortunate setback and rise like the phoenix into a new incarnation so magnificent as to make his previous activities look like the games of children. He intended to set this plan before her, she was an integral part of it. But not now.

"Did you say you had guests, Theo?" he asked. "Won't they think it exceeding strange that you absent yourself for so long?"

She started and gave a dismayed laugh. "I had forgotten them. Oh, Father, I had planned a triumphal entry for you. I thought first to put them in a merry, convivial frame of mind, with—with music and food and our brandy punch. But it's been a complete fiasco."

"Who are they?" he asked, amused.

"Who but Alstons, Alstons, Alstons! They don't approve

227

of me any more, or you. I thought to win them over, or at least to dazzle them into graciousness despite themselves, but——"

"But they won't be dazzled?" said Aaron.

"They're a long-nosed, spiteful, hidebound parcel of dolts!" she cried. "And I cannot subject you to their hostility. You'll have to get upstairs some way and stay there until they go."

Aaron chuckled. He perfectly understood her plan, and its dramatic possibilities tickled him.

"Oh, no, my dear. I shall not go skulking upstairs to hiding. We'll carry out your idea as you intended. I can manage the Alstons."

"Joseph will be very angry," she faltered, "and they'll be horrible; you've no notion. They're vexed enough with me already."

"Courage, my dear. A bold offensive is the essence of victory."

"But aren't you tired? You've been traveling so long."

"You know very well I'm never tired. I confess that I should like to make some slight improvement in my clothes before bearding your lions, but, as that is impossible, they must accept me as I am."

He rose and helped her off the slab, picked up the lantern, and held the gate open with the ceremonious courtesy which characterized him. She took his arm.

"One thing, though, Theo. Tell me exactly who is there and any pertinent details as to their recent life, that I may govern myself accordingly. It is ever well to know the enemy's weaknesses."

On their way to the house she gave him the briefest sketch of each Alston. On the porch he nodded, satisfied.

"Do you go in and have your butler announce me properly. I shall wait here until he comes."

The men had quitted the dining-table and were now with the ladies in the drawing-rooms, where they had deployed into several small stiff groups. Otherwise, everything was as Theo had left it. The banjos still twanged fitfully, though the black faces above them had a dogged, disheartened look. She saw with surprise that she had been but three quarters of an hour, and they accepted her murmur of apology without comment. She seated herself with Mrs. Young and William Algernon and held her breath.

Almost at once Cato appeared in the doorway, took two steps forward, and bowed to Joseph, who looked astounded.

"Maussa, I'se the nonor to 'nounce Mister the Vice-President," he said, in ringing tones.

In came Aaron, erect and smiling, blandly unconscious of the gasp that greeted him.

Joseph did more than gasp. He shot to his feet and directed at Theo a furious glare.

Aaron made straight for him, however, and seized his hand. "My dear Joseph," he said heartily, "I'm very glad to see you. I hope that my unexpected arrival is not embarrassing." And here he made the smallest deprecating grimace that had in it so much of sly humor, and yet so much of careless charm, that Joseph responded to it despite his resentment.

"Your presence in my house could never be an embarrassment," he said heavily, "though I confess I am astounded. I had no idea you were within hundreds of miles."

"No more was I until yesterday.—How do you do, Colonel Alston and Mrs. Alston." He went over to Joseph's parents, who looked uncertain.

Mrs. Alston sent Maria a glance of supplication for guidance, but Aaron did not allow her to wait for the answer. He riveted her with his eye, showing his beautiful teeth in a smile so compelling that the poor lady fluttered and at last timidly smiled back.

"How well you look, ma'am. I declare you look as young as your daughter, Charlotte." Here he favored that young lady with a serious admiring glance that had in it just enough boldness to make it exciting. "And I perceive that Miss Charlotte has grown into a most fascinating young lady since I saw her last. Egad, I never saw such eyelashes," he finished in an audible aside to Colonel William.

Charlotte immediately dropped the eyelashes in pretty confusion, thinking that Theo's father might be monstrous wicked as they said, but there was something about him— and he was unmarried, too. This unrelated thought startled her into a genuine blush.

"I have heard much about your unparalleled horse, Gallatin, Colonel. Even up North his successes on the turf are well known. How is his wind holding? Will he be able to take the handicap again, think you?"

Colonel William thawed with a rush at the mention of the magic name. And Theo, who knew Aaron had never heard of the horse until a few minutes ago when she primed him, stifled an impulse to hysterical laughter. How wondrous clever he was! He knew precisely the right note to strike with each one, precisely how gross to make his flattery, depending on the recipient.

He did not allow them a minute to get the upper hand, but mowed them down one by one with a blend of condescension and graciousness. He did not often choose to dominate a group, preferring to listen and profit from a less conspicuous position. But when he exerted himself, he could gather up any amount of different personalities and combine them into one harmonious chord, with himself as the keynote.

The Alstons were no match for him. He won Mrs. Young's heart at once by telling her that Theodosia had written him of little Eliza, saying that she was the prettiest of children.

With William Algernon he talked of Thomas's latest volume of sermons, and it developed that that serious young gentleman had not been able to procure the book.

"I shall send you it from Washington," promised Aaron. "It shall be my pleasure."

William Algernon was startled to find himself beaming and profusely grateful.

Until only Maria was left, rigidly disapproving, her thin face soured with disdain. Aaron let her be for the present and turned to his daughter.

"Theo, my dear, I am most desirous of leading Mrs. Young out to dance if she will be so good as to honor me. Can you get your niggers to play a reel? They do it better than anyone, I believe. At least Mr. Jefferson always says so."

"What!" Maria flounced around. "Surely the President does not listen to nigger music."

"Most assuredly he does, Lady Nisbett; he vastly admires it," said Aaron, which was true enough, but, knowing the lady's temperament, he added, "and both the Marquis de Lafayette and the Duc de la Rochefoucauld, when they were here, professed great interest in it"—which he had made up on the spot.

Maria continued to look incredulous and murmured that nothing—absolutely nothing—should induce her to dance to that heathen din. Still, she did condescend to look on while some of her relatives danced. The musicians cheered up and what they lacked in melody they made up for in rhythm.

So Theo's evening was, after all, redeemed from utter failure, and when the guests left, they took leave of Aaron quite cordially. Colonel William, indeed, even urged him to come to Clifton, so that he might see Gallatin for himself and judge of his wind.

"Stay as long as you can, my dear sir; you are always welcome at Clifton." He had quite forgotten Aaron's disgrace until, in the coach going home, Maria reminded him of it with acrid emphasis.

As the front door of the Oaks swung to behind the last guest, the three inside stood together in the moss-hung rooms. Theo looked up at her husband ruefully. "You see, Joseph, it was for Father that I wanted Ishmael and the barge, but I dared not tell you. Will you forgive me?"

Aaron laughed. "She's a minx, but I think you must forgive her. See how pretty she looks tonight."

She stood between them, small and delicate in her embroidered rose dress, an enchanting expression of mingled naughtiness and contrition on her flushed face. The men's eyes met, for once drawn into accord. Joseph's heavy face lightened.

"You're right, sir," he said. "I suppose I must forgive her."

Theodosia, laughing a little, dropped them both a curtsy.

Chapter Twenty-one

AARON could stay with them but a few days, it seemed. Then he wished to go to Statesburgh and greet Natalie before returning to Washington. In the Federal District his office protected him. No matter what charges lay against him, he was still Vice-President with duties to perform until March.

"Then what will you do?" asked Theo fearfully. She had been dreading to bring the question up ever since he came. Where would he go, and what could he do, when his term expired and the ten thousand a year with it? New York and New Jersey were alike closed to him.

"There are many things I could do," said Aaron. "After all, I am a not incapable lawyer." He had, in fact, never lost a major case. "I might hang out my sign in Philadelphia or Richmond. But I shall not. I have far more important things in mind."

Theo looked up in surprise at an unusual seriousness in his voice.

They were sitting on the wide front porch at the Oaks. Gampy played on the lawn below them, singing a vague little song to himself and dragging a wagon full of treasured stones from a pile on the driveway to another pile beneath the largest live-oak. It was late afternoon, and the slanting sun filtered through moss onto his curls until they sparkled with flame.

Joseph had ridden off to consult his overseer. It was quiet except for the warbling of a mocking-bird. The air smelled of burning stubble from the rice fields, and the smoky fragrance made Theo think of October at home. But there leaves were burned, and the air would be fresh and crisp. Here, as usual, it was hot. The one frost had not yet been repeated.

She waited for Aaron to continue. Instead he lit himself a

cigar, one of Joseph's finest that had been shipped direct from the Havana, inhaled it with sensuous pleasure, and leaning back in his chair said: "I suppose if I were truly master of myself, I should forswear tobocco. I confess it gives me keen delight. You should smoke, too, Theo. It would calm your nerves, promote tranquillity. You might try a little pipe, such as the nigger beldames use."

"Oh, Father," she laughed, "that would indeed be the final straw for the Alstons. I believe they would pitch me off the Waccamaw Neck into the ocean."

"I think the time is coming, my dear, when you may be quit of all the Alstons—except Joseph, of course—and they will then come groveling on their knees to claim relationship to you. Even if you smoke a pipe, or paint your teeth red, or wear a parakeet for a hat."

"What do you mean?" she asked, puzzled by his manner, for his usual bantering smile was absent.

"Mexico," he said thoughtfully; "and perhaps Louisiana; maybe even Kentucky and Tennessee. Who can tell? But certainly Mexico."

She sat up straight, staring at him, uncertain whether to laugh or not. "Father, what *are* you talking about? I don't understand a word."

He turned to face her, and now he smiled, though his eyes were still serious.

"I intend, my dearest Theo, to found an empire."

She sank back again, smiling. "Ah, yes. That is a charming dream. You will have two subjects, anyway, Gampy and I."

"You speak truer than you know, but you won't be subjects. You shall be the Princess Royal and Gampy, my heir. There will be millions of other subjects. I'm quite serious, Theo."

She gazed at him in growing alarm. Those hundreds of miles in an open canoe under the beating sun, might they not have a delayed effect? Or the fever? Sometimes the first symptom was wild talk.

He read her mind as he so often did, and his mouth quirked. "No, I'm not sickening from anything. I am, in fact, in rude health." He touched her hand with his long fingers. "See? I'm quite cool. As cool as one can be in your infernal climate down here."

He drew his chair close to hers. "Listen, my dear. I will make it as simple as possible. I know how your lazy little brain hates to work."

He paused and looked deliberately around to assure himself that there was no one within hearing and, satisfied, went on with quick earnestness.

"Spain is on the brink of war with us. It may break out at any time. That will be the best opportunity. But even if it does not, I shall go ahead anyway, as soon as my plans are ready."

"Plans for what?" she said slowly. "I don't understand you."

"To conquer Mexico," he answered, as blandly as though he was saying, "To take a cup of tea."

She gazed at him appalled; then she thought she understood. "You mean that the Government will send you at the head of expeditionary forces, that you will try to seize Mexico for the United States?"

"I mean nothing of the sort. The United States has more than enough land already. I mean to conquer Mexico for us, you and me—and Gampy."

"But that's fantastic, impossible!" she cried. Her heart beat fast, and again she felt fear.

"It is neither," he said calmly. "Already I have negotiated with England through Anthony Merry; they will give us ships. And I have also negotiated with Spain through Casa Yrujo. Spain naturally knows nothing of my interest in Mexico; they are enticed by the thought of regaining their lost Louisiana. Spain's enmity can be used to advantage."

Spain, England, Mexico. Concepts so tremendous as to be overwhelming, and yet he tossed them at her on that quiet porch with the casual deftness of a juggler pitching colored balls.

He watched her struggling to hide her dismay and smiled. "You will accustom yourself to the idea. There will be plenty of time. I must proceed slowly and with utmost caution. I can do nothing but pave the way until my term expires. Then I shall set out at once on a preliminary survey. I plan to journey through the Western States and down the Mississippi to New Orleans, testing the temper of the country. New Orleans will, I think, provide the natural base for my operations: particularly as Wilkinson will be Governor of the Louisiana Territory. He and I understand each other very well. He is a reasonable man."

"General Wilkinson!" she repeated, still more amazed. "He will be a party to this project?" She remembered the Commander-in-Chief of the United States Army as a pompous, arrogant man, much concerned with his own importance.

"Precisely," said Aaron; "and already I have found many

to view the project with enthusiasm, though I confess I do not outline to each one my ultimate goal as frankly as I do to you. One must use different nets for different fish. I need hardly add that I am trusting to your discretion as I do my own. You must never put a hint of this on paper. I shall give you a cipher which you may use on occasion, and we will refer to the whole matter as 'X.' "

"But I still don't understand it! How is it possible to found an empire in Mexico? You have no troops, no money. I know that I don't understand these things; I know nothing of statesmanship, or—or intrigue, but I cannot see——"

"You don't have to, my dear. You must trust me, for I do see very clearly. Troops and money will come. The Mexicans are ripe for revolution; oppressed by Spain, they will welcome a liberator. All they need is the certainty of succor and a leader. These I will provide."

His quiet, confident voice impressed her. He was capable of anything—anything. She had always known that. If he had at last found the proper theater for his genius, why should she niggle at him with her foolish fears and misgivings? And yet——

"Father"—she hesitated, searching for words. "These things you say—this plan staggers my comprehension, but if, as you tell me, it is possible, if it should come to pass, would it not be—treason?"

She waited unhappily for his answer, fearful that he might be angry and yet impelled by a half-forgotten memory: "All these lands will be part of America. We shall stretch from one ocean to the other, a mighty nation, unified, of one tongue. Does this mean nothing to you?" It had meant nothing then, submerged as she had been by her despairing love. But now she remembered the quiet thrill in Merne's voice.

"My dear," said Aaron, shrugging impatiently, "I cannot undertake to say what our fair Republic may consider treason; that is an elastic word. I've told you a dozen times that they have title to far more land than can be administered. That has been one of Jefferson's many grievous errors. In any case, I speak not only of the Western States, I speak of Mexico——"

He rose suddenly and, encircling her chin with his hand, raised her head so that he might look into her troubled eyes. "Where is that faith in me and my destiny which you have so often proclaimed?"

His nostrils dilated, his whole person seemed to expand. His gaze grew incandescent, exerting on her a hypnotic power.

"Look, Theodosia!" He turned her head and pointed through the drawing-room window. On a table before the window stood a small plaster bust of Bonaparte. "He is to be crowned Emperor in a few weeks," said Aaron softly. "Do you dare to doubt that I am at least equal to that little Corsican peasant?"

He waited, watching, holding her thus, until he saw in her transparent face that all other emotions had been subdued, leaving only an awed conviction. He was profoundly sincere, and yet as always a portion of him held aloof, savoring the dramatic perfection of this moment. Here on this remote plantation porch he had created for her a vision, as he had for many others, the shimmering gold seduction of a crown.

"We, too, shall be royal, my Theo," he added, very low. "Now you believe, don't you?"

"I believe that you can do anything," she whispered— "anything."

His hand dropped. He turned abruptly from her, began to pace the porch as though to ease his body of its fierce energy.

"You must help," he said presently.

"Yes, of course. How can I?"

"Joseph. The plan must be carefully presented to him. He will be part of it."

Her heart sank. Dazzled as she was by her faith, she was not so blinded as to think Joseph would be convinced.

"He loves you," said Aaron. "Sooner or later he will do as you wish."

A thought struck him, and he frowned. "Though since I have been here, I've been troubled. I have fancied that there was a cloud between you. You do not seem in complete sympathy. And I notice that you no longer share a bedroom. I trust this has no special significance."

Hot color flooded up into her hair. "I have not always felt very well of late, as you know, and I—I——"

"Ah, then it was not his idea," said Aaron, relieved. "I feared that he had perhaps heard something of your—your interest in Captain Lewis."

She gasped, shrinking back against the chair. "I don't know what you mean."

"My dear child, you need not play the ostrich with me. I'm not so stupid as you seem to think. There was unfortunately some gossip in Washington after you left. Nothing important, and I do not accuse you of infidelity, so you needn't look as though I were throwing stones at you. I simply

236

wondered whether Joseph had conceived any inconvenient ideas."

She sat very still. A hot current of pain ran through her. Aaron's knowledge, partial though it was, his cynical acceptance, the mention of gossip: these were ugly things: desecration. And yet, after all, no outside thing could really penetrate the shrine. That was a room in her heart to which no one but Merne had the key: not even Aaron.

"Joseph knows nothing," she said at last quietly. "And it was over a year ago."

A year without word. During it she had seldom dared to think of Merne. Only sometimes in the twilight or that hazy hour between sleeping and waking she saw his face.

"Naturally it has been a year," said Aaron sharply, "since Lewis left last July for the West."

"Is there—have you heard any news?"

In spite of herself her voice betrayed her, and Aaron was annoyed. "Only that the expedition left St. Louis last spring and was at once swallowed up into the wilderness."

No doubt he's dead, thought Aaron with satisfaction. The subject displeased him excessively. She had twice, under the influence of this lanky captain, both startled and disappointed him. It should never happen again. He would see to it that there was no further meeting—ever, if by some unlucky chance neither the Indians nor the wild beasts nor the manifold dangers of such a journey did not neatly dispose of the problem.

In the meantime he exerted his usual skill at forgetting the unpleasant and effaced the matter from his mind. There were topics of vital importance to be discussed.

Gampy, just then tiring of his game, raced up on the porch and clambered on his grandfather's lap. "See watch," he demanded, tugging at the gold repeater in Aaron's pocket. "See tick-tick." Aaron presented it to him, and laughed as the child held it to his ear with an expression of infantile rapture. "Pretty watch, nice big gold watch," he crooned.

Aaron twisted the soft curls and pinched the plump little cheek. "I'm glad to see that he speaks plainly. Have you taught him to read yet?"

Theo started. For once she found it hard to follow her father's mercurial changes of mood. He played now with the child, joggling him up and down, poking a teasing finger into the delighted Gampy's ribs, as though the child's amusement were the only consideration in the world.

"Well, can he read?" repeated Aaron. "And I trust you

and Eleanore are teaching him French."

"Oh, Father! He is only two," she protested.

Aaron stilled the child's laughter with a smiling headshake. "That's enough now, sir. You will play something quieter. We'll go down on the lawn and I'll build you a castle with your stones.—He is none too young to be learning the proper habits of study and application," he added to Theo. "He is a precocious child and will do us great credit if you are not too lazy to teach him."

"Castle, castle, castle!" shrieked Gampy, tugging at Aaron's hand. "Make castle for Gampy."

Aaron smiled and lifted the child high in his arms. "I shall make a castle for Gampy," he said, with emphasis; "not this little play one down here, but a shining palace big enough for Gampy to live in."

"And Mama, too?" said the child, interested.

"And Mama, too. And Father and I. But you must be a good boy and learn your letters. More than that, my little Gampy, you must learn how to be a prince."

"Prince," repeated the child, obediently, wriggling.

"It means nothing to him now," said Aaron to Theo, "and even you, child that you are, cannot yet comprehend the future that is in store for you. But you will. For destiny," he added softly, "can be carved into whatsoever shape we wish if the tool be whetted by indomitable purpose."

He left her then, allowing the delighted child to lead him down on the lawn. She watched them together, seeing the tender understanding with which he entered into the little boy's world and Gampy's adoring response.

Yes, she thought, he's right. He is always right. What dearer destiny can there be for me or Gampy than to follow where he leads? He is already so far above other men that how can I doubt that the outer world must at last recognize it?

Her course became clear. All other relationships faded or changed. Even with Merne there had been questions, uncertainty. But her love for Aaron permitted no question. It simply existed, as much a part of her as her hands. Life could give her no more precious gift than the happiness of being his daughter.

Chapter Twenty-two

❦ ❦ ❦

AFTER all, it took only two days to win Joseph over to the cause: two days of Aaron's restrained eloquence that hinted at far more than it told. But he was, as he had expected to be, immeasurably helped by Theodosia, who, secure in the knowledge of her husband's character, expatiated on the magnificence of their certain elevation.

He was to be Prince Consort and command wealth that staggered the imagination. The fabulous mines of Mexico would be theirs; rivers of jeweled gold were to be poured out to them by the grateful people. What were the paltry thousands which he wrested from the rice fields compared to this?

And when at first Joseph, sullen and shaking his bewildered head, remained obdurate, Theo wept: wept sincerely from disappointment and frustration, because the plan had now become hers too; she believed in it with every fiber of her body, and it was inconceivable that her husband should be so dense, so pedestrian.

Gradually he allowed himself to be impressed by the distinguished names tossed him by Aaron, names which Aaron truthfully assured him had promised backing.

"For war with Spain is inevitable," said Aaron, "and the instant it breaks out, we must be ready."

"There may be some truth in what you say," Joseph admitted grudgingly.

Theo and her father permitted themselves one quick mutual glance of satisfaction.

When Aaron departed, he carried with him Joseph's assurance that he would produce fifty thousand dollars whenever it might be needed.

Aaron went from the Oaks to Statesburgh and visited Natalie. He sounded out her husband, but, on finding the atmosphere unsympathetic, abandoned the subject so deftly that Thomas Sumter was unaware that he had been approached.

Then Aaron returned to Washington, where his high office protected his person from arrest, as it did in all States except New York and New Jersey. In these the murder charges still held. He finished out his term with a kind of dignified flourish that confounded his enemies. He presided over the trial for impeachment of one Judge Chase and did so, said a more sympathetic newspaper, "with the dignity and impartiality of an angel, but with the rigor of a devil."

The day after the conclusion of this trial, he took formal leave of the Senate and made a speech so moving, so skillfully compounded of pathos and courage that many of the senators were moved to tears.

Public opinion was softening; there were now many to think that he had been unjustly used. He might have settled in any State below the Delaware, but he had no longer the slightest interest in the East. During his forced journey to the South, Richmond Hill had been seized by his creditors and sold to John Jacob Astor for twenty-five thousand dollars. This sum did not begin to liquidate Aaron's obligations, so that the debtor's prison awaited him in New York as well as the murder charge. The West, however, beckoned—the West and the dream of empire.

Aaron set forth on his trip across the Alleghenies, then down the Ohio and the Mississippi to New Orleans. As he traveled, his enthusiasm increased. The country was ripe for "X"—the sublime glittering project. In every town and hamlet, in the lonely settlers' cabins, he found new adherents. He wrote to Theo constantly, using their private cipher, and she, relegated to the eternal feminine rôle of marking time and waiting for news, rejoiced at each report.

How trivial now seemed her past concern with the Alstons! What matter now their approval or disapproval! Buoyed by the certainty that she would soon be quit of them and deprived of her northern trip by Aaron's absence, she managed to find some pleasure in the planter's unchanging schedule. In the spring and fall one stayed on the plantation; summer—Debordieu Island. In the winter—Charleston for the prescribed round of festivity, the Saint Cecilia Musicals in January, soirées at the home of the Pinckneys or Rutledges, return hospitality at her own house on Church Street. February brought Race Week and the climax of Charleston excitement. The planters gathered from all over the Carolinas

240

to enter horses, to lay bets, and to cheer wildly at the success of their favorites. Theo sat in the Alston box near Colonel William, who during this period was reduced to a pulp of quivering nerves. He oscillated between the paddock and the grandstand, alternately wringing his hands and cursing the jockeys, or trembling with triumph and shouting encouragement. Theo continued unable to care very much about the outcome, but she managed to hide this and to show a creditable degree of the enthusiasm which was expected of her.

For the theater she did not have to feign enthusiasm. And though she privately thought both the productions and the actors far inferior to those in New York, she admired the graceful pseudo-Greek building on New Street with its white-and-silver interior, which set off the ladies' gowns to such advantage. Here she laughed or thrilled with the others to the drama of *Gustavus Vassa, The Mountaineers,* and *Blue Beard or Feminine Curiosity,* forgetting for a little while even the delicious consciousness of "X."

She and Joseph did not often discuss the project. There was little that she knew tangibly to discuss, and he was often absent from her in Columbia, where the House had appointed him its Speaker. It made her happy, however, to know that she might mention it to him. It would have been a weighty secret to carry alone, and the knowledge brought them closer together.

Sooner or later she knew that Aaron would summon her to a more active part in the project, and she waited with what patience she could, devouring his letters and training Gampy for his exalted rôle to the best of her abilities, in view of her son's extremely tender years.

She unearthed an exiled Spaniard in Charleston and began Spanish lessons with him, for the French and smattering of German and Italian which she already possessed would be of scant use in Mexico.

The call came at last, in the spring of 1806. "This time I wish you to accompany me on my trip to the West," Aaron wrote her, "and come alone for the present. Joseph and Gampy may follow later, if all goes as I expect. Prepare yourself to endure some hardships, and I want no mournful complaints about them. You will be surfeited with luxury in time."

She joined Aaron in Philadelphia, having left the Waccamaw with a heart fast beating with hope. Perhaps she need never see it again. Somewhere in the West a new home must be waiting, prelude to the magnificent one she would eventually inhabit. This hope lightened her parting from the baby; he would be well tended by Eleanore; and "It won't be for long, darling," she assured the solemn child. "Your papa shall bring you to me soon."

Eleanore came into the room on this sentence and exclaimed: "Nom de Dieu, Madame, what do you mean by that? You are not going to drag le petit across those horrible mountains! The savages will massacre him and me too. I do not go.'"

"Oh, yes, you will, my good Eleanore," said Theo, laughing. "You would not let Gampy move one foot without you, I know. You don't realize what is waiting for us all out there: a golden future. Ah, I can't tell you, but you must trust me."

"Pfoui!" snorted Eleanore rudely. "There is no future out there, nozzing but log cabins and savages and wolves."

Theo hugged her and laughed again. "You will see."

Aaron had warned her of hardships, and she was cheerfully prepared to accept them. But in his company the journey did not seem unduly rigorous. True, there were many days on horseback, and he traveled fast; still, at the end of them he always contrived to find remarkably comfortable lodgings at houses he had visited the year before. And at Pittsburgh a commodious flatboat awaited them. It was more like a floating ark than anything else, containing as it did four rooms, glass windows, and a fireplace.

When Theo expressed her surprise and delight, her father laughed. "Wait until you see Blennerhassett's Island; that will really amaze you."

While they floated down the Ohio, he told her something of the eccentric and wealthy Irishman who had built for himself a palace in the wilderness. Harman Blennerhassett and his wife were won over heart and soul to the cause, "As indeed is the whole West," added Aaron with satisfaction. General Wilkinson had promised to provide troops, General Andrew Jackson in Nashville was sympathetic, Jonathan Dayton and Daniel Clark were loyal supporters; and in New Orleans, gateway to Mexico, Aaron had piled triumph on triumph, winning over not only the French and Spanish elements, but the Catholic Church as well.

He had not, of course, presented exactly the same aims to each different group. There were many facets to the project: the colonization of the Bastrop lands on the Washita River suited some, the most timid; the disaffection and union of the Western Territory suited others; while only a very few had the vision and discretion to be trusted with knowledge of the ultimate goal, the liberation of Mexico from Spanish rule.

The Blennerhassetts were amongst the elect.

A thousand miles from civilization, sixteen miles from Marietta—still a rude frontier village—this enterprising Irishman had metamorphosed his hundred-and-forty-acre island into an elaborate estate that was part pleasure garden, part imitation of an English manor house, and part pure fantasy.

The virgin forest had been hewn and clipped into tortured figures. There were circles and mazes and arbors. There were artificial pools and several unsuccessful fountains where Blennerhassett's knowledge of physics had not been quite equal to his ambition. He had imported grass seed and fruit trees from England, and around an incredible expanse of lawn, peach, apricot, and pear trees stood as background to a formal garden.

In the center of the island he had built himself a twenty-two-room mansion which was actually three houses connected by covered porticoes. It was furnished, as Theo later discovered, with a luxurious abandon which far eclipsed Richmond Hill in its heyday. This creation had cost him sixty thousand dollars, not counting the purchase of the army of slaves whose unremitting labor had made his dream concrete.

As the Burr houseboat tied up to a wooden dock at the Ohio River island, Theo was even more amazed than Aaron had prophesied. The dock had been carved and painted into the semblance of a huge recumbent lion. And behind this monstrosity, upon a species of white-graveled plaza, there milled a horde of waving, cheering blacks. When Theo and Aaron descended the gangplank to a strip of red carpeting which had been laid across the lion and stretched into the distance toward the house, the blacks raised their right arms in a salute, then with obviously rehearsed precision pelted the arrivals with roses and daisies.

Two odd male and female figures detached themselves from the crowd. They came forward, bowing. Theo felt her hand seized and respectfully kissed. The lady before her executed a sweeping curtsy.

"Welcome, ma'am," said Mrs. Blennerhassett, adding in a piercing whisper, "We welcome our sovereigns in expectancy."

Dazed and battling a desire to laugh, Theo threw Aaron a quick look. His eyes were twinkling, but there was also in them a gratified gleam. She heard Harman Blennerhassett address him as "Sire" and saw Aaron bow response in a manner even more than usually courtly.

Her father took her arm and they progressed together up the carpeted strip, while Theo mustered all the imperial dignity which she could find at short notice.

"Let them play-act if it gives them pleasure," said Aaron in her ear. "It will be in sober earnest before long."

"I'll do my best," she whispered. "But my breath is taken away by all this. I fear I have not yet acquired the regal manner. What position will they hold in our—our empire?"

"He shall have a dukedom, and I have promised to make him Minister to the Court of Saint James's. He wants that above all else, as what Irishman wouldn't!"

She smiled, but checked it at once. Incredible and fantastic as all this might seem, it was none the less real. Had Josephine too smiled when her little corporal first said to her, "Some day I shall be Emperor of France, my brother King of Holland, another, King of Westphalia?" For them, too, there must have been a shadowy beginning, when the vision alone sustained them, the vision and Bonaparte's unswerving belief in his destiny. And here was more than dreams, the tangible result of the forces which Aaron was molding to his ambition.

She trembled in sudden excitement.

The excitement sharpened during the weeks which they spent upon the island. Aaron came and went gaining supporters up and down the rivers. On his frequent returns he brought with him new converts and these were a mixed crew —uncouth backwoodsmen, buckskinned scouts, plantation owners from as far south as New Orleans, Frenchmen, Spaniards, even soldiers in the white-and-blue United States Army uniform. Once General Wilkinson himself came, pompous and long-winded, with sly little eyes. And him Theo could not like, though she bestowed on him a careful courtesy, knowing that he was closest of all to Aaron and vitally necessary to the cause.

She grew fond of the Blennerhassetts. How could she help but be fond of people who treated her father with worshiping awe and extended to her the heady flattery of subject to queen!

She no longer was amused by their peculiar methods of dress. They both clung to the mode fashionable in Ireland when they had left it twelve years back. Mrs. Blennerhassett, with her brocaded panniers and sweeping hats loaded with ostrich plumes, was only slightly less bizarre than her husband, who wore red smallclothes and a white peruke constantly askew above his shortsighted eyes while he peered and puttered about his domain.

Perhaps it was just as well that Blennerhassett could not distinguish a horse from a man at twenty paces, for his fair lady sometimes cast upon Aaron glances whose warmth was not entirely attributable to her reverence for royalty. And Theodosia one evening was startled, upon walking unexpectedly into the library, to come upon a tender scene.

Aaron sat upon a sofa, and from the quick stir and mantling confusion upon Mrs. Blennerhassett's buxom face Theo was forced to suspect that until her entrance the lady had been nestling exceeding close. Aaron, perfectly composed, favored his daughter with the faintest quick droop of the right eyelid. Theo fled, murmuring apology.

Later, when she and Aaron were alone, he referred to the matter at once. "Perhaps, my dear girl, it would be as well if you knocked before precipitating yourself through closed doors, don't you think?"

"I'm sorry," she stammered. "But I had no idea—and Father, really——"

She was so accustomed to his charm for women that she never thought about it. She knew vaguely that he often indulged in amatory adventures, though he seldom allowed any of these to intrude on her notice. An affair with their hostess, however, under the circumstances seemed a bit dismaying.

Aaron laughed. "Don't be prudish, my dear, and pray do me the honor to believe that I know what I am about. If a few kisses can please the ladies and bind their loyalty to our cause, I see no reason to deny them. There is, to put it vulgarly, more than one way of killing the cat."

He looked at her with such a blend of affection and puckish humor that she ended by laughing with him; and then forgot the matter. In any event she made no more embarrassing discoveries.

The days slipped pleasantly by. Theo ignored peremptory letters from Joseph, demanding to know what she was doing and when she would return. She missed the baby, missed him achingly, but she knew that he was safe with Eleanore, and surely it would not be long now before she could send for him.

The tension and bustle on the island, meantime, increased to fever point. Fifteen large batteaux were being built. Mrs. Blennerhassett, aided by Theo, directed the purchase and temporary storage of vast quantities of flour and pork and meal. Kilns were built for the drying of corn. The island resounded with the din of preparation.

Down at Natchez boats were building, too. At a given signal, when the flotillas should be ready, they would converge—the glorious offensive would begin by water, while General Wilkinson would start the land march at the head of his troops.

"When will it be, Father?" asked Theo, seizing upon a rare opportunity for private conversation.

"The instant we declare war on Spain, or she on us."

"Are you certain that there will be war?" How could he be so calm, so contained?

"I am quite certain, my anxious one," he answered, smiling.

"But if there shouldn't be?"

Aaron shrugged. "If there shouldn't be, then we shall have to proceed more slowly; we shall then commence from my lands on the Washita. I have many strings to my bow." He patted her hand gently. "Come, Theo, patience, my child. An empire can unfortunately not be built in a day."

She subsided, reassured.

But Aaron was not so well satisfied as he sounded. The war with Spain was unaccountably delayed, and Sam Swartwout, his loyal young friend, had written him in cipher that there had of late been disquieting mention in the eastern newspapers, dark hints of a conspiracy in the West, a treasonable plot led by "an erstwhile high executive of this country who has fallen into disgrace." This premature leakage was unfortunate. Speed and surprise were essential to success now. He redoubled his energies.

And yet there were unavoidable disappointments. In October the war had not started; the preparations were not finished; there was still much left to do.

Theodosia awoke one morning to look through the red damask curtains of her bedroom and see a rowboat approach the Blennerhassett dock. In the bow sat a familiar stocky figure whose stubborn black hair and air of affronted belligerence were visible even at that distance. Theo gasped, leaning far out the window, hoping that her eyes had deceived her and yet ashamed of the hope. There was no doubt about it. She flung on her clothes and rushed out of the house to greet him.

"Joseph!" she called. "I'm so surprised and so delighted!" She put unusual warmth into her greeting, guiltily conscious that, though she was certainly surprised, her delight was tepid.

He gave her a brief kiss. "I've come to take you home," he said, frowning. "You pay no attention to my letters. I had never permitted you to go had I realized the situation."

"But you don't realize the situation; everything is under way," she began impulsively, then stopped. There was no use talking to Joseph when he wore that black mulish look.

"Come and have some breakfast," she said pacifically. "You must have had a hard trip."

A terrifying thought struck her. "Gampy's all right, isn't he? That isn't why you came, is it? He wasn't ill?"

"No, he wasn't ill. He's been on Debordieu with Eleanore. But he's fretting for you. You must come back at once. I'll have no more of this idiotic business."

"We'll talk about it presently, dear. Look around you. Did you ever see such a heavenly place?"

"Heavenly!" snorted Joseph. "Nigger's idea of heaven, maybe, ridiculous ostentation out here a thousand miles from anywhere, gimcracks, gewgaws, monstrous. I hear the man's crazy."

Theo sighed. Joseph was going to be difficult, was apparently firmly entrenched in the typical Alston refusal to be impressed with anything that was not Carolinian.

The Blennerhassetts welcomed the Prince Consort with their usual warm-hearted Irish verve. Their cordiality, however, sagged under the chill of Joseph's heavy silences. He was ill at ease, uncertain whether he was in truth seeing the inception of a mighty coup d'état, or whether he was being humbugged. He also had heard ugly rumors in the East, and they had made him very uncomfortable. Whatever the outcome, this was no place for Theodosia. The fever period in Carolina had passed. She must return with him to her rightful home.

For once she could not budge him. When Father talks to him, it will be all right, she thought.

But Aaron cruelly disappointed her. "I'm afraid you must go, my dear, though you know how much I hate to part with you. Matters are not yet matured. It would be unwise to bring Gampy until we have a settled place in which to receive him, and he needs you. You had better go back for a little while."

Her eyes filled with tears. "I thought I should never have to go back. I hate it there, and it is so far from you. I shall never know what is happening——"

"No tears, no nerves, no self-indulgence, my darling. You know I hate them," said Aaron, with brisk tenderness. "I

247

will keep you apprised of our movements, using the same cipher we have used before. Burn the letters as soon as you read them and hold yourself in readiness to join me instantly —with Gampy."

"I will," she whispered. "Oh, I will."

Mrs. Blennerhassett was loath to part with her. During Theo's last day on the island she could scarcely let her out of her sight. "I never knew that I could dote on a female as I do on you, Theo," said the good lady, for she had temporarily dropped her reverence for her "sovereign in expectancy" and felt for Theo a genuine affection. "We shall meet soon again, though, in Mexico," she added, her eyes beaming. "Sure, and we must drink to that." She clapped her hands and ordered a bottle of Madeira brought up.

She poured them each a glass, and Theo, half-laughing, half-sighing, allowed her hostess to clink it solemnly against hers.

"To Mexico," said Theo.

"To the fairest and sweetest Princess that will ever adorn a throne," said Mrs. Blennerhassett. Alas, that she should be fettered to such an ill-mannered boor as Alston! she thought, but this she could not say.

So, much against her inclination, but in obedience to her father's wishes, Theodosia left Blennerhassett Island and returned to the Waccamaw.

Chapter Twenty-three

THEODOSIA returned to the Oaks, but her spirit remained with Aaron. She refused to leave her plantation, fearful lest his letters might be delayed in getting to her, even by a single day. Her sleeping and her waking alike merged into a long feverish anxiety. What was he doing now? Had they started? What did the ever-mounting crop of rumors amount to? Was it true that he had been tried and acquitted in the Mississippi Territory? Was it true that General Wilkinson had suddenly turned traitor to the cause and denounced him? Or were these but the usual newspaper lies and speculations, influenced by politics and unworthy of notice?

She had received only two brief cipher letters from him, saying that all was well, and that no matter what she heard she must not be upset; for matters were progressing to his utmost satisfaction.

These calmed her for the time, but now in March it had been weeks since she had heard from him. Every day she sent the flatboat to Georgetown to await possible news there. And there was no news: even the newspapers were silent.

She had moods of wild hope. Everything must be going well. Silence was the best indication of it. The flotilla had started down the river; the Spaniards had ceded the west bank without a murmur; he was already triumphantly in possession of New Orleans. Perhaps they had crossed the Sabine on their way into Mexico. The news would be delayed, of course; Aaron would himself restrict it. He would have the power to do so. Power! Her heart swelled with exultation. She saw him already crowned, surrounded by a cheering people. "Long live the Emperor, Aaron the First!"

"It is so. It must be so," she whispered to herself a dozen times a day. But these moments of delicious optimism alternated with foreboding and despair. She grew thin and pale. Sleep eluded her.

Joseph spent most of his time in Columbia, acting, she thought angrily, as though his tuppenny-ha'penny office in the state legislature were of paramount importance. When he did return to the Oaks, he refused to discuss "X." The whole matter worried him exceedingly.

In April, her long uncertainty was ended. She was sitting on the porch in the warm afternoon sunshine with Gampy at her knee. The sturdy five-year-old was reading aloud to her, his small face puckered with concentration, his fresh little voice hardly stumbling over the long words. "The dog is an es-estimable animal, and by reason of his fidelity merits our admir-admiration."

"That's very good, darling," she said, smoothing his tumbled hair, which was no longer golden red, but a rich dark auburn like her own.

"Will Gamp be pleased with me when he hears me read so well?" asked the child. Under her guidance he had come to direct every effort toward the approval of the faraway grandfather whom he still remembered and loved.

"Of course he will," she answered, smiling. Oh, why don't I hear from him? The constant question tortured her.

Unconsciously she turned from Gampy, stared unseeing down the avenue of moss-draped live-oaks, trying by force of will to pierce through the barrier of space.

Suddenly she heard the gallop of hoofs and saw the headlong approach of a horse and rider. For one ecstatic, unreasonable moment her heart leapt with relief.

But it wasn't Aaron, of course. It was Joseph, returning from a trip to Georgetown. She had scarcely time to feel surprise at the fury with which he threw himself from his horse, yelling with even greater than normal impatience for a stable-boy to take the reins. He stamped up the steps, thrusting a newspaper at her. "Read that!"

She stared at him stupidly. His swarthy face was purple. His whole stocky body was trembling. Gampy gave a little cry and shrank into her skirts, hiding his face from his father's scowl.

"Read it, can't you?" shouted Joseph, directing a shaking finger at the paper in her hand.

She raised the newspaper, the *Richmond Enquirer*, March 27th, 1807.

"What has a Richmond paper to do with me?" she whispered.

"Damnation, take it! Look here! Can't you read?" Through his angry rudeness she heard the note of fear.

She stared at the jiggling lines of print.

> Last night the traitor, Aaron Burr, arrived in Richmond to await trial. He was in the custody of Colonel Nicholas Perkins and his band of courageous men, who have conveyed him on the perilous journey northward from Alabama where he was apprehended. He will shortly be lodged in the county gaol. Many of his fellow conspirators are also being brought to Justice. It is to be hoped that none of these will be allowed to forego their just deserts.

She raised her eyes slowly. The white porch columns tipped together, veered round and round in slow, sickening lurches. Her fingers contracted on the newspaper, crumpling it convulsively.

"It isn't true! It's another one of their lies."

"It isn't true," he mimicked savagely. "Nothing is ever true for you, unless you wish it so, or your father either. He's caught, my lady, d'ye understand that? Caught and jailed and soon to be hanged. This time he can't wriggle out as he did before."

He raised his riding-crop and brought it down with a whistling snap onto the porch railing. Flecks of white paint exploded from the gash.

Gampy gave a cry of terror and began sobbing. Theo gently pushed him from her. "Run away, dear. Go quickly." As the child stumbled out, she turned on Joseph. "How dare you speak to me like that of my father! How dare you!"

"How dare I!" he bellowed. "How dare you try to involve me in his treasonable plots and harebrained schemes! Thank God, my judgment was never impaired by his foul machinations."

She gasped; her eyes grew enormous. "You *are* involved. You believed in the enterprise, heart and soul. You've given money to it. You went to Blennerhassett's Island and were part and parcel of the project there———"

His furious glare became opaque, his fists clenched, but he said, with a sudden deadly calm: "You are mistaken, Theodosia. I have never been interested in your father's ambitions. Nor have I ever been to Blennerhassett's Island."

Her head jerked up. For a second, stupefaction overpowered her. She thought vaguely that she could not have heard aright. "You have never been to the island?" she repeated blankly.

"I have not seen Colonel Burr since he came here, unbidden, and forced me to give him hospitality a year ago last October."

The crumpled ball of newspaper fell from her hand to the floor of the porch, where a vagrant breeze scudded it over the painted boards with a faint, scratching noise. She watched it until it disappeared over the edge of a step, then turned on Joseph a look of such concentrated contempt that it pierced his anger.

"I shall do my best not to interfere with your charming little fiction." She walked rapidly away from him.

He clutched her by the shoulder. "Wait, Theo. What are you going to do?"

She removed herself from his touch, not violently, but as though he had been some inanimate object, a branch or a curtain, which interfered with her progress.

"I am going to prepare myself to go to Richmond."

"You cannot. I forbid it. I will not have any of my family mixed up in this disgraceful affair."

"Nevertheless, I shall go. And you need not consider me as belonging to your family if you do not wish to. I would prefer not to see you again."

He recoiled. The bluster, the fury were sponged off his heavy face. His shoulders slumped. "Theo, don't. You know I love you. It's for your protection, too. Your father is disgraced, worse than that."

"My father is not disgraced," she answered inflexibly. "That he could never be. If he is in trouble, I wish to be with him. I suppose, in view of this account, that he is really in Richmond. But the rest I do not believe. I'm sure that he is not under arrest. He has done nothing to merit that. Even Jefferson's hostility could not go so far."

Joseph heard her with renewed rage. How could she be so stubbornly blind? Her insensate belief in her father infuriated him. He barely mastered an urge to strike her, shake the white, contemptuous remoteness from her small set person.

"You're a fool!" he shouted. "You credit nothing which does not come from your precious rogue of a father. Here, perhaps you will believe his own words."

He drew a tattered sheet of paper from his pocket. She saw the familiar small handwriting and snatched it from him. As she read, he watched her with angry satisfaction. He knew the scrawled hurried lines by heart.

I am under arrest, to leave here tomorrow for the North. We will pass through Carolina in a week. My guard numbers nine. A small force can effect my release. Chester will be the best place for this.

A

"I don't understand!" she cried. "How did this get here? It's directed to me. Why did I not receive it?"

He was silent. He did not regret having intercepted her letter, but he did regret that his anger had betrayed him into giving it to her now.

She saw his expression, and understood. "You kept it from me," she whispered. "We could have rescued him, as he says, and now it is too late."

He was frightened at the change in her. He had expected anger, a sharpening of the contempt with which she had been regarding him, but not this stony despair. She sank into a chair and fastened her gaze on a corner of the carved-wood arm. Then her head drooped.

"He must have thought I had deserted him. He must have hoped, and waited, scanning each face, looking for friends, for those who believe in him—and there was nothing. Oh, how could you do that to him—and to me?"

Joseph touched her bowed head with a clumsy hand. "Be reasonable, Theo. What could we do? The Government has arrested him. How could I effect his release?"

"Of course, you could have. You have authority in this State. A score of men could have done it. But you're a coward. You have no loyalty. You think of nothing but your own skin. I despise you." She spoke with a toneless lack of emphasis that stabbed him.

"You are unjust, Theo," he stammeded. "I'm—I'm——" He closed his lips with a gulp. He'd be damned if he'd try to justify himself. He'd acted as would any reasonable man. He turned on his heel and stamped into the house, venting his anger by administering to Cupid a lusty kick as that small black boy, who had been hovering in the hall, neglected to scamper to safety with requisite speed.

Theodosia stayed alone on the porch. She thought: Just here he sat with me, on that golden October afternoon when he first told me of it—of "X." She saw again his transfigured face, felt the glory and the majesty that he had made her feel. Still behind her, on the table in the drawing-room, stood the little bust of Napoleon. "Do you dare to think that I am not at least the equal of that little Corsican peasant?"

She shut her eyes and slow tears welled from under the lids. She shook her head impatiently. He hated tears. How dared she weep and despair! "This is only a temporary setback," she whispered to herself. "He will extricate himself. They cannot do anything to him. He has done no wrong." She repeated this over and over like an incantation.

When Eleanore later came out on the porch to tell her that le petit had had his supper and was calling for his mother, she found her mistress dry-eyed and calm, but she noted her pallor, traces of recent tears.

"Is there bad news, Madame?" she asked sympathetically.

Theo nodded slowly. "Yes, bad news, but it is temporary. It shall be surmounted."

The maid lingered, curious, offering, with the liberty of a valued servant, "Monsieur Alston seems in a bad temper; he is shouting and bellowing like a mad bull."

Theo shrugged, her lips parted in a faint, remote smile. "Mr. Alston's behavior is a matter of complete indifference to me."

Eleanore started. Mon Dieu, comme elle ressemble à son père! For in that moment she had seen Theo's gentle prettiness freeze into a brilliant hardness. The lift of her chin, the jeweled flash of her disdainful eyes, these were Colonel Burr.

"Monsieur Alston is, after all, no match for Madame," said Eleanore to herself, astonished. "Let him roar and hit about as he will." This was a new idea to her. She had accepted Theo as a docile wife and daughter, except, of course, for that affair in Washington. But that had been simply une petite indiscrétion now far in the past, and never repeated. Madame lived like a nun, nor ever seemed aware of any admiration she might arouse.

Joseph softened his stand before Theo left for Richmond. He clung as long as he could to his authority. In public he violently repudiated any knowledge of the conspiracy and endeavored to maintain this pose in private as well. Yet Theo's icy indifference reduced him to misery. She had made preparations to take the mail coach from Georgetown, but on the night before her departure, he entered her room, scowling.

"I will not have you go by public conveyance. It is not fitting for an Alston," he said roughly, as though it had been her idea. "Pompey will drive you in the cabriolet."

She was on her knees beside a small cowhide trunk that she was packing. "Thank you, Joseph," she said, with distant politeness.

He shifted his feet and cleared his throat. "It's possible that I may join you later up there if I can arrange my affairs."

She knew that this was for him a painful concession, and she had a faint impulse of pity. But she had not forgiven him.

"If you come as a supporter, if you come to help, I shall be pleased to see you." She turned back to the trunk.

He watched her small bent back unhappily for a moment. Her loosened hair swung in long curling strands across the blue of her dressing-gown, she looked young and fresh and tempting. A vein throbbed in his temple. Damn it, she was his wife! How dared she run counter to his wishes! Why shouldn't he seize her by the loose shining hair, force her, subdue her, beat her until she cried for mercy?

She looked up in some surprise when she heard him draw a rasping breath.

"Is there anything more you wished to say to me, Joseph?" Her great dark eyes were questioning, and cold as the winter ocean.

Turning savagely, he flung out of the room.

It was dusk when Theo arrived in Richmond. The air was heavy with thunder. Stifling July heat pressed down upon the town. It was hard to breathe; dust rose thick from the streets, and yet those streets were crowded with people and there seemed a holiday feeling abroad. Through tavern doors came laughter and snatches of song. So numerous were the roisterers at the Eagle Tavern that tables had been placed outside on the pavement, and around them sprawled groups of men, clinking tankards. Spilled beer dribbled into the gutters.

As Theo's carriage passed down Broad Street, the crowd became so dense that the horses could not go forward. Twenty feet ahead of them a group of young people danced back and forth across the cobblestones to the whistled tune of "Money Musk." On Theo's right in the Capitol Square she heard the sputter and whish of fireworks.

She pulled her hood down around her face and, leaning from the carriage window, spoke to a man in buckskin breeches who stood upon the curb tapping his foot in time to "Money Musk."

"Pardon me, sir. Is there some sort of celebration? Why

are there so many people in town?"

The man touched his coonskin cap and laughed. "Celebration enough, ma'am. We've come from all over Virginny to see the traitor hung."

The people nearest him caught up the words. "Hang the traitor!" shrilled a female voice. "Hang him! Hang him!" Like a diabolic chorus the sinister cries of the mob swirled around her.

She shrank into the depths of the carriage. Panic struck through her, and she shivered in spite of the heat. She huddled into her cloak.

Oh, little Burr's wanted for murder, and little Burr's wanted for treason—
And we'll string him high on the gallows tree, no matter what the reason.

A raucous voice started the couplet to a jigging tune, and at once it was bellowed from a dozen throats.

Panic ebbed as anger gripped Theo. The street was still blocked. Pompey had got out, and was standing by the horses, imploring those nearest him to make way.

Theo thrust her head forth again. "How dare you talk of hanging!" she cried into the astonished faces outside. "Burr is no traitor. And he's not even been tried yet."

The man in the coonskin cap stopped singing. His jaw dropped. Her blazing eyes abashed him. "Why, sure, ma'am, he's a traitor. Jefferson says so."

"He has no right to say so," she returned furiously. "The President has no right to condemn any man unheard."

The dancers broke from "Money Musk" and crowded round the carriage. They muttered and stared. Pompey, momentarily deserting the horses, pushed his way to her. His black face was gray with fear.

"Don' talk like dat, Mistiss," he begged in a hoarse whisper. "Dey mought hurt us. I kain git de horses troo dem nohow."

"Where you want to go to, ma'am?" asked the man in the coonskin cap, who had overheard Pompey. Theo's words, coupled with her beauty, had had their effect.

She drew a deep breath and squared her shoulders. "To the jail," she answered quietly, "to see Aaron Burr."

There was a moment's silence, then somebody tittered. "They say he casts a spell over the females."—"Even a gallows bird can find comfort in a pair of soft white arms."—

"Give him a kiss for me, my lady," shrilled a fat wench, placing her arms akimbo and smacking her lips. This sally won guffaws; somebody slapped the wench across her broad buttocks.

Theodosia rose inside the carriage, her cape and hood slipped off, and she leaned far out the window, directing her words to the farthest of their stupid, goggling faces. "I am Aaron Burr's daughter. Will you kindly let me pass?"

The crowd fell back then, murmuring, whispering, their expressions changed to avid curiosity. The man in the coonskin cap gave her a look of grudging admiration, and he went to Pompey's aid. "Make way for this lady!" he shouted. The surging crowd obeyed. The news ran like wildfire over them.

The carriage rolled slowly down the street between rows of staring eyes, and stopped before a small red-brick building with heavily barred windows.

Theo stepped out and made herself known to the uniformed jailer who greeted her. Her small back was straight and her head high, but her legs were trembling.

No matter how I find him, I must not show my dismay, my terror, she thought. In a frenzied effort to anticipate the worst, she pictured him in a dark dirty cell, littered with straw; she saw him with his hair cropped, garbed in the soiled homespun uniform, dun-colored, which was reserved for prisoners. Would he be beaten, humiliated, trapped, his gallantry and courage for once effaced by this incredible degradation? She forced her lips to a casually affectionate smile. There must be no heroics—he would hate them.

Reality brought a rush of blinding relief, so that she swayed a moment by the door. For the jailer ushered her into a commodious room whose furnishings included tables, chairs, and a length of crimson drugget over the boards.

And her father! He was a trifle pale, his brilliant dark eyes showed fatigue, but he wore his familiar black silk suit, his neckcloth was snowily immaculate as ever.

She flung her arms around his neck, burying her face in his shoulder that smelled of tobacco and clear-starch from his fresh linen: an indescribably comforting odor which sent her straight back to her childhood, when the strength of his arms holding her, the blessed reassurance of his nearness, exorcised all woes.

It was so now. She had prepared herself to comfort and sustain. She saw with deep joy that that had been presumptuous. He was as always master of himself, of his environment, and of her.

"Father, darling," she whispered, and now that there was no longer need to be brave, her eyes swam with tears.

He kissed her cheek and laughed, saying with his own unique mixture of raillery and tenderness: "Welcome to the penitentiary, madam, and behold the jailbird: a pampered jailbird. I am far more comfortable here than I have been during a great part of my life. Many of the good citizens of Richmond keep me supplied with delicacies. Look!"

He pointed to a table beside the window, loaded with gifts. There were piles of oranges and apricots, baskets of raspberries, a pitcher of cream, a pat of butter; there were colored comfits, a box of cigars, and a towering bunch of red roses.

"A fair lady sent me these," said Aaron, pulling one of the roses from the vase, "with a most impassioned note. She would be surprised at the use I shall make of this one." He fastened it to the neck of Theo's dress. "Now, if you will smile, my pretty one, you will be lovely as I like to see you."

Theo managed a watery smile.

"That's better. I see you are surprised to find me like this. Poor child, did you really expect to find me beating my breast and wallowing in filth?"

She nodded ruefully. "Something like that. Thank God, I was wrong. But Father—that mob out there, they're horrible. They're all against you; they scream and rant about —about——"

"About my hanging," finished Aaron calmly. "I know. I can hear them. They will, however, be disappointed. I do not intend to be hanged."

She moistened her lips. "Are you—are you sure of the outcome?" She watched him fearfully as he walked back and forth on the strip of drugget, frowning.

"They have not a shred of real evidence," he said at last. "There is nothing to it save Jefferson's hysterical enmity, and fortunately John Marshall is on the bench. He is a just man and will not allow our magnificent President to intimidate him."

"But what happened? How did this really come about?" She asked the question which had jabbed at her since the first black moment on the porch at the Oaks when Joseph had shown her the newspaper.

He shrugged. "General Wilkinson, while accepting Spanish gold with one hand, has managed to inflame Jefferson against me with the other. It's very simple."

"I thought General Wilkinson was your friend!" she cried.

"He was to command your troops, he was heart and soul immersed in the cause."

"He was all that, and more, until he discovered that there would be greater profit in denouncing me."

She sprang up, clasping her hands together. "It's vile horrible treachery! And why should Jefferson listen? What is the malign fate that twists your motives, and presents you always to the world in a false, sinister light?"

Aaron sighed. In his heart he agreed with her point of view. Still, he would not allow his composure to be ruffled. The stoical acceptance of disagreeable events was as much a part of his nature as was the shrewdness which enabled him to circumvent them—when circumvention was possible.

"My dear," he said soothingly, "you have read to very little purpose if you have not remarked that such things happen in all democratic governments. Was there in Greece or Rome a man of virtue and independence, and supposed to possess great talents, who was not the object of vindictive and unrelenting persecution?"

"I suppose not," she said unhappily.

"Alston did not come with you?"

She shook her head, debating whether to tell him the full story of Joseph's behavior and decided at last to do so, that he might be forewarned.

"I suspected as much," said Aaron when she had finished. "I had no great hopes of rescue in Chester. I thought that very likely you would not receive the letter. And yet, I confess that at the time it was a grave disappointment."

How grave she would never know. He had attempted to escape from his guard and had announced himself to the gaping, bewildered people of Chester. When nothing happened, and he was ignominiously bundled back upon his horse, he had lost control of himself, had been reduced for one instant to a shaking, piteous mass of nerves. This memory shamed him as nothing else ever had. He buried it anew where it would not trouble him.

"I wish you to go out much in society here, Theo. Be gay and laugh. Never for one moment betray fears or agitation, or I renounce thee. You will go into a pleasant house on Clay Street. It is being lent you by the Clarks, who are disposed to be most friendly. Whatever the mob may think, the gentry have been kind and sympathetic. There are many Federalists here who despise Jefferson and incline to admire Burr. You will see."

Theo was thirsty for the reassurances he gave her, desperately anxious to believe that there could be no doubt of the outcome. And yet, for all the red drugget and the table and chairs, this was a prison. There were stout bars across the windows, and the jailer had locked her in. The grating of his huge brass key had made no impression on her at the time, but she heard it now echoing in her mind as a harsh symbol of defeat.

"I have no heart for gaiety. I fear I cannot pretend it. Let me stay here with you, Father—please." She put a pleading hand on his arm.

He took the small white hand and raised it briefly to his lips. "No, my dear. You came, I assume, to help me. And you will do exactly as I say. Mingle in society, present to everyone an unperturbed serenity. More than that, if you meet, as I believe you will, members of the opposition, jurists or John Marshall himself, your woman's wit will guide you as to the best methods of dealing with them. You have my permission to smile and coquet a little. When you choose, you can be irresistible. I hope you have brought some pretty gowns."

She shook her head, troubled. She had not anticipated any such part as this. But she understood him perfectly, and would do her best.

"I brought only simple clothes, except—wait—I believe Eleanore packed for me my new yellow brocade that I had made in Charleston."

"Good. Yellow becomes you, and if you are as pale as you seem to be now, buy yourself a pot of rouge. Rub a little on the lips as well. It enhances the whiteness of the teeth. Did you bring the diamond necklace?"

She nodded. She never traveled without it. "I have it here in my reticule." She loosened the strings and drew the necklace from its little leather bag.

Aaron lit the two candles which he had wrested from the unwilling jailer. She put the necklace gently down on the bare table where the light caught it. The diamonds shimmered and flashed yellow sparks. They stared at the jewels silently, both held by poignant memory.

Aaron touched one of the diamonds. "Poor little Miss Prissy," he said, with a flicker of sadness. "Another birthday has just passed, your twenty-fourth, and this time I gave you nothing."

"I want nothing!" she cried. "Nothing but your freedom."

"I shall get my freedom," he said, with confidence. "And you shall yet have magnificent jewels, opals and pearls and diamonds that will make this necklace look like the tawdry bauble of a barmaid."

She looked at him in quick surprise. "You have not then abandoned all hope of"—she cast a quick glance around, and whispered—"of 'X'?"

His eyebrows shot up. "How can you ask me that? Do you think me a weakling? I am ashamed of you. Here, take your necklace and flaunt it proudly." He gathered up the diamonds and poured them back into their leather pouch.

When she left him, Aaron knew that he had reinfected her with hope and confidence, a confidence that he quite sincerely felt himself. But there were undoubtedly difficulties. He foresaw a long legal battle, recriminations, accusations, the necessity for parrying the venomous many-headed serpent which Jefferson had let loose.

If only I had money, he thought, with a burst of anger. Money would have riveted Wilkinson's fickle loyalty, would even at this late stage shut the venal general's prating mouth. Aaron knew his man. The blustering turkey-cock could ever be swayed by self-interest His newfound patriotism and horror of what he now called conspiracy had coincided with the disappearance of Aaron's funds—the monies subscribed to the cause by Joseph and Blennerhassett and others.

Aaron's thoughts turned again to Theo's necklace. Upon consideration he decided that its forced sale would not bring enough to compensate for the pain of depriving her of it. Besides, it might be urgently needed later—when the trial was over.

He seated himself at his table, pulled a sheet of foolscap from a pile, headed it in cipher, "A New Plan for Royalist Government." He had become so accustomed to using symbols and numbers in places of letters that he no longer needed to consult a key.

He wrote rapidly: "The Mexican Empire under Aaron Burr will be a monarchy incorporated with the best features of democracy. Though unlimited power shall be firmly vested in the Emperor, the people will nevertheless have restricted representation in the government." He filled page after page with detailed analysis. It was an occupation which never failed to give him keen enjoyment.

Outside, the long-threatened storm exploded into thunderclaps and a torrential downpour. Lightning blasted an oak in a near-by field. The deafening crash rocked the jail, brought screams from two tipsy strumpets who were confined on the floor below.

But Aaron never even looked up from his writing-table.

Chapter Twenty-four

✍ ✍ ✍

THEO FOUND that Aaron had not exaggerated the numbers of his friends and supporters in Richmond. There were many who thought him a martyr to Jefferson's petty persecution. They rallied around the charming Mrs. Alston, deluging her with hospitality. In obedience to her father's wishes, she entertained and was entertained. There were nightly routs or musicales or dances. The town was crammed with visitors, who streamed in on foot, on horseback, in the stages, or in elegant Italian chaises. They slept four in a bed in the taverns, and in private houses the children were banished to the attics to make room for guests.

Besides the curiosity-seekers, there was a multitude whose presence was legitimate: witnesses, journalists, and an array of lawyers for both sides. There were distinguished names for the prosecution—the United States District Attorney, George Hay; that flower of oratory, William Wirt; and Alexander McRae, the Lieutenant-Governor of Virginia.

Aaron's own array of talent was no less impressive— Edmund Randolph and Benjamin Botts and John Wickham were minor stars revolving around the huge bibulous bulk of Luther Martin. With the latter gentleman's defense Aaron had not been pleased. It was perfunctory and, all too frequently, unintelligible because of his habit of enlivening the tedious court proceedings with copious swigs from a large black bottle which he kept concealed beneath his coat-tails.

"See, my dear, if you cannot induce in him a more serious attitude toward my fate," said Aaron on one of Theodosia's daily visits to the jail.

And she had succeeded brilliantly. The yellow brocade dress and the diamonds were bewitching. The rouge was unnecessary that evening. She had felt well and confident

The admiring glances, the little sympathetic murmurs which followed upon her entrance to the Richard Keenes' drawing-rooms buoyed her and gave her an assured sparkle. Luther Martin had come to her side at once, his eyes brightening. And she had charmed the old man with smiles and flattery, made him feel that he was a gay dog indeed.

"Egad, I'm half in love with the lovely Mrs. Alston," he told everyone, slapping his great thighs and reaching for his bottle. "Did I know no other good of Burr—and I do, mind ye—it would be enough for me that he has such a daughter."

And Theodosia, hearing this roar from the other end of the room, had smiled, and been well content: especially as the ultimate object was obtained, and Martin's handling of the case increased in fervor.

But every morning the carnival spirit, the gaiety, and the certainty that, after all, this was—as Aaron said—but a temporary embarrassment, were dimmed by the grimness of the courtroom. Each morning Theo entered the Capitol and was ushered to her seat in the gallery. Then, with the majestic arrival of John Marshall on the beach, the three imperative knocks of the gavel, the appearance of Aaron under heavy guard in the prisoner's box, her courage ebbed.

John Marshall's face, sternly imperturbable under the curled white wig, filled her with fear. A just man, Aaron had said, and not likely to be swayed by Jefferson's hostile pressure. Maybe not. But he was not sympathetic to the defense either. His cold judicial stare told her that. And where might he not conceive justice to lie? How could he or any man sift truth from the wicked welter of accusations brought forth by General Wilkinson and his cohorts?

And even if the judge was impartial, the jurymen all too obviously were not. When the counsel for the prosecution spoke, they leaned forward straining not to miss a syllable, they nodded as though unconsciously, they murmured to each other, and at the mention of the words "traitor," "conspiracy," or "treason" their eyes shifted to Aaron's impassive face with glances of collective hostility. When the lawyers for the defense countered, they relaxed and stared at the ceiling, either not listening at all or listening in but a bored manner.

Over and over again Luther Martin stumbled to his feet to check the interpretations which now one and now another of the witnesses conceived to have been Aaron's plans.

Once, General Wilkinson endeavored to bolster his tale of treason by alleging that he had heard that, besides desiring to split the Union and seize Mexico, Colonel Burr had conceived the idea of introducing "some of his desperate followers into Washington and at a given signal seizing the government, appointing himself President, and possessing himself of the public monies deposited in federal banks."

Here Aaron permitted himself a gentle smile and murmured to one of his counsel, Wickham, "'Tis a most ingenious idea. Would that I had thought of it!"

The young lawyer shushed him nervously, but at the same instant Luther Martin roared: "Objection, Your Honor. May I once again point out that we are not here concerned with General Wilkinson's fantasies. The prosecution is endeavoring to prove that the accused committed an overt act of war. Without this proof it cannot establish the crime of high treason. These chimeras which the witness fancies may have passed through my client's mind have no bearing whatsoever."

Judge Marshall nodded gravely. "That is quite true. The prosecution will confine itself to establishing that an act of war occurred."

The courtroom rustled and settled back. It was stifling hot in the small room jammed with people. Theo felt her head whirl and a sensation of faintness. When the court declared a recess, she got up and forced her way through the jostling crowd to the air. Sun beat down on the Capitol steps. She leaned against the wall and wished helplessly for water. She dared not go far, unwilling to miss one moment of the proceedings. She shut her eyes.

"You look faint, Mrs. Alston," said a cheerful male voice at her elbow. "May I help you?"

She started; the voice seemed familiar: the face, too, with its high color, small hazel eyes that, though sympathetic, yet had a mischievous gleam, tousled brown hair, neckcloth askew under one ear.

"Why, thank you——" she began uncertainly. Where had she met him? He was no acquaintance from the Carolinas, his Yankee inflection showed that.

"You don't remember me," he said, with a shout of laughter. "Oh, fickle Dulcinea! Have you forgot the banks of the East River? Have you forgot your first kiss, if I may be so bold?—Washington Irving, ma'am, at your service."

"Oh, of course," she cried contritely, laughing a little. "You must forgive me." She had a vision of the boy and girl, half-playful, half-enamored, experimenting together with the light sweetness of adolescent love. Richmond Hill and her seventeenth birthday! How happy I was!

Aloud she said, "That was so very long ago." In spite of her effort to be light, her voice faltered. "You have hardly changed," she went on quickly.

"Nor you, Theodosia, except to grow more beautiful." But this was not quite true: he found her much changed. She was beautiful enough, her great eyes as magnificent as ever, her hair as burnished and silken, but the dewiness was gone, the fresh sparkle. And though her face was still smooth and unlined, it had sharpened. When she did not smile, it was marred by a heaviness of expression which aged her. Joy and expectancy have deserted her, he thought, and immediately rebuked himself. How could one be joyful and expectant with a father on trial for his life?

"I see a bench down there in the shade," said he, indicating the square. "Let us sit there, and I will find you some refreshment."

"I dare not leave," she began. "I must be there when they convene."

"They will not do so for half an hour," he assured her. "The marshal told me."

She allowed him to settle her on a bench, declined his offer to procure her a glass of Madeira from the tavern across the square, but gratefully accepted the cup of water he brought her.

"So you, too, have come to gape at the pillorying of an innocent man," she said sadly, turning to him.

Poor Theo, he thought with sympathy. Does she really think him so innocent? His writer's brain was fascinated by the new angle which he might glean from this meeting. He longed to probe her, to uncover for his delighted inspection the motives and emotions which animated her. But he did not wish to hurt her. Though the boyish love he had felt for her had long since vanished, it had left a residue of sentimental interest: a pleasing nostalgic pang.

"I have not come to gape. I am reporting the trial for the *New York Chronicle*."

"Oh." She accepted this vaguely. "You have then become a writer, as you meant to be."

"Not as I meant to be." He laughed. "Not yet. But I shall."

"Tell me truly"—she turned on him with sudden vehemence. "Do you think it is going all right—for Father, I mean? I hear so many conflicting opinions. I dare not know what to believe. I can't always understand what happens in there." She pointed to the Capitol. "It goes on and on. There is so much legal talk. They all contradict each other. And that beast of a Wilkinson—how can they listen to his monstrous lies!"

If they *are* lies, thought Irving cynically. But he had no admiration for Wilkinson, and, though he did have many doubts about Aaron's guilt and ultimate fate, he could at least give her one truthful reassurance.

"Your father is superb. I admired him particularly at his first encounter with the General in court. Colonel Burr looked him full in the face with one of his piercing regards, swept his eye over his whole person from head to foot as if to scan his dimensions, then coolly resumed his former position. There was no appearance of study or restraint in it, no affectation of disdain or defiance, nothing but a slight expression of contempt. I know of no other man who could have withered a treacherous enemy so cleverly. The General, for all his bombast, collapsed like a balloon."

"Oh, I know!" she cried. "Father is wonderful, always. But you haven't answered my question. There can't be any doubt of the outcome, can there? Sometimes——" Her voice sank. She shut her lips over the rest of her sentence: "I can't help feeling frightened." That would have been disloyalty, disobedience to Aaron's express commands. She had forgotten for a moment that Irving was a journalist: one of the howling pack that had already done their best to rend Aaron.

"How silly of me to ask such questions!" She straightened, and her voice had a false briskness that Irving thought pathetic. "Of course there is no doubt of the outcome. An innocent man cannot be convicted. I mean simply, how does it appear to you as an observer? You will, I trust, furnish your paper with an unprejudiced account."

"Most certainly," he answered kindly, glad that this committed him to nothing. He moistened his lips, considering best how to find the answer to a multitude of questions which plagued him. Where was her husband? Had they really been on Blennerhassett's Island or no? Above all, what, in so far as she knew them, had been Colonel Burr's real intentions? She held the key to all these matters. Matters he and his confrères had speculated upon and discussed pro and con night after night, after the day's session was ended. He ached with curiosity.

It was maddening to sit there beside her and to know that, by clever tactics, by invoking the ghost of their faraway little love affair, or indeed by downright bullying, he might wrest

266

from her so much valuable information. And yet he could not. Her dignity, her air of remoteness, and, paradoxically, her vulnerability constituted a shield. He knew that she was scarcely conscious of him, now. Her eyes were continually raised toward the Capitol Building, her fingers plucked at a small lace handkerchief on her lap: scarcely conscious of him as a person, sitting on the bench with her, and not conscious of him at all as a man. This piqued him slightly, for women did not usually treat him so. And yet was it not that same impervious quality in her which had intrigued him years ago? He had been unable to pierce it then, and now he no longer had the urge to try.

The town clock struck, and Theodosia sprang to her feet. "I must get back."

Irving offered her his arm and escorted her to the courtroom. When they entered, the prisoner was already in the box. Irving, watching with alert interest, saw the quick look that flickered between Burr and Theodosia.

Why, she worships him, he thought, startled. And he, in his cool, self-centered way, worships her. That was more like the signal of parted lovers than a look of filial affection.

The idea interested him. He reached for the quill pen provided for members of the press, pulled the bottle of ink toward him and made some quick notes before settling back to listen to the proceedings. The trial had been exciting enough before by reason of the magnitude of the charge, the number of persons involved, and the former high standing of the accused. Now, after his re-encounter with Theodosia, it had developed overtones which intrigued him mightily. This is far better than the theater, he told himself with delight. His bright hazel eyes darted from one face to the other, speculating and weighing.

Next day he had abundant new cause for interest. Matters went badly for Burr. The prosecution produced witnesses from Blennerhassett's Island: a groom and a gardener who made damaging admissions. There had been great preparations on the island—the storing of food, the outfitting of boats.

"Warships, might they be called?" the prosecutor suggested. Well, no, not unless you called flatboats warships.

"But there were guns?" Oh, yes, for sure. There were plenty of muskets and ammunition.

"And Colonel Burr had raised a sizable army to use these muskets and ammunition?" Yes, a good number of men had enlisted with Colonel Burr.

267

A murmur ran around the courtroom. The jury was fixed by the prosecutor's triumphant eye: here was the beginning of the necessary proof; it remained but to show that those muskets had been fired, then Burr's goose would be cooked for sure.

Everyone in the courtroom knew the value of this evidence. Everyone tilted forward straining to see Burr and how he took it. Not a muscle in his indifferent face quivered, however. He sat relaxed, a trifle pale, perhaps, but no more so than could be explained by the continued and choking heat.

Irving alone of all the crowd looked, not at the prisoner, but at Theodosia. He thus happened to see a flash of naked emotion on her face. And the emotion astounded him: he had expected consternation, dismay, fear; and he saw instead utter amazement followed by joy. It couldn't be joy, unless she had lost her reason, he thought dumbfounded. He then perceived that her dilated eyes were not fixed on her father as was their wont, but on a point beyond Burr's head. Turning, he followed her gaze.

There was a newcomer. A tall gaunt man with fair hair, leaning against the wall. And his eyes were riveted on Theo as hers were on him. It was for this man, then, that her face was illumined with a bewildered joy that transformed it; had transformed it, for now, as Irving turned to look at her again, her eyes were cast down, but even across the dozens of people who separated them, he could see that her cheeks, even her neck and the square of chest exposed by her dress, were scarlet.

Now, what is the meaning of this? thought Irving. Can it be the husband? Does one ever betray so much emotion at beholding a husband? He listened a moment to the evidence, which had once more bogged down in technicalities and required no attention, then he jogged the arm of the journalist next to him. "Tell me, pray, do you know the name of the long fair fellow who stands over there against the wall? He in the green coat?"

The other looked and jumped. "Gad, man! That's Meriwether Lewis!" He hissed it so loud that it brought a rap of the gavel and an angry look from the bench.

Irving gave a surprised exclamation. "The conquering hero, no less? I've heard much of him and his triumphant return last month from his expedition with Clark. He is Jefferson's favorite, is he not?"

"He has been appointed Governor of the North Louisiana Territory," returned the other significantly, but in a more cautious whisper. "So you may judge whether Jefferson is pleased with him! The President has doubtless sent him here in his own stead to watch the trial."

Then, why, by all that's infernal, does Mistress Theodosia Burr Alston blaze with delight at the sight of her father's enemy? Here is something vastly peculiar. Irving mused pleasurably over this new mystery. Impossible to imagine two men more different: the one, tall, taciturn, disdainful of the recent honors and acclaim which had been heaped upon him, had risked his life to enlarge and unify his country; while the other——

Irving glanced at the prisoner. Well, whatever the truth of these particular charges against him, it was clear that Burr cared not a rap for the future of the United States. His vision was bounded by self-interest. True he had fought brilliantly in the war for freedom—but then so had many another young man from motives no more lofty than adventure and personal advancement.

I verily believe that Burr has not an ounce of patriotism, thought Irving, nor any deep emotions at all, except perhaps one.

He turned instinctively to look at Theodosia and uttered an exclamation of concern. Her color had faded into a ghastly white, her upper lip glistened, and, while her head fell forward, her small body slumped.

Irving sprang to his feet, but already a score of people had seen her plight. There was a buzz of sympathy. "She's swooned, poor little thing," said a voice, "and no wonder. Such a strain, and in this heat."

Two men carried her outside, and Aaron, who had also started forward without thought of his confinement, was pushed down by the two guards on either side of him. He bit his lips and, flinging back his head, saw Lewis's tall form hurrying through the door opposite.

For a moment his face contorted. His fingers clenched, they wound themselves in the ruffled white neckcloth at his throat. There was a sharp sound of tearing linen. The guards looked at their prisoner in astonishment. "For sure he feels all this more than he lets on," one of them whispered, and the other nodded.

The gavel sounded, the courtroom quieted. The cross-examination of a dull witness proceeded. Aaron once more became impassive. He did not look at the empty chair where his daughter had been sitting.

When Theodosia reached the air, her eyes opened. "I'm all

right now," she murmured, struggling to hold her head up. "But I think I will lie down for a little. Will somebody please call my carriage?"

"Your carriage is here, Mrs. Alston, and I will do myself the honor of seeing you home." Lewis took her arm, dismissing the hovering spectators with a curt gesture of his chin. The carriage door shut them in.

"Merne," she whispered, hardly yet daring to believe, "Oh, Merne—I never thought to see you again."

She had fainted for pure joy. From the instant of seeing him in the courtroom, she had lost realization of the trial, even of Aaron. Her long-submerged love had rushed upon her like a suffocating torrent. She had felt in that moment only—Thank God, he is alive. He is near me. He will help us. Everything will now be all right.

Lewis smiled grimly. "I am hard to kill, Theodosia. I'm sorry I startled you so. I didn't think how unexpected my appearance would be to you."

She gazed at him hungrily. He was thinner, who had always been lean. His skin was weathered dark as oak. His hands were seamed, rough with calluses. She touched one softly.

"Merne, you're so cold, so still. Are you not glad to be back? Did you not do all that you set out to? Did you find the other ocean?"

"Yes, the other ocean and mountains and great rivers."

"Were there savages? I never dared think of them. I have been so terrified for you."

He gave a short laugh. "There were savages, and amongst them the truest, most loyal friend a man could find, Sacajawea. Without her we could have done nothing."

"A woman," she said quickly. "And were there other women, Merne?"

He shrugged. "Other women, of course. Lights-o'-love, a French trollop or two in St. Louis."

She shrank against the cushions, staring at him miserably. He had not looked at her once since they entered the carriage.

"Oh, what is it, my dear?" she faltered after a moment. "Why do you speak so harshly to me? You hurt me."

"I'm sorry for that," he answered coldly. "Can you expect me to be merry with a woman whose father has attempted to wrest from the Union those very territories which I have labored for four years to bring into it?"

"That's not true!" she cried. "He was interested only in Mexico!"

"And anything else he could lay his hands on," said Merne bitterly. His anger, though she could not guess it, was as much for himself as for her. Why did she still have the power to disquiet him? He had thought himself cured, their love safely relegated to the status of a vanished dream. Yet the sight of her in the courtroom had moved him profoundly.

"You don't understand," she said urgently, her first swift resentment passed. "If some of the western territories should break away, it would be their own doing. They have no feeling of allegiance to Washington. They are too far away. They *wish* to form another nation."

Her flushed earnestness touched him. He turned and looked at her ruefully. How well her father had trained her! She had acquired all his dexterity for proving that black was white.

"I trust you are wrong about that," he said, with a faint smile, "since I have just been appointed Governor to those territories you assure me are ripe for revolt."

"Oh—!" She was startled. She glanced at him quickly. Somehow she had never pictured him as an important figure, for all her love. He had been merely a captain, a secretary, or the leader of a hopeless little expedition into the hinterland. Now he was to be Governor of a tract as large as Europe. Why should he? she thought, suddenly angry. What had he done to merit such honor, when a man like her father could be condemned to prison? But Merne was a friend of Jefferson's, Aaron's bitter enemy. In the bliss of seeing him again she had forgotten that.

"Why did you come to the trial, Merne?"

He hesitated and her hope that he would answer, "To see you, to help you," perished.

Instead he pointed through the coach window, saying, "Is this your house? The carriage has stopped." When she nodded coldly, he added, "May I come inside with you? I have something to say."

It was cooler inside. Merne stretched out his long legs and watched her seat herself stiffly across from him before the dark fireplace. Suddenly the memory of their parting engulfed them, the feel of each other's arms and lips. They could not look at each other.

Perhaps, he thought, if we had been truly lovers, we should be sated now. This unrest and feverishness would not leap at us yet again. His jaw tightened. There must be no repeti-

271

tion of the rapturous and inconclusive days in Washington. Surely at last they were beyond that. He had been sure of it until he saw her. He had come to the trial at Jefferson's request, fully sharing in the President's hostility toward Aaron and prepared to proffer new evidence against him. He had encountered the ragged edge of the conspiracy as he passed through St. Louis, had talked with a handful of men, who, indiscreet in their cups, had furnished him with many details.

"Go down there, Merne," ordered Jefferson, "and demand to be sworn in. I like not the shilly-shally and hair-splitting which Marshall allows. The man should have been hanged long before this. You are in high favor with the people, and your appointment as Governor will give weight to your evidence."

He had consented gladly, ignoring the thought of Theodosia. What if it hurt her? What if she hated him? He had not reached his present position without incurring enmity. Her father was a scoundrel and a menace to the country. It had seemed simple.

And now, alone with her, he felt himself blurred with sentimentality—with passion: his purpose blunted.

"I came down here to give new evidence against Burr." He flung it at her roughly.

Her eyes widened; she shrank to a listening stillness like a wild thing scenting danger. "What new evidence?"

"Matters I came upon in St. Louis," he answered briefly.

"But you won't give it—you can't——"

"Why not? Because you and I have known love? That is the reasoning of a fool—or a woman."

Have known love, she thought with anguish. Does he mean that? Is it all past? Has he come here simply to injure us? Somehow I must check this new danger: danger from the one person I trusted to help.

"You're a Governor now, a great man. I should not be surprised that you no longer feel—feel affection for the daughter of an impoverished prisoner. I was doubtless more attractive as the daughter of a Vice-President?"

"Rubbish!" he exploded. "Don't play the hypocrite with me, Theodosia."

She was silent. Her thoughts ran together in panic. What was this new evidence? He came from Jefferson, he had been out West. Whatever he said would be listened to avidly. The prosecution had so far been able to produce few witnesses more important than the grooms and gardeners they had heard today. This would be different. If he no longer loved her, she had no weapon. She was helpless and shamed before his cold implacability. Suddenly she looked full at him, and their eyes met. Her heart leaped with relief. She gave an inarticulate cry. "You do still love me, Merne! You can't lie to me now! I see it! I know it! Listen——"

She ran to the corner of the room, seating herself at the pianoforte. Her fingers stumbled a little and then grew sure; her voice throbbed with her desperate desire to reach him, to conjure the old emotions from the past by the sure magic of their music.

Water, parted from the sea ——

He listened, at first resentful. She meant to soften him with this cheap trick. It was unworthy of her—childish. Women —always hankering for the past, refusing to let it die decently. Then gradually, as he listened, his resentment fell away. A peculiar thrill ran through him, as though his spirit trembled on the verge of discovery. It seemed that his consciousness expanded far beyond the limits of the shadowy room in Richmond. He feared to move or breathe, for behind the thinning mists revelation dwelt. "Almost I can see, in another second I shall understand the whole——"

Once in the Mandan country, two years back, he had stood alone at sunrise upon the summit of one of the gigantic rocky mountains which reared their mighty bulk out there across the continent, and this same feeling had come to him then. The expedition's trials and dangers had diminished to nothingness. The mountain winds had brought him peace, a momentary glimpse of the eternal cosmic verity—as her small unconscious voice did now.

Let my heart find rest in thine ——

But she sang of love, human love, while he in that blinding instant knew—as she most mercifully would never know— that she sang also of death. Love and death intermingled, the two edges of the same sword. Tenderness and a great pity held him.

Theo's hands fell from the keys, her brilliant eyes sought his face. He came to her and kissed her gently as he would have kissed a child.

She caught his hand. "Merne, promise me that you will do nothing to hurt Father—promise me."

He sighed, and turned from her a little. The moment of

illumination was gone. Life slid back into its neat, appointed course. Love and death, foreboding and rapture, they made no sense, he thought, with faint disgust. How had he managed to read all this into a piece of sentimental music?

"I can't promise, Theodosia. I came to Richmond for a purpose. To do—if you will forgive the cant—my duty. Our love cannot alter that."

"You're cruel and hard!" she blazed, flinging her head back. Then she added in a softer voice as a new hope occurred to her: "At least, Merne, come with me and talk to Father. You scarcely know him; you are prejudiced. If you will just talk with him, you will see how you have misunderstood——"

Poor baby! he thought. She believes her father to be some sort of wizard; that a few honeyed words from the fascinating little Burr will enslave me.

He smiled at her sadly. "If you like, I'll go with you. But it will do no good."

Already she had darted for her cloak and tied its brown ribbons beneath her chin. "He will be back in—in the penitentiary by now. Call the carriage, please. It will be quicker. The mob knows it. They let me through."

He complied silently, already regretting his agreement.

Together they passed the staring guards on the ground floor of the prison. The jailer, sprawling on a stool before Aaron's door, greeted her courteously: "Good afternoon, Mrs. Alston. You're early, ain't you? He won't be expecting you yet. Who's the gent?"

"A friend of mine," she answered quickly. "I will vouch for him. We shan't be long."

The man touched his cap and unlocked the door. It swung silently open on its well-oiled hinges, disclosing Aaron in the center of the room at his writing-table as usual. But his position was not as usual. His head, that she had never seen anything but jauntily erect, was slumped on his arms. His shoulders drooped, they seemed shrunken. He looked defeated—and old.

Theo uttered an instinctive cry of pain and his head jerked up. As he saw her companion, a greenish light flashed in his eyes. It was gone in a second, vitality flowed back into him and a subtly sneering defiance. He sprang lightly to his feet.

"This is indeed an honor," he purred. "I trust you have recovered, Madam, from your indisposition in the courtroom. Though I see that you are still so weak that you need an escort."

She was frightened by the venom in his tone. He who could

always control his feelings, when that control was to his advantage, must not give way to hostility now. She knew that he had always disliked Lewis, but she had no conception of the bitterness of his jealousy. How could she, when he did not admit it to himself?

But Merne understood. The pattern that seemed to change had yet been inexorably laid down during their first clash in Vauxhall Gardens. It had not changed.

Theo stood uncertainly between them, as she had stood then, and their hatred for each other crackled past her. She had been a fool to bring Merne here without first warning her father, she realized too late. How could she say to him, in the presence of that tall, quietly disdainful man: "Father, show him your goodness, your true nobility. Make him understand that you are incapable of wrongdoing. Win him over with your golden persuasive tongue, as you have won so many people."

Aaron moved, and reseated himself. "To just exactly what am I indebted for the very great honor of this visit? The pleasure, perhaps, of gaping at an interesting prisoner, or simply that you cannot tear yourself for one moment from the company of Mrs. Alston?"

"No!" cried Theo sharply. "Father, don't talk that way. Captain Lewis has some—some sort of evidence, or thinks he has. He felt he must testify. But I knew, if he could speak with you, you would make him realize that he must have been misinformed."

"I have no interest in any evidence which this gentleman may wish to proffer."

"But it will injure you! He is to be Governor of Louisiana, he is Jefferson's friend. The jury will listen."

Aaron lashed out at her with sudden fury. "And you, too, listen to what he says, don't you, my dear? This Governor of Louisiana, this friend of Jefferson's, he is no doubt a far more seductive subject to listen to than a disgraced traitor, an emperor without an empire, the murderer of Alexander Hamilton, the betrayer of his country. You had better attach yourself somehow to the tail of this new comet. It's unfortunate that you happen to be married, it is not? Yet, with patience and ingenuity, perhaps even that obstacle may be surmounted."

She shrank, clutching blindly at the back of a chair.

Merne, white with disgust, turned on her too. "How can you continue to idolize such a man——"

Her eyes slid past him blankly to rest upon Aaron's face.

How terribly hurt he must be, she thought, how desperately unhappy! He has never been unjust to me before. Can he think I would desert him, I who love him more than anything in life? She saw him again as he had been when they came into the room, slumped, defenseless—old, and a painful terror closed around her heart. He must never be vulnerable. Never! Always he must be shining, invincible. Nothing mattered compared to that.

And now the echo of Merne's angry question reached her. Her body stiffened. She raised her chin, looking at him as though he had been an offensive stranger.

"I had rather not live than not be the daughter of such a man," she said quietly.

Aaron drew a sharp breath. There was triumph in his face, a fleeting shame and gratitude. She went over to him and knelt beside him.

Merne watched them, and his throat grew dry. This was a love that he could not understand, and its object he thought dismally unworthy. But into that bleak prison room it had brought beauty. And there are many kinds of love; who was he to judge?

"You win, my Theodosia," he murmured. "Destiny shall deal with your father, as it will in any case, but I shall not meddle."

He rapped softly on the door to attract the jailer. The two Burrs, torn from their deep preoccupation with each other, looked up at the sound.

"Good-bye," said Merne. "No, you needn't worry." He answered the frightened question in Theo's eyes. He smiled ruefully, made her a small brief bow. "I shall leave Richmond tonight."

Chapter Twenty-five

𝒟 𝒟 𝒟

THE TRIAL dragged on during the sweltering August days. Joseph appeared for a week, ill at ease and grumpy. He tried to persuade Theo to return with him at once, and she ignored him. Not only ignored him, but seemed, in a curious and alarming way, to be unaware of his presence. He occupied a room not far from hers in the borrowed house; they occasionally dined together when she was not with her father; but her eyes looked past him; she answered politely, chatted about the weather, even expressed some courteous appreciation of his coming—all without giving him the slightest feeling of contact. There was no hostility in this blankness. There was no emotion at all.

Joseph made a few half-hearted attempts to clear his own name, suffered an extremely uncomfortable interview with Blennerhassett. The Irishman was now also imprisoned and standing trial with his "sovereign in expectancy," and, while he remained loyal to Aaron, he did not scruple to hide his contempt for Joseph.

Joseph regretted having come, though he was relieved to see that the trial was progressing more favorably for Aaron than he had expected. He took himself home again, heartily sick of the whole matter, and more profoundly uneasy about his wife than he had ever been. She dwelt in some remote borderland where all human relationships—save one—seemed shadowy. In her feverish concentration on her father, even concern for her child seemed not to touch her. "He is all right with Eleanore," she said. "He does not need me as I am needed here."

And as for me, thought Joseph, she never considers my rights or needs at all. And he traveled alone back to his plantation.

On September first the long ordeal ended. It had, after all, been impossible to prove that Aaron had committed any overt act of war. That he had intended to do so, no one doubted, but in the absence of conclusive proof of an overt act, the law could not touch him.

Had it been given, even Meriwether Lewis's testimony would probably not have affected the outcome, because no act of war had occurred. The conspiracy had been checked before it had matured.

The verdict was unaccompanied by any demonstration. The courtroom was weary of the proceedings. From the moment of hearing Judge Marshall's calm summing-up, no one could fail to guess the result.

The jury took but a few minutes, then, shuffling their feet and staring at the floor, they returned sullenly to their box.

"Not guilty because not proved," said the foreman, with ill grace.

Theo repressed a cry of joy, but Aaron leapt to his feet to protest against this ambiguous "Scotch" verdict.

"Either I am guilty or I am not guilty!" he cried. "I demand that the jury alter the wording of its verdict."

A lengthy and bitter verbal battle ensued. The judge, jury, counsel, and Aaron all took part to a buzz of interested comment from the spectators. The high moment of acquittal petered out into something like a cat-fight. After an hour of acrimony, the jury consented to a compromise. The verdict was accepted as rendered, but entered on the record simply as "Not guilty."

Chief Justice Marshall bowed briefly to Aaron and disappeared. The jury trailed out, still grumbling, followed by the prosecuting attorneys.

Aaron's guards touched their caps, swung open the door of the prisoner's box, and he was free. He was congratulated, of course, Luther Martin clapping him on the back and emitting roars of triumph. His Richmond supporters wrung his hand and suggested immediate celebration at the tavern. Theo clung to him, laughing a bit hysterically, giddy with relief.

Washington Irving, approaching the father and daughter to offer his own congratulations, thought, There is something spurious in all this. It doesn't ring true. Though he has been grudgingly acquitted here, what can he do now? Jefferson is not appeased. There will be more persecution. The people believe him guilty. Moreover, they say he is heavily in debt. Poor Theo. She has hitched her wagon to a very dim star.

He clasped her hand, murmuring his congratulations while his eyes were warm with sympathy.

Theo saw the sympathy and resented it. Why should anyone dare to pity them now? Aaron was exonerated.

The burst of elation, the happiness of triumph, were shortlived. During the weeks that followed, it became all too clear to Aaron that escape from the gallows in Richmond conferred no such certainty anywhere else. Ohio and Mississippi indicted him on the instigation of Jefferson. He had wriggled out in Virginia, wriggled out even from a subsequent anticlimactic trial for misdemeanor there, but there were other States. In New York and New Jersey he was still wanted for the "murder" of Hamilton. A Baltimore mob tried to lynch him on general principles——

"Apparently there is not a jail nor a gallowstree in the States but yearns to tender me its gentle hospitality," he told Theo. "Can such popularity be deserved?"

Theo was too sick at heart to answer. She had passed beyond outcry at the injustice done him. The unrelenting persecution now seemed to her like a formless black monster. One did not expect justice from a monster: one tried one's puny best to escape.

"Yes," said Aaron, reading her mind, because of late they had discussed this only solution. "I shall have to go abroad for a while. Without my presence here, they will cool down or find another quarry. In England I shall find supporters, and in France."

His eyes narrowed, and she knew that he was thinking of Napoleon. Let him but once establish contact with the great conqueror, and he felt confident of enthusiastic support. Here they were provincial and panicky: they had no vision. In the Old World it would be different: the Emperor would understand.

"Jerome Bonaparte, whom I entertained at Richmond Hill, is now King of Westphalia," he remarked, pursuing this line of thought.

Theo brightened. "And surely he will be hospitable to you in return, will help you to see his brother."

Aaron had no doubt of it. Gradually Theo again found hope. Aaron had never lost it. "X" was, after all, still possible. Europe would provide the proper theater for the next act. The necessity for exile was perhaps only a blessing in disguise.

With decision reached, they were both galvanized into action. The Swartwout home in New York was opened to them. The brothers Swartwout had never wavered in their faith and affection. Aaron arrived at night and was smuggled to an upstairs room which he dared not leave during the weeks of negotiation for a passage to Europe.

The lack of money, as usual, made the situation even more uncomfortable than it would otherwise have been. The Swartwouts gave what they could; a handful of the disbanded Burrites were entrusted with the secret and contributed, but the total was not enough to pay his passage and allow him to live decently on the other side.

"If only the people who owe you money—would pay," wailed Theo one evening, as they bent together over the table in Aaron's room mulling yet again over the inexorable figures.

"Why should they?" asked Aaron cheerfully. "I do not pay the people to whom I owe money either."

"All the same, I'm going to try again." She rose and put on her cloak. It was one of many discreet and humiliating calls which she made in New York. She must infallibly conceal his presence here, and yet sound out his former friends, and, while trying to extract money from his debtors on the one hand, avoid his creditors on the other.

Nor was she very successful. Intimates from Richmond Hill days sent down word by their servants that they were not at home. Or, if they received her, it was with cold politeness which changed to glassy silence at any mention of her father.

"I know, my dear," said Aaron. "It's quite useless. Your efforts have been wonderful, but it is quite useless."

She sat down beside him with a weary sigh. If only Joseph could help! But that resource was cut off; for even if he were willing, he was no longer able. He had given fifty thousand dollars to the cause and it had melted away. Moreover, Jefferson's recent Embargo Act had crippled him badly. Rice might no longer be shipped abroad, and, without that plentiful revenue, he was much embarrassed for ready cash. Every letter informed Theo of the unpleasant fact.

"Well," she said, sighing again, "there's only one thing left to do. We must sell the necklace."

Aaron silently put his arm around her and drew her head to his shoulder. He had reached that conclusion some time before.

Samuel Swartwout undertook the commission. A Spanish Jew on Pearl Street, crying to Heaven that it was robbery, nevertheless handed over a hundred guineas. It was not a quarter of its worth, but Aaron accepted it with thanks.

Passage was booked on the packet *Clarissa*, bound via Halifax for Falmouth. It was booked for G. H. Edwards. The vessel would sail June first.

On the night of May thirty-first, Aaron and Theodosia sat together and watched the June morning of their separation dawn above the chimney-pots and tiles of the city. They had had wine for dinner, far more than was their wont. Now, as the moon paled, the hazy courage the wine instilled had worn off. They had said all the casual farewell things that people say when they wish to forget the real anguish before them. There had been welcome last-minute details. She had packed and repacked his cowhide chest, folding his suits and frilled shirts with loving care. The chest was marked "A. B." in brass nails, an oversight. "A. B." were not the initials for a gentleman named G. H. Edwards. The nails had been uprooted and skillfully replaced. Before the trunk was closed, Aaron laid across the piled clothes, just under the lid where it would be uncrushed, Theo's portrait painted five years ago by Vanderlyn. They both stared down at the unframed canvas.

"It shall never leave me for a moment," said Aaron softly. "I shall talk to it. When I write you, I shall prop it up before me and imagine you with me."

"Oh, Father, if I only could go with you——"

He shook his head. "You know how dearly I wish it too. It is impossible."

"Yes, impossible. She would impede him: even had there been enough money, even had she been willing to desert her child. Could she only have taken Gampy too——"

"It won't be for long." Aaron used the reassurance they had been giving each other since first the decision was reached.

It brought no comfort now. Theo leaned her head against the wall, staring out the window. The glimpse of harbor over the roofs was changing from gray to blue in the waxing light.

"If only I could believe in a benevolent God and Heaven ——Don't you ever feel the need of those, Father? Don't you ever fear death?"

"No," he answered her after a thoughtful moment. "I don't fear death. I wish to avoid it as long as I can. But bless me, my dear, we must all die. And when it comes, let us at least die game."

"Yes, I know. But there is scant comfort in that."

"On the contrary, my child, there *is* comfort in that. Courage is a religion in itself: the only religion which is real

281

to me. I do not know whether death is final, but it will be interesting to find out some day. New projects have ever attracted me, as you know." He laughed, the bantering, tender laugh which had never failed to elicit her quick response.

She tried to smile, but she could not. She put her hands to her face to hide the rush of tears. "We're fooling ourselves. It will be a long separation. I know it. I feel it."

He pulled her close to him, her head fell against his shoulder. He smoothed back her hair, drew out his handkerchief and wiped her eyes. "And if it should be, will that change our feeling for each other? Will time or distance diminish our affection?"

"No," she whispered, "nothing could do that: not even death, I think."

"Well, then, no more tears or forebodings, I entreat you. I cannot stand them just now."

He rose and paced quickly up and down the rug before her and turned to the kettle which purred gently on the hob beside a small fire.

"I'll make you a cup of tea, my dear," he said briskly. "It's curious how many sorrows may be alleviated by a glass of wine, a cup of tea, or a good cigar. No, it's true. Don't look at me as though I were an unfeeling monster. There is much solace in the little things of life."

She accepted the steaming cup and choked down some of its contents. "Dolly Madison said something like that to me once."

"And Dolly was right. She is a clever woman." He went to the window and stared out at the risen sun.

"It's time, isn't it?" she said hoarsely.

He nodded. "So wish me Godspeed, Theodosia, but remember we have been parted many times before. This is no different because my journey is longer. Discipline yourself; never relax your habits of study and thought. Train Gampy for the high destiny he may yet achieve, and write to me, as I will you, constantly."

His eyes glistened; he kissed her quickly on the forehead and smiled at her. It was that smile—tender, seductive, brilliant—which comforted her after he was gone. It made him seem young and supremely confident. It banished fear. He had known great misfortune, he had been cruelly used, but it was over now. This time in this new venture he would succeed. Her desolation lightened.

Far out to sea with all sails set the schooner *Clarissa* sped merrily toward Europe, and on the poop deck Mr. G. H. Edwards, huddled in a greatcoat, strained his eyes for a last glimpse of American shores. He had embarked upon a four-year exile.

Chapter Twenty-six

THEODOSIA traveled back to Carolina, using the public conveyances, as there was no vessel in New York Harbor ready to sail for the South. She did not write Joseph of her coming, knowing that she herself was traveling with the mail and would reach the Waccamaw at the same time that a letter would.

It was June, and Gampy was no doubt at Debordieu with Eleanore, but even of this she was not sure. She hired a carriage at Conway, where she left the mail coach, and drove down the Waccamaw Neck to the Oaks. Here she would learn of the whereabouts of her husband and son.

The Oaks was deserted; no black children were in sight around the wide white steps. The blinds were drawn, and the house at first sight gave an impression of blank emptiness. This she had expected. Joseph would not be here during the fever season; he might be at Columbia, Debordieu, or Sullivan's Island. But the servants could tell her where, of course. They would be on their "street," and she debated asking there first, but on impulse tried the front door and found it open.

The drawing-room, with its furniture shrouded in dust-cloths, its rugs rolled, seemed cool and faintly inviting. She sat down to rest a moment on the swathed sofa, and looked up, startled, at the ceiling. Above her head there was a murmur of voices, a woman's throaty laugh.

The blacks, she thought angrily. Can they possibly have the effrontery to use the bedrooms? She ran upstairs. The murmurs came from Joseph's room. Without hesitation, without the slightest presentiment, she flung open the door.

For a blind instant she thought her surmise was confirmed. There was a flash of amber-colored skin and a scream. "Niggers——" The epithet strangled, unuttered. She stood paralyzed, staring. I'm going to be sick, she thought, with impersonal interest. She put her hand to her mouth to choke down the sensation of retching.

Not "niggers" in the plural, but Venus and Joseph. Vaguely she saw his sweating face, white as paste, his coarse hair ludicrously mussed, clutching his dressing-gown around him, his eyes popping at her. She saw him but vaguely because her entire attention was concentrated on Venus. The girl in a white shift had a savage beauty. If she had felt shame for a second, it was gone. Her tigerish eyes were yellow with malignancy and triumph. She tilted back her head on its long column of throat, the color and texture of yellowed ivory. And she laughed.

"Welcome, Mistiss. You'm onexpected, enty?" Her insolence was alive, like a beast springing.

From the moment we saw each other, it has been leading to this, thought Theo, and abruptly she became calm. The first nauseating shock vanished. The girl has always hated me, been jealous of me. She thinks she has her revenge now.

"Theodosia——For God's sake. What are you going to do?"

She turned and contemplated Joseph. He was in real anguish, in an agony of remorse that transcended shame. Even though he had been caught in the most embarrassing situation known to man, he had recaptured some dignity. He no longer looked ridiculous.

"What is there for me to do?" she said quietly.

Venus darted forward, her thin, voluptuous face raised defiantly. "Yo' speak truth. Yo' kain' do nothin'. You'm no wife. You'm cold as graveyard stone. Ober and ober yo' go way off and leave him. Always yo' pleasure yo'self. Dat's howcome yo' los' yo' man."

"Shut up, you bitch!" Joseph dealt her a clout across the mouth.

She fell back against the bedpost, her lips swelling, but still defiant. "Yo' kin hit me effen yo' want ter, it ain' gwine wipe out the feel of Venus's arms about yo'. Yo' got me in your blood, Maussa. She ain' nothin' to yuh."

Joseph did not hear her. "Theo," he mumbled, "don't look at me like that. It was a madness you can't understand——"

There came a flicker of doubt into Venus's sneering eyes. She had been so sure of her power, of her revenge. In her slender golden body she had thought to possess the sure instrument of revenge against her slavery, against the white woman. And now she wasn't sure. The white woman should have been screaming, ranting, livid with fury. This quiet silence—what did that mean? She kain' do nothin' to me, thought Venus frantically. She kain' make him have me lashed, or sell me to the Floridas. I'll git a conjuh that'll work. I'll kill myself—or her. Her eyes narrowed. There were poisons——

"Go now, Venus," said Theodosia. Her voice held neither anger nor contempt. To her own amazement she felt none. A curious detachment had descended on her. She saw that the girl was seething with hatred and fear, and it did not touch her; she even felt a twinge of pity.

Venus stumbled over to Joseph, tugged at his arm in frantic appeal. "Don' let her do nothin' to me. Yo' promise me I kin hab clothes an' a fine new cabin. Yo' promise me I could live like buckra. Yo' kain' go back on dat, Maussa." Her long, nearly straight black hair fell forward, hiding her convulsed face. She buried it on his arm.

He shook her off. "Get out, nigger!" He spat the last word at her, giving it its full force of insult.

Venus lifted her head. "I ain' no nigger," she panted. "I'm a Berber. I'd be a princess in my own land." She flung her slender arms upward. "I wish God would strike yuh both daid."

She was terrifying. Joseph stepped back involuntarily, then, quickly recovering, raised his clenched fist. Before he could strike, Venus gave a choking cry, her thin shoulders quivered, and she stumbled out through the door.

Joseph sank on the bed and buried his face in his hands.

"Has this been going on a long time?" asked Theo, in a voice devoid of all emotion.

Her quiet frightened him as it had Venus. He made an imploring gesture.

"I suppose I should have guessed it long ago. I've been very stupid," she added.

"It hasn't been long," he muttered. "Only a couple of months. She was sitting outside her cabin one night—singing. There were flowers in her hair. I was lonely——"

"You needn't explain it to me, Joseph. I am quite aware that men take mistresses. But I wish it had not been one of your own slaves and in our own home."

Her cool voice augmented his shame. He had tried to forget, during these weeks of blind passion with Venus, that she was one of his slaves. He thought of the disgust with which his father or brothers would regard any intercourse

286

with the slaves. It happened, of course; that fellow on the Santee was debarred from Charleston society because of it. But it was contemptible. It was her fault—that brown devil with her luring voice and her thin, passionate lips!

He sprang up. "I'll sell the bitch tomorrow!"

"No." Theo seated herself quietly and shook her head.

He went on, unheeding. "She shall be sent down to the barracoon in Charleston. The factor will take charge of it, see that she is bought for a distant plantation. You wanted me to do that once before. I wish I'd heeded you. Oh, Theo—with all my soul, I wish you had been spared this humiliation—and I too," he added with a groan.

She surveyed his self-abasement with maternal tolerance. Having no physical love for him, it was easy for her to forgive. Her first reaction had sprung from the hurt to her pride and revulsion from an ugly episode. And there was truth in Venus's accusation: she was not a good wife in the conventional sense. Poor Joseph, she thought, as she had so many times.

"I don't want you to sell Venus," she repeated gently.

He raised his head, wondering what punishment, then, Theo deemed the girl deserved. Whatever it was he would comply. A wife so sorely humiliated might make any conditions.

"I want you to set her free, Joseph."

His jaw dropped. "What!"

"Yes. Give her her freedom. She's like a mountain lioness from the back hills, trapped and caged. It is because she is caged that she's dangerous. And she is dangerous; she always has been. I think slavery is wrong, anyhow, but for those others it does not matter: they are stupid, and they are better cared for by us than they could manage for themselves. Yes, I know. We must have field hands, or what would become of the rice? But Venus is no field hand."

"She would bring me a very good price," said Joseph. He was dazed by her magnanimity.

"You can afford to forego the price.—Oh, yes, you can."

"But what would she do—where would she go?"

She was silent a minute; then she said: "I think you should buy her a passage to the North, Boston, perhaps, and give her a little money besides. Up there she will find her own level.—And don't tell her it was my idea. Let her think that she has won this great victory over me and her hatred will vanish at last."

"You're wonderful, Theo," he said humbly.

His humility did not last long. In an hour he was blustering at her for having stayed North so long, and how dared she stop at the Oaks during the fever season! Even one night might be dangerous.

"You were here, willing to take the risk yourself," she pointed out.

He reddened and was momentarily silenced. At any rate, she must go to Debordieu as soon as the sun was up and sleep with her windows tight shut against the night air.

"Of course," she agreed. "I'm aching to see my child. I've longed for him constantly, but——"

But your father came first as usual, thought Joseph bitterly, but he did not say it. They did not mention Aaron after she had given him the bare facts of his sailing. Joseph was relieved. Good riddance. The stormy petrel had finally departed to a safe distance from whence he could no longer foul the family nest. He showed restraint in not laboring this viewpoint. Gratitude kept him silent. Theo had shown incredible generosity in her treatment of Venus and himself. He would show equal generosity by never referring to her disgraceful father. They would start afresh.

His hopes were realized except for one thing. Theo settled quietly back into life in Carolina. She ran his households more efficiently than she ever had. Indeed, with Venus gone, the blacks became more amenable to her rule. She did the necessary civilities to his family: without enthusiasm, and on both sides with nothing more than chilly politeness, but still she did them. She spent much time with Gampy, tutoring him, playing with him. To Joseph himself she was invariably charming. She consulted his wishes and bore with his ill temper.

But she retained her own bedroom, and the door remained shut. And he could do nothing. Her health was poor, as it always was on the Waccamaw. She suffered from headaches and a recurrence of the kidney complications which had accompanied Gampy's birth. She seldom complained, but she proffered this as excuse for the shut door. He grew to feel that, besides this, her refusal sprang from his guilty affair with Venus. She had forgiven it, had been angelic in her forbearance, yet it was not surprising that a pure delicate woman, herself naturally chaste, should recoil from this memory. It made a barrier that time alone could surmount.

So thought Joseph, saving his pride, and she let him think so. It didn't matter what he thought, so long as she escaped the embraces which had always been revolting and would now be unbearable. She felt some guilt for this final complete denial of conjugal rights, but none for the secret occupation which consumed every free minute she dared snatch: the dispatch of letters, to everyone who might have influence to remove the persecution against Aaron.

When, in the spring of 1809, she read of the election of James Madison to the Presidency, her heart beat high with hope. Had not Dolly once said, "Of course, I am Colonel Burr's friend"? That charming blue-eyed lady would not be cold as were these ingrates. And she could do anything with her Jemmy.

Theo sharpened her quill and bent again to the task.

> Madam: You may perhaps be surprised at receiving a letter from one with whom you have had so little intercourse for the last few years. But your surprise will cease when you recollect that my father, once your friend, is now in exile; and that the President only can restore him to me and to his country.

Her pen flew over the pages of entreaty, but she warned the good lady that "Mr. Alston is ignorant of the step I have taken in writing to you."

When the answer came, it was cruelly disappointing. Dolly wrote affectionately. It took careful re-reading to discover that the sweetness concealed denial. There was nothing that the Madisons could do "at present" except tender good wishes and affectionate remembrances, etc.

In truth, Madison was far too harassed in attending to other legacies from the Jefferson administrations to concern himself with an unpopular exile.

This was a blow to Theo, who had counted on Dolly's friendship. Still, Aaron's letters were encouraging. He was enjoying himself in London; had met a vast number of people in high places, many of whom were sympathetic to "X." Lord Holland and the Earl of Bridgewater had received him cordially. He made long visits to Jeremy Bentham, the philosopher, a kindred spirit. There was no cause for worry.

Theo kept these precious letters locked in a small casket which she carried with her everywhere. She wrote voluminous answers and bribed little Cupid to smuggle them off the Waccamaw to the northbound mail. This procedure was unnecessary, for Joseph was often absent, and, if he had intercepted one of her letters now, he would have looked the other way.

But Theo took no chances. He had once concealed a letter, one of such importance that had he not done so it might have changed Aaron's life. She could not trust him where her father was concerned.

On the fifth of October, 1809, Theo was reinstalled at the Oaks after a summer of short trips in search of coolness and health. Debordieu had not seemed to answer. It had been oppressed this year by a nearly constant land breeze tainted with the swamps. She had gathered up Gampy and Eleanore and a handful of servants and tried various up-country resorts in the Carolinas—Rocky River Springs, Greenville, Chevalos—without finding permanent relief at any of them.

Now, with cooler weather, her spirits lightened a little. It was not disagreeable to rest at the Oaks. It was the hour for lessons. She and Gampy were secluded in the library. The seven-year-old was hunched over his little desk, laboriously writing at her dictation.

"Amo, amas, amat," said Theo. "Take heed, darling. You will have to recite all this from memory presently."

He nodded, frowning with concentration.

I shall have to get him a tutor soon, she thought. He learns so rapidly that he will be beyond me.

She looked at the curly brown head proudly. If only her father might see him now. She treasured every one of Gampy's sayings and precocious doings to send to Aaron, who never failed to comment on each one with lively interest. Even three thousand miles away he showed more interest in the boy than did Joseph, she thought, not quite justly. Joseph was fond of his son; yet he saw him but seldom, and he did not understand that severe displays of paternal authority frightened the little boy, who kept out of his way as much as possible.

"Now conjugate the whole verb for me," she suggested, seeing that he had finished.

Gampy had obediently begun, when they were both startled as a shrill scream came from the porch outside, followed by the excited chatter of black voices.

"What in the world——" began Theo, laying down her Latin grammar.

The door burst open, and Eleanore rushed in, cap awry, gesticulating wildly. "O Madame, il y a un sauvage dans le jardin!"

Mother and son stared, Gampy's eyes round with excitement.

Then Theo laughed. "Nonsense, Eleanore. There are no Indians on the Waccamaw."

"Moi-même, je l'ai vu! He is vilain et féroce, with fezzers in his hair, and a gun. Mon Dieu, he will shoot us all."

"I hardly think so, Eleanore. But, come, show me this Indian."

"Me, too, Mama. Let me come, too," wailed Gampy, as she motioned him to stay there. "I want to see an Indian."

"If he is a friendly one, I will call you," she promised.

The shrinking Eleanore led the way to the porch. "Voilà, Madame!" She pointed a trembling finger.

"It *is* an Indian!" cried Theo, surprised and interested, though certainly not a hostile one, for his gun was slung across his back and he had one hand upheld in greeting. His long hair was twisted on top of his head and skewered with an eagle feather, but his dress was the conventional fringed buckskin suit of the backwoodsman. He wore beaded moccasins, but she had seen those, too, on many white men out West. His copper-red face was unpainted and serene.

He advanced quietly down the lawn, ignoring the scared black faces that peered at him from around the corner of the house.

"Ciel—sauvez-vous, Madame!" screamed Eleanore, tugging at Theo's arm.

"Certainly not," said Theo impatiently. "Stop making such a fuss. I cannot imagine what he wants, but he has a good face."

The Indian now mounted the steps toward Theo, and Eleanore gave a stifled gasp and fled.

"What do you want?" Theo stood still, staring into the impassive dark eyes that, now that he had gained the porch, were a foot above hers.

"You Mrs. Alston?"

She nodded, puzzled.

He silently slid his hand into his leather jacket, took from it a letter, and held it out to her.

It was inscribed, "Mrs. Theodosia Burr Alston," in an unfamiliar handwriting. She made no move to take it. Her brain darted over a score of possibilities. It must be something to do with Aaron, of course. This peculiar messenger might have come from one of his remaining supporters out West: but it could be some kind of trap. Devious and many had been the instruments of his persecution already; this might be a new device.

"Where do you come from?" she asked, temporizing.

The Indian held the letter rigidly out in front of him "From setting sun, beyond Great River," he answered "And how did you get here?"

"Follow trail over plains and mountains. One moon since.'

"Ask him his name, Mama." A small excited voice from behind her betrayed that Gampy, unable to bear the suspense any longer, had crept out on the porch and was staring at the Indian in openmouthed fascination.

The Indian turned his head a fraction, and a faint smile softened the grimness of his face as he saw the boy. He touched his breast. "Wabasha. Me Sioux Chief."

"Then what in Heaven's name can a Sioux Chief want with me?" she cried, half to herself.

"Read——" He indicated the letter. She took it from him now, still wary.

The Sioux folded his arms against his chest and stared, expressionless, out over the lawn.

Theo broke the red seal, noting with increased disquiet that it had been impressed with a governmental insignia She saw the date, "St. Louis, September first, 1809," and then she knew: knew before she turned the closely written sheets, and saw at the bottom, the signature, "Merne."

The letter dropped to her lap. The name penetrated her heart with a pain that she had believed conquered. I won't read it, she thought violently. He has nothing to do with me. This is some new injury against Father.

True, he had been merciful according to his lights in Richmond; he did not give evidence, whatever it was. But she no longer felt that the evidence could have been harmful. Aaron had been acquitted. He would have been so, anyway, she thought now, secure in the calm of certainty. Her doubts, her suspense, her pleadings with Merne seemed shameful in retrospect. She revolted from the memory of her attempts to force his love: a love which he no longer wished to feel.

"Why don't you read your letter, Mama? Who's it from?" Gampy, having examined the impassive Indian from all angles, now pushed against her knee curiously.

Yes, of course I must read it, she thought. This is ridiculous. But not here. She must be alone. "Go back to the library, Gampy," she directed, "and wait there. I'll be with you in a minute."

She went to her own room and locked the door. She unfolded the paper with determination. How strange that she had never seen his handwriting before! It was clear, bold, and very legible. The letter began abruptly.

The Indian who brings you this is my trusted friend. I did him a favor once which he is now repaying. I cannot trust this message to the mails.

I am going to die, Theodosia. I cannot tell you how I know it, but I do. I might tell you of a vision I had, the second-sight of my Scotch forebears. I might tell you of the prophecy of a Mandan woman. These Indians see many things we do not, and they often see the future true. This may be folly and superstition. But for me, I know that the trail is nearly ended.

I want to see you once again first. I shall be with you in mid-October. I shall not embarrass you; it will be for a few hours. I am on my way to Washington to try to clear my name.

President Madison has seen fit to question my expenditures out here. He questions my honor. It seems that I have made many enemies, who do not scruple to slander me.

Is there something familiar to you in this, Theo? Yes, I also see the parallel. You called me hard and cruel in my judgment of your father. Perhaps I was. In my own consciousness of rectitude, I thoughtlessly assumed that the opinion of the majority must be justifiable: that there can be no smoke without fire. Now I am no longer sure. I am discovering for myself that lies may be as effective as truth.

Had I one human being on whose unswerving loyalty I could count, as he could count on you, I would call myself blessed. I feel this now, who never did before. I have always gloried in my internal solitude. Even you have never touched it.

And now I am lonely. I am thirty-five, yet I feel old and finished. I do not say this to arouse your pity—God forbid! I am trying to explain to you and myself why I must see you. It is a yearning of the spirit. Our love has never reached fruition; it has been tainted time and again, by desire, by anger, by the sordid, and even the grotesque.

And yet it has been love. We were, I believe, meant by Heaven or destiny or what you will to be together. That we have never been is the result of the strange compulsions of the human heart. You had—you will always have—a greater love than I. I, too, had other loyalties.

I think that somewhere and sometime there will be a state where these different loves will not conflict. It is one of the things I wish to tell you of. I cannot write them.

I have lain under the stars. I have listened to the voice of the waters—the rivers that you love. The wilderness has taught me. I think I can make you understand, too.

MERNE

Theo sat quietly, the letter in her hand. He who had never needed her, who had repudiated her love the last time they were together, he needed her now. He was in trouble and lonely. How gladly would she see him! They might meet now, at last, untroubled by passion, unclouded by obscure resentments.

"Mid-October," he had written. He had already started, then. He would be here in a few days. They could be together, not only for a few hours, but he must stay at the Oaks. Joseph would be pleased to entertain the Governor, and Joseph knew nothing of their association. In any event he could have no objection. She and Merne had no relationship to which a husband could object. That was finished.

She discounted Merne's premonition of death. That was a morbidity she had not expected from him. It was born of loneliness, and perhaps illness. The fever gave one fancies like that. How often she had seen it!

She read the letter again, then, leaning over the fire, put it on the embers, where it flared up brightly and was gone.

The Sioux was standing where she had left him, on the porch. She approached him smiling. "Governor Lewis says you are his trusted friend. I thank you for bringing me the message. Come in and I will give you food and drink. You must stay here as long as you like and rest."

The Indian's calm eyes surveyed her. "I will eat, then I go."

"Not at once. I will give you a room. You must rest some days."

"No, I eat, then I go. Back to my own people. I like it not here."

Theo could do nothing with him, except order the mutinous servants to provide him with food. They sidled past him warily. Cato flung the dishes of rice and roast meat at him, as though he were tending a crouching panther. They had worked up a pleasurable fear of being tomahawked, and they resented the dark-skinned visitor's acceptance at the buckra dining-table.

A faint amusement flickered in Wabasha's face, but he said nothing at all. Theo sat down beside him and tried to draw him out. Gampy, more than ever fascinated with this

294

interesting break in his monotonous life on the Waccamaw, hovered beside her.

"Governor Lewis is on his way East," said Theodosia. "By what route is he coming?"

"Boat down Great River to Chickasaw. Then trail."

"You mean he will follow the Natchez Trace?"

Wabasha grunted.

"Do you think he has reached the Alleghenies yet?"

The Indian did not answer. He speared himself half a wild duck, picked the bleeding flesh neatly off with his fingers. The rice, which he had never seen before, he did not touch.

"Has the Governor been ill—sick?" she asked, trying again.

For a moment she thought there would be no answer to this either. Wabasha consumed his duck in silence. She sighed, when suddenly he raised his head and looked at her.

"Sick in body—no. His spirit is sick. The Bird of Death has touched him."

"The Bird of Death?" she repeated blankly. "What do you mean by that?"

Wabasha shrugged. "Great white bird from the North. When it touches with its wings, we die. My people know. Governor know too."

Can it be that Merne has really let himself become infected with this heathen folly? she thought, dismayed. It is as bad as the blacks'.

"How can this be if he is not sick?" She spoke with matter-of-fact briskness, suddenly conscious of Gampy's sharpened interest.

"All trails lead to death," said Wabasha. "It matters not which one he travels. White bird comes for all. For him it will be soon."

Theo rose abruptly, with a gesture of impatience, but Gampy, his small serious face pillowed on his hands, stared at the Indian across the table. "Is it ugly—the bird?" he asked. "Does it scare you?"

Wabasha pushed back his plate and wiped his mouth. "Not ugly, little one. His feathers are deep—soft."

Gampy considered this, and nodded. "Where does he fly to?"

What morbid tarradiddles are these? thought Theo. I must stop it. Gampy should not think of such things. And yet she waited for the Indian's answer.

"He flies to the land beyond the cold. A good place."

The boy accepted this with the same unchildish quiet. "I wouldn't be afraid," he said.

Theodosia saw a change in the Indian's face. A ripple that vanished at once, not pity or sympathy, but a softening. A shiver ran through her.

"That's enough, Gampy," she said sharply. "Don't bother our guest with foolish questions."

"But I want to ask him some more about the good place where the bird goes."

"You don't know what you're talking about, darling. What does he know of such matters?" She was careless whether she affronted the Indian or not. It was necessary to efface that unnatural old look from the child's face. "If you want to ask these questions, save them for the Sabbath; the rector will explain to you."

But he doesn't, Mama. I can't understand what he says. He uses long words. I don't like him. I like Wabasha——"

They both turned at a soft sound. The Sioux Chief had risen. There was quiet force in his tall figure. "I go," he said, with simple dignity. He raised his hands shoulder-high, palms upward. "May the Great Spirit be ever near you." He added strange and yet musical syllables: invocation or farewell? Theo could not tell, though she felt their message, and they had beauty.

Gampy struggled to run forward, crying, "Please don't go, Wabasha." Theo put a gentle arm around the boy and held him back.

The Indian, with quick soundless step, disappeared through the door.

At once Eleanore, who had been hovering nervously in the hall outside, burst in on them. "Ciel!" she cried. "He is gone, then, le sauvage! He vanish into the forest like a shadow. What did he want with you, Madame? Is he dangerous?"

Theo smiled faintly. "No, he was not dangerous. He brought me a message from the West."

"And he told me about the Bird of Death," added Gampy softly.

Eleanore stared. "Bird of Death! Qu'est-ce que c'est que ça? Death—la Mort——" She made the sign of the cross, her voice rose: "But then he will attack us! He has his men hidden in the forest, he goes to get them. We shall be massacred yet, Madame. You will see."

"That's silly, Eleanore," cried Gampy. "Wabasha was a good man, wasn't he, Mama?"

"Yes." Theodosia tightened her arm around his thin little body. "But he said many foolish things. He is not a Christian, you know. He is very superstitious, like—well, like

296

our blacks here. You know how they believe in conjuh?"

Gampy shook his head stubbornly. "It's not the same. And, anyway, conjuh does work sometimes. Old Maum Chloe can make it rain, and she can make cows sick, and——"

"Oh, Gampy, darling, that is just coincidence. It just happens that way. Now you know there isn't any big white bird. And no one can foretell another's death, or his own. I want you to forget all that folly."

She kissed the troubled face. "We are expecting a guest," she added, with a change of tone. "We must make ready the blue room. Eleanore, see to the linen and have the floors polished. Gampy, you may help me pick flowers to put in the vases."

"Who's coming, Mama?"

She hesitated, startled at the uprush of joy in her throat. "Meriwether Lewis, Governor of the North Louisiana Territory, an old friend of mine."

She had forgotten Eleanore, whose anxiety about the Indian was removed by this interesting disclosure. "Ah, ça, Madame!" she gasped. "Encore de jeune homme!" What remarkable people, these Americans! They have une affaire, they part, and do not meet for years. They send messages by red Indians, they come to stay in the husband's home. But it will do Madame good. She has had so much trouble, so much worry with her father, and Monsieur Alston, too, avec cette sale négresse. Eleanore, of course, had come to know about Venus.

"Madame will want some new clothes," she suggested, with an expression which could only be described as a respectful leer. "She has nothing pretty enough—assez séduisant—for the receiption of a—a Governor."

Theo frowned. "You don't understand. It is not like that now. All that you are thinking, c'est fini. Governor Lewis is an old acquaintance who finds it convenient to stop off here on his way to Washington. C'est tout."

"Certainement, Madame." Eleanore was unconvinced. More than ever unconvinced, as Theo, after all, sent one of the servants to Charleston by boat with the rice, with instructions to bring back five yards of embroidered India muslin, two yards of gold ribbon, and the latest fashion papers. She noted sympathetically also that Madame spent much more time than usual before the mirror.

She came into Theo's room one morning with the cut pattern of the new dress, for trying on, and found her mistress at the dressing-table peering anxiously into the greenish glass.

"Soyez tranquille, Madame, vous êtes toujours belle." She took up the brush and began brushing the long curling hair with soothing strokes.

"I found some gray hairs," said Theo. "I pulled them out, but more will come. And I am sallow."

"This terrible climate. It ages one. But he will not notice. He will still think you lovely."

This time her allusion went unreproved. It was true: she still wanted him to think her lovely. Each day since the receipt of his message, her longing had grown. She awoke to think—Will it be today?—and retired each night with an ever-mounting weight of disappointment.

Everything was ready. Flowers were renewed each day in the blue room, the fire laid on the hearth. Cupid or one of the other black boys kept constant watch at the gate. They had orders to scamper to the house with warning at the first sign of a horseman on the river road. She was sure that he would come on horseback. Merne had ever disdained a lumbering coach.

But no one came. No one but William Algernon and Polly Alston to pay a brief call. Theo was in a fever of impatience while they sat languidly sipping rum punch and making civil conversation on the porch. Suppose this should be the moment of Merne's arrival, now, with this critical brother-and sister-in-law to witness their meeting! They would have to pretend again, she and Merne, as they had so often been forced to pretend, that they did not know each other well, make formal greeting, guard their eyes from each other. They must meet as strangers, or the family tongues would be yapping.

She controlled her desire to be rid of these two, forced her tongue to civil inquiry—"How is little Eliza?" and, "Are you indeed going to Charleston so early this season?" and, "How is Colonel William's health now? Joseph and I were much distressed to hear that he had had a touch of ague."

And as she talked, her glance slid past them down the drive, her fingers pleated a fold of her skirt.

"And when will Joseph be back from Columbia, this time?" asked William Algernon.

She caught sight of Cupid scampering toward them, and her heart hammered. She rose abruptly, sank back again. Cupid turned off toward the quarters.

"I'm sorry," she said to their surprised faces, "I thought

298

someone was coming. Why—I don't know when Joseph will be back. Perhaps next week."

"Joseph is becoming of great political importance," remarked William Algernon, helping himself to more punch.

"You must be proud of him," added Polly amiably. "Very like he will be Governor of the State yet."

"Perhaps he will," said Theo. Would they never go? Just now, as dusk was gathering under the hanging moss and the porch was shadowed, he would be most likely to come—at the end of a day's ride.

But when the Alstons had gone, trundling away in their chaise for the hour's drive to Rose Hill, he had not come. She lit all the tapers downstairs, so that the house might blaze with welcoming light. It was not yet too late to hope. Though most horsemen would not brave strange roads in the dark, Merne was different. How many strange dark roads he had traveled! She thought of the expedition. How little she knew of the other part of his life! She had asked him nothing of the great and successful adventure during their brief unhappy interview in Richmond. It would be different now. They would have leisure to talk. Just to talk, she thought. He is my friend: no longer lover. I don't want that, nor does he. Now that he has acknowledged his injustice—I can talk to him about Father. He will help me, tell me what to do now. The joy of speaking of Aaron to Merne! Of receiving sympathy and help, where there had once been bitter hostility. She clasped her hands hard against her chest. Oh, why doesn't he come!

She sat down to write to Aaron, but tonight words crept slowly. She dared not write, yet, of the matter which was consuming her heart. After Merne had come, she would tell Aaron, make him understand that Merne had changed; she would at last melt bitterness from between those two. But tonight she could not write.

She had made a map, a rough, inaccurate sketch, worked out from such maps as she could find, of his probable journey. If only she knew more details! If he had left St. Louis, then—he must be here now, or here. She made tiny marks on the paper. Wabasha had said he would follow the Natchez Trace into Tennessee, then Nashville, and down through the northeast corner of Georgia into Carolina. She could not be sure of the route, and there might be any number of hazards to cause delay. Her own journey West had taught her that.

The hall clock struck midnight before she dragged herself reluctantly up to her room. "Tomorrow, then," she told herself. "He said mid-October and this is only the twenty-third. It is folly to expect him yet."

She snuffed her candle. That night she dreamed of him. He was standing beside the mighty river; the sound of its rushing waters deafened her ears. As she came to him, he held out his arms, and she felt his kiss with a rapture greater than any she had ever known. "I knew you'd come to me," she said, laughing, and turned without surprise to see her father with them, too. He was young and smiling, as he had been in the days at Richmond Hill. "Now I am happy," she told them, and, though her voice was lost in the roar of the flood, she saw that they understood.

The dream dissolved into trivialities. But a springing fountain of joy remained. She awoke with it.

It's an omen, she thought, half-ashamed of the superstition. Today he will surely come.

She sang that day little snatches of popular songs. She played with Gampy, delighting the little boy with her nonsense, joining him in a picnic on the lawn. He begged to take their lunch down the river "to a new place," but this she would not do. Nor leave the house a second.

She appeased him with stories, and even, careless of the giggling servants, chased the squealing, ecstatic child round and round amongst the giant live-oaks in a game of hide-and-seek.

"I didn't know old people could run so well," observed Gampy, after she had caught him.

"I'm not really so very old," laughed Theo, out of breath.

"I guess not," agreed Gampy dubiously. "Anyway, you don't look it now. You look awful pretty."

"Do I, darling? That's because I'm happy, I guess."

"Why are you happy?"

"Because—because——" She broke off and stared down the avenue of live-oaks. This time surely she would see Cupid come running with the news. There was no one, only the murmur of a little wind in the trees as it stirred the hanging gray fronds.

Gampy had lost interest. "It's almost night-time, Mama; maybe we better go in. It's cold."

"Oh, no," she cried, "it isn't late yet. The sun won't set for hours."

"It has set," he objected, astounded at this denseness. "Look over toward the river. It's all gone. Let's have more games in the house, Mama. It's cold."

300

She drew him to her, sheltering him with her arm. Silently they walked back to the house.

As the days went by, she did not laugh again or play with Gampy. Though she read to him and supervised his lessons with her usual loving care, there was no more gaiety.

On the first of November, Joseph returned from Columbia. He was glad to be home, pleased to see Theo and the boy, anxious to get out and inspect the condition of the rice fields. After he had eaten, he announced that he was going to the overseer's house to confer with him. "Here are some of the latest newspapers from Columbia," he said, dropping a sheaf of them on the table before her, "though I believe there is nothing of special interest." He went out.

Theo turned the papers over listlessly. It was thus that she came upon an item.

GOVERNOR MERIWETHER LEWIS OF THE NORTH LOUISIANA TERRITORY MOST FOULLY ASSASSINATED
> The Governor on his way east, near Nashville, was set upon by bandits and shot. Every effort is being made to apprehend the murderers.

There was more, but she did not read it. She gave a small whimper like a frightened child. She uttered no other sound, but sat rigid holding the newspaper and staring out the window into the gathering dusk.

Chapter Twenty-seven

AARON SPENT four years in exile, years of diminishing hope and ever more stringent poverty. The first fair promises of the great in England faded into evasions, into boredom, and then into suspicion. In the end it became necessary for Lord Liverpool to write a bland note, the purport of which was that Colonel Burr's presence in England had unfortunately become embarrassing to the Government. He might have passports and free passage to any port he wished, but he must avail himself of them.

So Aaron tried Sweden, then Germany and Paris. He ingratiated himself with many, he pursued several desultory love affairs, and he oscillated between a giddy social life and actual hunger when the sale of his watch or of some coins he had bought as a present for Gampy saved him from starvation. But the plans for "X" were at a standstill. Indeed, in Europe, except for the initial interest of some English noblemen, they never began.

When Aaron reached Paris, he made many abortive efforts to gain audience with the King of Westphalia. The former Jerome Bonaparte ignored him, no less completely than did his imperial brother. Aaron kept up his spirits as best he could. He wrote Theo determinedly cheerful letters that hid his disappointment. He kept a journal which she should see some day and laugh over, when they were together once more. He was outwardly cheerful, but his health, for the first time in his life, was poor, and he longed for home. He was, moreover, worried about Theodosia.

There had been a silence of many months in the winter of 1809, and though, when he finally received a letter, she wrote in her usual vein, telling him of her efforts to insure his reinstatement, telling him news of Gampy, telling him how desperately she missed him, yet there was a note that disturbed him. She had abandoned their carefully maintained playfulness, their fiction that all was well with him. She implored him to come home.

> Risk anything, make any sacrifice, but come home. Or, if the worst comes to the worst, I will leave everything to suffer with you. The icy hand of disappointment falls upon my heart to smother every spark. Do not frown at these complaints. Oh, my guardian angel, why were you obliged to abandon me? How much I need your counsel and tenderness . . .

Aaron read these letters anxiously, puzzled by their extravagance. He knew that her health was none too good, but he felt in her a despair that went deeper than physical discomfort: a profound unhappiness for which he knew no source.

He determined to come home. He felt his fiber deteriorating. He was aging—at last he knew it. And he longed for the two who were of his blood, Theodosia and the child. He spent many futile, miserable months in trying to obtain a passport, and when finally, in March of 1812, he obtained passage from London for Boston on the *Aurora*, war rumors were thick between the United States and England.

The British had been secretly inciting the Indians to revolt; they had attacked American ships; they had kidnaped four thousand American seamen and impressed them into the British Naval Service; besides this they had instituted a virtual blockade of American waters. The South felt that these conditions were intolerable and was clamoring for war. New England held that compromise was possible. President Madison also endeavored to stem the rising tide of public hysteria. But the old enmity and jealousy caused by the War of Independence sprang up again. Twenty-nine years had not been long enough to lay them permanently.

Aaron had little love for the America which had cast him out, but none at all for England which had done the same. He stood upon the *Aurora's* deck and watched the gray line of land fade into the horizon.

"I hope never to visit England again," he said to the kindly captain, who had finally consented to ship this inconvenient and unpopular passenger, "except at the head of fifty thousand men. *Insula inhospitabilis,* as it was truly called eighteen hundred years ago."

303

Captain Potter grunted. "I hope this tarnation war don't catch us in mid-ocean. The *Aurora* will be captured sure. She's none too fast."

Aaron laughed. "Have no fear. Our present administration will never declare war. We are totally unprepared. We have neither men nor money, and I believe but twenty warships. I treat the country's war prattle as I should that of a bevy of boarding-school misses. Show them a bayonet or a sword and they will run and hide."

He was wrong. War was declared between England and the United States on June eighteenth, but by that time the *Aurora* was safe in Boston Harbor.

The *Aurora* was safe, but Aaron was not. The government prosecutions still hung over him. Two of his largest creditors in New York held judgments against him: it was necessary not to be recognized until they could somehow be appeased. So Aaron borrowed an old-fashioned wig and clothes that were too large for him. A rather shabby Mr. Arnot slipped back into his country in much the same way that Mr. Edwards had sneaked out of it four years before. This was not the triumphant return they had pictured, he and Theo. But at least he was back on the same continent with her. Let him once reach New York and their meeting would not be long delayed.

Aaron hid for some weeks in Boston and then decided on a bold move. A letter from Samuel Swartwout in New York encouraged him. The Government was far too busy with its war to bother about a penniless exile. Even his creditors might be kept quiet for a time. So Aaron sold his few remaining books to Harvard College to secure passage money and sailed for New York. He took lodging on Nassau Street and hung before the door a modest tin sign bearing only his name. He inserted a line in the newspapers, saying, "Aaron Burr has returned to this city and resumed the practice of law." Then he settled back to await results.

These were highly gratifying at first. Clients flocked to him. People were curious; they reminded each other that, after all, he had been acquitted. Anyway, it was all years ago. Even the duel was no longer interesting, and whatever else little Burr might or might not be, no one had ever questioned his legal ability. The creditors stayed their hands while they waited to see whether he could make some money.

Aaron's spirits soared at once. On the strength of two thousand dollars in fees he wrote exultantly to Theodosia. They would buy back Richmond Hill. Everything should be as it used to be. "These dark hours through which we have passed will be all forgot," he wrote. "They are forgot already. You and Gampy and I will yet realize our glorious future. I await your arrival with the utmost impatience. Kiss the boy for me and tell him that I have many little gifts with which to amuse him. As for you, hussy, I have bought you some topaz earrings. You will be a veritable houri in them."

He mailed this letter on June thirtieth and walked buoyantly back to his dingy little law office.

The letter reached Theo two weeks later at Debordieu Island. She lay on the bed in the octagonal back room of the beach cottage. She lay utterly still, her unwinking gaze fixed upon the boards which formed the ceiling.

Joseph brought the letter to her. He knelt down beside the bed and put it gently in her hand. Her fingers did not move and it slipped to the sheet.

"It's from your father, Theo." His voice held a new softness, his heavy face was drawn and haggard.

"From Father?" she questioned vaguely. "Read it to me." She turned her head painfully on the pillow. Her eyes, no longer swollen with weeping, but expressionless as black glass, rested on him quietly.

"I don't want to read it," he cried hoarsely. "He doesn't know."

She reached for the letter, holding it between her fingers. "No, poor Father. He doesn't know about Gampy. He doesn't know Gampy's dead." She gave a small high laugh. "I didn't think I'd ever be able to say that. It doesn't seem to mean anything any more. Isn't that queer?"

Joseph got up and poured a glassful of medicine from the bottle by the bed. He held it to her docile lips and she drank unquestioningly. Then he called Eleanore.

The maid ran in, her black wool dress hanging slack upon her once ample body, her eyes rimmed with red. "Elle est pire, monsieur?" she whispered.

He nodded. "She is more feverish."

He walked through the house onto the porch. The ocean lay there in front of him, quiet and gray-blue in the twilight. He dropped down on a step and stared at it dully.

There must be someone who could help her. He could not reach her. During the first ghastly days after the little boy died, the women of his family had been there—Mrs. Alston and Sally and Polly. She had refused to see them, as she refused to leave the room where the child had died.

Gampy was buried at the Oaks in the family burying ground. Joseph had understood her anguished refusal to be present when the small coffin was placed, but he had tried to persuade her to go to the burial service with the family. All Saints' Parish Church had been beautiful with flowers, and the words of the service had given him a little comfort. They might have helped her too. But she would not go.

There had been wild grief at first, an agony of tears, far less terrifying than this devastating quiet that had now settled on her. Day after day she lay on the bed, gently answering when spoken to, but without will or life of her own. Sometimes, when Joseph tried to rouse her, she gathered herself together as though she listened. But not to him—straining for some voice he could not hear, when all that broke the silence was the monotonous crash of the surf.

Gampy's illness had been so cruelly short. He came into the house from playing on the sands and his teeth were chattering, his small body shaking with chill.

"It is the ague again," said Theo, troubled but not really anxious. "He should not have ridden back to the plantation with you last week. Even in the daytime, there is fever about."

"Give him the Peruvian bark," said Joseph.

"I think not." She put her hand on the child's head, frowning. "I don't believe that bitter concoction does any good, and he hates it. I shall try calomel."

"The bark is better," argued Joseph irritably. "All the family use it for chills and fever."

"And does it stop them?" she asked. "The agues go for a while, but they come back. I believe that stuff is useless."

He did not persist. It was true that the swamp fever came and went. Gampy had had it before. This time it did not go. The fever rose higher until the child's body was like a red coal to the touch. The chills became ever more violent and the lull after them brought no respite. And now Theo in a frenzy of fear used all the remedies she had ever heard of. They dispatched servants to Georgetown for a doctor. He came too late, and if he had not, thought Joseph, what more could he have done?

At dawn of the third day Gampy, who had been mumbling incoherently, opened his eyes and smiled up at Theodosia.

"Do you remember Wabasha?" he whispered, "and the white bird, Mama?"

Joseph thought the child still delirious, as he had been

for hours, and could not understand Theodosia's sharpened terror, the anguish of her voice which she strove to steady.

"Don't think about such silly things now," she murmured, holding the little boy closer.

His fever-brilliant eyes looked up at her with the same unchildish earnestness. "I see the white bird. He's beautiful."

"No, darling," she cried violently. "There's nothing here. Your sickness makes you fancy things."

Gampy shook his head. "It is, you know," he said softly. "I'm not afraid, Mama. You mustn't be—either." He sighed once and his eyes closed.

Joseph had started forward in answer to Theo's frantic cry, but the child turned his head upon her breast and was still.

Joseph rose and paced heavily up and down the strip of shale before the house. The coarse beach grass tangled around his legs. He swore and kicked at it in a futile rage. He was sick at heart and riven with pity for Theodosia. If he could have helped her, he would have stayed. But she didn't want him or anyone, and he longed to be out of this house of painful memory. He had work to do.

The month before he had been embroiled in an unpleasant matter. The country was seething with war preparations, and he had been elected to the command of the Sixth Brigade. To his rage the officers who were to serve under him had dared to write an open letter of protest to the Charleston papers. They questioned the legality of his election, hinting that he had bought his commission, and wound up with the long-delayed thunderbolt: "The reports in circulation against you as having knowledge of, and agency in, Burr's conspiracy would deter us from serving under you."

He had answered hotly, denying all knowledge of the conspiracy, but the rumors had persisted. His officers were insubordinate, and matters looked none too hopeful for the gubernatorial campaign on which he was embarking.

Aaron's return to the country disquieted him. What new embarrassment might he not suffer from his father-in-law's presence? Still, for Theo's sake, he was glad. If anything on earth could rouse her, he knew that her father could. And Aaron must be told.

Joseph, who had little imagination, nevertheless realized the bitter shock that the loss of the little grandson would be, and he wrote to Aaron as simple and human a letter as he had ever written in his life, and he held the letter until

Theodosia was well enough to add a few words.

He brought her writing-desk and pen to her bedside. "You must write your father, Theo."

She turned on the pillow. "I know. I've been thinking of him. But everything goes well for him now. He is happy."

"All the same you must tell him."

She took the pen which he put in her fingers with the same mindless obedience she had shown since the day of Gampy's burial. He watched her painfully forming words, and while she did so, her strained body again held an attitude of listening: uncanny and heart-rending. She wrote as though she scarce knew what her hand was doing. He took the letter from her, half-afraid to see wild gibberish there. But there was none.

A few miserable days past, my dear father, and your late letters would have gladdened my soul; and even now I rejoice at their contents as much as it is possible for me to rejoice at anything; but there is no more joy for me; the world is a blank. I have lost my boy. My child is gone forever. He died on the thirtieth of June. My head is not now sufficiently collected to say anything further. May Heaven by other blessings make you some amends for the noble grandson you have lost.

She handed Joseph the letter, turned her face to the wall, and relapsed into quiet.

After a few weeks she began to get up a little. She wandered around the cottage or out onto the beach. Sometimes she sat for hours looking out over the ocean. It was impossible to walk far: she tired at once. Though she ate a little food when they brought it to her, she grew emaciated. The small bones jutted from beneath the skin that had been so white and now was tinged with yellow. At times she was possessed of a great thirst which nothing would quench. But when the apothecary from Georgetown forbade her to consume so much water, she obediently tried to limit herself.

"She has renal disfunction," said the apothecary, and fed her quantities of mercury. She accepted this as she did everything else. What did it matter? Only out of the shadowy borderland there gradually crystallized one human desire: to get back to Aaron. He will not like me like this, she thought sadly. He hates disease and ugliness. And she made more decided efforts to get well. Tomorrow perhaps I can start, she thought. But it was apparent to everyone that she could not stand the journey.

The days slipped by. Beyond her little island the States resounded with war. The American Navy accomplished a series of brilliant victories. On August nineteenth the frigate *Constitution* demolished the British *Guerrière*. The country roared delight and saw hope of annexing Canada, a prize for which it yearned.

Joseph, now safe in his command, a brigadier general, unpopular with his men, but protected by unquestionable authority, caught the infection. He saw himself a military genius, assailing Quebec, as Aaron had done years before in another war with England. He alternated hopefully between Columbia and Charleston, now promoting his possible military glory, now his political aspirations. For it began to seem as though his chances of being elected Governor were brightening. He mourned for his son and worried about Theodosia, but he was caught up by the bustle of activity, and the pangs were dulled.

No bustle touched Theo now, however. Day by day she slipped farther from reality. Dreams were her companions. Sometimes she talked with Merne, sometimes with Gampy. She was not often unhappy. Sometimes, when she looked at the ocean, she thought of how delicious its cool gray waters would feel about her body. The coolness and the peace would support her like the softest bed. One could drift and cease to struggle. Father would scold me for morbid fancies, she thought. And she saw him suddenly: his brilliant, mocking eyes softened to tenderness, his voice hiding his anxiety with bantering tone, as it would be now, if he were with her:

"For shame, Miss Prissy. Sickly vapors and megrims. You must accept what comes in life, since you cannot alter it. Where is your courage?"

"Oh, Father," she whispered, "how am I to get to you?"

For an instant her brain worked clearly, as it had not in months. Why was she still down here separated from him— the only being who held her to life?

She had not long to wait. Aaron in New York had been delayed in sending for her by a combination of circumstances. He could not come himself; though New York had accepted him on sufferance, he dared not risk arrest elsewhere. The war, too, made arrangements difficult. Money after the first short burst of prosperity was again scarce. And Joseph, to whom he wrote increasingly preremptory letters, was not helpful, writing that Theo's health did not permit of moving her, that she could not make the journey alone, and that he himself could not leave the Carolinas as yet.

In this dilemma Aaron turned to Timothy Green, physician and his former agent, the Timothy Green who had served him well in South Carolina before the election of 1800. Aaron used all his persuasive powers, invoked old friendship and promised liberal reward—sometime—if Green would undertake the journey. Timothy Green was now an old man nearing seventy, disinclined to move from home. But he accepted the commission at last and arrived on the Waccamaw Neck on the third of December, having previously visited Joseph in Columbia and told him of Aaron's proposed arrangements.

Joseph was not pleased. "It was unnecessary for Colonel Burr to send an emissary to bring Theo," he told Green angrily. "Mrs. Alston is not fit to travel, and if she were, I or one of my brothers would take her."

Green was embarrassed by his reception and he conceived an instant dislike for this overbearing man with disagreeable manners, but he persisted politely.

"Colonel Burr is very much alarmed by reports of Mrs. Alston's health. Indeed, she has not been well enough to write to him. I have some medical knowledge and can care for your lady on her journey. Colonel Burr feels that she will do better up North with him."

Eventually Joseph gave in. "If she wishes to go, you may make suitable arrangements. I cannot come to the Waccamaw until after the election next week. You will scarcely find passage by then, anyhow."

And with this grudging permission, Green proceeded to Debordieu. He was horrified by his first sight of Theodosia, whom he remembered as a gay pretty girl. When he entered the beach cottage, she was lying in a chair in the front room, gazing out through the window at the ocean. Had it not been for her beautiful hair, which was bunched on top of her head with no regard for fashion, he would scarcely have recognized her.

Theo turned at his step and gazed at him quietly without surprise. This woman is very ill, he thought, dismayed, as he advanced smiling.

"Greetings, Mrs. Alston. I am Timothy Green, do you remember? I come from your father. I am to bring you to him."

Her eyes closed as though the effort of seeing him hurt her, then opened again.

"I'm glad," she said slowly. "I want to go to him. He's all I have now, you know. The others have gone: the others that I love."

You have a husband left, madam, thought Green, but after seeing him, I'm not surprised you don't count him.

"How soon can we go?" she asked, in the same faint voice that seemed to come from far inside her, pushing past her lips with effort.

He pulled up a chair and put his fingers on her pulse. It was weak and rapid. "As soon as we can find safe passage. But you must get stronger first. Your father will be distressed to see you so spiritless."

The shadow of a smile curved her pale mouth. She straightened. "Yes, I must get better quickly. He likes to see me healthy and gay. I mustn't be a drag on him, especially now that he is so successful again. He is at Richmond Hill, I suppose. It comforts me to think of him restored to all his honor, once more taking his rightful place amongst the highest in the land."

Green stared at her astounded, then turned away in embarrassment. Incredible that she should believe that Burr might ever be restored to Richmond Hill. The poor fellow was barely kept from debtors' prison by the constant efforts of his remaining friends. The first demand for his professional services had subsided. He was living, to put it bluntly, on charity of one sort or another. He missed many a meal, unless people asked him out. Though Burr would never brook a hint of sympathy, it was sympathy or pity which he now inspired. It was pity which had persuaded Green to set out on this increasingly uncomfortable commission.

"How does he look?" asked Theo, with a faint animation. "Though I need not ask: he will never change. Always he is fresh and vigorous—young."

Green shook his gray head and held his tongue. He thought of the man as he had last seen him in the dark cramped room which he called his law office, crouching over a desk in the old characteristic manner. But now the thin shoulders were stooped. He had grown shabby and more than a little wizened, and about him—plain to be seen—the impalpable aura of defeat.

Green looked at the pale little ghost opposite him. Poor thing, it will break her heart when she finds out the truth—if her heart is not already broken, and I believe it is. She can stand no further shock. In fact, I fear——He did not finish the thought, but sighed heavily.

During the next few days he did what he could for her, but her malady baffled his scanty medical knowledge. There was fever and thirst and a wasting away. She was very weak, and he dreaded the task of getting her back to her father. Still he persevered, and luck favored him, for a pilot boat that had been privateering on the high seas put in at Georgetown for repairs.

This little schooner was named the *Patriot*, and she was built for speed. She was commanded by Captain Overstocks and carried a sailing master as well. She was to make a hasty trip to New York with her booty—her guns stowed away below decks. There was every prospect that the voyage would take but five or six days. True, she was small, scarce sixty feet over all, and her accommodations were poor, but Green was relieved. The *Patriot* seemed made to order for his purpose. He engaged the cabin for Theodosia and Eleanore, and a bunk in the fo'castle for himself, there being room, since most of the crew had been dismissed in Georgetown.

With this done, Green wrote to Aaron:

GEORGETOWN, S.C., *December 22nd*, 1812

I have engaged a passage to New York for your daughter in a pilot boat that has been out privateering, but has come in here and is refitting merely to get to New York. My only fears are that Governor Alston may think the mode of conveyance too undignified and object to it; but Mrs. Alston is fully bent on going. You must not be surprised to see her very low, feeble and emaciated. Her complaint is an almost incessant nervous fever. We shall sail in about eight days.

TIMOTHY GREEN

He debated giving the Colonel a fuller hint of Theo's condition, then decided against it.

It remained now but to await Joseph, who on the tenth of December, after a hot battle, had been duly elected Governor of South Carolina: not elected by the people, with whom he was unpopular, but by a harassed legislature.

The new Governor arrived at Debordieu on Christmas Day. The beach cottage was damp and cold and there were no festivities, though the servants had pinned a few bunches of holly to the candelabra and boiled a plum pudding. The memory of Christmases at the Oaks with an excited child to celebrate them was too poignant.

In the afternoon, however, William Algernon and Polly, the only other members of the family on the Waccamaw at the time, had dutifully endured the long drive over from their plantation. They were depressed by the gloom of Debordieu and impatient with Theodosia.

"She should rouse herself," said Polly to Joseph, after leaving Theo's darkened room. "It's cruel hard to lose a child, but it has happened to many, and one must make an effort for those who are still here. Just now, too, that you have come into high position, you need a helpmeet."

Never before had she dared criticize Theo to Joseph. The family had a nervous respect for his touchy temper. But really——What sort of governor's lady was this, lying silent and helpless in bed, protecting her strength? And for what? To leave her husband—as usual—and go to her disgraceful scamp of a father. It was exasperating.

Joseph did not answer. He tugged at his whiskers and frowned gloomily, as he helped himself to Christmas eggnog. He resented Theo's indifference to his new office. She seemed to have no conception whatever of the importance to which he had attained. He only dimly realized himself that half the pleasure of victory lay in the thought of her startled admiration. At last she must see the true worth of the man she had married: solid accomplishment compared to treasonable chimeras.

But Theo had received the news with the vague, gentle smile which was now her habitual response to all demands on her attention. "How splendid, Joseph," she had said politely, and turned from him to slip back into the borderland which she preferred.

"You should be more stern with her," pursued Polly: "awaken her to her responsibilities."

Her husband nodded agreement, and as Joseph still said nothing, Timothy Green came to Theo's defense. "Mrs. Alston is very ill, ma'am. She cannot rouse herself so easily as you suggest. And she must have a change of climate."

Polly shrugged her plump shoulders. "Oh, Theo has ever been in search of a change of climate," she said, good-naturedly enough. "It is no secret to us that she has never liked the Carolinas."

Why should she? thought Green, when the climate has killed her child and ruined her own health. But he held his peace. They were to sail in five days.

On Thursday, December thirtieth, Theodosia was carried

313

to the largest plantation barge, which lay waiting in the creek behind Debordieu, and rowed around the point into Winyaw Bay. Timothy Green and Joseph sat with William Algernon in the cramped stern. The latter had come at Polly's suggestion in order to add a semblance of family ceremonial to the leave-taking, and accompany his brother back to Rose Hill after the parting was over. "For Joseph will want a bit of cheering," said Polly hospitably. "He is always most downcast after Theo leaves him, though goodness knows he should be used to it by now." She refrained from adding that it was beyond her what Joseph had ever seen in that sickly girl, who had brought him little but trouble and inconvenience. Still, poor thing, she had been pretty enough, and there was no accounting for masculine taste.

Eleanore, in her black stuff dress and newly starched white cap, sat in the bow with Theo's head on her lap. The Frenchwoman watched the receding shores of the Waccamaw Neck and was glad. "May le bon Dieu grant that we never see that sinister country again," she murmured. She looked with loathing at the six sweating black backs as they hunched over the oars and chanted their song:

"Rowdah, yowdah. De weary, weary load."

She thought of the first time she had heard that chant: ten years ago, in this same barge, when she had come to the Carolinas wtih Madame. Only then there had been a curly-haired baby in her arms, le pauvre petit Gampy. Her rough red hands trembled and she turned her head quickly toward the bay.

The *Patriot* lay at anchor by the bar awaiting them, her hold bulging with rice from the Alston plantations. Joseph had seized on this excellent opportunity for sending a shipment to New York. Captain Overstocks protested vehemently. He wanted no sluggish, laden ship to handle. The *Patriot* was not built for heavy cargo, and she carried already besides her dismantled guns the spoils from successful captures amongst the Leeward Islands.

Governor Alston, however, insisted and Overstocks at length gave in, for it went against his Yankee shrewdness to turn down good money, and the rice would sell dear in New York. So the Captain loaded her with thirty barrels of the polished white grain, stuffing them somehow into a hold already crowded with booty—raw silk and ivory and silver ingots.

The schooner sank very low in the water.

"She'll no come about sweetly if we hit heavy weather," grumbled the sailing master.

"She'll do anything I want of her," retorted the Captain, "and I'll thank ye to hold your tongue."

"I like not sailing with women, women in black too—'tis ill-omened," persisted the other, gloomily watching the approach of the plantation barge. "The crew's muttering, what there is of them. They say we'll no make port."

"Ye claver like an old woman!" roared the Captain, and stumped angrily to the rail where the Alston party was boarding.

Theo was helped down the companionway to the cabin, which was cramped and dingy, with two tiny portholes and two rude bunks. It smelled of tar and bilge water, but it had been roughly tidied for her and was moderately clean. She subsided on one of the bunks, with her eyes closed, while Eleanore made her as comfortable as possible, and Joseph directed the disposition of the baggage. There was not much of this: a bundle of linen, a cowhide chest, and the casket which contained Aaron's letters and various papers which he had entrusted to her before he left America.

When all was finished, Joseph made a sign to Eleanore, who vanished. Green had stayed above decks, and William Algernon had not come on board at all, but had remained in the barge.

Joseph stood by the bunk looking down at Theo. Greenish light from the porthole flickered across her shut face. She seemed hardly more than a child, lying there so small in her black dress. It did not seem possible that she had once lain with him and borne him a son. All traces of wifehood and maternity were gone. Though she was nearly thirty and wan with sickness, there was an ageless quality about her. He thought of the laughing, heedless girl whom he had first seen on a June night twelve years ago, and the memory was bitter.

Life has dealt hardly with her, he thought, and yet she has something of that untouched beauty she had then: untouched by me, or even her child, impervious to anything but her insensate devotion to her father. The familiar anger stirred in him. There's always been that between us: always she leaves me for him, as she is doing now. This illness, and all the others which she has proffered as excuse, the one argument no man can fight—they are but evasions. She recovers fast enough when she has her way.

He drew his breath sharply, and she opened her eyes.

315

"You are angry, Joseph? You look so black." She smiled up at him faintly, though pain twisted her mouth. "Don't be angry now, when we say good-bye."

Suddenly blood rushed to his forehead and pounded in his temples. "You're not going!" he shouted. "Do you hear? I won't have it! I forbid you to go!"

Her wide dark eyes remained fixed on him patiently, as though he had not spoken.

"Don't you understand me?" he cried furiously. "You're not going! It's madness! Suppose this piddling vessel is captured by the British. It's not fitting for the Governor's lady to travel like this. And I *am* the Governor, though you seem to think nothing of it."

An echo of the old pity touched her. His blustering anger that always had sought to mask his jealousy and the doubt of his own worth. Once she had been able to reassure him, responding as best she could to his need. That was long ago. She had no strength for Joseph now, or for anything left on earth, save one.

There came a thundering knock on the cabin door, and Captain Overstocks' rough voice. "The breeze is fresh, the tide nearly on the turn, Excellency. We must be off."

Joseph scowled. He went to the door and threw it open, angrily roaring at the astounded captain: "You'll be off when I say so, and not before—damn your impertinence!"

He slammed the door and turned on Theo.

"Get up! Get your maid to help you. You can get well here on the Waccamaw if you will but try."

She focused her eyes on him slowly. His voice hurt her ears, so that a moment passed before she could respond. "I must go, Joseph. The path to him is the only one left me. Nothing but death can keep me from him, since he has sent for me."

She spoke so low that he had to bend close to hear, and yet he suddenly knew that it was final. There was no use trying to fool himself, he could not combat her. His rantings, his puny commands could not reach her. She possessed a stronger force.

"It's a dangerous trip in wartime," he persisted, "and you are not strong enough to stand the voyage." But he had lost conviction.

"Perhaps—but I must go. I have never failed him when he wants me." She sighed and, turning wearily from him, added in a whisper, "I've failed you and Gampy and Merne —but never him."

316

What did she mean by that? She was feverish again. Who was Merne? The question slipped through his mind and vanished as the cabin door shook under renewed pounding: a fanfaronade of anger. The Captain's respect for the Governor had been swallowed up by rage at being ordered about on his own ship.

"Let be! I'm coming!" shouted Joseph. He bent over his wife. "God speed you, Theo. Write to me at once upon your arrival."

She nodded. With effort she raised her hand and touched his cheek.

"Farewell, dear Joseph."

He kissed her pale forehead and left her.

How should he know that this parting was final? There had been so many partings. He knew her to be ill, of course, but now he half-shared the family's conviction of hypochondria. And despite his angry argument, he had no serious fears for the vessel's safety. He had written a safe-conduct for her, in case they should encounter the British fleet. And the British did not war on sick women: they would let her pass. He would have word of her arrival in a fortnight. He returned to his executive offices in Columbia, and plunged into work.

The *Patriot* skimmed out of Winyaw Bay with a fair wind. For two days she made nothing of the blue sea miles. On January second they were off Hatteras when the wind changed. The gentle rolling swells wrinkled and broke into angry crests. Choppy waves began to snap at the *Patriot's* hull like snarling dogs. The sky darkened, and vagrant snow flurries swirled through the rigging.

"There's dirty weather making," said Captain Overstocks, and he gave the order to shorten sail.

In another hour the schooner was laboring, groaning, over mountainous seas, her decks shivering under the constant pounding of green water. And the wind was still rising. Overstocks shoved the helmsman aside and took the tiller himself, dismayed to feel how sluggishly the vessel responded to her helm. And he cursed the rice cargo. Undermanned, as they were, no hands now could be spared to heave it overboard, even if they could have managed the barrels in this tossing, furious sea. Sweat started from his body and face, and was frozen by the icy wind and spray.

Below in the cold cabin Theodosia had been dreaming of Richmond Hill. There was happiness in this, for soon she

317

would be in Richmond Hill again. It would be June, of course, after the ship had made port, and the roses in bloom as they always were. Yellow roses. Aaron would put them in her room while she slept, so that she might wake in her white bed and be delighted with the fragrance. Roses yellow as gold—as Mexican gold. That was why his crown was golden like the roses.

It will be my birthday, she thought, and I will wear the necklace. I will look pretty, and Father will tell me so. Perhaps he will be so pleased with me that he will let me dance with Merne.

She smiled a little, and though her body under the heavy bedcovers braced itself to the violent pitching of the boat beneath her, she knew nothing of that.

Merne is so tall, but he will dance with that same quiet grace with which he walks. We will dance the valse together. And then the musicians will play our song, "Water, parted from the sea . . ."

Soon I shall see my river again—the Hudson. All my life has been mingled with rivers. The Potomac—warmth and sunlight, the rich ecstasy of romantic love, laughter, and kisses. The Ohio—a blare of trumpets, ambition, and action. I was a queen there on the Ohio—"Your Highness." The Waccamaw—ah, but that is as ugly as its name, fetid and sinister. I hate it, but I don't have to think of it now. I'm going back to my own river. From the windows of my white bedroom I shall see it when I wake in the morning before Father calls me downstairs to study. I must remember to tell him how well Gampy is doing with his lessons. He knows as much Latin as I do. Father will be delighted with Gampy. He is growing tall. Maybe some day he will be as tall as Merne.

A tremendous wave seized the *Patriot* and the little ship moaned and twisted like a woman in labor. For a moment Theodosia opened her eyes to see the blackness of roaring water against the portholes. A single tiny oil lamp swung free from a plank overhead. It lurched back and forth in grotesque rhythm with the rolling of the ship.

Above the straining, creaking confusion, she heard a terrified sound. It was Eleanore, kneeling on the tilted planks, a crucifix in her hand, her eyes fixed upon her mistress.

"Madame, j'ai peur," she whimpered. Her lips moved incessantly. "Sainte Vierge, aidez-nous . . ."

What ails her? Theo thought. She's ugly. This place is ugly too. It's dark and cold—and there is so much noise.

Her eyelids closed again. At once she saw Richmond Hill: a soft glow illumined it and it became transparent so that, in an indescribable way, she could see the whole of it at the same time. She saw each separate dark green leaf upon the box trees, each quivering yellow chestnut frond. The white pillars shone in the June sunlight, and yet within the house she saw the peaceful beauty of its ordered rooms. Every detail of the familiar furnishings was as vivid as the warm, cleanly stables where Minerva beside the other horses munched contentedly upon her oats. There was a feeling of laughter and delicious expectancy. There was music in the drawing-room, and the perfume of roses was in her nostrils.

A soft blissful feeling stole over her. She could no longer see those whom she loved, and yet she knew that they were there—waiting.

"Mrs. Alston!" A harsh voice jerked her back. Timothy Green bent over her, shaking her shoulder. "Mrs. Alston—we are in great danger!"

Danger! She repeated the meaningless word to herself, resentful of its intrusion. What a silly word, like the clanging of a bell. But the bell clanged louder and nearer until it exploded thunderously.

She struggled up onto an elbow. "What is it?" she cried. But her voice was lost in the rushing and crashing about them. Beneath the din there was another sound, a sinister measured pounding from behind the bulkhead. Now, acutely aware, she realized that this pounding had been going for a long time.

"What's happened?" she cried again.

Timothy Green's wrinkled old face was white as his hair. "One of the guns has broken loose. It's battering our sides in," he shouted. "We're leaking badly. The Captain doubts we can ride out the storm."

As he spoke, he wondered why he had roused her with warning of their peril. They were helpless, only Providence could save them. Yet as she struggled to her feet he assisted her, supporting her with one hand while she clutched the bunk rail with the other.

Eleanore was useless. She lay on the pitching floor and moaned.

Another wave hurtled itself upon the *Patriot*. The ship heeled over and slid down as though she sped thankfully for the ocean bed. Theo, thrown to her knees, waited instinctively for the vessel to right herself again. But she did not: she lay on her beam ends, quivering like a hurt animal.

319

"We're sinking, ma'am!" cried Green. "The cargo's shifted."

A sinuous curl of black water oozed from beneath the cabin door and spread silently over the floor.

Eleanore threw herself forward onto Theo, clinging to her neck. "Nous allons mourir—Madame. Nous allons mourir——"

Theo put her arm around Eleanore and drew the woman's limp body close. For an instant a spasm of mortal fear shook Theo and passed, leaving a faint astonishment. Death. Can it be that I am really going to drown? The sea to which all rivers flow: all life, all rivers run to the sea.

Her arm tightened around Eleanore. The woman buried her face in Theo's long flowing hair. Already it was half-wet, for the water reached to their waists.

What was it Father said once—long ago? He laughed, and yet he was utterly serious: "Courage is a religion. Since we must all die—why, bless me, my dear, let's die game."

She shut her eyes.

The *Patriot* lurched sideways and settled lower. The sea rushed in with a soft hiss.

Theodosia lifted her head and smiled a little. For she saw Aaron standing before her on the steps of Richmond Hill. She held out her arms to him: "Don't be unhappy. I'm home at last where I've longed to be. I'll wait till you come. Merne and Gampy are back there inside the house. I shall be with them."

And it seemed to her that Aaron's face and Richmond Hill were transformed by golden pulsations of light.

But in the cabin there was darkness.

The *Patriot* rolled sluggishly for the last time as though weary of her fruitless struggle. With a long sigh she nestled slowly into the welcoming depths of the tranquil, omnipotent sea.

THE END